# GONE FOREVER

## THE FIRST JACK WIDOW THRILLER

## SCOTT BLADE

Black Lion Media

PUBLISHED BY BLACK LION MEDIA.

*Back in 2014, Lee suggested I write my "own" Reacher.*

*It was a great suggestion. Thank you.*

1

Sheriff Deveraux was shot in the head in a town I tried to forget—Killian Crossing, a small town in nowhere, Mississippi. Until eighteen hours ago, I hadn't thought of this place since I was seventeen, which was the age I ran away from home. I never had a second thought about it. I wasn't the type of guy who looked back. I looked forward because I had thought that everything that mattered was ahead and not behind me.

I was wrong. Because eventually, the past always catches up.

It was the early morning hours. The sun wasn't even peeking around the corner yet.

I stood over Deveraux, who was bound up tight in hospital sheets and blankets like she was being held prisoner by the hospital bed. She either lay dying or recovering. I wasn't sure. I'm not a doctor, but she looked bad.

A nine-millimeter bullet shot to the front of her head should've killed her instantly, but it didn't. The shooter must've thought she was dead because he left her lying in a ditch on an abandoned road to nowhere in front of her police cruiser. I closed my eyes and imagined the cold blue lights still flashing in the heavy rain and washing over her body.

The shooter had shot her and driven away without leaving behind a single clue.

A gunshot to the head doesn't always cause death. It's all about relativity and physics—that and the size of the bullet. Most handguns are low velocity, but low velocity doesn't mean less damage. A high-velocity round fired into the head might leave a victim with less damage because of its steady speed. This appeared to be the case for Sheriff Deveraux.

A high-velocity round, higher than from most handguns, had burst through the front of her head, right side, torn through flesh, cracked her skull, and stayed lodged in there somewhere.

A bullet damages a human skull in two ways. First, the bullet causes damage on impact; a direct blow will draw first blood. The track of a bullet destroys everything that it meets, creating a permanent cavity. But if the bullet yaws or twists or turns or spirals while on its course, it can trigger the energy transfer to increase, and the cavity left behind is much, much greater—absolutely devastating. It can leave a crater—like a meteor slamming into the earth.

The second way a bullet causes damage is the initial shock wave, then the body's tissue surrounding the bullet's path gets caught up in a fleeting vacuum that usually is exponentially larger than the bullet. The bullet's flesh crater gets stretched and distorted and then restructures itself several times, like a blob, until the tissue cavity returns to its original position, or at least tries to.

I had seen a lot of gunshot wounds in my career, and a lot of them were headshot wounds. And I had seen a lot of dead people. I had seen people shot and stabbed and blown up all over the world. Some of them I had shot myself—nothing new to me.

Some people that I had seen shot survived, and some didn't.

Sometimes gunshot wounds that don't appear to be as bad as others are fatal, while others that bleed like a runaway firehose are not. Gunshot wounds are like commercial real estate. Everything is location, location, location.

I'd seen straight-on headshots pass through a guy's head and come out the back, and the guy lived. I'd even seen a bullet bounce off a chief petty officer's skull once. All he got from being shot in the head was a fractured skull, a major headache, and a newfound respect among the rest of us. Professional NFL football players had experienced worse. Nothing surprised me anymore.

Some bullets fired straight and true and enter and exit. Others could penetrate a man's skull and then ping pong around inside his body, tearing and ripping through every piece of tissue, muscle, and organ that it encountered, like a pinball machine, lighting up every *ding* and *bing* along its path.

Headshots are much more difficult to predict. The skull is like a sealed capsule. It cradles and protects the brain. Nothing is ever getting in until the capsule opens, and the only way to open one is to crack open its wall of thick bone. Inside the capsule, there's hardly room to move around. There's little space inside the human skull for anything other than the brain. If a bullet ping-pongs around in there, the damage is almost always catastrophic.

But if the bullet hits the skull dead-on and fires right through, sometimes the victim will survive, live through the process, and even recover to live a normal life. Not a common result, but it happened.

Sheriff Deveraux wasn't that lucky, not yet, but she was a fighter.

No one knew I was there. I had walked in past relaxed hospital security, past video surveillance cameras that were obviously not being monitored by anyone. I had to recon the halls in order to find her room. And now I stood over her in her hospital room in the early morning hours.

I walked in, right past a deputy sheriff who was supposed to be guarding her while she recovered. Instead of doing his job, the guy had been fast asleep on a sofa in the hallway right across from her room when I arrived. The staff must've pulled it out of the waiting room and set it directly outside her room for the deputy to sit on. They should've given him an uncomfortable chair instead, and then I wouldn't have been standing over her while she was so vulnerable.

I could've killed her and gotten away with it, easy as anything.

The deputy slept, sitting straight up. A cold cup of coffee rested on the end table next to him.

One of those old TVs, shaped like a massive box that couldn't fit underneath a Christmas tree, hung from a steel fixture at the top of the wall inside the waiting room across from him. It was at an angle. At some point the deputy must've sat there, wide awake, watching TV, because he was angled in the sofa's corner so that the TV was in his line of sight.

The local early, early morning news aired on the screen. No sound. But I could see that they hadn't gotten the story about Sheriff Deveraux being shot, not yet. The local news was based out of the next county because Killian Crossing was nothing more than acres and acres of forests and woods and a small, dying town. The only things here worth noting were the decommissioned train tracks and the long-abandoned army base.

I walked over closer to Deveraux's bedside and gazed down at her.

Life-preserving hospital machines pulsated and hissed and whirred nearby, a steady symphony of mechanical sounds. The room was smaller than some prison cells but larger than the bunk space on a naval Seawolf-class submarine. I would know because I'd seen them both.

Deveraux breathed in and breathed out. She wore a green hospital gown. IV tubes ran into the veins in her arm and strung up to an IV drip.

She didn't move or make any sign that she was aware of my presence, or anything else, for that matter. The only sign of life that she gave off was her breathing. Her head rested on a pile of white pillows. Her eyes were calmly closed, no twitching or racing like she was dreaming, which was not a good sign.

Other than the hospital machines and the IV drip and the wide, hospital-white bandages that wrapped tight around her head, she was exactly as I remembered her, a little older and a little grayer. But those were the only differences.

She still had thick hair that could fill a bucket. Her skin was deadly pale, but it always had been white.

I reached down and took her right hand in mine. My hands were like baseball gloves, and they dwarfed hers.

She liked to be called "Chief." I remembered that. She liked it, even though there was no such thing as a chief sheriff. It was just sheriff.

I whispered to her. I said, "Chief."

My voice cracked like I hadn't used it in months, which I basically hadn't.

I don't know if she heard me or not. Then I said, "It's me. I'm here."

She made no sound. Only the whirs and blips of the hospital machines responded to me, like they answered for her.

"It's been a long time since I left." I paused a long, penitent beat, and then I said, "I made a lot of mistakes. I shouldn't have been silent for so many years."

I paused again and stared at her face, a face that I hadn't seen in sixteen years, but I hadn't forgotten.

"I bet you wonder where the hell I've been. Well, you'd be proud and pissed off at me all at the same time. 'Cause I joined the Navy and got into trouble, but that ended up getting me a job."

I rubbed my thumb around the palm of her hand, hoping that she'd feel it, hoping that she'd wake up.

"I'm sorry it wasn't the Marines. I know you wanted me to follow in your footsteps, become a Marine like you did, but I became a cop like you. Sort of.

"I got booted out of the Navy. But then the NCIS recruited me. They said the same shit that people used to say my whole life. You know. I owed it to myself to use my gifts. Put my temper to good use—blah blah.

"I finally listened. They sent me off to college and NCIS training and then right back into the Navy. A civilian, technically, but I got all kinds of undercover work. Guess because I was expendable.

"After my first year, I had to train to become a Navy SEAL. Can you imagine that? Me, a nobody, turned college graduate to frogman? A boy from Mississippi."

I paused a long, long beat, waiting for her to open her eyes, to say something, but she didn't.

I said, "I wonder if you'd even recognize me. I wonder if you'd even know me."

The machines continued to whir and beep, and one made a nearly silent whistle, but there was one other sound from behind me at the door—the sound of slow scuffing shoes on tile.

A deep, southern Mississippi voice said, "Freeze! Now, ya hold it right dere!"

I stayed quiet. I didn't recognize the voice, but I knew the accent.

The voice said, "Turn 'round! No fast moves!"

I turned back toward the door and saw the deputy who had been asleep on the sofa. He stared at me from behind the barrel of his department-issued Glock.

The early morning hours of the hospital room must've shrouded me in just enough shadows to cover my face, because when I turned around completely, the sheriff's deputy jumped back a little like he had seen a monster. I wasn't a pleasant-looking man, not in the wrong light, and darkness was the wrong light.

I'd been told that in the darkness, I looked like something out of a nightmare. I'd been told that if I walked into a casting call for an actor to play the killer who comes out of the swamp and never dies, then they'd hire me on the spot. That's one thing that made me perfect for the SEALs. The best weapon that a SEAL has in the field is his mind. But being scary looking wasn't a bad thing either, because fear and intimidation were just as valuable as bullets and bombs. Being able to terrify enemies in the dark has benefited me all over the world. But I wasn't trying to scare this small-town deputy, so I said, "Relax."

The deputy said, "Hands up! Keep 'em where I can see 'em!"

He was in his early thirties, maybe not the best specimen for a cop, but I didn't know the guy. It was just a first impression, like an occupational habit. He visibly trembled.

He had what looked like a Glock 41, which was a standard law enforcement sidearm.

I was stationed at Coronado Naval Special Warfare in California —technically. But only technically, because I was undercover, and my assignment had been to pose as a former SEAL.

My CO had me dishonorably discharged, with a made-up criminal record, the whole nine yards. I spent a year growing out my hair and beard just so I'd look the part. Like a Navy SEAL has-been. All part of an operation that I spent a year preparing for. Of course, I wasn't there now. The investigation was all wrapped up anyway, but I got the news right at the end of it that someone shot Deveraux. So I left.

Before that operation, whenever I wasn't investigating a crime, they often stationed me in various places to maintain my cover. The SEALs are a relatively small military outfit, like a family. We had known each other or heard of each other, or we all knew a guy who knew the other guy. It wasn't very productive to put me into hot spots as an undercover operative and then pull me out when the job was done, because eventually, the other SEALs would figure out that I wasn't one of them.

I always had to go all the way. Sometimes I had to go all the way to the edge, close enough to see over it.

I had to go where the SEALs went and train when they trained.

The Glock 41 was a big step up from the old guns that this county had issued to its police force many years ago. Back when I lived here.

The Glock was a weapon that all military forces respected. You didn't have to like them, but they made fine handguns.

I kept my hands outward, palms open, and facing him. I stayed calm. Didn't want him to shoot me out of some sort of deep-down primal fear, like being afraid of the dark.

He said, "Step into the light."

I stepped forward, one big step.

He stepped back in conjunction, but a smaller step, staying out of my reach. He looked at my arms and surmised that I could swivel fast, with little effort, and grab the gun right out of his hand. Then he put more space between us, and he backed out of the doorway even farther into the hall.

A nurse stepped out from around a corner. Probably heard the commotion. She was a black woman, about forty, with a cheerful demeanor about her and a friendly face. She wore loose, blue scrubs with blue tennis shoes that looked new and more like they belonged on the feet of a teenager who cut lawns for a summer to buy them, which made me suspect they were a gift from a teenage son.

She said, "Wayne, what's going on?"

The deputy said, "Now, you stay back, Gloria."

Gloria said, "Who's this guy?"

"I don't know. But I'll find out. Now, who are ya?"

Gloria said, "Son, you can't be in here. There're no visitors in critical care."

She seemed to dismiss the sheriff's deputy and his Glock. Maybe she knew him on a more personal level than just the way small-town people knew each other.

The hospital was for the entire county, and that was the only reason that it was even big enough to have a critical care unit. The state must've funded the construction of this hospital. It wasn't here sixteen years ago. And the equipment was relatively new, with new-looking rooms and hospital beds. Only some corners were cut. Accessories were better described as hand-me-downs or secondhand: the TV in the waiting room or the old furniture, like the sofa.

The deputy said, "Damnit! Gloria! Get back!"

The nurse shot a look of shock at the deputy named Wayne, which must've been his first name because his nameplate read LeBleu. I took a glance at it.

Wayne LeBleu was a funny-sounding American name, but not for Mississippi and especially not the deep parts far from major cities, like the northeast corner. Here, the nearest city on a map that mattered was Memphis or Atlanta.

I stayed quiet, just watched their back-and-forth. I don't think that they saw my eyes because my face was still in darkness.

LeBleu said, "Turn around, sir. Face away."

He wanted me to turn back to facing away from him. I knew what that meant. In my experience, it meant one of two things. Either a bullet in the back or handcuffs. Here, it meant handcuffs, which I dreaded. I had been in handcuffs before, and I had a feeling that I'd be in them again and again. I didn't want to reject his command because he had that Glock 41 pointed at me, and he was a cop. I was taught to obey the cops. I twisted, slowly, and pivoted on my right foot.

He said, "Slow now!"

I grinned because this was slow for me, but I did as he asked. I adjusted my speed to virtually standing still.

Finally, I faced away from the two of them, but I craned my neck and looked back over my shoulder at them. I was ready for the cuffs.

I GREW up in Killian Crossing without a father but still lived a good childhood.

Killian Crossing is the stereotype of a small town—the back of beyond. It was rural but never dull, not under the surface. On the surface, things seemed quiet, but take a closer look. And small towns have their secrets, like shadows stalking them.

I never lived in a city until I was seventeen, but I'd never been country or rural or redneck, or however you want to describe someone from a rural area in the South. People from small towns don't grow up to be that way, not always and not mostly. Small-town life isn't like the movies.

Mine wasn't.

In a small town, there was plenty to do and plenty that needed doing. We had to do for ourselves. I fired guns, hunted animals, fished, built campfires, survived out on my own, and I learned survival in some of the most rugged terrain available. The United States Army used to have an elite training base out here for Army Rangers; the Seventy-Fifth used to send the best of the best here to train for a time, back when I was young and before. It was quite a big deal for us. This town was built up around the base. No other real economy to speak of. And it only got worse over the years since the base closed, and no major road passed through— no reason for anyone to stop.

The closing of the base almost killed the town, and it may yet be a slow death. Many southern towns are in a sad state of disrepair: crumbling roads, closed stores, sunken economies, abandoned high schools, wastelands of empty plazas, shopping malls, grave-yards for old trains, and like Killian Crossing, forgotten military bases.

Parts of Mississippi are like the third world. It took leaving the state for me to see that, because like I said, I knew no better until after the day that I fought with Sheriff Deveraux and left.

I grew up to be a big guy. It was a genetic thing that was, in part, a mystery to me. My mother was my only family. My father, I had never known.

At six, I was tough—got into my first fistfight back then. Kids learned quickly not to mess with me. If they left me alone, then I left them alone. I wasn't a bully. I hated bullies, a viewpoint that I never lost. Some of the other kids would pay me for protection from bullies. My first enterprise was born and my first sense of capitalism. I made a good profit in elementary school protecting smaller kids from the bigger ones. They paid me part of their lunch money like a recovery fee—a fine enterprise for me. I didn't have many friends. Not really. I was like Frankenstein's monster —everyone was afraid of me, and I was misunderstood. Not to forget that I looked like him. I was much bigger than the other kids.

The school's coaches loved me. All the way through school, they tried to get me to play football, and eventually, I did. I played for one season until I broke another kid's jaw, not intentionally. The coach instructed me to tackle him—no holding back.

All season, the coach had been riding me, accusing me of not giving it my "full potential." He said that I had feral eyes. I'll never forget that. Feral. I'd never heard that word before to describe another human being. It's a great word. Feral.

It described that experience better than any other word because, for a few seconds, I lost control of myself. I went into a rage. I ran straight at this kid. He stood cocked down low on the line of scrimmage, in the ready position, less than a second after the center snapped ball—less than half a second.

No one was blocking him, and our quarterback stayed wide open, baiting him, but instead of charging the quarterback like the coaches had trained him to do, he simply stood there, frozen, with his feet still firmly planted in the dried dirt. He had a clear shot.

He lined up the quarterback in his mind's reticle, and he knew it —but something that he saw in his peripheral stopped him dead in his tracks. Something feral.

He had seen me. The sight of me running him down had frozen him solid. In his quivering eyes, I could see the sheer terror that overcame him as he stared at a hulking goliath running him down like a freight train.

I ran behind the quarterback from the opposite side of the line. I ran past the other players and ran right at the kid. Headed straight for him. I was a fifteen-year-old freshman, and he was a seven-teen-year-old senior, but he was right to be terrified of me. I suppose that was the natural order of things.

The kid had no time to retreat, and he knew it. In that split second, he had time for only one thing—which was to fear for his life.

For the first time in my life, I performed an action that I'd never even thought of before. I achieved a feat that eighteen years later would save my life. Never had I trained to do this move, not then and not now. And now I had learned a lot of combat moves. But this was all genetic, some kind of ancient warrior gene that lay dormant in my bones until that second. I ran at the kid, full speed, with no intent of braking, no flinching, and no hesitation. At the last microsecond, I reared my head back, contracted my neck muscles and shoulder muscles like a snapping turtle coiling his head back into his shell, and then I catapulted. My head whipped forward in a violent slingshot motion like a cannonball, and I felt my skull lunge forward, and my helmet whipped and crashed into the kid's face, straight through the open-faced part of his helmet, and shattered the bones in his nose and jaw. If his helmet hadn't had the hard plastic faceguard on the front, the adults might've been cleaning up that kid's face with a bucket and a shovel.

I delivered a colossal headbutt.

The force behind my blow had sent broken parts of his helmet flying off his head. His face mask broke into pieces, and I had broken more than that. The kid's nose splintered and cracked, his front teeth sprayed out of his mouth: two white incisors and three broken canines. His chinbone had pierced through his skin, and his jaw snapped and split, everything broken.

Parents and school officials rushed the field to the kid's side as he lay crying and wailing like a dying animal. Paramedics had to rush the kid off in an ambulance.

Two things happened after that: I never played football again, not in high school, not in college, not in the Navy, and that kid never looked right again. I never meant to hurt him seriously. Later, I heard he had to wear a steel wire for six months. I heard he never breathed right after that. I learned a serious lesson about my strength, and I could never bring myself to play a full-contact sport again. But I learned the headbutt was a powerful weapon to have in my arsenal.

Standing there, in Deveraux's hospital room, it was no mystery to me why Deputy LeBleu and Nurse Gloria had that look of fear I was so used to on their faces when they saw me in the light.

I stayed quiet and waited for them to speak.

Gloria muttered something that was like, "Wayne, who is he?"

"Gloria. Get back! I'm tryin' to find dat out. Now, what are ya doin' standing over the Chief like dat?"

I said, "Relax. I'm not here to hurt her."

He asked again, "Why are ya here? Who are ya?"

I cleared my throat, not as a response or a comment, just because I needed to. I said, "I wanted to see her."

"Turn around and face me. Hands where I can see 'em."

He never put handcuffs on me. Not yet. I guess he wanted to get a look at me first.

I turned, slow, and faced their direction. I moved slowly enough so that he would feel reassured that I would not make a move, which I could have. Easy as anything. I could've sidestepped into the hospital room, grabbed the big, heavy hospital door, and waited for the deputy to follow with his Glock. Once he was in the doorway, I could've slammed the hospital door right into his gun hand. I could've broken his fingers at the knuckles with one good heave of the door, cracking bones in between the door and the frame, but I would not do any of that.

I moved my hands slowly up by my head, the surrender position.

"What the hell are ya doing here? Why you standing over the Chief?"

"Visiting her."

"Why?"

"She's my mother."

Gloria asked, "That's your ma?"

I swiveled my head and looked at her with my hands still up. I said, "Yes, ma'am."

The deputy asked, "Chief has a son?"

I didn't answer.

LeBleu kept his Glock out, but he lowered it to a safe, pointing position at the ground. His finger stayed near the trigger. He said, "Lower your hands."

I lowered my hands back down to my sides, but I left my palms out so he could see them.

"Step out into the hall. In the light."

I stepped farther into the hall.

Gloria said, "You look just like her. Look at his face."

The deputy took a good long stare at my face and then my eyes and back down my torso. He said nothing.

Gloria said, "No offense. But you must get your size from your daddy. Because your ma is tiny."

I smiled and said, "I never met him, ma'am, but you're probably right about that."

She nodded and looked back at the deputy.

He said, "Let me see some ID."

I kept one hand out extended as a gesture of submission, and with my other, I reached into my back pocket and pulled out a slightly bent and extremely used, dark-blue US passport. I reached it out slowly and handed it to him. He stepped closer and took it. Again, I could've swiped that Glock right out of his hand, easily. But I wasn't here to cause problems.

He sifted through the pages and studied them. His face turned to curiosity. He was glossing over all the foreign stamps that I had on my passport. There was a lot. Every page was drenched in faded stamps from foreign countries. The thing was practically filled up. I had traveled to a lot of places, and most were on there, but some weren't. Some places that I had been to were classified, and I wasn't supposed to be in them. It was a need-to-know sort of deal.

He said, "Tehran? Where da hell is dat?"

I smiled and said, "Iran."

"What da hell are ya doing there? Isn't that our enemy?"

"Not right now. They haven't been our enemy in decades. Not really. It's more of a PR problem than an actual enemy."

"What you mean? An enemy is an enemy."

"No. Not really. Just because some of them don't like us doesn't mean they are our enemies."

He didn't respond to that. He asked, "What you doing with these stamps? Are you military or something?"

"Something like that."

"Well, what exactly?"

"Navy."

"What? Like a seaman?" he said and chuckled. He had said "sea-man," but he had meant "semen," or he had said "semen," and he had meant "seamen." I wasn't sure. I never was, but it was a joke that I had heard a lot, and so did every other Navy guy in the world.

He said, "I was in the National Guard."

"Then we're brothers," I said, but I didn't consider us that, not even close. But it's good to add that kind of kinship to a conversation when you're face-to-face with a redneck deputy pointing a gun at you. We weren't family. I didn't consider the National Guard the same as the Navy. My only real family was dying twelve feet behind me.

The deputy flipped to my ID and stared at it, and then read my name out loud. "Jack Widow."

I nodded.

He waited a beat and then was about to say something, only Gloria interrupted and said, "I need to check her vitals. You boys want to move this conversation down the hallway? Let me do my job and let her have some quiet?"

The deputy flipped my passport shut and holstered his weapon. He returned my passport back to me, and I slid it back into my pocket.

He said, "Let's head down to the cafeteria. Grab some coffee."

I said, "Sure."

He led me down the corridor, and we looped around a couple of corners and made our way outside the cafeteria.

I stopped at the soda machine, reached into my pocket, and pulled out a five-dollar bill, wrinkly. I force-fed it to the cash reader and waited for a second for the machine to take it. Then I pressed the button for bottled water. A brand owned by the Coca-Cola Company came tumbling out.

I picked it up, twisted off the cap, and sucked down a long swig from it like it was a canteen out in the field after a long day of humping my gear, which was one reason I was grateful to have it. I had packed nothing for this trip. Literally, the brass pulled me right out of my assignment and told me about my mother being shot, and I left straight away. No packing anything. No planning what to wear. I'd have to think about that later.

Having nothing to carry, I had to admit, felt good. It felt liberating.

LeBleu motioned for me to follow him over to the cafeteria, which was closed, but the lights to the dining room were still on.

We sat at a table near the window. I sat with my back to the wall, an old habit that I'd formed long ago.

Beyond the bright dining room, the area with the checkout windows was completely dark. Way back in the kitchen, I heard sounds of clinking silverware and clattering plates and banging pots and pans like the kitchen crew were here, prepping for the morning breakfast crowd.

LeBleu drank coffee. For a while, there were no sounds between us, except for the slurping sounds he made when he drank his coffee.

Finally, he broke the silence and said, "My name is Wayne LeBleu. I'm your ma's number two. There used to be another guy, but he retired years ago and picked up and moved to Florida. No one has heard from him since."

I nodded. I remembered the other guy. I said, "Tell me about what happened to my mom."

He sat back in the chair and stared out of the window. It was still dark, but the sunrise was only around the corner. He said, "Ya ever heard of a place called Jarvis Lake?"

I shook my head.

"Well, the town is called Black Rock, but the lake is Jarvis. The whole town is built up on it. But the lake is what people know best. It's a tourist spot. Sportfishing once a year. That sorta thing."

"Yeah?"

"Well, yer ma is friends with the sheriff there. And one of our girls, who went off to college, drove that way last winter. She never made it to the school, and she never came home."

He drank from his coffee and said, "And the girl's mother got all up in arms about it and hounded yer ma for weeks. Yer ma had gone through all the proper channels for this sorta thing, but no one was helping us. She decided to look more into it. On her own. She called the sheriff there. You know, to check up. He said to call the FBI. So, she did. They gave her the runaround. Turns out girls have gone missing passing through that county for years. It's the weirdest thing. They just vanish without a trace. Yer ma hounded the FBI about it, but they said their investigation went to a dead end and that the girls who've been missing over the last five years are all of age. The FBI swears they are just runaways. Nothing they can do about grown women who leave Mississippi and never return. Nothing they can do without evidence."

"How many girls?"

"The FBI knows for sure how many have been reported, but yer ma thinks it's something like a dozen or so."

A long pause fell between us. He drank the last of his coffee out of the paper cup, and half crumpled it, set it down on the tabletop.

I asked, "She was digging around about the missing girl, and Black Rock is at the center of the whole thing?"

He nodded.

I asked, "And then someone lured her out to a dirt road and shot her?"

He nodded again, looked down.

I followed suit and stared down at the table. I was angry at the guy who shot her, at myself for not picking up the phone to call her, not once in the last sixteen years.

"Any idea who she was meeting with?"

"Of course not. If I knew, I'd be the first banging down his door!"

I nodded. I believed him. He may not have been top of his class at the academy or in the National Guard, but he was loyal, a good soldier, and that was equally important. Small-town cops are like that. He had been with my mom for years, and she didn't keep him around for his southern charm. She kept him around because he was loyal and dependable and a good cop.

I said, "This road?"

"Yeah?"

"Take me to it."

WE DROVE in the rain to the place where my mom was shot in the head less than forty-eight hours ago. Neither of us spoke, not a sentence or a word for the entire ride.

The place where my mom was shot in the road was exactly what LeBleu had described it to be, and exactly nothing more. It was dirt, shaded dark from when it had rained, almost like dried mud. The road was abandoned. And if I had to guess, because I couldn't remember ever being on it before in my life, it led nowhere. It was just a forgotten dirt road. Small towns were full of them. They were developed and bulldozed for reasons that I didn't quite understand. Other than mud riding or teenagers riding their bikes up and down them for some place to go, I saw no value in having them.

I got out of the police cruiser, front passenger seat, which was new for me. Even though I was a cop, I got arrested a lot with bad guys I investigated and thrown in the back of NCIS police cruisers because, in most cases, the arresting agents never knew that I was a cop. Most of them never knew that I was on their side. This was to protect my cover. They were never told. Only a handful of agents in the Naval Criminal Investigative Service knew of my existence. And only a handful in my unit could even have identified me.

I stopped over the spot where my mom was shot, and I stared at the space. I got down on one knee; blue jeans dipped in the mud. I reached my hand down and felt the dirt. There was nothing to see, nothing to feel. No tracks left—no evidence of any kind. The rain had washed everything away as if it had never happened.

I said, "Why the hell did she come out here? Who could've convinced her to come out here for a secret meeting in the middle of a rainy night?"

"Son, I got no idea."

"Where's the bullet casing? Did you guys find it?"

He said, "The shooter took it with him. That's what we figure. Believe me, we were all out here all day looking for it. I was on my hands and knees, looking around. We figure maybe the rain washed it away, but no way. We woulda found it."

I nodded and said, "Wouldn't have mattered, anyway. The rain would've probably washed away fingerprints, but you're probably right. The shooter took it with him."

He reached out and put a hand on my shoulder and said, "We're going to find this son of a bitch. Don't you worry about dat."

"Take me to the station. I need to look at her office."

I got up and walked over to the car and got in. LeBleu got in next. He fired up the engine, and we drove off.

THE POLICE STATION in Killian Crossing was exactly the way I remembered it—forgettable. It was the same location and the same old white paint. The front of the station was constructed with enormous glass windows that looked like they built the place to be a storefront and not a police station, which was exactly right. I remember it was originally a small paint store, but what does a tiny little town need a paint store for?

I said, "This place looks a hundred years old, still."

LeBleu said, "It is a hundred years old. It's still got da third bathroom."

"Third bathroom?"

"You know. For black people?"

I nodded. I never realized that was what the third bathroom was for. I had forgotten that it came with three. There was a men's, a women's, and a janitor's closet that actually had a toilet in it.

I changed the subject and said, "I don't remember you from when I was a kid. Are you from here?"

"Nah. I'm from Tennessee. But I'm from a similar small town just like dis one. I moved here for da job. Yer ma hired me."

We pulled into the police lot, parked, and got out. I followed LeBleu through the police station. The interior had the same old telephones with dull buttons and long curly cords, brown splintery desks with steel legs, and black vinyl chairs that rolled on worn-out plastic wheels.

There was a green leather sofa in front of a secretary station that doubled as the county's dispatch. The furniture was prehistoric, like it was all built by the dinosaurs from the Jurassic age and then handed down to their offspring and then inherited by humans, and now they sat in this office.

Two other patrolmen were standing near a coffee machine, waiting for it to brew a fresh pot, and wondering who the hell I was.

Both patrolmen wore crisp, tan uniforms. Both were about the same height, same age, and had the same cop demeanor and same stance, the same haircut even. They could've been brothers.

I scanned the rest of the station and compared the people in the office with the number of patrol cars out in the lot. This must've been the full crew, with maybe one guy off today. The math added up. And maybe they had a couple of guys on reserve, like civilian deputies.

I moved my attention to the walls and the doors and the windows. There was a framed copy of the US Bill of Rights, blown up to be about three by four feet. It hung over the center of the room, next to my mother's office door. None of the interior walls were blank spaces. Every inch of real estate was covered with a plaque or a sign or a copy of Mississippi statutes or an inspirational poster with cop jokes, like a photo of a cop pulling a guy over that read "A cop pulled me over and said, 'Papers!' So I said, 'Scissors, I win!' and drove off." Or another one had a picture of a SWAT team pointing their assault rifles at a Chihuahua. It read, "FREEZE!"

I had a feeling that my mother had something to do with the posters. She always had a sense of humor like that.

LeBleu said, "Guys, dis is Chief's son, Jack Widow. Dis is Gary and Greg Ferges. They're brothers."

I nodded, realized that I was right, and we all shook hands.

One of them, I didn't know which, said, "Don't worry about the Chief. She's going to pull through."

The other brother said, "The doc said so."

They reminded me of Rosencrantz and Guildenstern from *Hamlet*—interchangeable as well as lying through their teeth. I knew it, and I'm sure that they knew I knew it.

I ignored them and asked, "What did the state police say?"

LeBleu said, "They're sending a guy. But he won't arrive until next week."

"Next week!"

One brother blurted out, "Because she's alive." Which implied that they were waiting for her to die before they would commit to sending someone to investigate. I clenched my fists in anger. No one saw.

The other brother slapped him in the bicep and said, "He means they want to wait until she wakes up. That way, she can give a statement like a witness. No reason to come investigate now. We've already run a crime scene analysis. There's nothing."

I nodded, but I didn't like their answers. I looked around the room and judged them, which I didn't mean to do, but my mother was dying in a hospital bed, and I had plenty of experience with police work. No one was going to find the shooter. I'd have to do the heavy lifting myself, which was fine by me because I wanted to be the first person to find him.

"They'll send a special investigator if she doesn't... uh... if she don't change conditions," LeBleu said and then stopped.

I said, "I got it. I want to look at her office."

"Of course. You can just go right in."

I turned and went in. Flashbacks of being a little boy ran through my head. I remembered growing up here, playing around the police station, playing with my cop toys in the corner while my mom ran the station. I remembered reading books and her checking them off my reading list in the third grade. And I remember having a little yellow plastic desk in the corner of her office. She kept it there even when I grew up, a bit of nostalgia from my childhood. I remember she gave me a rotary phone that was plugged into nothing. I used to pretend to take important calls on it when she was on the phone, playing that I was conducting police business. Meanwhile, she was conducting actual police business on a real phone or sorting files or filling out paperwork. I remember her being pissed off at me for ripping her papers to shreds one day when she was out.

She had kept the room virtually the same, but my little desk was gone.

In the corner, there was a small, outdated library of books on criminology and pathology and forensics and law on a little black shelf, which was the same shelf that she had there when I last stood in this office. The books were the same: old, hardbound things that she had decades ago. The shelf was old now, but still stood proud. I remember helping her put it together. It was a big deal for me because it was our first furniture-building project.

One thing about me that people find odd is that I love to read books. I almost always have a book with me. Usually, they're secondhand paperback books. I read them all the time. I'm addicted to them. I enjoy going to those tiny bookstores that sell used books—an all but extinct American find.

I read old things, new things, fiction, and nonfiction. I read just about anything.

Right now, I had in my back pocket a worn-out copy of Stephen King's *Misery*. It had black binding and several creases in the spine. The book had the cover of the old movie from the late eighties or early nineties—I wasn't sure which. The pages were stained yellow and smelled like old trees, a smell that I loved.

I took the book out of my pocket and tossed it on my mom's desk and sat in her chair and went through everything that was out and open. I found nothing of interest, only official documents.

Her desk was well-organized but cluttered at the same time. My mom had a sense of chaotic organization that I always loved about her, but it wasn't a trait that I shared. No one would consider me an organized person. The only reason I had always had organized quarters in the Navy was because I had never owned much—my uniform, my dress uniform, my medals, and BDUs. I only owned two pairs of jeans and four T-shirts, for when I had shore leave. I never owned fancy clothing.

A single photograph sat on my mom's desk. I stared at it. It was a photograph of my high school graduation, one of the last times we had seen each other. We stood together for the last time as a family in a photo, just the two of us. It made me feel about as horrible as a man can.

I turned my attention to her computer. It was an old thing, like the rest of the office. I clicked the keyboard, and the screen lit up. The background was the Marine Corps logo. My mother had started out as a Marine cop and then returned home to become a local cop. Once a Marine, always a Marine.

The computer had no password. It just opened to a Microsoft Windows screen. I searched through her desktop. I spent about thirty minutes doing that. I searched through files and Microsoft Office documents. I looked for anything interesting and recent— anything that would lead me to a clue as to who she had met with, but I found nothing.

I waited to go through her emails until the end of my search of the local files.

I opened her emails and started to look through them. I spent more time on this, but I didn't search too far back because whatever might be there wouldn't be far in her email history. I spent about forty-five minutes doing that.

I found the chain of emails from the FBI's local field office in Jackson, Mississippi. Some agent there had said that he appreciated her inquiry into the missing girls, but it was still an ongoing investigation, and they were already working around the clock on it. But they had been doing that for five years apparently, and without any results.

The response seemed generic, a complete blow off as if the guy was saying, "Hey, lady. Let the big boys handle it."

I'd seen emails like this one before in my career. Bureaucracy was full of bullshit, generic rejection responses.

The only real information that was important was that my mom had mentioned the missing girl's name: it was Ann Gables, which made me think immediately of Anne of Green Gables. Not sure if there was a correlation or not. Not sure if Ann's parents had liked that novel or if it was a coincidence. Or maybe they didn't even know about the novel. Maybe they named her after the TV show.

After this email, there were no emails of interest about Ann Gables or the missing girls or the town of Black Rock.

I leaned back in the chair and thought about what to do next. But my thoughts were interrupted because the telephone rang out at the station. Deputy LeBleu answered it. After a few moments of talking, he hung up, stepped into the room, and stood in front of me.

He looked at me and said, "Dat was the hospital. Yer ma is awake."

WE SPED through the streets that I had known as a boy. LeBleu didn't use his sirens because traffic was light. We ran stoplights and signs and blared through a school crossing.

We stopped in the hospital parking lot and left the car parked in the emergency vehicle section.

I followed LeBleu through the sliding doors of the emergency room, and we walked past security and back to the critical care unit and then around another corridor to my mother's room. We passed the sofa that LeBleu had fallen asleep on.

Two nurses and a doctor in scrubs stood in the doorway.

The doctor came up to me as soon as she saw me and held her hand out.

She asked, "Are you the sheriff's son?"

I nodded.

She said, "I'm afraid that I have bad news."

I stayed quiet.

She said, "Come with me. Let's have a seat." She gestured to the waiting room, which was empty, and she pointed at a seat.

I shook my head and said, "Just tell me."

She nodded and said, "The bullet lodged inside your mother's skull. It didn't kill her, what usually happens with this kind of injury. Sometimes we can operate, but not this time. We've conferred with experts from Jackson Memorial and even called the Air Force hospital down in Biloxi. The doctors at both locations confirm that an operation wouldn't be worth the risk. Because of the location of the bullet, she'll definitely not survive it."

I stared at her forehead for a long moment, unable to move my eyes away from it. Finally, I asked, "What're the chances?"

"Of survival from the operation?"

I nodded.

"Zero. I'm not exaggerating. It'll kill her. One hundred percent certainty that an operation will kill her."

"What are her chances without?"

The doctor paused a long, forlorn beat and took a deep breath and said, "Not much better."

"Give me a percentage, doc."

"I don't know. Maybe ten."

My shoulders sank, and my eyes slumped down. I stared at her nameplate, didn't even read it.

She said, "I'm afraid the bullet will probably kill her. It's only a matter of when. All we can do is make her comfortable."

I looked down at the floor and stared at that universal hospital tile for a long moment. No one interrupted me.

Finally, I asked, "How long?"

"I think hours. I'm really sorry."


I said, "Chief."

I sat near her as she lay dying.

I wanted to tell her that she had a fighting chance, but I didn't want to lie to her.

The nurses and doctors and X-ray technicians were working around the clock to keep her alive. She knew that, and I knew that. I could see it in her eyes. But all she cared about was seeing me for the first time in sixteen years. Her face lit up when she laid her eyes on me. And I couldn't help but return a smile. I was happy to see her.

My mother was a fighter. She had always fought and won. This time, she could fight but there was no winning. It was over, and she had no fight left. Her understanding of this was written behind her smile. I could see it, but I didn't say it. No point.

I don't even think that the doctor had to tell her that she was going to die. She knew it.

Out in the hall, the deputies and the doctor and the two nurses stood near the nurses' station, waiting in case we needed anything or in case my mother had pain, but she didn't complain. She never had. Even on her deathbed, she smiled at me like she was staring at an angel, but I was the one looking at the angel.

My mother was devastatingly beautiful—a fact that I had to cope with my whole life. It caused me a lot of grief when I was a kid because I had gotten into my fair share of fights at school with the other kids who would make comments about her. They used to call her a MILF and a cougar—negative words, in my opinion, at least when they were used to talk about my mom. But I put a stop to that quick.

In my early teens, only new kids made the mistake of making those kinds of comments. Once I corrected them, they never did it again. My mom would discipline me for putting kids in the hospital whenever they said something rude about her. It became a cycle—they'd make snide remarks, I'd correct them, and she'd punish me, and so on. In my later years, I learned to accept their comments as the way of the world. Boys were going to make rude comments about her, and there wasn't a lot that I could do about it. She had taught me that violence never solved anything, but it did. For me, often using a little violence got the job done.

Suddenly, a nurse that I hadn't met yet, and one that I thought wasn't familiar with the situation, came in from the hallway and asked, "Is everything okay?"

Her scrubs smelled of cigarette smoke. It wasn't overwhelming, but it was beyond faint. I figured that she'd just started her day. She probably had one last smoke before she clocked in for her shift.

The nurse was perhaps thirty years old and shaped like a raindrop—small top half and heavy bottom half. She had short, blonde, slightly curly hair and piercing blue eyes, her most noticeable physical feature. She must've had colored contacts on top of her real blue eyes because they were unnaturally blue, like the Pacific Ocean, which I had seen a thousand times.

I said, "Everything's good."

The nurse turned back to the hallway and walked out of the room, where the doctor greeted her. I could hear them speaking but couldn't hear what they were saying, exactly. I imagined it was something like, "Leave them alone" or "They're fine" or "Stay out of there."

Then they must've told her that I was the Chief's son because she stared back at me in disbelief.

I turned back to my mother, ignoring them. I looked at her with the gentlest expression I could muster. I didn't want her to think that I hated her or that I was still mad at her after all this time. She looked back at me and smiled wide. Her hair was thick and black, with long gray strands. She'd always had long, thick hair. Now it was draped across the pillows that propped her up, pouring over the fluffy layers like black and gray lava spilling out over hills and crevices and rocks.

She looked at me and struggled to sit more upright. I reached down and held her hand in mine. Again, I noticed that it was such a tiny little thing in my giant hand.

She asked, "How are you?"

These weren't exactly the first words I expected to come out of her mouth. But what are you supposed to say after your only child returns to you after having left for sixteen long years?

I said, "Save your strength."

Without letting go of her hand, I grabbed a couple more pillows and layered them behind her. She fell back against them and rested there like a turtle on its back.

She said, "I'm fine. Your mother was a Marine, remember?"

I smiled at her but gave no verbal response.

She coughed for a long minute, and the staff stared in through the window again, but then she relaxed, and they went back to talking to each other.

I asked, "Are you okay?"

"I'm fine. I told you. Quit asking about me. I want to know about you. I can't believe that you're here."

She said it euphorically, which made me realize she was probably very doped up on painkillers, maybe morphine.

"Where else would I be?" I said, and then I paused for a long beat and said, "I'm so sorry I never called."

"Hush. Say nothing about it now. It's my fault."

I shook my head and said, "No. It's my fault. I was stubborn and proud—maybe. I should've called you. I have no excuse."

"Forget it. I knew where you were."

"You did?"

"Yes. In the Navy."

"You knew that?"

"I knew. I've got connections still. Ya know? Perks of being a Marine. I followed your career for a bit. I almost called you several times. But I knew you had a right to never want to see me again."

"I didn't think that you knew."

"I knew. I'm very proud of you."

"Do you know everything?"

"I don't. I lost you a few years ago. You were in special operations?"

I nodded and said, "Something like that."

"Tell me. What were you doing?"

I paused a beat. I had told no one exactly what I had done, not that it was some big secret, not anymore. Once a case was closed, and convictions were handed out. It didn't matter who knew what; I suppose. I said, "I joined the Navy. But I had trouble. You know..."

"Taking orders? You always were stubborn."

"Yeah. I was about to drop out. My four years were over."

"What happened?"

"I was recruited by someone else, a different organization."

"NCIS?"

"Yeah. How'd you know?"

"They called me once. Background investigation."

I nodded. It made sense. For the kind of undercover work that I was doing, they must've done an extreme background check. They probably even called my seventh-grade teacher and asked how many times I had detention.

I nodded and said, "NCIS recruited me. Sent me to school. Trained me. I worked for them for about eight years."

"What did they have you doing?"

"Special Ops. Like you said. You got it."

"Investigations? That's what you were always good at."

I nodded, said, "Sometimes."

"Undercover work?"

I nodded again.

"Where? SEALs?"

"Why do you think that?"

"Your body. Look at you. You must be in the gym every day!"

"No. They made us train hard."

She said, "Wow! My boy is a SEAL? Team Six?"

I nodded, and then I said, "Actually, DEVGRU, but yes. The same."

She smiled at me with a wide, coat-hanger-shaped smile. She said, "I'm so proud of you." A few tears started to trickle out of her eyes.

I said again, "I know. I know. I'm sorry that I never called you."

"Don't you be! Don't you worry about that! I deserved it!"

I shook my head and said, "No! You didn't!"

I didn't cry, not my nature, but I was about as close as I'd ever been. I had run away from my past and from my mother over an argument, and I had never looked back—one stupid argument. At first, months went by and then a year and then two, and before I knew it, years had gone by. I guess out of sight was out of mind, and I had been blinded. I should've called. I should've done so much more, but it was too late now.

She said, "It's in the past now. Live your life. I'm so proud of you."

I stayed quiet.

"Listen to me. I've got to tell you something."

"You really should rest."

"Listen. Okay?"

I nodded.

She said, "You're a good man."

She paused. The room filled with a heavy silence. Then she said, "I'm a proud woman, but the hardest job I've ever had was being your mother. Raising a boy without a daddy is tough, even for me. But I did all right. Look at you. A Navy SEAL and a cop at that."

"It's because of you," I said.

She nodded and smiled. "I taught you about weapons long before those frogmen did."

"You did. You taught me everything I needed to know years ago. You're the reason why I got through SEAL training."

"That's not 'cause of me. It's your genes. It's your heart. You've got warrior in your blood way down deep. Like your grandpa," she said, then paused and said, "Like your daddy."

I ignored the last part and said, "Either way, I never rang that quitting bell because of you. Every time I heard it ding and another guy quit, I wanted to follow. But I couldn't. You instilled that in me. I never gave up."

She said, "I trained you how to fight like a Marine. How to speak like a Marine."

She stopped, paused, and took a breath. She said, "How to treat a lady. How to take care of yourself. I taught you how to think for yourself."

She coughed again for several minutes, and then she righted herself and said, "I raised you to do the right thing. But there're things you do, things that you naturally are, that I never taught you. You're the smartest person I've ever known. You're honorable. The only other men I've loved almost as much were your grandfather and your daddy.

"That's what I regret. I regret never telling you the truth about your daddy when you were young. I never should have lied to you."

I squeezed her hand and said, "Don't worry about that now. I'm the man I am because of you. Not some guy I never met."

She said, "Use your talents for good. I want you to help people."

She clutched my arm like she was having an attack. She coughed a bit until it subsided, almost as quickly as it had come on, and then she began breathing normally.

I breathed in and breathed out in relief.

We were both quiet again for a long moment until she said, "Since the day you were born, I tried to raise you the best that I knew how. I'm only one parent. I tried my best to be your mother and father, but there's no good substitute for a real father. I want you to understand that I had my reputation to think about. I left here when I found out I was pregnant with you. I drove down to the Gulf Coast. You were born, and we lived there for almost a year, but I didn't make enough money to stay there. Biloxi had little jobs. It was all hotels and casinos. I worked in one of those resorts for months, working security. Imagine, I had been a cop in the US Marine Corps, and there I was, a single mother, pregnant and working security in a casino."

She chuckled lightly and then continued, "I couldn't make enough money for us there, so we returned home and have been here ever since."

I listened.

She paused again. I thought she was about to have another coughing attack. Instead, her voice cracked and went up in pitch, and her eyes brimmed with more tears. I hadn't seen my mom since high school, but I had known her for eighteen years before that. I had seen her enforce the law, beat up guys three times her size, take down criminals, solve murders, and look at the vilest things imaginable done to people by other people, but I had never seen her shed a tear, not until today.

She said, "Please don't hate me. I don't want you to hate me. That's why I'm trying to explain my reasons. I want you to understand why I lied to you about your father."

I reached out and caressed her forehead lovingly. I squeezed her other hand and started to speak, but she went first.

"The voters in this town can be judgmental," she said. "This is the South. And I needed my job back to give you the best life that I could. I lied to you. I lied to everyone. I didn't want them thinking I had gotten knocked up by a drifter. I didn't want them thinking that your mom was a slut, and that's exactly what they would've thought.

"But mostly, I didn't want to lose you. I lied, and I kept lying, and the years rolled by. Before I knew it, I had lied so much and so often that I believed my lies more than the truth."

She paused again. She closed her eyes for a moment and breathed in deeply, hesitating as if she had a long-held secret she was reluctant to share. "I don't know why I lied to you for so long. Really, I don't."

Another hesitation before she said, "I told you that your father was dead. That he died in combat. A war hero. I lied to you. Your father's alive."

"I know, Chief. You told me this before."

In fact, she had told me this in our last conversation, which was why I ran away to begin with. But she didn't acknowledge it. She acted as if she had forgotten that her confession, all those years ago, was what drove me away in the first place. She had lied to me my entire life. Everyone in the town, all my friends, everyone had thought that my father was some war hero who died in combat, but there was no such person. She had told me the truth. We had argued. She said things, and I said things. Simple as that. I ran away thinking that my entire life had been a lie. But time had passed, and now I was only angry at myself for not coming back sooner.

I said, "I was stupid to run away."

She shook her head and said, "No. You did the right thing."

I disagreed but didn't answer.

She said, "He's not dead, and he never abandoned us, not really, not on purpose."

I stayed quiet. She'd told me this before.

"Truth is, he doesn't know about you, but not because he left. Because I never told him." She paused longer this time, maybe waiting for some kind of emotional outburst from me or a sign that I was furious with her. I could see that she had carried the guilt around for years, that she'd never told me the truth until now, and then when I left, she carried more guilt because she'd never told me it wasn't his fault until now.

I remained silent. No reaction, no outburst, just a calm quiet. I think that my silence stung her worse than any expression of rage or anger or spite would have. There weren't many things I regretted because I wasn't that kind of guy. Regret was something that simply wasn't in my nature because it was like a sponge—it soaked up all your time and thoughts.

She said, "I wanted to tell him. I looked for him when I found out I was pregnant. He was in the Army, and then he rolled out and became a drifter, which is typical for ex-military guys, back then. I wanted to find him and tell him about you, but I didn't have the chance. Not when I was further along in my pregnancy."

She stopped cold and stared at me with those huge, pleading eyes. I could see that she didn't want me to hate her, and it broke my heart even to think that she believed I would.

I said, "I don't care about him. I only care about you. He's ancient history."

She breathed a long sigh of relief that could've extinguished a candle on the other side of the bed. And then she said my name like she always had—last name only, military-style. I cocked my head and stared into her eyes, thinking to myself that this might be one of the last times I ever saw life in them. But I was wrong. It would be the very last time.

"I was so afraid of what you would think of me. I meant to tell you so many times."

I felt my heart wrench and twist behind my ribcage. With a lump in my throat, I said, "I love you, Mom."

"I love you, son," she said and smiled. Silence fell between us. She must've started thinking about my dad because she laughed and said, "He didn't own a thing. Not one item to his name except for a toothbrush he kept in his pocket."

I thought about this for a moment. A toothbrush? I guess that would be one thing a drifter would need if he wanted to keep his teeth clean. It made sense.

A drifter would need a toothbrush, money, and identification.

"A toothbrush," she repeated, and then her chuckle quieted and vanished. A moment later, a hearty smile spread across her face as if she remembered a lost love. Her eyes stared past me into the corner of the room and moved up to the ceiling.

Suddenly, she laughed out loud.

I asked, "What?"

"Your name. Jack Widow."

"Yeah?"

"You never asked where it came from?"

"It's not from him?"

She shook her head, and I wondered if the morphine drip was kicking in overtime. Then I knew why it was so funny because she said, "It's the name of a marijuana plant."

I laughed and said, "You named me after pot?"

"Sorry. I had to give you a last name."

"Why not use his?"

She said nothing for a moment, and then she said, "I can't remember."

"Don't worry about it. Jack Widow is fantastic weed," I said, but I didn't know.

She laughed and then struggled to sit up straight without the pillows, reaching her arms out to me like she wanted a hug. I leaned forward and held her tight. She felt so delicate in my arms.

She pulled me down closer to her and whispered in my ear. "I love you, Widow."

I asked, "Chief, who did this to you?"

She said, "I can't remember."


LATER THAT NIGHT, my mother died in her sleep. I watched her fall asleep, then sat back and reminisced silently about my happiest memories of her. I'd lived a good life here, a good childhood. Halfway through the night, she coughed in her sleep, only a few times at first, and then the cough grew louder and louder. I felt her hand squeeze mine for a moment, and then she was gone. Every part of her was completely still, and her hand had gone limp in mine. I never got the nurses or the doctor because I couldn't bring myself to let go of her hand. I don't think that they wanted to come in and bother me, either. She died as peacefully as anyone could. I leaned forward and brushed her hair from her face with my fingertips, combing it downward and to the side. I reached up and felt her face. Her skin was already turning cool, and the lines in her face had relaxed. She had passed on.

I had no time for mourning. Now I had something to do—find the guy who shot her and make him pay. But first, I had to bury her.

3

THE FIRST DAY, I didn't make any arrangements. Instead, LeBleu took me to my mom's house. I spent the afternoon and the night going through her stuff and reminiscing. A childhood that I had all but forgotten washed over me like a tidal wave. I didn't know how to feel, and my body couldn't keep up with the emotions that would come. That night must've been what it was like for addicts to go off their drugs cold and have extreme withdrawals.

A flash of sadness and happiness and anger and then guilt rushed through my mind like the great flood. It didn't last for forty days and forty nights, but it sure felt like it. I cried. I screamed. I broke stuff. And I cried some more. No one came to the door, and no one called the house to disturb me, which I had expected. But I was grateful that no one did.

In the morning, the house phone rang from its perch on a long countertop. I walked to the kitchen and picked it up. I said, "Hello?"

A male voice said, "Hello. Is this Jack?"

"Yes."

"Jack. I'm sorry to be calling on this terrible day for you."

I stayed quiet.

The voice said, "My name's Chip Weston. I'm a friend of your mom. I'm her attorney. I'm so terribly sorry for your loss."

"Thank you."

"I need to see you today. I know you're dealing with a lot, but it's important."

"Can it wait until tomorrow after the funeral?" I asked. "Or the next day?"

He paused, breathing heavily on the other end of the line. "Your mother insisted on special arrangements, and I need to go over them with you. She left some instructions for you regarding her burial. Unfortunately, I must see you before that. Today."

"What kind of arrangements?"

"I need to talk in person. It's a legal thing."

I held the phone close to my ear for a moment and listened to the fan overhead as it whirred and spun and shook under the ceiling.

"One hour," I said.

I dropped the house phone back in its cradle and walked back into the living room. I slumped down on the sofa, sank into it, and stared at the wall. My mother didn't believe in having a television. I was supposed to entertain myself by learning and doing things when I was a kid. Television was a waste of brainpower, she used to say.

The night before, I had tried to sleep on the bed in my old room, which was still the same as the day I left. My mom hadn't changed a thing as she had cleaned it, dusted it, and sprayed scented air fresheners. The walls were littered with posters and photographs. A desk in the corner had an old Compaq home desktop computer sitting on top of it, which probably didn't even turn on any longer. In addition, a mountain of plugs was cluttered underneath the desk and led to a surge protector that was no longer plugged into the outlet on the wall.

There were posters of baseball and football players, a poster of Michael Jordan dunking a basketball, a couple of old rock bands, and one very old Sports Illustrated swimsuit calendar. I had been a teenage boy, after all. But the good stuff was at the top of my closet in an old Reebok shoebox.

One of the first things that I had done when I got here was, I walked into the house and scanned everything. I had let my mother's bedroom sweep the old memories out from under the rug in my mind, and I let them consume me. The last thing that I had done before I lay down for the night was, I got out that Reebok shoebox, pop the top, and pull out my old Playboy magazine collection. I only had a couple of issues, but one of them I had been very proud of. It was Miss Pamela Anderson's first issue—a prized possession back in the day. I thought about taking it with me when I returned to my post, but in the end, I decided to leave it.

I hardly slept at all. Maybe I got a few hours just from being exhausted, but that was it. I stayed awake most of the night listening to the creaks in the attic; the wind beating gently on the shutters, and the occasional thump of a pinecone falling against the roof and rolling down over the shingles.

Suddenly, my burner phone rang. I answered it and said, "Hello."

A female voice said, "Widow, everything okay?"

The voice belonged to Rachel Cameron, the special agent in charge of Unit Ten. That was her official title. She was my commanding officer, but I didn't think in civilian terms. I thought in military terms, part of the reason why I'm good at blending in with the SEALs.

I said, "She died."

Cameron paused a beat. I could hear the sincere concern in her breathing, and then it echoed in her voice. She said, "Jack, I'm so sorry."

No one called me Jack. This was a tactic that she had been trained to do somewhere in some conference or convention among the special agents of the Naval Crime Investigative Service, or maybe even the Department of the Navy. She'd been trained to speak a certain way during times of grief for a sailor or agent, just as she'd been well trained on how to speak with prisoners or members of the public.

I doubted that it was intentional. I was sure that she said it out of habit.

Cameron was older than me but by less than ten years. I had no friends. Not really, because I was always undercover, and my friends were temporary. Most of my unit never knew who I was, all but Cameron, the unit commander. As far as I knew, she was the only one who ever knew the real mission parameters. We had to keep it that way so that I could be effective in the field.

Cameron said, "Anything that you need?"

"No. Thanks for asking."

"Take all the time that you need. The bad guys here aren't going anywhere."

I stayed quiet, and she came back on the line and said, "Widow. I mean it. I think that you should stay there, maybe take a month, and sort out your affairs. You never take vacations. We don't have anything for you here, anyway. Not now."

"Thanks. I think I will."

"You know that I mean seeing your family and taking care of your mother's affairs, right?"

I didn't answer.

She said, "Let the police handle everything else."

Of course, she was referring to the bullet that killed my mother and the man who fired it.

"Don't worry. Mississippi's finest are on it," I said, with a hint of something in my voice. The phrase "Mississippi's finest" wasn't easy for me to say. Not so far.

I knew that she had picked up on it, but she didn't mention it. She said, "Okay. Good. Call me if you need anything. I'll give you a call in a few days. Your job will be here waiting for you."

I clicked off the phone without saying goodbye. The mobile phone had been a throwaway phone even though the Department of the Navy had a much bigger budget than other departments of the government. They had given me a throwaway phone, but it wasn't cheap.

The NCIS had a nice-sized budget. A fraction of a fraction of the NCIS's big budget was a black budget, which meant that it was secret, and it went to a secret section called Unit Ten.

Unit Ten was a special unit designed to investigate the special forces of the Navy and the Marine Corps. We were a small unit of about a dozen agents. Most of them worked support, while a handful of special operatives worked undercover. I was one of the latter. I was the first to make it into the Navy SEALs, and I didn't know any of the other undercover agents. We were kept separate. Being kept in the dark was a part of the job.

The black budget over my unit meant that the burner phone I held in my hand was a brand-new iPhone with all the bells and whistles that one could have on it. It didn't even have a case on it. I was certain the thing had cost more than a thousand dollars, but it wasn't my money. Personally, I hated cell phones—always have. If I was going to carry one, then it was going to stay thin. I slipped it back into my pocket and forgot about it.

4

Killian Crossing was a small place, but like many towns, it had a lot of lawyers. Most of the county lived within the town's limits, so all the court's business was handled here.

I walked along Main Street, past the sheriff's office. I walked over to four low buildings. In the back of one of them, the one on the corner with odd red-and-yellow awnings hanging over the sidewalks, was the law office of Chip Weston. His walkway was around the side, past four small shrubs. I followed the stony path to the back, naturally skipping over the gravel and placing each foot on flat stones.

He waited outside his door to greet me.

Weston was a forty-year-old man of average build, average height, but slightly smaller than average weight. His figure was out of proportion for his height. To say that he had dainty hips would've been an understatement. My first impression was that he could've doubled in a drag show down in New Orleans, and he would've made a killing dressed up as a woman. I dismissed this observation as quickly as it had come on in order to avoid any uneasiness between us.

Up close, I saw Weston had a reader's stare with circles around his eyes to match. I imagined that when he left his office every day, he probably went home, poured a scotch, neat, and sat back to immerse himself in a book.

He had thick, curly black hair, graying around the sideburns.

Weston had learned of my mother's death the same way as the rest of the town—on the front page of the tiny little newspaper that a local guy named Robbie Mile printed out of his tire shop.

Robbie had inherited his tire business from his father. Tires were the only things that his father had ever done. Robbie had gone to school for two semesters to be a journalist, and it was rumored that he had wanted to leave and move to New Orleans to work for the Times-Picayune, but that dream was stomped out, way back in high school when his dad passed away and left him a small business to run and a mountain of debt to manage. He could've turned down the business, watched the bank foreclose on his dad's building, and let the IRS seize everything else, but that wasn't something that sons in the South did.

Since Robbie would never have the chance to write for a major paper, he decided that our community needed a publication. He started his paper, and it did reasonably well. The people here picked it up at the local diner and a few other places. He charged nothing for it, but he turned a small profit off advertisements from out-of-state companies like BP and T-Mobile.

The paper was usually boring and only one page—front and back—but the townspeople talk about it all the time. It was the only news that many of them cared about knowing. A lot of the small towns in Mississippi had a real isolationist feel to them, like the rest of the world not only didn't matter but didn't even exist.

Today's headline read, "Chief Gone."

I had glanced at it in a pedestrian's hand, on my way through the town to Weston's office. I didn't need to read it because I already knew what it would say. It'd announce my mother's passing and funeral arrangements, set for tomorrow morning, and it would probably talk about her many years of service to the community and her dedication to her job and to her son, name not given. I knew that because everyone loved her.

The funeral home had taken my mother's body away from the hospital early in the morning. They drove her to their funeral parlor, which was the only one in town, the Ford-Elder Funeral Home.

The oldest son of the Elder family had gone to school with me, way back when. He'd gone off to college after I had run away from here, and he had graduated four springs later. He majored in business administration so that he could take over the family business—another example of how sons took over their fathers' businesses in the South. One generation followed the next, and the cycle of small-town life continued. I wondered what that was like.

I walked into Weston's office. He held the door open for me, let me walk through, and then greeted me with a hot cup of coffee in his hand.

He held the cup out to me and asked, "Coffee? I made a fresh pot."

I shook my head and said, "Not now." Which was unusual for me. I like coffee.

He shrugged and motioned for me to follow him.

There was no secretary in his lobby, but there was a desk for one. I wasn't sure if he had an assistant or not. I'd never been in his office. The truth was, I had never met him before. I'd heard the name, but that was it. I didn't know how big his firm was. Maybe there wasn't enough business in town for him to keep a staff. Maybe fewer lawyers would've helped.

I'd seen my fair share of courtrooms. Part of the job of being an undercover cop is that from time to time, you have got to make court appearances.

I'd also seen television shows with law offices as part of the sets. Cop shows and dramas about lawyers were popular with guys in the Navy stationed out far from home. That was if you were lucky enough to be stationed near civilization where you could get regular TV shows.

The offices in those shows could usually be found behind large, heavy, and beautifully polished oak doors. They were always fancy, with dark oak paneling and big leather chairs.

Weston's office couldn't have been farther from this Hollywood image. It was a rinky-dink, two-room office with wallpaper the color of pea soup. His doors looked like planks of wood scavenged from a ship's wreckage. His desk was a rusted steel thing with one drawer and two empty slots where drawers had once rested. He had three chairs in the room, two on my side of his desk and one on his. His chair was the nicest of the three, but it was still a piece of junk. It had a faded brown cushion on the back; the stuffing pouring out of two gaping holes like it was trying to escape a hell that no man had ever known.

He gestured toward the guest chairs and said, "Have a seat."

I sat. He followed suit, sitting across from me. He placed his coffee cup down on top of some legal papers and looked up at me.

"How are you holding up?" he asked.

The concern in his voice seemed sincere. Something unique to small-town folks was that they were genuine in their concerns. Not to generalize, but people in bigger cities usually had an air of minding their own business about them, as they lived in their own bubble.

I looked at Weston, and then I said, "I'm okay. She went peacefully."

He nodded like he had expected that. But I guess everyone who knew my mother would've expected her to not make a federal case out of death. Then he leaned back in his chair and opened his one steel drawer. The springs hissed and whined as they stretched with the drawer's movement. After it was opened, he reached into it and pulled out a thin, stapled document.

He released the drawer. It slowly retracted itself to a closed position, like it was spring-loaded.

He flipped through the pages and began to read to himself. After a few moments, he looked up at me and said, "This is your mom's last will and testament. I know this seems like bad timing on my part, but in it, she expresses two basic issues, time-sensitive issues. First, you're to inherit her house, the money in her savings account, and all her possessions. The second part is how she wants her remains disposed of."

I cocked my head and moved my focus to him instead of the backside of the papers.

He kept his eyes on her will and continued reading the second part.

"These are her own words," he said, and cleared his throat. "I don't wish to be buried." He stopped and looked at me.

I nodded, and he continued.

"I've arranged it with the Ford-Elder people that they're to bury an empty coffin at my funeral. My funeral is for the townspeople. It's for them to grieve and move on."

He took a moment and swallowed. Then he continued, "The funeral home is going to have me cremated, and my ashes will go to my son, Jack Widow. I want him to take them and scatter them across the old train tracks. This is important. That train, the one that used to barrel through our town every night at midnight when Widow was a kid, it meant something to his father and me. I want him to scatter my remains across the decommissioned tracks. I can't explain more than this."

*Across the train tracks?* I thought. I knew what tracks she meant, but I didn't understand why.

"Tell my son that I love him. And I loved his father. Scatter my ashes and let me go. Tell my son that his father was a drifter. He must've seen the beauty in the world, enjoyed the freedom of being free. I want Widow to live his life like that. There's a huge world out there. Go see it. Tell my son to follow his nature. It will guide him."

Weston stopped reading and looked up at me.

He said, "That's it."

I nodded and thought about the train tracks. I knew about them but wasn't sure of the significance. There used to be trains that would barrel through town every night at midnight. The trains were stopped and decommissioned years ago. But they used to barrel through at high speeds, shaking everything around like an earthquake. Something that couples liked to do was to make love near the tracks. Something about the rush of the speeding train combined with the movements of lovemaking made for quite the experience, or so it goes.

Then I started to realize where this line of thinking was headed. My mom and my dad must've been a serious thing. They made love to the rushing train. He had been a drifter, and one day he was gone, like the train. She had told me that he had no idea about me. Still, he could've stuck around. I guess I couldn't be angry with him since I don't know the details of their relationship.

I decided to listen to her advice on the matter and let it go. This wasn't a line of thinking that I wanted to continue having. No man likes to think about his mother in that way. But I understood it. She had met a man, fallen in love, and he had left her pregnant. She had never told him. I didn't question her motives. I just had to accept them.

He paused, like he was waiting for me to say more. He said, "You don't have to do any of this. I must abide by her wishes because that's the law, but you don't. The house will have to go on the market. There's nothing I can do about that. She left the profits from the sale to you. I'll set them up in a savings account for you."

He was silent for a moment, and then he said, "Are you okay?"

I nodded.

"Well, I have her ashes here. Are you okay with scattering them?"

I felt so much emotion inside that I didn't know how to act. I simply nodded again.

He pushed the last page of the document to me and handed me a fountain pen.

"This acknowledges that I've given you a reading of the full contents articulated in her will and that you agree to carry out her wishes."

I leaned forward, grabbed the pen, and signed the document in solid blue ink. Didn't care to read it.

He reached back and picked up a square-shaped box that I hadn't noticed before from the top of a filing cabinet. He said, "Her ashes."

I reached out, took the box, and opened it. Inside, there was a clear plastic bag with my mother's remains. She'd been three feet from me ever since I sat down, and I hadn't even noticed.

I stood up and shook Weston's hand and exited the building, carrying my mother's ashes.

I TURNED east and headed toward the railroad tracks.

It was mid-morning, and the town was up and full of life. I walked the downtown streets and turned and zigzagged. I avoided as many people as possible. I didn't want to stop for anyone because then I'd have to stop for everyone, not that anyone recognized me. Better safe than sorry.

I walked past a diner and the local hotel and the bars. I went beyond the banks, a gas station, a public park, a second gas station, and the grocery store. I kept my head down, avoiding everyone's gaze. No one was looking at me because they recognized me. They were looking because I was a stranger to them.

I walked for twenty minutes and stopped at an intersection with a traffic light—a steady stream of cars passed by. I'm not sure if anyone recognized me. No one honked or stopped. In a small town, everyone knows everyone. Even though I hadn't stepped foot here for sixteen years, I still had the crushing feeling of being trapped by a complete lack of freedom.

I couldn't explain it, but it was a new feeling. Maybe I had gotten used to being a stranger everywhere I went, everywhere that Unit Ten had sent me. But now I was back in the most familiar place that I'd ever known, and all I wanted was to leave.

I kept my head low as best I could and tried not to make eye contact with anyone, but there was no way for me to stay unseen. I stood out. That was the other reason why I thought surely someone would remember me, because I could be spotted in a crowd in less than the blink of an eye.

The most I had weighed was two years ago, when I had gotten up to two hundred forty-five pounds. That was because I had to beef up for a particular assignment. I was going to spend more than a summer in the desert. I knew that I would come out of the desert weighing about thirty pounds less. And I did. That's why I had decided to tack on excess weight. Undercover work was more than playing a part. You've got to look it too.

Walking by an abandoned and out-of-date playground reminded me of a summer when my mom had me doing all kinds of grunt work for the city—real push-and-pull stuff. I mowed public lawns, trimmed hedges, planted trees, and uprooted dead ones. I did most of the city's landscaping around the public buildings, including around the high school and its football and baseball fields.

This abandoned playground was one place that I had worked. I spent a summer in charge of cleaning up trash around it. She called it beautification. Which at the time, I had thought was a made-up thing. It turned out it was a real thing in most cities. There was a beautification department.

I was thin back in those days. I was consuming five heavy meals a day just to keep up with my hunger from all that work in the sun. I used to eat a lot of fast food and tons of protein and drank gallons of water.

Besides being big in high school, I also had thick, long black hair like my mother. She liked my hair long and let me grow it. She said it made me look Native American, like one of those old painted warriors. I was a little sad when the Navy forced me to shave it off.

Of course, now it was long again because of my last assignment. Not as long as it was way back in high school. Back then, it was long enough that I could've said I was in a garage band, and people would've believed me. Now it was down to my chin, maybe six inches or so down along my face.

My skin was sun-beaten and rough from being in Southern California for the last year.

The cars and pedestrians continued to go by. I ignored them.

I hugged the box with my mother's ashes close to my chest like a football. I crossed the intersection and headed on toward the train tracks. I still remembered where they were, even though it had been more than sixteen years since I had seen them.

I walked between a two-story building and an abandoned post office and then came out onto a small open field. And there it was. The railroad tracks ran straight through the center of town, north to south. It split the town in half, east and west. There had literally always been a right side and a wrong side of the tracks. What that had meant was there was the white side, and there was the black side. Most of our black population lived on the wrong side. From the looks of things that hadn't changed, not one bit. It wasn't something that I was ever particularly proud of, but it had been that way long before I was born, and I guess it would continue.

Grass and weeds had grown thick over the rail bed. The trains had stopped running when I was a kid, long ago. There was no evidence left of them except for the old, rusted tracks.

I surveyed the nearest street that crossed over and headed to a needless railroad crossing. It ran west to east. On one side of the tracks, the old train warning sign still stood upright. The broken bottom half of a warning sign stood on the opposite side for oncoming traffic. The top half of it had vanished long ago. Probably taken out into the woods and used for target practice by local kids.

I stomped through the overgrown grass in the clearing and made my way to the tracks.

The middle connecting planks were mostly intact, but a few of them were split here and there. Nearly a dozen years of neglect had seen to that, which was about when they were decommissioned.

The rocks in between the lines had kept their off-white color. Not much would erode them, anyway. Rocks never changed.

I walked along the tracks for a while, then stopped at the crossing road and turned my head to look both ways. There were no cars in sight.

I looked to the east. That had always been considered the bad side of town. It was mainly small project housing and a couple of abandoned factories. An old sign on the side of the street caught my eye. It was once blue and reflective, but now it was mostly peeled away, and the letters were faded. I could still read it because I already knew what it had said.

It read, "Kill n 4 Mil s Ah ad." The translation was "Killian Army Base was four miles ahead."

Killian Army Base was an old, abandoned base that this town had been built up around half a century ago. My mother had never spoken too much about it, and I never asked.

The sun was just past the ten o'clock position in the sky. The May weather was cool for this time of year, down to sixty degrees. It felt more like early spring than the preface to summer. Once summer arrived, the weather would be hot and humid and probably rainy.

I took a deep breath and held out the box. I opened it and pulled out the bag containing my mother's ashes. It was heavy, more than I had expected.

I tossed the box on the ground and watched it roll a couple of times before it went off the road. I wasn't worried about littering. No sheriff's deputy would've said anything about it, not to me and not on this side of town.

Next, I pulled her house keys that I'd been using out of my pocket and used the jagged edge to tear the bag open. I started at the top and sawed a narrow hole down to the middle. Then I returned the keys to my pocket and stood still for a moment.

I gauged which way the wind was blowing. I didn't want to scatter my dead mother's ashes into the wind and have them blow back on me. That would've been a very bad experience.

After I found the right direction, I ripped open a wide hole, twisted back, and then whipped the bag around like a fisherman casting a net. One powerful swing and the ashes released into the wind and were carried off. My mother had been here, and then she was gone.

It was only a matter of seconds until she was spread out into the wind over the tracks.

I watched her blow away until she was gone from sight.

I stood there, breathing, taking in the scenery. This was the town I had grown up in. It had once been my home.

I pulled out my mom's house keys again and stared at them. Then I reared back and threw them as hard as I could. They flipped and spun through the air in a northwest direction. I lost sight of them in the heavy grass.

I never carried a wallet anymore. It was too easy to forget about a bank card or an old driver's license that could be used to identify me when I was undercover and supposed to be someone else.

Also, I never liked the bulky feeling in my pocket. I used to keep my bank card and my driver's license in my back pocket, but now it was the same, except I didn't have a driver's license, only my passport.

I pulled out my burner cell phone and switched it on.

It had a full charge and a strong signal. The phone's wallpaper was some generic crap. I looked at the time—9:55 in the morning.

I thought about her last words to me. She'd tried to tell me about my father. I didn't care one way or the other about who he was or even if he was still alive. An ex-Army vet and now a drifter?

That's basically what I had become.

A wave of understanding came over me like a force. For the first time since my mom's small hand had gone limp in mine, I felt something like direction and purpose. The feeling swept over me, steering me like a compass, pointing me the right way. I probably would never meet my father, but I could follow in his footsteps. After all, I was basically a drifter already. Might as well embrace it.

Then I had an idea. That's how I'd find my mother's killer. LeBleu had told me about Black Rock and Jarvis Lake. I'd start there. I'd wander into town like a drifter. That would be my cover story. An ex-military drifter was believable. These are hard times.

Playing the part was something I was good at. Being undercover was something that I was good at. Being an investigator was something that I was good at. Only, I used to do it for a paycheck. Now I'd do it because it was personal.

## 5

I WALKED on the side of the road back toward downtown. I passed by the diner, the sheriff's station, and the outlet stores. I passed by people that I had never known and a few that I remembered from long ago. I passed them without a second glance or a second thought because they were in the past now. I walked like a man possessed, which reminded me of that old TV show called *Kung Fu*—the show about the wandering stranger. Or *Rambo*. In the first movie, old Sly was an ex-soldier who wandered the landscape. That was a good comparison, only I have a mission to find my mom's killer, and Rambo was without a mission.

I continued west and walked the timeworn main thoroughfare out of town. Cars passed me by. I think that a couple of the drivers recognized me because they slowed, but no one stopped. They took one look at my face, at my demeanor, and left me alone, something that I was accustomed to. I walked forty-seven minutes straight at a steady pace, with no break and in no rush. I was surrounded on both sides of the track by a thick green-and-brown forest of low-hanging trees. The ditches along the sides of the road were dry along the beds and covered in layers of grass along the tops. Gravel had sunk into the bottoms of the ditches, probably washed in from the road by the rains—this state had rainy summers.

At that moment, I started to feel trapped. Even though I had traveled the world on Uncle Sam's dime, I had barely seen any of my homeland. More than that, I had never had a life of my own. I was a citizen of an America that I had barely seen, and I had more sights to see and places to visit. There was an entire frontier out there, filled with mountains and rivers. There were huge cities, and there were deserts. There was the countryside, and there were parks. There was a forest, and there were hotels and music. There were historical places, and there were plenty of roads and tracks and paths. There were graves, and there were places where legends had been born and where they had died. I wanted to see it all.

I stayed straight on the only road that led out of this place—one way in and one way out. I placed one foot in front of the other and stuck out my thumb, headed for answers.

I headed west. Jarvis Lake was to the west. That was where my mother was looking for Ann Gables, so that was where I'd start looking for her killer.

It wasn't long before I heard vehicles approaching. I craned my head and looked over my shoulder. Two pickup trucks came up behind me, stirring up small clouds of dust as they came.

The first one was a brand-new crew cab, a white Silverado. It pulled a small trailer.

The second truck was an old, beat-up thing, probably a Ford. I wasn't sure because there was no logo on the grille. It was the ugliest truck I had ever seen. Some of the body had been slapped together from other dead trucks. The thing looked like it had just driven out of a junkyard. The guy in it had his left arm hanging out of the window. From his fingertips to the middle of his bicep was a long stretch of rugged, sun-beaten skin. He pulled up alongside me and leaned over in the seat. The passenger window was down.

He looked at me and asked, "You need a lift?"

I bent down to see into the cab, looked him over.

The guy wore gray slacks, a plaid shirt with a pack of cigarettes in the front pocket, and a genuinely concerned look on his face. He was middle-aged. He looked like he had lived a hard life but managed to keep a good outlook. He smiled at me, showed some crooked teeth and some empty slots where there had once been teeth.

His right arm was draped across the top of the steering wheel at the twelve o'clock position, like he had been driving with the bottom of his forearm instead of his hands.

I said, "I'm headed out of Killian Crossing."

"Well, you're going in the right direction."

I stayed quiet.

He asked, "Where to exactly?"

"West. Jarvis Lake."

"Get in. I'm headed dat direction for da next half hour or better."

I opened the door and got into the truck.

The guy was a safe driver whenever he had a passenger in his truck—that was evident. As soon as I sat down, he returned his hands to the nine and three o'clock positions.

No traffic behind us, yet he still used his signal like he was going to merge and looked over his left shoulder for a good, long second. He hit the gas, the engine roared, and the truck sped off, leaving a cloud of dust behind us.

"What's your name?"

I twisted in my seat and craned my head as far back over my right shoulder, as far as it could go. I gave the end of Killian Crossing one final, hard look. Then I turned forward in my seat and reached up to grab the seat belt. I pulled the seat belt out of its holster and down across my chest and clicked it into its latching mechanism.

I turned to him and said, "Widow."

## 6

I HAD MADE it about sixty miles from my hometown with the guy in the old junkyard truck when he let me out. I had a clear direction of which way I was headed, and it was no longer the way that he wanted to go. He was headed south. He dropped me off at a gas station off Highway 118, near the corner of a road called Blackwell, a big, paved road with blacktop that was completely empty. No landmarks in sight, just the gas station, and flatlands, probably farms. Mississippi's major agricultural export was sweet potatoes, even though most people thought cotton.

I stayed at the gas station for a spell. Inside, I used my debit card and bought a bottle of water and one of those gas station sandwiches. Not the healthiest thing, but I was starving since I hadn't eaten all day or the night before. At the checkout, I stared at the roadmaps displayed in front of the counter and wondered if anyone ever bought those anymore because it seemed like everyone had smartphones with Google Maps. I paid for my items and then went outside and sat on the curb. I ate my sandwich and drank from the water bottle. I drank nearly half the bottle in one long pull.

Highway 118 ran parallel with Interstate 48, which was just over the horizon, not even a hundred yards from me. I figured I would get a lot farther a lot faster if I could hitch a ride on the interstate, so I finished my sandwich and threw the wrapper into a trash bin, then crossed over the highway and walked to the interstate along some decent roadside scenery. The grass was green and freshly cut and smelled of springtime. I walked across a vast field and heard the rush of cars on the interstate, traveling fast, as you would expect on a busy freeway. I heard *Whoosh! Whoosh!*

Semitrucks and big rigs hauled goods at high speeds to destinations that I could only guess at. Gas trucks, oil tankers, trucks hauling limbless trees, and two trucks filled with brand-new Dodge Vipers rocketed past me, shaking the smaller vehicles. The eighteen-ton trucks versus the four-cylinder compact cars were like big bullies toying with small kids. Some trucks headed east and some west, but all had destinations to somewhere, a definitive purpose and route. Mississippi was just a state to pass through. It always had been and always would be.

I climbed a hill on the side of the interstate and began walking along the shoulder up on the westbound side. I walked with the traffic and stuck my thumb out, hoping for a ride. I walked about four miles, glad that the summer heat hadn't set in yet because I had walked for just over an hour, and not a single car had even slowed down for me.

I had retracted my thumb long ago as well as thrown away my empty water bottle. I didn't usually litter, but the ditch I tossed it in was already filled with trash. I didn't think my water bottle would make much of a difference and figured that any local wildlife living there was probably used to the trash anyway.

I walked on for another ten minutes. I started to think that maybe public transportation would've been better than hitchhiking. Then my mind wandered to the question of why America had no high-speed train system like Europe or Japan.

Maybe one day, just not yet, I suppose.

Just when I was about to give up hope of ever getting a ride, a blue Ford Fusion with a nice coat of wax glimmering in the sunlight pulled off the road in front of me. It stopped so abruptly that the tires skidded smoke, and the smell of rubber packed the air. The brakes howled as the car halted to a stop on the shoulder a good forty yards away. I scrambled toward it. I saw that the driver must've had second thoughts because the brake lights went off at one point, like he was about to speed off before I reached the car. He had probably seen me in the rearview mirror. Although my clothes had been relatively clean when I left town, I still looked like something out of a horror movie. A giant hitchhiker with disheveled hair was not the kind of guy that drivers preferred to pick up. Then again, these days, the hitchhikers risked as much as drivers. I had heard stories of hitchhikers being murdered by killers who drove around looking to take advantage of lost, nomadic travelers. Generally, as a hitchhiker, you were at the mercy of whatever driver was kind enough to stop. Drivers could be choosers, but riders less so.

Still, I wasn't a dream-come-true hitchhiker. But if there was such a thing as a driver who sought out hitchhikers to murder, I doubted he'd pick me up, because I could handle myself. That was something any idiot with two eyes could see.

I didn't want to lose this ride, so I picked up my pace and jogged the rest of the distance to the car before he changed his mind. I reached the passenger door and grabbed the handle. I pulled at it, but it sprang back into place, making a snapping sound. The door was locked.

I paused a moment and stared at myself in the reflection of the window. The window buzzed down a crack. I felt a blast of air conditioning rush out. I stooped down, and the cold air caressed my face as I peered into the car at the driver.

The guy driving wasn't a guy at all, but a young, attractive girl. She must've been at least ten years younger than me, maybe more. No way would her parents let her drive this long stretch of interstate alone if she was.

I said, "Thanks for stopping."

She looked me up and down and then back up again. I could see the hesitation and the worry in her face and even a hint of fear. She was probably thinking, *Oh my God! What have I done?*

I smiled the friendliest smile I could muster and showed my teeth like in the pictures I had seen in dentist offices on Naval bases all over the world. I even had a tooth pulled in the Navy because I had broken it while I was on a ship out on the Indian Ocean. The ship rocked like things do on the sea, but it wasn't so bad. The tooth that was broken was a wisdom tooth. Later, when I was docked in Australia, a local dentist pulled out the other three. He said that I didn't need them, and my other teeth would look better. He was right. A couple of years later, the extra space in my gums had allowed my other teeth to shift apart and straighten a little.

I had broken the tooth in a fistfight with five guys who didn't like me but liked picking on a young, female seaman recruit named Jessop. They had taken it upon themselves to harass her about her sexual preferences constantly. They accused her of being a lesbian.

She was one of the ten females that we had on-crew with a ship of one hundred seventy-three. They taunted her like stupid frat boys. Unfortunately, hazing is a natural part of military life. But sometimes it goes too far.

One day, I had seen it happen. One guy, with the same rank as me at the time, had broken into seaman Jessop's footlocker and stolen her underwear. He had filled the inside lining of her panties with hot sauce from the mess. I saw him doing it.

I did as I always did in a situation like that. I broke his nose. He was lucky I didn't break more. His buddies didn't take too kindly to that, and they ganged up on me. One hit me in the jaw with a wrench, breaking my tooth.

Of course, that didn't work out for him or the others because I broke bones on all five of them.

I got into some trouble for that. My punishment was basically extra duties since the Navy didn't want Jessop to file a report on the situation, and the five guys didn't want the incident in their files, either. Somehow, I ended up the only one who was punished, but I figured two broken arms, seventeen broken fingers, two broken right kneecaps on two different bodies, and one broken nose, not to mention the busted egos, was punishment enough for them. Our commanding officer at the time figured it wasn't worth shining a light on our company for such behavior.

Of course, seaman Jessop was grateful to me, and it turned out that she wasn't a lesbian. I can attest to that—personally. I ended up spending three steamy nights with her on shore leave.

That uniform didn't do her any justice. Out of uniform, she had cleaned up nicely. Later on, the first night, I found out exactly how great she looked out of uniform and out of clothes.

The girl driving the car asked, "Where ya headed?"

Suddenly, I realized that I didn't have a cover story. Usually, I was given a new identity and backstory—this time; I had none. I couldn't tell people what I was doing. I had to think. Why would someone go to Jarvis Lake?

She repeated, "Where ya headed? You don't know?"

I looked at her. Worry crept across her face, so I blurted out, "Oxford."

Then I thought, fishing, that's why someone would travel to Jarvis Lake—sports fishing. But I had already said Oxford, and why would anyone go there? University.

I was thirty-three years old, but I had hoped that maybe she would believe that I was some sort of free-spirited college student backpacking across the state, going back to school, even though I had no backpack, no luggage, and nowhere to carry fresh clothes.

It was the middle of May. The spring semester had ended, but maybe I was returning to school for summer classes after a two-week hiatus.

She wore a Mississippi State University jersey. On the front of it was a picture of a cartoon bulldog, their mascot.

"You a bulldog?" I asked. I continued to smile, but not too big, not enough to frighten her.

"Sure am. Graduate school. Working on my master's in psychology." She had a thick southern accent. It sounded almost cliché, like it was rehearsed.

She clicked the button on her door. I heard an electronic lock snick as the passenger door unlocked. I pulled the handle and the door opened. I dumped myself down into the seat. Getting into her car was a tight fit. I spent several seconds trying to find the latch to ratchet the seat back.

She watched me fumbling around for a moment and then said, "It's on the bottom. Center."

I found the bar for the seat mechanism and pulled it up. The seat skidded all the way back as far as it would go. It wasn't enough room for me to recline, but it was enough to enable me to fit my legs into the footwell and shut the door. My knees rested against the dash, but I didn't complain. At least I wasn't walking anymore.

I looked at her and said, "I appreciate this. I've been out there for over an hour. I was beginning to think that nobody'd stop."

She nodded and smiled and began to drive forward. She merged with the traffic, taking us off the shoulder and up to a comparable speed with the other cars.

She glanced my way and said, "Don't forget to buckle your seat belt."

I nodded and pulled the belt around my chest.

She asked, "Are you a student?"

"Yes."

"Not to be mean, but aren't you a little old to be in college?"

"I was in the military first. You know. GI Bill?"

"Right. Smart man," she said. Then silence fell between us.

We rode without talking for a ways. She feared me. I could see it in her demeanor—shaking hands, nervous glances, and she kept looking at her glove box. I decided it was best to break the ice before she pulled over and kicked me out or pretended to get gas and drove off as soon as she sent me inside for an energy drink or a water bottle or a soda or whatever.

I said, "I wouldn't have thought I'd get a ride from a beautiful young woman. Isn't it kind of dangerous for you to be giving rides to strangers? Especially ones that look like me?"

She smiled and then said, "I figure I'm safer with a big guy like you than I am on my own. You know, because of all the abductions in this county."

*Abductions*, I thought.

I asked, "You've heard about them?"

Maybe she knew more about this than I had been told so far. So, I asked, "What do you know of it?"

"In this part of the state, it's been happening for years and in three other counties nearby. Young girls. Sometimes people say that grown women have gone missing too.

"A girl from my school drove through here by herself a couple of years ago. No one has seen her since." She paused a beat, and then she asked, "You haven't heard about it?"

I shrugged, kept it to myself. A key to undercover work is to say as little as possible. The fewer lies that you tell, the less that you've got to remember.

"She was a really pretty girl."

I stayed quiet.

"It's been happening for so long that it isn't even on the news anymore. It was like national news the first year, but now it's just another girl gone missing. Oh well. It's just Mississippi. Who cares about them rednecks, right?"

"It is that bad? How long has it been going on?"

"Five years or so. Now it's like an urban legend."

"Your parents are okay with letting you drive this interstate on your own?"

She paused a beat, and then she said, "There's a gun in the glove box."

I stared at the dash and realized why she had glanced over at the glove box.

"Are you sure you should've told me that? What if I'm the culprit?"

She smiled and said, "Nah. I knew it wasn't you when I saw your eyes. They're nice eyes. A good man's eyes. Besides, you're too obvious to be the bad guy."

I nodded and said, "Gee, thanks."

"It's a compliment. You know girls like bad guys."

I shrugged, changed the subject. I said, "My name's Widow."

"What kinda name's that?"

"Last name."

"The military thing."

"Right."

"Jill," she said. "Nice to meet you."

I nodded.

"Are you in the Army now?"

"I wasn't in the Army. I was in the Navy. But I'm not active anymore."

"You still go by your last name?"

I said, "Yeah. My mom started it when I was little. She was in the military. You know how it is. Military family."

She nodded and looked back at the road.

There was more silence in the car as we drove in the fast lane. I looked out the window and stared at the terrain as it brushed by. Then I saw a highway sign that read, "Tupelo 65 miles."

"You don't really go to school, do you?"

She didn't buy it. So, I told the truth. I said, "No."

"So, where're ya headed, exactly? Because I'm turning south at Tupelo."

"I'm going west. Jarvis Lake."

"What's there? Wife? Kids?"

I laughed and said, "No way! I'm going on vacation."

"Without luggage?"

"I'm a drifter."

"Without a bag? Don't you guys usually carry a backpack with all of your possessions?"

"I'm new at it."

"Why did you lie to me?"

"Sorry about that. I figured you wouldn't have given me a ride, and the truth is really quite boring."

"It's okay. I understand that. People misjudge other people all the time. I think we should be kind to each other. Especially strangers."

I nodded.

She asked, "So what was that in your back pocket? Looks like a book."

"You were looking at my back pocket?"

"I wasn't trying to check out your backside. Just noticed the bulge."

I smiled, leaned forward, and jerked a book out of my pocket. I said, "It is. Stephen King."

"I like him."

"Yeah, he's good."

She looked at me strangely and then asked, "What are you? A drifter who carries nothing with him but a book?"

I hadn't thought about that so far. I guess drifters usually did carry a rucksack with them everywhere. I said, "Yeah. I like to read."

"What? Do you just stop at diners and read your book? Drink coffee and move on?"

I thought about it for a long moment. I hadn't imagined the drifter life all the way through. It sounded... good. I said, "I like it. My grandpa read a lot."

*Grandpa?* I thought. I guess to her; I was an old man, like a grandpa. I remembered when I was in my early twenties; I had thought that people in their thirties were old.

"Do you read a lot?"

"Sometimes. At least a book a week. Out on Naval ships, it can be quite boring on your downtime. I read a lot," I said, and that was true. I did read a lot. I liked to read.

"What are you, like a genius?"

"No. Far from it. I like to read and learn things... facts. And I like numbers. My mother started it. Way back when I was young. She had me read every book she could get her hands on. I kept at it when I was in the Navy, being out at sea and in strange, foreign ports with no friends," I said, slightly bending the truth, because the reality was, I had plenty to do in the Navy. But there was no reason to tell her I spent my career solving homicides and studying dead bodies and pursuing police work.

She nodded, and I stayed quiet. Then there was silence for a spell.

We drove on for another hour through the rest of Marion County, about fifty-two miles. She was speedy but an alert and cautious driver.

To break the silence and to retrieve more information, I casually said, "Before you let me out, I wanted to ask about those abductions. I'm just curious. What're the cops doing about it?"

"Not much. The FBI's involved, but they've been involved since the beginning. They came to my university the first year and handed out pamphlets and emergency numbers to call in case we saw anything. They even opened a temporary field office in Brownsville. I think it's still there."

She paused a beat and checked the fast lane in her side mirror. Then she signaled a lane change and moved the car over, pulling to the left. She accelerated, and the little four-cylinder picked up speed. I felt the engine purr, not a roar like a V-6 or higher. It purred as a small car does, a house cat compared to a V-6 leopard or a V-8 lion.

"They said that over ten girls had gone missing, and all of it was in this area. These four counties, I mean. Guess they never found any evidence. That's why we're supposed to ride in pairs like a safety carpool, but I've been driving back solo. That was when my father bought me the gun and taught me to shoot."

*Ten girls*, I thought. *And still no answers.*

We drove on in silence again, only for a good long while. I stared out the window and calculated the facts so far. I had a missing girl from my town. My mom started to get involved. And somebody shot her for it. Somebody that she trusted must've lured her out to that road. And now she was dead. I would get answers.

## 7

Jɪʟʟ ᴅʀᴏᴠᴇ around an interstate cloverleaf and successfully merged into the southbound traffic. She headed to the nearest exit into Tupelo, where she glanced over at me and said, "Sorry, I didn't drop you off on the road before the intersection. I forgot it was so close. I'll let you out at this gas station coming up. Maybe you can catch someone who's going to Jarvis Lake from there."

"Don't worry about it. It was nice enough of you to give me a ride this far. I'll be fine."

She followed a sign for the gas station and pulled into the lot. She pulled up to the pump and put the gear into park. Then she killed the engine. She turned in her seat to me and leaned over the center console to give me a hug. The seat belt quietly stretched with her contorted body.

I hadn't expected her to hug me, and my body locked up for a moment, a reaction to being touched unexpectedly, I guess, like a reflex.

"It was nice to meet you. Good luck."

"Do you want me to pay for your gas? Pay you back for the ride."

She smiled at me, and then she said, "You really are the sweetest guy. No thanks."

I pulled the door lever, got out of the car, and stretched my legs and arms out as far as they would reach. I enjoyed the feel of the stretch, feeling like I had been crammed into a cargo box and had just gotten free. I looked up at the sun to check the time; I didn't have a watch. It was in roughly the half-past-three o'clock position, but I wasn't sure. My mother had taught me to tell direction and time by the shadows on the ground, not the sun, but the Navy had taught me about telling the time this way. I wasn't very good at it. Not very precise, but I could guesstimate. Of course, it only worked in the daytime and when there were shadows and sunlight. Today was a sunny day, so there were plenty of shadows. Then I remembered that I had that fully charged burner phone in my pocket, so I figured why use the sun like a pioneer would when it was easier to look at the home screen to see the time? I didn't need the sun to tell the direction either, because I already knew which way was west. It had been clearly marked on the interstate signs.

I reached into my pocket and pulled out my phone and touched the screen. It lit up.

I ran my finger across the screen and checked the time, 3:36 p.m., and then I searched through the call log. The phone notified me that I had five missed calls, a few voicemails, and even some text messages. I had given LeBleu the number to this phone before I left. Not sure if I should have or not. Most of the missed calls were from his office. I assumed all the voicemails were as well—no reason for me to listen to them. I didn't want him to know what I was up to. So, I ignored them and clicked the power button. The screen returned to black, and I slipped it into my back pocket.

I didn't need anything from the convenience store, but I decided it was best to go to the restroom while I was near one. I headed inside and used the bathroom. Afterward, I walked through the store and peered through the window. I watched as Jill's car pulled away from the pump. It drove onto the blacktop—the tires making that slow rolling sound—and then she sped away and was gone from sight.

I stepped outside and looked around the lot and saw four cars parked under the gas station's cover and four drivers of all different ages and sizes pumping gas. I could've approached any of them and asked for a ride, but I wasn't too keen on that tactic. What if they thought I was panhandling before I even got a word out?

People are immediately defensive when approached because they're always getting hit up for change by panhandlers. It was a big problem in Mississippi. I remembered that. Poor states have many people looking for handouts. Not that I was against it. A guy has got to do what he's got to do.

I figured it was best to let one of the customers approach me. If I asked, then it'd only be a matter of time before a driver complained to the clerk behind the counter, and then he'd call the manager—or worse, the police. They'd think I was some sort of vagrant. Next thing you know, I'd be getting a ride, all right, but in the back of a state trooper's car, handcuffed probably, and I hated being handcuffed.

And all of this because I needed a ride west. No, I was better off heading back to Interstate 278 and walking until someone pulled over and offered me a ride.

I began walking out of the lot and back to the interstate on-ramp.

As I walked out, I saw an old fuel truck of medium size with faded symbols along the side. I could make out the writing as the truck crossed between the pumps. It read, "Jackson West Airfields—Caution Jet Fuel in Tank."

*Far from Jackson*, I thought.

I shrugged, passed the old fuel truck, and didn't give it a second glance. I continued onto the interstate.

The on-ramp was steep and short. Walking up, it was a short workout, like stair climbing. At the end, I headed north so that I could turn on the cloverleaf and go west. I hugged the shoulder of the overpass as best I could. It wasn't very wide, not wide enough for a car anyway, which I thought was supposed to be the point of a shoulder.

As luck would have it, I only had to walk for two more minutes because just before I turned onto the loop that took me to the westbound lane of Interstate 278, I heard a horn behind me. I turned to see the fuel truck from the gas station. It had caught up with me. The truck slowed to a stop a few yards behind me. There were no cars behind it, so the driver hadn't even bothered to pull over onto the diminutive shoulder. He just stopped in the middle of the lane and honked his horn.

I walked back to the passenger side, conjured another smile, and eyed into the window.

The guy behind the wheel was an old, white-haired man in a bright-red cap and gray overalls, like a mechanic wears. There was a faded blue patch on the upper left breast of his overalls with writing on it. I couldn't make it out from this distance, but figured it was probably his name stitched into the fabric.

Sitting in the passenger seat, at attention, was a black-and-white border collie. It was old, with hints of gray hair showing through the black in its fur.

The dog didn't growl or jump up when I leaned against the window. It simply waited for its master to speak. This was a well-trained dog. They were quite the pair—must've been together for years. The dog was probably his age in terms of dog years.

The guy was ancient, well beyond the age of retirement, probably a great-grandfather with a dozen grandkids running around somewhere, maybe spread out all over the state, maybe the country.

I grabbed the door handle and pulled the door open. It squeaked loudly, as if no one had ever opened it before. The first thing that hit me from the inside of the cabin was a musty smell. Not bad but not great either. It smelled like he had been living in his truck, which was entirely possible.

The bench seat was made of old, worn leather. I didn't know what color it was supposed to be because it was so old that the shade was indiscernible. I guess it might've been light brown originally.

The dog's fur was all over the place. It was a longhaired border collie, which was a medium-sized dog. This one was maybe forty-five pounds. Not a small dog, just smaller than I thought a border collie would be, but then again, I'd never seen one in real life.

The guy spoke first. He said, "Howdy."

His voice was squeaky, and I immediately knew why. His incisors were gone, and the rest of the teeth he had left were rotting so badly that they were a brownish color. He needed to see a dentist, and soon. The inside of his mouth looked like the remains of a bombed city just after the bombing had taken place, and it was still smoldering. His breath hit me like a gas grenade. Didn't anyone ever tell this guy how bad it smelled?

A thought occurred to me right after the smell of his breath swept across my face. I thought, *How the hell does he eat? He must be on a soup-only diet.*

I made a mental note that if I was going to be hitchhiking, I'd better start carrying gum or breath mints or Tic Tacs. At least that way, I could offer some to whatever driver picked me up. I could ask, "Would you like a piece of gum?"

Polite conversation. No one would think it meant anything, and most people wouldn't turn down a free stick of gum. It would spare me from having to endure the stench of bad breath. I imagined it was going to be a long ride with this guy, if all I could focus on was his breath.

I said, "Hi. How's your day going?"

"It's going pretty good so far—nice weather. So, you need a ride?" he asked. There was a kindness in his voice and in his face. Now I knew exactly why no one had mentioned his bad breath to him— his demeanor was such that it immediately made a person look right past his flaws. This guy glowed like an angel, just the way you would expect a loving old grandpa to glow.

I said, "I would surely appreciate one."

"Hop in. Let's get goin'. And don't mind Link. He won't bite. Move over, Link."

The dog moved over. It didn't bark or snap or dismiss his command. It was perfectly obedient, truly a good dog.

Link moved to the middle of the bench, making the effort seem like a great struggle. Then he curled up and rested his head on the seat. He didn't pay me any more attention, not even a sniff. This dog had this "if it's okay with my master, then it's okay with me" attitude, like his master's approval was gospel.

I got into the truck, closed the door, and grabbed for the seat belt, but it was not there. I grinned and tried not to look like it was a big deal, which it wasn't.

The old guy noticed the move and said, "Sorry, son. Dere is no seat belt. I hope dat's okay. I promise dat I'm a good driver."

"No problem."

I believed the old guy. Grandpas were usually excellent drivers, until they got too old, lost their reaction times. Slow and safe was a statistical reality about old guys, so I didn't doubt his claim. I was more surprised that he hadn't replaced the seat belt, especially considering that he was dressed like an airplane mechanic. I guess airplane mechanics and car mechanics had different priorities. To an airplane mechanic, a seat belt at thirty thousand feet was completely unnecessary, more of a placebo to give the passengers peace of mind than to save their lives. When a plane drops out of the sky at thirty thousand feet and plummets to the ground, the last thing that'll save a passenger's life is a seat belt. A car is a different story. Cars don't reach speeds of hundreds of miles per hour and travel tens of thousands of feet above the ground, and cars barely deal in gravity when compared to airplanes.

He said, "I'm really not supposed ta pick anyone up. Insurance BS. But ya looked lost out here, and I got a long drive still. I'd sure like da company."

I figured that the old guy didn't have many passengers. He had a kind of loneliness about him. His voice hung on the word "sure," and it came out with a slight whistle at the beginning. He grinned wide. That was when I realized that one of his bottom front teeth was broken, not chipped. It was broken in half, and he'd never fixed it.

The air produced by his windpipes must've hissed right through his missing incisors and then scraped across his broken tooth, creating a distinctive whistle, especially with his pronunciation of the letter "s."

I was having quite the luck with drivers today. My first had been an old man missing his teeth but in good spirits, and now I had another old guy with messed-up teeth, again in great spirits. I wondered if this was the life of a drifter.

I looked over at him and said, "I appreciate you stopping."

"Son, where ya headed?"

"West. To a place called Jarvis Lake."

He smiled at me, wide, and chuckled. He said, "Well, I'll be damned. I'm headed dere. It's about twenty-five miles west. I'm going to da little fishing town next to it called Black Rock. You can ride with me all the way if ya want."

"Thank you. That's fantastic. What a stroke of luck."

"Where's your bag?" he asked.

"What?"

"Luggage? Doncha have a bag?"

"No bag. Just me."

He asked, "Where do you keep your toothbrush?"

A quick burst of laughter flung out of my mouth. I had to stop myself. I laughed because; it seemed to me; a toothbrush was the last thing on his mind.

He said, "What is it?" and smiled.

I shook my head and said, "Nothing. I just realized I forgot my toothbrush." That part was true. I'd have to get one.

He didn't ask any further about it. He just hit the gas, and the fuel truck picked up speed and slid over to the truck lane. He wasn't a slow driver; that was for damn sure. That had been a large miscalculation on my part. He pushed the ancient truck as hard as it would go. It wasn't struggling with the gas pedal's sudden request to jump forward, but it didn't quite jump to life like Jill's Ford Fusion had.

He repeated Jill's question and said, "I tought hitchhikers always carried a bag. Ya know, with camping gear or a sleeping bag or somedin'. So ya can sleep out under da stars. Ya don't look very prepared if ya don't mind my saying so."

He hung on the "s" sounds in "saying so," and the whistle followed.

"I'm new to this. I just rolled out of the military. Guess I didn't really think it out that far ahead."

He nodded. He didn't seem surprised, but then again, I doubted that much of anything surprised him.

We continued to drive down the interstate. The old guy was fast, but he wasn't heavy-footed because he kept the truck at a steady seventy miles per hour, the maximum speed limit.

Some of the other vehicles on the road drove faster, and some drove slower. At one point, we got stuck behind two eighteen-wheelers. One drove in the fast lane at a slow speed, and the other drove in our lane at the same slow speed. I thought it was the responsibility of the truck in the fast lane to speed up, pass, and then move back over to the truck lane if he was going to continue to drive slowly. But the driver of that truck seemed not to be concerned with such formalities.

We drove in silence for about twenty minutes until I finally broke it. I asked, "Is there an airport nearby?"

The old guy said, "No. I work at a small airstrip outside Jackson."

"Are you headed to Jarvis Lake for business or pleasure?"

"Not exactly either. It's fer work, but I plan on doing some fishin' while I'm dere."

Another whistle.

The old mechanic looked back over his shoulder behind the seat to a narrow rear cargo space between the front bench and the back wall. It was an area that was too small for a back seat, but it was unusually wide for a single-cabin truck. It was as if this truck was specially designed or customized.

I leaned back and peered into the cargo space. A worn metal tackle box and a couple of fishing rods were folded up against the rear wall. It looked like he was prepared for some major fishing on the lake.

"What kind of work will you be doing on a lake?"

"Flying boat."

"Flying boat? You mean a seaplane?"

He shook his head, and then he said, "Common mistake, son. Everyone calls dem seaplanes. A seaplane is a plane dat can land on water. I mean, technically yer right dat dat's what I'm going dere fer, but dere are two types of seaplanes. Da one everyone dinks of is basically just a seaplane or a floatplane. And da second is like da plane dat I'm goin' ta work on. It's a flying boat or a super scooper. It's one of dose water bombers. Ya know, fer fighting forest fires from da air. Dey are da large planes. Da fuse-lage on dem is shaped like da hull of a boat. It's a boat dat flies. Sometimes dey're fer transporting cargo, but mostly nowadays, ya usually see dem as water bombers."

I nodded. Of course, I already understood the difference between a seaplane and a water bomber. I'd seen a water bomber once when I was stationed in South Korea.

He said, "Anyway, I'm meeting a guy wid a flying boat."

"Why's this guy flying a water bomber to a lake in Mississippi? We don't have any forest fires."

"It's some rich fella. Probably oil money. Maybe flying his buddies out ta a remote lake fer some fishing. I've never had anyone fly a flying boat out ta a lake before, not fer recreational use, but a seaplane, sure. Dey're probably carrying a small boat stored in da hull, or da guy has a big crew dat he's bringing wid him. Dese planes can usually hold two pilots, one jump seat, and maybe eight passengers on a bench in da back."

"So why does he need you to drive to the lake?"

"Look at dis vehicle. I'm driving fuel out dere for da plane. No available fuel in Black Rock for da rich guy ta use ta refuel da plane. I dink he's flying from da Gulf or somewhere. Gonna need fuel ta return."

I nodded. It made sense. The rich guy needed to refuel, so the old guy was meeting him there.

Then the old guy said, "My name's Hank, by da way. Hank Cochran. I was in da Coast Guard fer twenty years; den I retired. Now I work as a mechanic at a small airstrip in Jackson. Dat's my story. So, who are you?"

I said, "Widow, first name, Jack."

Hank gave me a wide smile. The sight of his missing teeth and the smell of his bad breath rushed out at me again, but his smile was full of warmth. And we continued on.

## 8

JARVIS LAKE WASN'T a place that I'd ever heard of before yesterday, at least not that I could remember, but it echoed in the chambers of my mind. I looked out the window of the fuel truck, and my lips moved inadvertently. I whispered, "I'll find who did this to you, Chief."

"Did ya say somedin'?"

I turned, breaking free from my thoughts of revenge and said, "Thinking out loud."

"I do dat all da time. Well, actually, I talk ta ole Link here, but he don't say much back." Hank let out a chuckle, and Link looked up after hearing his name.

"Good boy, Link," Hank said.

The dog wagged his tail.

I gazed out across the horizon through the front windshield. The land was mostly flat and covered with tall pine trees. I calculated we were getting close to the off-ramp for Black Rock.

I stared out above the trees. Portentous, dark clouds filled the sky, foreshadowing terrible events ahead.

Great. It looked like those clouds would turn into a thunderstorm.

It was the month of May, and Mississippi was a rainy place in late spring and through the summer. It was a part of the hurricane belt and experienced a lot of rain from the Gulf.

The old guy stared out at the horizon. He squinted his eyes, and then he said, "Whew-wee. Looks like a storm rollin' in."

I stayed quiet.

"Son, good ding ya ridin' wid me ta Jarvis. I'm stayin' in a nice cabin on da lake while I wait fer Mr. Caman ta arrive."

"Caman?"

"Da rich fella wid da flyin' boat. His name is Caman. He won't be arrivin' till tomorrow or da day after dat. I'm headed dere early so I can get in some fishin'. I wanted time ta use his cabin. I've never stayed dere before, but he said it would be okay. I saw it on the internet. It's two stories wid four empty bedrooms, so I've got plenty of room. You could stop in wid me and stay until da storm passes. I can't imagine dat he'd object ta dat. He's a foreign fella, but he sounded real nice on da phone."

I thought for a moment. A home base would be advantageous while I started to get the lay of the land.

"Link and I'd be happy ta have some company. Dese storms usually only last a night. In da morning, dere will be some good fishin'. You could help me reel some in. I got an extra rod."

I looked back out at the clouds. A silvery lightning bolt flashed across the underbelly of one of the bigger ones, and the thunder cracked a split second later. It echoed with plenty of sound and fury through the sky, like a ripple through the water.

I looked back at Hank and said, "Sounds great."

He smiled.

We saw the off-ramp to Black Rock and took it. We drove about two miles through a heavily wooded area. Magnolias grew on both sides of a dusty old road. It wasn't a rocky road—the drive was smooth enough—but I could tell that it hadn't been black-topped in over a decade. The road ended in a fork less than a mile from the southeast corner of the lake, where the lake branched off from the main body and snaked inland for a half mile.

To the right-hand side and up on a hill, there was a sign that read, "This way to Jarvis Lake Houses." To the left-hand side of the fork, a sign read, "Black Rock/Jarvis Dam."

Up on the right-hand side past the signs, there was a small compound, like one of those I'd seen on the news whenever the ATF or the FBI or the DEA was there and gearing up to raid the place. It was a series of scruffy mobile homes and crumbling buildings bunched together like a giant wagon train, with no fence and no signs of life.

The mobile homes perched way back and away from the street. Past them, farther east and toward the trees, there was a new-looking white brick house with hunter-green shutters. It looked like it could have been the headquarters for the whole thing. In the back and sloped way down about forty yards from the house was a large, freshly painted white barn. It was brand new, like a recent addition to the compound, and there was a long dirt track running up to it from the road. The barn had shiny new motion sensor lights installed high on the corners that glimmered and reflected sunspots like flashes from a distant handheld camera or sniper scope.

The most striking part of the compound was an enormous Confederate flag flying high above the trees, right in an open field near the track. It was attached to a gigantic steel flagpole. It looked as if the people living here had spent their life savings on it —and no money on their mobile homes.

The flagpole was massive, soaring above the magnolias, pine trees, and even the heavy oaks. The steel was polished to a shine that glimmered with or without sunlight. It was the most majestic flagpole I had ever seen, and I had seen plenty of them on bases all over the planet.

"Da lake is dammed up on da west side. We'll be drivin' across it if we go inta town, but we're headed dis way ta da cabin," he said and pointed to the right-hand side.

I nodded.

He turned the steering wheel and headed up the hill on a road that was paved but falling apart. It had been pushed up and cracked all over the edges by the roots of a patch of enormous oak trees growing side by side.

I saw where locals had cut down the limbs of the trees so that they didn't grow into each other. Only the limbs that faced outward, away from the road, grew into long, majestic branches that reached toward the sky.

The old gears of the fuel truck whined and clanked as Hank shifted them to climb the hill. A small part of the hill shot up steep, but once we climbed over it, the land became flat again.

We drove down a winding lane that hugged the corners and curves of the lake for about five miles, and then I saw the water from the road. A razor-thin beach composed of sand and rocks knotted the shoreline. The water reflected the stormy sky like a cheap painting hanging in a southern diner somewhere.

Another lightning bolt crackled overhead, lit up the lake, and reflected on the water. For that two-thirds of a second, the entire lake was bright white until it died back to the dull reflection of the dusky clouds.

I said, "We'd better hurry and unload everything as soon as we get there."

Hank nodded.

We arrived at the house. A patch of thick trees hid it from the road. Tangled behind the trees in the shrubbery and vines was a black iron bar fence cutting off access to the backyard. But behind the trees, there was a walkway next to a small clearing of green grass.

My eyes landed on what Hank had called a cabin, but was more like a huge lake house. I imagined a cabin as a tiny one-bedroom log-built thing with a brick fireplace, but this house was huge. Hank had said it was on the large side, but he should have said it was massive. It must have been four thousand square feet.

The building was brick on the front, but the rest of the house was made of wood, probably real and probably oak. It looked sturdy, like it could withstand hurricane conditions, but I doubted that full-blown hurricane-force winds blew this far north, not category five winds anyway.

The rain from a hurricane could make it here, but not the strong winds. By the time a hurricane blew this far inland, the distance and the amount of water it released over the land reduced it to a tropical storm.

Hank pulled the truck up to the side of the house on a small gravel driveway. He threw the gear into neutral and stomped on the emergency brake, locking the vehicle in place. Then he killed the engine.

He said, "Do ya mind unlockin' da house fer me? I need ta bring in my gear."

"I can carry your stuff in for you."

He nodded gratefully, and we exited the vehicle.

Hank held his door open a little longer than I did to allow Link to crawl out. The dog's black-and-white fur blew in the wind as he walked behind his master.

The storm approached our position fast. The air smelled like stale rain, and a sea smell hung in the breeze as if we were out on the open water.

I looked up over the horizon of the lake and saw that the clouds had closed in. I could see a blanket of rain on the far shore. It had already started raining on that side over the town of Black Rock.

I went to the driver's side of the fuel truck and opened the door. I pulled Hank's seat forward and grabbed all the gear behind it. I grabbed a suitcase in one hand and the fishing rods and tackle box in the other. Then I closed the door and walked up the gravel driveway to the side door that Hank had left open for me. The door led into an enormous kitchen area with a big island countertop in the middle of the room. There was expensive cabinetry with black chrome handles on everything. There was a gas stovetop, and a refrigerator built into the wall. The doors were constructed with a new wooden finish, and they matched the walls, virtually blending in.

It was a spectacular kitchen.

Hank said, "Just put dat fishing gear down by da door. I'll use it tamorrow."

I nodded and set everything down. Hank came over to me and took his suitcase. It was one of those wheeled suitcases with a handle that popped out of the top. Good for airports. He set it down, the little wheels touching the floor like the landing gear for a jet. Then he pulled the handle up, extended it to its full length, and walked off with it. The wheels rolled across the tile, clicking as they hit the grout lines.

"I'm goin' ta bed. I'm gettin' up early in da morning so I can get some good fishin' in. Hopefully, da rain will have let up by then. Please join me out on da dock behind da cabin. Dat's if ya want ta fish," Hank said in a cheery voice like he was talking to his grandson, which I could have been—technically.

"See you in the morning."

"Ya can sleep in any of da rooms upstairs dat ya want. I'm going ta sleep downstairs. Back bedroom. Da stairs aren't good on my knees."

He yawned a loud, old-guy yawn, his open mouth exposing his missing teeth again. He turned and left me alone in the kitchen.

Link barked at me like he was saying goodnight and scurried behind his master. They disappeared together down the darkness of a long hallway and into the bowels of the house.

I took out my burner smartphone and switched it on. The screen lit up. I saw more missed phone calls. Probably LeBleu was calling to check on where I had gone. But I couldn't tell him. After all, I wasn't here to arrest anyone. I was here to find my mother's killer and the missing girls. If possible.

I checked the missed call log and confirmed it was probably LeBleu or somebody from his station because the area code matched. I put the phone back in my pocket.

I thought about what my life would be if I lived this way permanently. A drifter. Off the grid.

I'd be a hard man to find. I would have no phone. What for? And I don't have a Facebook page, no LinkedIn, no social media, no usual email, no mailing address—I had nothing.

Most people wouldn't understand the attraction to that kind of life, but I did.

I knew exactly the feeling of being trapped and wanting nothing more than to leave. In the first half of my life, I had the burning desire to get up and go—forward momentum. I never felt right unless I moved forward, but this part of my life had been stationary. I grew up in the back of nowhere in Mississippi. I never knew what else was out there in the world, but I had always wanted to.

One day, my mother told me the secret about my father and that she'd lied to me. We fought, and I left. Never looked back. But the ugly truth of it was that I used my anger for an excuse to leave, and I never called. I should have.

I closed my eyes and stared at a picture of my mother in my memory of the last time that I had seen her sixteen years ago. I let this image linger for a while. I opened my eyes and switched off the phone to conserve the battery. I hadn't thought to bring a charger. I could buy one tomorrow. It'd give me a purpose to walk around and survey the town.

I walked up the stairs to the second floor and entered the first bedroom that I came to. I collapsed on top of a made bed. I didn't turn it down or anything because I was beat from the long day. I didn't even take off my shoes. I just slept on top of the covers.

WARM SUNBEAMS FELL across my face through the window. I opened my eyes sharply and was wide awake. I sat up in bed and reached over to the nightstand, picked up the phone, and switched it on. The battery was still charged. The phone powered on, and the same missed number of calls and text messages showed. No change. It was 6:35 a.m. I left the phone on and slipped it into my pocket. I kept it on silent and left it that way.

I got up and straightened out the bed from where I had rumpled the comforter by sleeping on it. I left the room as I had found it.

I walked downstairs and found that Hank and Link were gone. The fishing gear was gone as well. They must've gone out on the dock.

I went into the kitchen and opened the fridge. It was stocked with bottled waters, sodas, and condiments, but no food. I wouldn't take the food anyway, but I didn't think anyone would mind if I grabbed a bottle of water. There was plenty of it—two cases.

I picked up a bottle, opened it, and gulped it down in about sixty seconds. I stopped for breath just once. I was parched. Afterward, I looked for a trash can and found it near the corner closest to the sink, hidden in a cupboard that pulled out. I pulled on the handle, and the whole thing came rolling out on a cheap-looking white plastic track.

I crushed the bottle and trashed it. Then I stopped and eyeballed the side door that I had entered through the night before. It was on the far wall, just in front of an entrance to another room. I glanced at another door at the rear of the house. That one had to lead to the backyard. I walked over to it, exited the house, and closed the door behind me.

Outside, the air was pleasant. A cool breeze blew in from the lake. I stretched my arms out to full length in the morning sunlight, walked farther into the yard, and gazed out over the horizon.

Closer to my line of sight, a single tree grew tall near the edge of the property line. There was a long shadow trailing from the roots off in a westward direction. A stoned-in grill stood at the edge of the house on a long cement slab, with steps going down a short hill to the grass. The sky was clear and deep blue and sunny, with no storm clouds or clouds of any kind. The high trees created a green barrier around the lake like an old fortress wall, thick and reinforced in some places and eroding in others. Rows of low buildings outlined the northwest corner of the lake, like a painting of an American landscape.

That was the small town of Black Rock.

A good-sized dock, big enough to anchor a seaplane and as new as the house, protruded from the shoreline out over the lake. Hank sat on the tip, loosely holding a fishing rod that extended up and out over his head. The fishing line disappeared far off into the water. He sat hunched over on top of an old cream-colored bucket. The lid appeared to be tightly sealed underneath his small frame. He planted his elbows near the tops of his knees. The end of the fishing rod's long handle was firmly planted into a large gap between the boards on the dock below him.

His dog rested behind him. It was curled up, as it had been in his truck. I liked dogs. I always had. Dogs were an important part of small-town life.

The edge of the water was about a hundred feet from the back of the house, and the dock began about fifteen feet before that. It stretched out about sixty-five feet across the water. There was no railing to keep someone from slipping in, but I doubted anyone would need it. I could see the bed of the lake from where I stood. The water was shallow, at least this close it was.

The dock comprised a platform, the wooden pillars beneath it, the boards, and the nails. I kept thinking of it as a dock, but I wasn't sure if I should've been calling it a dock or a pier. I was sure that no one would call it a wharf. It could have been a pier, but it was thick enough to anchor a seaplane to the end, so I thought that a small dock was a better description.

Hank had invited me to join him in fishing, but I didn't want to fish. I had no interest in it. If I ever wanted to eat fish, I would just look for a seafood restaurant and order from the menu. I hung back near the house and took a moment to plan my next move.

My phone vibrated in my pocket. I pulled it out. It was reminding me I had missed calls and voicemails—five of them. I didn't even bother to look through them. Instead, I touched the screen and opened the settings menu. I switched the phone to airplane mode. Now no one could call me. I clicked the power button on the top of the phone, and the screen went dark. It was now in standby mode. I slipped the phone back into my pocket.

I started thinking about my next move, where to start, and quickly concluded that the best thing for me to do was to walk around the lake, down the southwest side, back down the road to the fork, and take the road into town. I was already here, so it made sense to look at Black Rock.

In town, I could buy new clothes and a cell phone charger, plot out my route, and get a bite to eat. I could find out about the local sheriff, too. I needed to make contact at some point.

I made it down to the edge of the lawn and the beginning of the dock. That was when I noticed a hiking trail worn in the soil from foot traffic. It looked like it might go all the way around the perimeter of the lake. I didn't know the actual stats for Jarvis Lake, but I could see that it was long. It wasn't like one of the Great Lakes, but it was an enormous lake for Mississippi.

I looked left, looked right, and then I paused. Running straight toward me was the most beautiful woman I had ever seen. Not just in real life, but in movies and the internet too. She was breathtaking. She jogged the track at a brisk pace.

She was tall, like a gazelle, maybe five feet ten inches, and she was lean—flat stomach, muscular shoulders, and muscular legs, like a professional runner's, like an athlete. I thought she should have been in one of those fitness magazines. She must've been a runner her whole life, probably track in high school and then college.

As she neared me, I realized I had been staring straight at her. My gaze had never let up, not for a second. In normal situations, when I was caught staring at a woman, I glanced away, like I had only been glancing. This trick wouldn't have worked here because she had seen me staring at her from just a few yards away, and she hadn't flinched, not even a little. She kept on running toward me. She was probably used to guys staring at her. In fact, she probably expected it.

She wore a tight gray-and-white outfit, runner's clothes. The tight gray pants stopped just below her knees, and her tight white short-sleeved top accentuated her shape. She had incredible breasts, not too big but far from small—perfect. Her white-and-red laced-up running shoes looked brand new, still stiff from never being worn and clean like they were straight out of the box.

Her hair was long and blonde and pulled back in a tight French braid. She had long bangs, and the tips touched the top of her eyebrows. She had an Eastern European look about her. If she hadn't spoken to me if she had just run right by without saying a word, I would've thought that she was from Eastern Europe. For sure. No doubt about it.

She stopped three feet from me. She continued to run in place, shuffling from one foot to the next, and then she bent over and placed her hands on her knees. She panted hard with long recovery breaths, then stood up tall and pulled earbuds out of her ears. She held the ends in one hand and stared at me.

She must've been around forty years old, an older woman, older than me anyway. I hadn't considered forty to be old; after all, I was thirty-three. Seven years wasn't much of a difference.

Her lips moved, and she gave me the biggest smile—all white teeth.

She was magnificent. Her eyes were green and bright, and her skin was tan and smooth. She took good care of herself; that was for damn sure. She was so beautiful that I became overwhelmed with the urge to bow to her like I was some peon, and she was royalty. She was the queen, and I was nothing but her servant.

She said, "I haven't had a man stare at me so hard since I was in college."

I gasped because, to me, it seemed like the whole experience had been in slow motion. From the second that I saw her to this moment, I had been suspended in time. I couldn't speak. The only thing I could do was stand there, breathing like I was the one who had just run miles around the lake.

She said, "Are you okay? Do you need a doctor?" She smiled at it like it was a joke. I wasn't sure why.

I recovered, and then I said, "Widow. My name is Widow."

She said, "Sheldon."

Then she paused for another deep breath and asked, "Are you here fishing?"

I shook my head.

"Visiting?"

I shook my head again.

"Tourist?"

I said, "Kind of."

There was a pause between us, and then she said, "Okay. Well, nice talking to you, or not, such as the case may be." She smiled, returned her earbuds to her ears, then jogged away.

I watched her run off. I would've been lying to myself if I didn't admit that I stared at her rear as she went.

She turned back to look at me only once, but that one look meant a lot. She was gorgeous. She had talked to me, and she had looked back at me, and it felt good. I smiled.

A voice from behind me said, "Aren't ya glad dat ya decided ta stay on da lake wid me?"

I spun around and saw that Hank and Link were standing on the dock staring at me and having their own little chuckle over my behavior, Hank for obvious reasons and Link because Hank was excited. They were about fifteen feet away, the old man with nothing in his hands but a pair of pliers, and the dog at his feet.

I smiled and said, "Yes, I am."

Hank said, "Sit by me and fish."

I said, "I'll sit with you a while, but I don't fish."

Hank nodded. He returned to the edge of the dock next to his fishing rod, and Link followed and sat down next to him.

I joined them. Hank sat on his bucket, and I sat down on the dock. The bottoms of my shoes touched the water before my legs had even dangled all the way down, so I had to pull them up and sit cross-legged.

Even sitting down, I towered over Hank and Link. It must have looked like Frankenstein's monster sitting next to the elderly blind man that he met in that old black-and-white movie, except that Hank wasn't blind.

I shook off the imagery and asked, "Catch anything?"

Hank said, "Oh, sure. I caught t'ree fish already. Look in da bucket over dere."

I glanced in a second bucket beside me. There were three enormous fish covered in ice.

I said, "Nice."

We exchanged no more words for a while. I studied the water and then the opposite shoreline. There were trees and rocks and more trees. Next, I scanned the northwest side of the lake. I saw piers full of boats and watched as people launched their vessels into the lake. I scanned past them and studied the low buildings. Most of the town seemed to be bunched up in the same rows of buildings. From this distance, I couldn't tell what they were, but I knew that there must be banks, a fire station, bait shops, motels, bars, cafés, a school, a police station, a clinic or two, and of course, a church. This was the South, and the South was a very religious place. I looked to the east of town and saw a group of buildings clustered together like a small military complex. One building was two stories, and the others were one. From this distance, they looked expensive. A shiny coil of barbed wire fencing surrounded the place like a prison fence. It created an impressive quarantine perimeter around the complex.

I asked, "Hank, what's that compound across the lake? The one that looks like a prison."

Hank raised his hand above his eyes like he was saluting. He used it to block out the sunlight and squinted to see across the lake.

He said, "No, dat's da Eckhart Medical Center. It's a research complex or somedin'. It's one of da only other economies here. Da biggest group of da townsfolk make deir money from tourism and fishing. I would say about fifteen percent of da town works for da Eckhart Medical Center or gets deir business from dere."

"Why the prison fence around it?"

Hank squinted again and asked, "How da hell are ya seeing dat detail? Dat fence is so tiny from here. I can't even tell what it is fer sure."

"I have good vision. And good hearing. I always have."

Hank said, "I dink dat dey do research on animals dere or somedin'. Dey don't want any escapin' or any environmentalists breakin' in. I've heard dat dey've had problems with activists in da past." He'd whistled every "s."

I said, "Big fence. What kind of animals do they have in there? Bears?"

"I never really dought about it before."

I shrugged. A moment of silence fell between us, and then I stood up. My legs had fallen asleep from sitting cross-legged. I shook one and then the other, trying to get the blood circulating again.

I looked down at Hank. He hadn't noticed that I had stood up until he saw my immense shadow move over him like an incoming predator. He stared directly up at me with his head completely cocked back.

He said, "Are ya leavin' us?"

I nodded and said, "Thank you so much for the ride and a place to crash for the night, but I'd better be on my way."

He put his fishing rod back down in the crack between two boards and stood up. He extended his hand for a handshake and smiled warmly.

He said, "Good luck, son. Come back if ya need a place ta stay tanight."

I shook his hand as gently as I could and thanked him, then turned and looked at the back of the lake house.

I could walk around the side of the house, take the road back to the fork, and walk into town along the road, but I took the jogging path that Sheldon had run along. It looked like it snaked all the way around the lake. This route had two bonuses that I could see —it was scenic, following the lake. Plus, Sheldon might turn around and run back this way, in which case I could see her again. I walked over and left Hank, Link, and the lake house, thinking I would see none of them again.

Part of me wished that had been true.

## 9

I WALKED along the jogging path, following the same winding route and heading in the same direction that Sheldon had taken before she vanished into the forest of pines. It took me forty-four minutes to make it around Jarvis Lake to the edge of town.

I reached the outskirts at around 8:30 in the morning, and I was hungry. I hadn't even thought that if I had stayed with Hank for another hour, he would've probably cooked us some breakfast. Old grandpa types were like that. At least that was what I had always believed. My grandpa had died long before I was born. My mother was a lot like him, I think.

I paused and took a break from walking without even realizing it. My feet stopped, and I stood there on the outskirts of town. I looked around, still half buried in my thoughts.

The jogging path had led me into a clearing that merged with the road heading into town. The track, neatly manicured here with a fresh synthetic material that looked like sawdust, became a part of a paved sidewalk that paralleled the town's main street.

I shook off thoughts of Hank's trout breakfast and got something to eat that wasn't trouty. I had plenty of money in my bank account, and a town, no matter where it was in the United States, was bound to have restaurants, cafés, and fast-food joints. Eateries were as American as apple pie. I didn't imagine there was a town anywhere that didn't have a place where you could get a good, hearty breakfast —especially small towns. Small towns relied on tourism. They relied on outsiders to come in and pump cash into the local economy.

Black Rock was a fishing town, so it relied heavily on the lake to generate income. Naturally, it would have seafood restaurants and a diner or two.

I decided I should stop for breakfast and then shop for new clothes and a cell phone charger. I walked into town and noticed a lot of out-of-towners, tourists, and vacationers. They were mostly older white men and mostly from Mississippi or Alabama or Louisiana or Tennessee or Georgia. The accents I had hated to hear in movies were prevalent here. The men drove around in big fuel-guzzling pickups and wore polo shirts, sunglasses, and ball caps. They all had beer guts and tan lines. They were the faces of southern anglers with money to spend. Black Rock prospered on their money, so I knew that there would be some good southern cooking here.

I walked into the heart of town. The traffic was moderate, and everyone seemed to be already awake. I walked on past street-lights and past a tiny florist shop with an awning shaped like a giant rose petal over the door, an ice cream shop that hadn't opened yet, and a bakery that smelled of fresh beignets. I moved beyond the town's municipal buildings and saw a courthouse with a sign out front that read: "Public Safety Complex."

It looked like the town had housed all its public safety services under one roof. The courthouse was obviously here. In front of the building, there were a couple of cop cars parked in the lot. In the rear, under a standalone carport, there was an old fire truck, a shiny red thing that looked to be about thirty years old. I guess they got little use out of it. But the city had taken good care of it, like it was more of a spokesperson rather than a functional fire vehicle. They must have washed it constantly, taking it to the local school and allowing the kids to hang on it for pictures. The kids probably took turns ringing the siren. It might've been the only time anyone ever heard the damn thing.

Black Rock had so far portrayed itself as a quiet town. Any ruckus in the area probably took place on the lake.

I looked back at the cop cars, studied them briefly. A pair of Dodge Intrepids. They were old, maybe ten years, but like the fire truck, they were well-maintained. The Dodge Intrepid was not an uncommon vehicle to be used by police departments. Of course, the Ford Crown Vic was seen more often, but for a small town like this, budget was everything. The Dodge Intrepid police package was probably lighter on the city's budget, and that they had little ground to cover made it viable to keep the same cars for ten years. I was sure that it was equally important to keep them in proper working order.

I left the Public Safety Complex and walked around the town longer, deciding not to stop for breakfast for at least another half an hour. I wanted to scan the town for all the options that it offered. Plus, I wanted to plan my day, so I ventured on.

Cars and trucks drove past me at a slow speed, the drivers intrigued by the transient who walked among them.

As I walked, I discovered that the town had at least three different Christian churches. I saw no other religious house of worship to speak of—no synagogues, no temples, no shrines. I wasn't surprised. The South wasn't famous for its tolerance of religions outside of Christianity. It wasn't even tolerant of many denominations of Christianity.

In my experience, though, the South was far more open to pluralism than its reputation conveyed. I had grown up with kids who had gay parents or were gay themselves. I knew black kids, white kids, Asian kids, and Hispanic kids. And my small town was not unlike Black Rock.

Not all the people who lived in Killian Crossing had been Christian. We had Jewish people, atheists, and even a Buddhist family. No one in the town ever protested any of their beliefs. It caused no friction, wars, or feuds. Everyone had gotten along fine, but I had never seen a building of worship that wasn't a Christian church. I'm sure that there were some in places like Jackson or Biloxi, but not in Killian Crossing and probably not in Black Rock.

Still, something about this town felt different to me. Something was missing, and it was eating away at a part of my brain like a pilot fish swimming close to the great white shark, cleaning it by nipping away at the small parasites that festered on its sandpapery skin. I was the shark, and this small something was nipping at my brain like a pilot fish, only I couldn't tell what it was.

I stopped and shrugged to no one but myself. I was hungrier than I thought and needed to eat.

I abandoned my survey of the town and went straight for breakfast. So far, I had seen a diner that was about three blocks in the opposite direction. I pivoted on my right foot and swung around as if one of my old Recruit Division Commanders had shouted, "'Bout face!" Then I headed back in the other direction, back to the diner.

I walked on until I returned to the corner where I had seen the diner.

The sign on top of the building read, "Roy's Red Dinner."

The spelling was wrong— "diner" is spelled with one "n," not two. When I entered, sat down, and opened my menu, I realized they knew it was spelled incorrectly. Part of their gimmick, I supposed. The first page on the menu had a cartoon drawing of a short, fat, bald white man with a pitch-black mustache, the owner and founder. The caption beside his character read, "Roy."

Next to Roy's cartoon picture was a story entitled "The Red Dinner." It explained that when it first opened, the diner's sign was spelled wrong, and it stuck. It was originally called the Red Dinner because the outside of the building was a bright-red color. The paint looked redone, and recently too. It was bright red. The story said that Roy had owned the diner for twenty-five years until he passed away five years ago. His daughter now ran the place.

I skimmed past the rest of the story and gazed at the food options. They had lots of breakfast items to choose from. They were all egg-based, which was fine by me because all I was in the mood for was eggs and bacon.


WHILE I WAITED TO ORDER, my mind wandered. I thought about my mom again. We used to be tight. She used to take me hunting and fishing. She'd take me to work, which isn't that unusual. However, her job was solving murders. And she'd get me to help her.

I was a little boy solving crimes with my mom.

I remembered one time she had taken me to a murder scene where the body of an old man was sprawled out underneath a white sheet.

"Who killed him?" she had asked.

I said, "I don't know."

"Look around the room."

"I can't see the body."

"You don't need to. Often the details in your surroundings give away more clues than a dead body does."

I tried, and then I said, "I can't."

She said, "Yes, you can. You can do anything you want."

I was only ten years old the first time she took me to a crime scene like that. Looking back on it, I understood how someone could see it as unorthodox, even borderline immoral. But my mom was training me for something.

My mom had seen more of life and death than most people. She had three decades of experience in solving murders. She had insight into a world that most people didn't know about, and I think she wanted to prepare me for it.

The same way that Robbie Mile's father had taught him about tires and cars, my mom taught me about solving crimes, about righting wrongs.

I was ten years old, and I was looking at a murder scene after the fact. I looked at the room. It was a motel room way off Interstate 72, exit 131B to the north. We were almost at the end of my mother's jurisdiction. The Tennessee border was only seven and a half miles away.

I remembered closing my eyes and reenacting the crime scene in my head. With virtually no details of the dead man's appearance, I saw a man, two empty beer bottles, and a glass of wine on the tabletop. A condom wrapper laid on the floor near the trash can. Shampoo suds dried near the drain in the tub. Globs of shower gel remained on the tile. I saw a toilet seat left in the down position. I saw a piece of wadded tissue paper in the trash can. Inside it was a chewed-up stick of gum.

There were subtle signs of a struggle—disheveled furniture, a skewed lampshade, and a rumpled bedspread, like someone had been rolling around on the bed. But the only thing that showed definitively that a struggle had occurred was the bathroom mirror. It was shattered.

My mother said, "What happened here?"

I kept my eyes closed, still scanning the room in my mind. I said, "The guy was shot."

Never opening my eyes, I pointed at the wall behind my mother and opposite the bed. Blood had splattered high on the wall and on the corner of the ceiling.

I said, "There's blood splattered on that wall. Someone lying underneath him on the bed shot the guy. The killer fired the bullet at close range and diagonally, probably through his gut. It exited through his back and sprayed blood at an upward angle. That's why it's so high on the wall. And there's stippling."

My mother asked, "And what's that?"

I said, "Can I see the body?"

My mother paused a beat and then she pulled back the sheet, and I looked at the body. Then she returned the sheet and said, "Okay. Now explain."

I said, "Burns on his skin from gunpowder. That's how I know he was shot in the gut. It also means it was a close-range shot."

She asked, "What kind of bullet? What kind of gun?"

I shook my head. Then I said, "I do not know."

I heard her frustration, but she had said nothing. It was there in her breathing.

She asked, "So who killed him?"

I opened my eyes and asked, "Where's his wallet?"

"We found it outside in the bushes."

"His car?"

"Gone."

I asked, "Was the money gone?"

She nodded, and then she asked again, "So who killed him?"

I said, "A prostitute. He wanted to go straight to adult business after they had a few drinks. And he drank beer out of the bottle, and she drank wine by the glass. Then he refused to pay her up front, so she pulled a small-caliber gun out of her stocking or from a nearby purse or from wherever a woman might hide a small handgun. She shot him right in the gut—point-blank."

My mom asked, "And then?"

I said, "Then she rolled him off her and grabbed his car keys and his wallet. She ran outside, took money out of the wallet, and stole his car."

"Any chance it was self-defense? Maybe the guy refused to pay and then forced himself on her?"

"Maybe. But either way, that's up to the prosecution. And this guy's dead. The woman isn't. I doubt the prosecutor will let it go as self-defense."

She nodded. "My job is to solve, not to judge. Always remember that, Widow. I don't want you to act outside of the law."

I stayed quiet.

She paused and then said, "Good job. Every man is innocent until proven guilty. Judgment is up to a judge and jury, not a single man."

"Do you want coffee?" a voice asked.

I looked up from the menu. An older waitress with deep-set brown eyes and a warm smile on her face stood over me, gazing down.

She held a jug of steaming coffee in her right hand and had an old white coffee mug in her left. The mug looked like it had seen its fair share of dishwashers. It was worn, faded, and had tiny cracks on the exterior.

I looked up at her with a smile. She had said the magic words. What Navy man doesn't drink coffee? I said, "Please! Let me get a coffee. Black. And two eggs, four pieces of bacon, and four pieces of toast."

She smiled and turned and disappeared behind a counter piled with beverage machines and coffee makers and mugs. Menu items like pies and cookies were displayed in glass containers. Soon she came out from behind the display with my coffee—black, a single cup, and placed it in front of me. She handed me a set of silverware in a napkin that was rolled tight and held together by a thin sticker like the seal on an envelope. I ripped through the sticker and placed the utensils in front of me.

I drank the coffee. It was good.

About twelve minutes later, the food came. It smelled good.

It was served in a red ceramic dish. I guess the whole theme of the diner was red—red dishes, red walls, everything red. I wondered why the coffee mugs were white and not red, but I dismissed my curiosity almost as fast as I had raised the question.

I was more interested in eating.

AFTER I FINISHED MY BREAKFAST, I asked the waitress about the area. She explained that the town's economy was based on the lake, which was obvious. It was the next part I was more interested in. She told me that there was a medical research facility that played a smaller role, and then she didn't say another word about it. She told me she had grown up here in Black Rock and was retiring here in a few years.

*You're probably going to die here*, I thought. Not on purpose, not with any kind of intentional meanness, but thoughts came and went, and there wasn't anything I could do about it.

I glanced at her name tag. It read, "Hazel."

I asked, "The medical place? Is that the compound that's surrounded by the barbed wire fence?"

She nodded and said, "It's called the Eckhart Medical Center. The town's only clinic operates out of it. Dr. Eckhart has been great to us. Before the doctor, we all had to drive to Oxford for serious afflictions."

"It's a hospital?" I asked.

"No, it's a research facility. They do research on animals or something. But the lower north wing is set up as a clinic and emergency room. There's a twenty-four-hour staff. The doctor keeps business hours and is always on call."

I nodded and said nothing.

She paused and put the check down in front of me, and then she asked, "Will there be anything else?"

"Where's the nearest Radio Shack?"

She looked at me with a blank expression and then said, "There's Cellular Citi. It's the only electronics store in town. They carry all kinds of stuff. It's like a small Best Buy. Want me to draw you a map?"

I smiled. "That would be great."

She set her tray down on my table, pulled out a pen, tore a clean sheet off a notepad, and began drawing on the paper. It took her about a minute to finish. She handed the map to me.

I accepted it and smiled again. And then she left.

I looked at the check. The bill was $9.55. I reached into my pocket and pulled out a ten and a five, stacking the bills on top of the check. The five made it a fifty percent tip, but I had the money and figured she could use the extra.

I stood up from the table and held the map in my line of sight. I stared at it and memorized the exact route she had plotted out for me. Then I crumpled the paper up and left it on the table. The map was etched into my memory.

My mind worked like a computer. It always had. I could visualize anything that I'd seen before or imagine anything with great detail just by closing my eyes and concentrating.

I left Roy's Red Dinner and walked on to the electronics store. I wanted to get that charger for my phone.

USING the map that the waitress had drawn up for me, it took me over ten minutes to walk to the store. The place smelled like it was once a laundromat. Instead of tile, it had a thick blue carpet that was stained from God knows what. Not the cleanest store ever.

I went straight to the counter and pulled my phone out of my pocket. It took the clerk all of two minutes to find the charger I needed. I paid for it and left the store.

After the store, I didn't have a plan of attack as far as which direction I needed to go. The left seemed as good a direction as right, so I decided that from now on, if I got confused about which way I wanted to go, I'd pick left.

I turned left and walked through the town. I've got to admit that I was understanding the appeal of the drifter life. Being a stranger in a strange place was appealing. It was like I was on the frontier. I was an explorer in a place that I had never explored before. It was freeing. Being told about a place and experiencing it for myself were two completely different things.

I walked through town—past the bait shops, the bars, two seafood restaurants, a used car lot, a used boat lot, and a shabby-looking museum, which was closed today. The town had a quaint, small-town feel to it. Quite touristy, if you go for that sort of thing.

I stopped walking and found an outdoor café. I sat at a table and ordered my second coffee. The waiter brought it and left. He didn't ask if I wanted food.

I took some time and thought about my plan of attack. Where would I start? I had no leads, except that the sheriff knew my mother, which wasn't much. Plus, I needed to speak to the sheriff without blowing my cover.

## 10

It was the middle of the afternoon, and I had spent hours simply observing. I hadn't moved from the café. The same chair. Same table outside. I tossed a couple of bucks on the table since I had taken it up all day. Then I stepped onto the sidewalk and headed east.

I had seen a motel on the east side of town about a block from the lake. I figured it was a good idea to get a room. I had no idea how long this would take, and I wasn't going anywhere until I found my mother's killer.

I walked past the store where I had bought the phone charger, passed some parked cars, and crossed the street. On the left-hand side of the street, there was a series of townhouses with privacy fences, black iron bars on the windows, and patriotic signs posted in the yards.

I walked on until I came to the end of a faded entrance to the parking lot of a Super 8 motel. I cut across the lot, went up to the office door, and pulled it open. A bell dinged above my head. It was attached to the door, an ancient but time-tested warning system.

A tall, wiry man with one crutch came limping out of a side room. He saw me and nodded. He wore a yellow trucker's cap and a thrifty gray polo shirt.

He limped over to the counter and went behind it and asked, "Can I help you?"

I said, "Can I get a room for the night?"

He looked down at a clipboard and studied it like it was a patient's chart. Then he said, "I have a single room all the way at the end. Number fourteen."

I said, "Works for me."

He nodded, turned, and grabbed a key off the wall.

He turned back around and said, "$27.50."

I pulled out a wad of money and peeled off a twenty and a ten and handed them to him.

He just stared at me for a moment, and then he said, "Hope you don't expect me to walk you all the way down there. I got a bum leg."

I shook my head.

He handed me the key and asked, "Anything else?"

I said, "Change?"

"I ain't got no change," he said and pointed to a sign on the wall that read, "Exact change only."

I grinned and nodded and turned to step out onto the sidewalk, but he cleared his throat and interrupted me.

I turned back to look at him. He had the guest registry turned toward me. He tapped his old, frail finger on the paper and said, "Sign in. State law."

I returned to the counter, took the blue ballpoint pen from his hand, and stared down at the paper. I paused for a moment and thought back to a lesson my mother had taught me before the

NCIS. One time, we had taken a trip to New Orleans to watch the Saints play the Cowboys. We had stayed off Bourbon Street in some old, rundown hotel with fake balconies and shutters. The whole place was painted pink, but it had faded to an orangish tint.

I shrugged and began writing the first alias I could think of. I didn't like to give out my name. I signed the register: Jeremy Shockey. Shockey had played for the New Orleans Saints during the Super Bowl in 2010. They won that year. I figured the old man might recognize the name, but I doubted it'd make any difference. I didn't think he'd call me out on it.

I put the pen down, smiled, and walked out of the office and down the sidewalk to room number fourteen.

It was the last room. There was no upstairs. No neighbors above. There was only the neighbor in room thirteen.

As I crossed in front of room thirteen, I saw the door was ajar, just a hair, maybe an inch. I saw an eyeball peering out at me from the darkness of the room. The shades were drawn, and the lights were off. The sun filled the terrain with its last light, but room thirteen remained dark. Whoever occupied that room didn't want anyone to know that he or she was there.

The second I stepped one foot in front of it, the door slammed, the dead bolt locked into place, and the chain rattled as it swiped across the top of the door. I wasn't offended. Maybe the occupant was an old woman or a timid person. In a seedy motel like this one, I wasn't exactly the neighbor dreams were made of.

I was a scary guy, but my clothes were normal. I was wearing an ordinary green T-shirt with an abstract design and baggy blue jeans. Typical casual clothes.

I was surprised at the generosity of the people I'd met in the last two days, especially Hank and the girl who had picked me up yesterday. The rides I had gotten so far were from people who seemed genuinely nice and friendly.

I slid the key into my door and turned it. The door opened, and a cloud of thick dust seeped out. The air was stale. It didn't smell bad, just unused, like an attic.

I entered the room and shut the door behind me. The lights flickered on. The room was in decent shape with old and worn furniture, but the bed was made, and the carpet was relatively clean and free of spots.

I slipped the key into my pocket. It was early, around sundown, but I was tired. I supposed I was emotionally drained from my mother's death, plus my investigation. And I still thought about my job. I had left an assignment, although it was over. I had literally been in California two nights ago, ending one undercover investigation, and now I was neck deep in another.

It was too early to sleep, so I returned to the diner. Sometimes, waiting was more productive than searching.

## 11

I sat at Roy's Red Dinner once again in a corner booth with my back to the wall—an old instinct, which meant I had a cone of only about ninety degrees to watch over.

It was about ten past eight in the evening. I knew this because there was a giant clock on the back wall above the counter. It had little cartoon hens drawn above or beside or beneath each of the quarter-hour bars. There was a large red rooster just underneath the twelve o'clock position. Probably years ago, Roy or his wife or his descendants had seen the clock in a garage sale and thought it would fit the little diner. And since everything was red, it did.

A young Hispanic girl about twenty-one years old approached my table. She was the evening waitress; I guess. She looked new. It was something about how she walked, as if she was confused about what her section was and where things were. She was also a lot more energetic than her counterparts. Maybe she hadn't yet been corrupted by years of complacency. She wore a fresh smile on her face.

Her name tag said, "Maria." It was silver with bold black letter-ing. It looked new and gleamed in the light, reflecting my face behind the letters in an obscure way. I felt like I was looking onto the surface of a spoon.

She stopped in front of my table, her notepad at the ready. She was tiny, probably five foot two.

She said, "Hey there. Are you ready to order?"

She had said "hey there" in that way that I've heard a woman say from time to time when flirting. I hadn't expected that, and she had meant it. I could tell. So, I smiled and said, "I'll have the cheeseburger plate. No fries. Just the burger. And coffee."

She looked up from her notepad and said, "Be right back."

I nodded, smiled. She walked away. She returned with water and coffee, placed both down on my table, pulled a clean spoon out of a plastic covering, and slid it into the coffee.

Pointing a finger toward the inside of my table, she said, "Sugar is there. Do you need cream?"

I said, "I like it black."

She turned to walk away, stopped, looked back over her shoulder, and winked at me. You don't have to be an expert in body language to understand a wink. I would've been smiling harder if it weren't for my circumstances.

I shrugged and took out my cell phone again. And once again, I ignored the missed calls, voicemails, and text messages.

I logged into my NCIS email account. I never liked modern technology that much, but I knew how. It was required for my work—naturally. I understood the ins and outs of mobile devices, the internet, and social media as much as everyone else. There was just something ingrained in me that preferred the old ways. I liked to speak to a person face-to-face, not by text message, and I never cared to share my every single thought or feeling on social media. Never saw the point. Feelings and thoughts were private, and they were pretty much meaningless. Thoughts were merely impulses and electronic signals firing in the brain. They reflected nothing about you. Only your actions and words spoke about you. Whenever someone asked me if I had Facebook, Twitter, or one of those networks, my standard answer was, "I don't tweet!"

I did like getting instant sports news. While I waited for my food, I checked the news in sports. Germany was doing well in soccer. It was rumored that the Cleveland Cavaliers might get back their star player, who had left the team to play for Miami for the last decade. It hadn't happened, but that was the journalist's prediction. There wasn't anything else of interest in the sports arena.

I turned to the news headlines and browsed through the articles. There were articles about the president's low job approval ratings, the bad economy, and something about civil unrest in the Gaza strip, basically nothing new. I saw an article about a raid by the DEA and the Mexican Federales on a major compound on the coast of Mexico and then a story on the rising stock prices of bottled water. Another article talked about the CEO of Starbucks promoting an idea to pay for college tuition for its employees.

The DEA thing looked the most interesting, so I clicked on the link beneath the article, and the web page loaded. The story talked about a man named Oskar Tega. Apparently, seven days ago, the DEA and the Mexican Federales had enough evidence to arrest criminal mastermind Oskar Tega finally. They had connected Tega to a string of secret operations all the way from Mexico to the south of Florida. DEA agents had raided his coastal compound on the Gulf of Mexico and found it empty. Then twenty-four hours later, one of Tega's secret locations was discovered—a bit too late because it had been burned to the ground.

The article said that the men who had already been arrested in connection with Oskar Tega had called the locations *granjas*. My Spanish wasn't very good. I knew people who spoke perfect Spanish, and I had taken some classes in high school, but I didn't recognize the word.

Maria came by and smiled at me.

She dropped off the obligatory red plate with my cheeseburger, placed a bottle of ketchup in front of me, and then asked, "Can I get you anything else?"

I asked, "Do you speak Spanish?"

She looked at me, and her smile turned to a look of disappointment. She said, "Oh, baby, you aren't like these racist idiots that live here, are ya?"

"No. No way," I said.

She smiled again.

"I'm just wondering if you speak Spanish."

She said, "Sí. I remember most words. I'm not from Mexico though. I'm from Texas. But my grandma and I used to speak Español. My mom, she only spoke in English, but she understood it just fine."

I handed her my cell phone after I enlarged the section with the word, I wanted translated. Then I asked, "Can you tell me what this word means?"

She grabbed the phone gently with one of her hands, leaned in toward it, and studied the text. Then she said, "This word means 'farms.' Oh, I heard about this. This guy Tega is some kind of drug kingpin. He escaped capture, and they think he fled to Cuba. But his men are here in the US. They've been visiting all of his farms and taking their product out, and they leave no witnesses. There was this town in Texas. Tega's men went there a few days ago and took back whatever drugs were there. Then they murdered all of his employees and left half of the town on fire. It's like what the Germans did in World War II."

A puzzled look must have fallen across my face, because she immediately responded.

She said, "You know? Like when the Russians would raid German villages and instead of finding prisoners and supplies, the Germans had burned everything to the ground and left their ruined homes behind. They made it impossible for the Russians to use any of their supplies."

I said, "That's called scorched earth, and it wasn't the Germans— it was what the Russians had done to the Germans."

She said, "Yup. That's it. Well, enjoy your burger."

I nodded.

She walked away from the table.

I continued reading about Oskar Tega.

Police thought he was in Cuba, and they weren't sure how he'd gotten out of Mexico without them noticing. They guessed by boat, or possibly he'd chartered a plane or already owned one. There was a large docking space at the end of a pier on his property. They figured he had cast off in a yacht possibly days before. The DEA assumed he had bribed his way past SEMAR, the Mexican Navy, or had gotten past the US Coast Guard on the outer perimeter. Tega was a well-connected man. Now no one knew where he was.

I took two big bites from my hamburger. One. Two. It was more than halfway gone. I had an enormous appetite and was hungry. Hitchhiking and tourism were hard work.

I put the burger back down on the plate and clicked on the internet search bar at the top of the screen. I typed in missing girls from Mississippi.

The circle icon spun around and around, showing that the browser was searching, and then several results came back— missing children, missing girls, murders, and so on.

I added the word "north" in front of "Mississippi" and clicked the search button again. The web browser searched and came up with links to articles like "The FBI Baffled by Missing Girls in North Mississippi."

I clicked on one link, and it took me to an article that was about five years old. I skimmed through it. It told the same story that Jill, the grad student from yesterday, had told me. Missing young girls. Most of them driving along the freeways and highways. All of them had left one destination and were expected at another, but never made it. Sheriffs, local police, and the FBI had all been involved. The investigation had gone nowhere and remained open.

Some reports claimed the girls were abducted by hitchhikers, but that was nothing but speculation. Some of their vehicles had been found abandoned, left in ditches or in shopping mall parking lots. In my experience, one thing that a young girl never did was leave her car behind. The reports said that some of the girls' vehicles had never been found.

I took two more bites of my cheeseburger and finished it. I slid the plate away and drank some water.

I turned off the phone and put it back in my pocket.

Maria returned to check on me.

She grabbed the plate off the table and asked, "Do you want anything else?"

I said, "No, thanks. Just the check."

She slid the check over to me and winked. As I reached for it, her index finger brushed against the top of mine like she was purposely trying to touch me.

I looked up at her and smiled.

She walked away.

I flipped the check over and saw that below the total; she had written her phone number with a smiley face underneath.

I smiled. I placed a twenty-dollar bill on top of the check, a generous tip, but the service was well worth it. I committed her number to memory and got up from my booth and left the diner.

## 12

Before I returned to my motel room, I walked around the town for two more hours. I wanted to get a good look at the nightlife. I stopped at a couple of dive bars. One was a country western bar. The band there played a few rock 'n' roll songs; only they made them sound like country. They weren't too bad, some local band that I had never heard of and would most likely never hear of again. But it was fun.

The second bar was a juke joint filled with aging hipsters. Both bars were busy, not completely packed, not wall-to-wall people, but busy. I seized the opportunity to grab a beer and ordered a single at the hipsters' bar—no shots, no hard liquor, just the one beer. I didn't want to be inebriated.

After I left the bars, I walked down to the lake and gazed out over the calm water. I felt the breeze blow warm, soft air across my face and neck. Jarvis Lake was a man-made lake, and man-made lakes were calm. No reason for high wave activity. Across the lake, I saw various lights from the houses and cars. A few boats were peppered across the surface of the water. Tiny lights blinked, showing their location and telling other boats that there was a boat in their path.

Nearby, a dock was loaded with plenty of nighttime fishermen. I heard voices and laughing in the distance. I looked to my left and saw the Eckhart Medical Center. I walked toward it, curious what went on there.

Black Rock was a relatively poor town. The buildings were old but taken care of and definitely used. Not too many of them were newer than ten years. Most of the newer businesses were probably operating out of old, remodeled buildings.

The Eckhart Medical Center was the one exception. The buildings were nice—and expensive. They were painted white—a fresh-looking paint job—and had closed green shutters on every window. None of this was really all that unusual, but the security was something that troubled me.

I walked closer to the perimeter of the complex. I got as close to it as I could without raising suspicion. Not that it had a posted guard or anything, but there was tall, barbed wire fencing all around it except at the front. The only places where this security was lacking were the two entrances. One of them was a dark entrance with a small glass doorway and no visible markings or signs. Staff entrance, I guess. The second entrance was an automatic double door with a flat black rubber mat in front. The sign above the door read, "24-Hour Community Clinic." According to Hazel, the waitress, this was the town's primary source of health care.

Both Hank and Hazel had said that animal research went on here. That explained the extra security measures—animals. But what animals required security cameras and a barbed wire fence? Maybe the security was more to keep activists out rather than keep the animals in.

Something else dawned on me, maybe because I had seen both the daytime people and the nighttime people. I had seen no minorities—not a single black person, no Asian people, no foreigners, and only one Hispanic. Black Rock was a small town, but there had to be a few thousand people living here. How could they all be white? This was 2014, not 1955, but Maria was the only minority I had seen. Every bar, diner, café, store, or street where I had walked so far, I had seen only white people. The South, especially Mississippi, had a poor reputation for being racist and segregated. That might've been the case forty or more years ago, but in my experience, Mississippi people were as tolerant as anyone anywhere now.

It was odd.

I shrugged off my curiosity about the Eckhart Medical Center and turned and headed back to the motel.

BACK IN MY ROOM, I sat down on the bed and realized that I had forgotten to buy new clothes. Guess I was going to have to wear the same clothes tomorrow. But I didn't want to sleep in them again, and I didn't want to wake up and wear dirty clothes. I took them off and washed them in the sink. I'd never tried it before, but I figured it'd work as well as anything. For thousands of years, mankind, or more precisely womankind, had washed clothes in streams and rivers.

I washed my jeans first with shampoo out of the little bottle from the shower. I nearly used the entire bottle on my pants. I wasn't sure if it would make a good detergent, but it had to be better than wearing them dirty.

I rolled the jeans in a towel to soak up some of the moisture and then tossed them over the shower rod and left them there to hang and dry. Next, I took off my shirt and rinsed it in the sink. I used hand soap for the rest of my clothes and save the remaining shampoo for my hair. The shirt was much easier to wash than the jeans. The fabric was cotton and soaked up the soap faster than the jeans. I let the hot water run and lathered up both sides of the shirt with the soap. Then I rinsed it and wrung it out and stretched the ends in opposite directions, so it didn't wrinkle as it dried. Finally, I hung it up next to the jeans. Then I cleaned my socks and left them on the side of the tub.

I washed my face in the sink and decided that I was beat. I wanted to sleep. I could take a shower in the morning and put on clean clothes, although they may not be completely dry.

I discarded my underwear. No reason to clean them, and I certainly didn't want to wear them again. I took them off and threw them in a wastebasket in the bathroom.

Before I went to bed for the night, I looked in the mirror and smacked my head. *Great, Widow! You forgot to get a toothbrush!*

Guess I had a lot to learn about the nomadic life. In the Navy, I'd just ask for it or go hit the commissary. I went to the bed, pulled the covers back, and slid in. I reached over and clicked the button on the lamp. The lights shut off.

I woke up at 1:37 in the morning. I knew this because I checked my cell phone before I got up and out of bed to see what all the noise was. That was when I met Dr. Chris Matlind and the three guys who wanted to do him bodily harm.

I heard voices and shouting and what sounded like roughhousing through the wall. Some dialects were so thick that they sounded like muffled cartoon voices.

I wasn't sure what was going on at first.

I got out of bed, went to the bathroom, and grabbed my pants. They were still pretty damp. With no source of heat to dry them, I didn't expect them to be dry enough to wear yet, but I had to put something on. I couldn't go over and confront my neighbors wearing no pants. I slipped the jeans on and buttoned and zipped them. No belt. No shoes. No shirt. I was getting too angry to bother putting them on. I didn't even check to see if my shirt was dry.

I got a glance at myself in the mirror. I was still half asleep. My face looked groggy. My legs and thighs were now damp from the jeans. I had gone to bed with my hair down, so now it hung down across my face. I looked like something out of a nightmare, like a caveman with one idea on his primal brain: kill. Not going to lie, I felt that way, too.

I stormed out of my room, barefoot, and over to room thirteen, next door. The door was halfway open. As I approached it, I heard the voices more clearly. One guy spoke articulately, even sounded educated, a little like an elitist, only his voice was nasal, like he was pinching his nose.

He said, "Please, don't hit me again. You fractured my nasal bones." Only his voice was filled with nasal sounds.

Another voice said, "You broke his nose, Daryl." The tone was the opposite of compassion. It was pleasure.

A different voice, a deeper voice said, "I know what he meant, Jeb. Now grab his arms. This city boy is going in the truck."

The nasal voice said, "I only want her back. Please don't hit me again. Just give her back to me, and we'll leave."

A third voice, an unknown voice, said, "Daryl, let me hit him with the bat."

Daryl said, "No, Junior. I think Pa is gonna wanna talk to him without breaking bones. 'Sides, we ought to put him in the truck instead of carr'n' him."

Jeb said, "Yeah, Junior, he is cohop'ratin'. No reason to hit him with the bat. Not yet."

*The word is "cooperating,"* I thought, reactively, like my fourth grade English teacher.

Before I even opened the door, I heard the frustration from the guy I assumed to be Junior, an audible expression, like a loud sigh from an ungrateful child.

Then I kicked the bottom of the door with my left foot, not hard and not soft. Just enough to swing the door open slowly in a kind of dramatic scene, like when the door in a haunted house creaks open and the occupants stop and stare. A big part of dealing with potentially violent situations is using tactical strategy—not something I learned in the Navy, but my mom had beaten it into me, literally. She had taught me to always fight with my head first and then, after all avenues of theatrics, diplomacy, and cerebral tactics had been exhausted, I always had the other way of handling a potentially violent situation.

The door creaked open. I hadn't surveyed the scene as well as I should have because it wasn't until the door was all the way open and I was committed to the plan that I realized these guys might have guns.

*Stupid, Widow,* I thought. Rookie mistake. Not a mistake that a SEAL-trained operative makes.

But then I could see these guys completely and felt better. They didn't have guns, and they didn't have knives, at least not in their hands. If they had guns, I figured, they would have pulled them on me. And they would have pulled them on the poor guy whose nose was gushing blood. Why threaten him with fists and a baseball bat if they had a gun, they could pull on him?

They stood still, frozen with fear. I knew the look of fear on a man's face. I had frightened many opponents. Mostly guys of equal stature or rank or mental fortitude, not like these guys. I had fought schoolyard bullies and rednecks before when I was a kid. These three would've fit into those two categories like a bad cliché.

They wore clothes that were practically interchangeable. Blue flannel. Green flannel. Sleeves torn off. One white, grease-stained T-shirt. One trucker hat. All wore work boots. All wore dirty ripped jeans. These guys were rednecks, no doubt. Their smell could only be described as stink.

One of them, the one called Junior, held an ancient-looking Louisville slugger. It reminded me of a book I liked to read at sea —*The Walking Dead.* It was technically a graphic novel, but I'm not that fancy. There's a bad guy in that series named Negan, with a baseball bat strapped with nails and wire. He called it Lucille. Excellent series.

The end of Junior's Louisville slugger was stained and partially splintered. It had been used before.

On whom? I wondered.

I didn't know the answer to that question, but I knew it wouldn't get used on me. That was for damn sure.

The men looked alike except that one was missing all of his teeth, save for one that dangled in the front like it wouldn't be much longer before he lost that one too. One guy was fatter than the other two, but they all looked like they had won their fair share of hot dog eating contests.

The guy on the left-hand side was obviously the leader because the other two looked at him for direction. Maybe he was the oldest brother, Daryl, if they were brothers. They might've been cousins.

Small gene pool.

The guy in the second position was Junior, no doubt about that, because he held the bat and had only the one tooth. He must have been the lesser brain, the Curly of the bunch.

The guy standing behind the victim had to be the one called Jeb.

The victim was a short, wiry guy. Short brown hair. Looked to be in decent shape but apparently not much of a fighter. He had that gym look like he worked out, but I doubted he had ever had a real fight in his life.

A pair of glasses lay on the floor near his feet. One lens was shattered and cracked. I guess they had hit him hard in the face. Once to shatter his glasses and knock them off his face and then again to break his nose or fracture it.

The three brothers or cousins or whatever they were stared at me. The jaw of the one behind the victim dropped.

Long, black strands of hair fell across my face. They could probably only see my eyes and no other facial features, just the darkness around my face.

I spoke first and said, "Guys. I'm trying to sleep next door. You aren't being very neighborly."

The one called Junior spoke with a stutter in his voice. Maybe from fear. He said, "You should mind ya business. So ju-just go back into ya own ro-ro-room, and we just forget we saw ya."

The three guys paused like they were waiting for me to reply.

I didn't.

The one called Daryl said, "Now you listen, fella. We don't have a beef with you. You just go on back to your room, and we'll forget like Junior here says."

I sized the three of them up in less than a second. Then I spent five more seconds looking them up and down, making it obvious that I was doing it.

I said, "Fellas, it looks to me like you're not wanted in this man's room."

I turned my head and looked briefly at the doorframe. It was splintered. One of them had kicked it in. Then I stared back at them, violent thoughts flashing in my eyes.

I said, "You broke into this man's room. Attacked him. You're trying to kidnap him. And all of that would have gone fine, but you made one fatal mistake, one colossal mistake."

Finally, Jeb spoke up in a sarcastic, idiotic tone. He asked, "Yeah? What?"

I said, "You woke me. I don't like to be woken up. Not by three inbred idiots like you."

"What ya gonna dew 'bout it?" Junior asked.

He stepped away from the others, lowering his bat. He was making room for a swing—their second mistake.

The room was small. I stood in the doorway. Not even all the way in. Just in the doorway. From Junior's position, he would have to reach over with his left hand, grab the handle of the bat to reinforce the swing, and then pivot with his right foot and step forward with his left. Next, he'd have to swing the bat with full force and swing it high.

If he managed not to hit Daryl on the upswing, then I'd still have the three to four seconds it would take for him to execute the move correctly because he'd have to check back and make sure that Daryl was clear of the swing. Three to four seconds was a long time in a fight. It was time that I would take advantage of. In less than a second, all I had to do was step back and out of the doorway. Back into the night.

Not even a second after I processed the thought, Junior acted. His brother Daryl had seen what he was going to do. I saw him give Junior a nod, a signal that said, "Go for it!"

Junior reached over, grabbed the bat with both hands, pivoted, and swung. Daryl ducked back and fell onto the bed so that the swing would miss him, which it did.

In the last bit of the second that it took for Junior to swing his bat at my head, I stepped back. The bat collided with the inside of the doorframe. Hard. Two feet away, the window, set low on the wall, shattered. Cheap glass crumbled away like dust.

Imagine swinging a Louisville Slugger as hard as you can without pausing or stopping at a telephone pole. The force from the resistance of the thick telephone pole would ripple through the bat and fracture or even break the bones in your wrists and arms and fingers. And that was exactly what happened to Junior.

I heard the bones in his hands and wrists crack and shatter. He wouldn't be swinging that bat for a long time. That was for damn sure.

His fingers dangled from his hands, and the bat fell to the ground.

Like a crazed killer, I stepped into the room.

Junior dropped to the floor and started wailing through his tooth-less mouth. He sounded like a dying animal. His right hand was better than his left. He reached over and cupped his left, crying like a baby.

Daryl looked up at me and reacted. He lunged at me, swinging a right hook my way, but I had long arms with a long reach. I swung a right uppercut. I was faster than him, and while he had to lunge at me, I could stand my ground and still reach him. My right fist caught him dead center in the nose, crushing it. His right hook grazed my left shoulder and did zero damage. It was like a mosquito bite. Less than a mosquito bite and more like pocket lint.

I pulled my punch back and watched as he fell back onto the ground. He grabbed at his nose and screamed when he touched it. Blood gushed from his nostrils in a red, flowing river, and his nose was bent away from his face like a clock hand pointing to a quarter after the hour.

I wasn't sure if the short, wiry guy they were attacking really had a broken nose, but Daryl's nose was broken—that I knew for sure. He was lucky it was still attached to his face. He was lucky that shards of it hadn't gone into his brain and killed him. Perhaps the only reason that hadn't happened was because he had a tiny brain, if he had one at all.

I stared back over at Jeb—the last man standing.

I grinned.

He held tight onto the short, wiry guy, using him as a human shield like I was pointing a gun at him.

I stepped closer.

"What do you say, Jeb? You want a shot at me?"

He started trembling. I knew this because the guy he held onto shook with him. Jeb peered over the guy's shoulder at me. He begged, "Don't hurt me, please!"

I said, "Here, Jeb. I'm going to give you a chance to make up for your boys."

I knelt down and picked up the bat. I leaned it against my shoulder like a batter lining up for a home run swing.

Then I said, "I'd say that, so far, it looks like strike two for you."

I pointed the bat down at Daryl. He and Junior were both rolling around on the floor, holding their broken appendages, but Junior did something stupid. Truly stupid. Like a dumb animal. He tried to get back up. He must've known that I could see him, because I was staring right down at him.

I swung the bat in a quick backswing. Not full force, not even close, but far from a light tap. I hit Junior square in the mouth as he was trying to get up on one knee. That was when I knew how important that sole tooth had been to him, because he screamed in agony when it came flying out of his mouth from the force of the blow. The bat hit him right in the mouth and broke that tooth off. His head whipped back, and he fell back on his ass. But the first thing that happened was his screaming.

Jeb looked on in horror. The screaming died down to a whimper. And then I pointed the bat back at Jeb. I flipped it in the air and caught the tip in my right hand. The handle stretched out to him.

I said, "Take it. Go for strike three."

Jeb stared at the bat like it was a trap.

"I'm unarmed. You could be the hero."

Jeb walked slowly backward, trying to retreat, only there was nowhere for him to go. I blocked the only exit.

I stepped forward and over Daryl.

Jeb said, "No. No. I don't want to. Please, just go."

"Take the bat."

He stayed quiet. He looked down at Daryl. I knew that Daryl, who was behind me now, was trying to get up.

*These guys just don't learn*, I thought.

I flipped the bat in the air again and caught the handle, and then I pivoted around like I was taking a golf swing and clubbed Daryl right in the nose with the thick end of the bat.

I didn't do it like I was hitting a long drive, and I didn't do it like hitting a baseball. I hit him like I was putting hard enough to break whatever cartilage and bone remained in his nose, but not enough to kill him. I didn't want to have to drag a dead body out of there.

He screamed almost like no other scream that I had heard before. Almost.

In the same fluid motion, I spun back around and faced Jeb and his hostage.

I pointed the bat at him again.

I said, "No one is going to help you. Let this guy go. Then, drag your boys out of here, or I'll take this bat and make it strike three. Okay, Jeb?" His attention came sharply into focus when I said his name. So, I said it again, "Jeb, if you choose option B, I will hurt you worse than I did them. Much worse. What's it going to be?"

He shook his head violently. He said, "Let me go. I promise we'll get out of here."

"Good choice. I knew you were the smart one."


IT TOOK Jeb about three minutes to help his two fallen comrades back to their truck. Not bad.

I watched as they piled into a brand-new F-150. They fired up the engine and sped away, leaving a cloud of dust behind them.

The truck had a large, transparent decal of the Confederate flag covering the rear window. It was the truck from the redneck compound with the mobile homes and that giant flagpole I had seen earlier. The taillights faded away.

I walked back into the motel room and stared at the short, wiry guy they had beaten up. I asked, "Are you okay?

The guy had stuffed tissue into his nostrils and was looking at himself in the bathroom mirror.

Without looking at me, he said, "Thank you."

"You should go to the clinic. Get that nose looked at. You might need a doctor."

He looked at me and smiled. Then he said, "It's only a nasal fracture with some profuse bleeding. Not a big deal. I'm a doctor."

I nodded. Stayed quiet.

He walked over to me, kept his head tilted back to stop the bleeding, and then reached his hand out, offering me a handshake.

Even though his head was tilted back, he still could look straight up and see me. He was about five foot nine. I towered over him. I reached out and took his hand and shook it.

He said, "My name is Chris Matlind."

I could clearly see that the guy was shaken up, now that I had the chance to look him over. Worse than shaken up—he looked terrible. His face was unshaven and unkempt. His hair was unwashed, and he smelled. It wasn't as bad as the stink of the greasy rednecks or Hank's musty smell, but it was far from a pleasant scent.

The room was cluttered. Dirty clothes were piled in one corner. There were two big suitcases, one black and wide open. It was almost empty of clothes. The second one was still neatly closed in the far corner. It was pink with a green flower pattern. I had never seen a more girlie-looking suitcase and was surprised that a man would have such a thing.

I said, "My name is Widow."

He asked, "Did you mean what you told those guys? I mean you made it seem like you were only intervening because they had disturbed you."

"They did wake me. But I wasn't going to let them take you."

He nodded.

I stayed quiet.

Then he asked, "Aren't you going to ask what's going on?"

I said, "Nope. None of my business."

A defeated look came over his face, like he needed me to be interested, desperately. I shrugged and asked, "What exactly is going on? Why were those guys trying to take you out of here? You must've done something pretty bad for a few fat rednecks to break down your door and try to kidnap you. Do you owe them money or something?"

"I don't owe them money."

He stopped talking. A look came over his face, a look like he wasn't sure if he could trust me. Then his eyes welled up, and he seemed to be about to burst into tears. I reached out and put my hand on his shoulder. His T-shirt was soaked in blood from his nosebleed. I tried not to touch that part of his shirt.

I said, "It's okay. You can trust me."

He said, "They have my wife. She's a hostage."

## 13

I SAID, "Coffee. Do you drink coffee? I find it makes for a good way to have a conversation. Over coffee. That's what normal people do. We'd better get coffee. You got a car?"

Fearful, Chris said, "No! We mustn't!"

"Get coffee? I know it's late at night, but I'm awake. You're awake. And I saved your ass. So, you're going to explain to me what the hell is going on. Let's get coffee or water or whatever you want."

Matlind said, "No, I mean about the car."

I asked, "You don't have a car?"

"Yes. Well, I do, but they have it."

I asked, "They have it?"

He nodded.

He said, "The mechanic has it. It broke down eight days ago."

"Is that diner in town open all night?"

"I'm not sure, but I can't go there. They're in on it too."

"What? The thing about your wife?"

He nodded.

"Do you know if it's twenty-four hours?"

"I don't know."

"Let's find out. I'm tired. I had a long day, and you have a story to tell. Don't worry. No one will mess with you as long as I'm here."

I left Chris for five minutes and returned to my room. I grabbed my shirt. It was dry enough. I slipped it on and then my damp socks, and then my shoes. I laced them up and walked out of the room. I shut my door but didn't bother to lock it. What would be the point? There was nothing in it. No valuables. No belongings. Nothing. And the room had nothing worth stealing.

I reentered Matlind's room and asked, "Ready to go?"

He stood up from the bed, released his nose, and pulled out the tissues. The bleeding continued, but it wasn't as bad as before.

I asked, "Is your nose broken?"

"Yes. It isn't too bad though. I can't go to the hospital. They don't even have one here—just a clinic. If the local doctor sees me, he'll insist that I get driven to the nearest hospital, and that's probably in Oxford. I can't take the chance of being sent away. I have to find my wife."

"Okay. Okay. Let's deal with one problem at a time. First, we have to fix your nose."

He nodded.

I asked, "Do you have any medical tape?"

He shook his head.

I asked, "Do you have any duct tape?"

He replied, "In my suitcase. Over there. With my tackle box. I like to fish."

I stood up and walked over to the suitcase he had pointed to. I searched through it and found a small tackle box and a travel-sized fishing rod. I grabbed the tackle box, popped open the lid, and peered in. I saw hooks, fishing lures, and a small roll of duct tape. I grabbed it and walked over to Matlind.

I said, "Move your hands away from your face."

He followed my instructions. I took a good look. It wasn't the worst nose break ever, but he was lying about the pain. It must've hurt like a train wreck or like he had been run over by a steamroller.

I lied and said, "It's broken, but not too bad. I'm going to have to set it. We can use the duct tape to act as a kind of field dressing. It will work just as good as any medical dressing you'd get in the emergency room."

He asked, "How do you know that?"

I said, "I've been in the military my whole life. I've seen a lot of broken noses and much worse. Now hold still."

He nodded and then said, "Do it."

He breathed in deeply and held his breath, giving me a signal to go for it.

I put the roll of tape down on the bed behind him and reached out with both hands. I grabbed, pulled, and snapped his nose. It cracked, and then the nose was back in place.

Matlind squirmed and tried to escape from me. For a moment, I think he had forgotten that I was trying to help him, but then he stood still. He was taking quick breaths for the pain, but he said, "Now the duct tape. I'm ready."

Quickly, I peeled a strand of tape off the roll and strapped it to his face. Horizontally. Nice and tight.

I stepped back and got a good look.

I said, "That'll work fine. Doesn't look great, but then again, any dressing on your face won't help you win a beauty contest."

He nodded and said, "Thank you."

"Now, let's get to the diner and talk about your wife."

He agreed and stood up and checked himself in the bathroom mirror, then grabbed a new T-shirt and a fresh button-down shirt. He took off his old shirts and exchanged them for the new set.

Probably couldn't stand looking at the bloodstains.

We left the motel and walked downtown and back to the diner.

It was eight minutes past two o'clock in the morning.

## 14

THE WALK to the diner was peaceful. It was a pleasant night outside. The stars glowed in the sky—or what ancient philosophers, modern poetry graduate students, and mothers everywhere would've described as twinkled. The wind blew softly around us, carrying the sound of rustling leaves in the tree branches overhead. From a distance came the sound of barking dogs. The lake was several blocks away, but the smell of the water wafted on the breeze.

Power lines hung overhead, and streetlights lit up the sidewalks. Not that we needed to use the sidewalks. There wasn't a car on the street—not one.

It was a ghost town.

I wasn't familiar with the local liquor laws, but I imagined that this was a dry county after 1:00 a.m. because the South was full of them. I'm sure that the bars and liquor stores had stopped serving long ago. So, no one was out on the town. No reason unless you wanted to grab a bite to eat at the diner.

Roy's Red Dinner was one of the few buildings lit up. A neon red light traced the roof and colored the night sky a shade of crimson. Above us, the red glow beamed off the bottom of the low clouds.

Matlind and I entered the diner. We were among the few people in the place. I didn't see any reason to make the waitress walk farther than necessary, so we seated ourselves at a booth near the kitchen.

Matlind held a menu in front of his face. It trembled in his hands. I knew he was starving—had to be, because his stomach growled loudly, and his face was sunken like he hadn't eaten in days. But I doubted he was really looking over the menu. I doubted he would order any food. It looked more like he was trying to hide his face from the staff.

I didn't need a menu. It was memorized in my head. I knew the items, at least the good ones. I knew the prices, with tax.

After another minute of waiting, Maria burst through the kitchen door, full of pep. She smiled at me, didn't even look at Matlind, and then walked over to our table. She said, "You're back."

I said, "We just needed to get out and grab some coffee."

She said, "You must really like coffee."

I said, "I do. Who doesn't like coffee?"

She nodded and then looked Matlind up and down.

He never looked past his menu. Never acknowledged her. He was still hiding his face.

She asked, "What's with your friend?"

I said, "He's shy. Can you bring us a couple coffees?"

She nodded and smiled and walked away.

I turned to Matlind. He moved the menu downward and looked at me.

With a tremble in his voice, he said, "She knows who I am. The whole town is in on it."

He looked paranoid, but I stayed quiet.

I said, "Tell me what happened."

Before he began, Maria returned with our coffees. She saw Matlind's face and recognized him—I was sure of it—but she kept quiet, walked away, and never offered to take our orders. She knew we weren't there to order food.

Matlind looked at me and began. He said, "Eight days ago, I married the most beautiful woman in the world. Her name is Faye. She and I met a year ago at a hospital. She's a nurse, and I had just gotten out of medical school. I'm a doctor. I guess I told you that."

I nodded and stayed quiet.

"Faye and I worked on the Gulf Coast. We got married on the beach. Decided to go on our honeymoon. She has a mother who can't travel—medical reasons. She lives in Chicago. So, we thought we'd make our honeymoon a road trip. We wanted to drive through rural places and take in the scenery. We were really going to take advantage of it. We had two weeks, and we were in no rush.

"Faye is really into history. She loves old towns and dives, and I love to fish. We thought we would detour off the interstate and make our way to Jarvis Lake. I had a friend who drove through here once. He told me about fishing."

He stopped, paused a beat, and then took a sip of coffee. It was straight black. No cream. No sugar. Like mine.

I followed suit and took a pull of mine. Good. Like before.

He made a satisfied expression, as if he had just tasted the nectar of life. He said, "So we drove into town. We got a room at the motel. The cabins were all booked, or I would have gotten one of those."

I nodded and thought about how the "cabins" were really huge, not what I considered cabins at all.

Matlind took another sip of coffee, followed by another satisfied look. He said, "Faye and I checked into our motel, and then we drove into town. We walked along the lake. We—"

I interrupted him. I asked, "I thought you didn't have a car?"

He said, "I said I don't have one that works. I'm getting to that part."

I nodded.

He said, "We walked along the lake. All the way around, it followed a jogging path. We sat a couple of times. It's really beautiful. Very rural and quaint. We stayed out near the lake for a long time, the entire morning. Before we realized it, it was noon. We walked back to town.

"And that was when we passed the redneck headquarters, the one near the fork on the south side of the lake. Has the giant Confederate flag?"

I said, "I saw it."

He said, "That was where our trouble started with the occupants of the compound, three of which were those guys you met in my motel room. The bastards who broke my nose."

As he said this, he reached up with his free hand to dab his makeshift nose splint. He winced slightly at the pain, and his eyes shut tight and then reopened. They watered. I could see the agony rush across his face, but he didn't complain. He toughed it out. He was taking it like soldiers I'd known.

He said, "We walked out along the road, right next to the compound. The mobile homes were all quiet. But as soon as we were alongside them, they were full of life, almost as if we'd tripped an alarm or something. Everyone who lived there ran out to see us. The men. The women. Even the children came outside and stared at us. I'm telling you I've seen nothing like it. I'm from the South. I was born in Georgia. I live in Alabama. Hell, I graduated from Southern Alabama. And I've seen nothing like that before. Those rednecks stopped whatever the hell they were doing and came outside just to stare at us."

He began tearing up. The agony on his face turned to sheer terror. He was white with it.

He said, "The looks. The looks on their faces were like nothing I had ever seen before. It was like we had reverted back to a time before civil rights. Before apartheid even. It was like we had gone back to the time of slavery."

I followed, but wasn't quite getting it. Why were they staring at the Matlinds so hard? What the hell did slavery have to do with it?

"I was scared that they would not let us leave. But all they did was stare. Some of them stood on their porches. Some of them came all the way to the edge of their properties. They just stared.

"We froze with terror. I knew they had guns—rednecks have guns. But they didn't even need them. There were dozens of men in the family. Big, fat guys like the ones you met. I thought for sure they were going to lynch us."

I still wasn't quite following. Why would they be interested in a young white doctor from out of town?

Matlind wasn't noticing the puzzlement on my face because he kept on with his story. I saw in his eyes that he wasn't even seeing me. He stared right at me, but he wasn't seeing me. He was visualizing the story as it unfurled. It caught him up in it so much; I doubted that he'd ever be able to shake it off.

"We stood there frozen for a good five minutes. And finally, I grabbed her hand tight and told her we'd better go. We didn't run. We just walked away. And no one came after us. No one followed. They didn't pursue us. I was certain that they wanted to do bad things to us. I had no doubt. But they didn't chase us. They just let us go."

Then he was silent. He looked up at me. Genuine fear swam in his eyes.

He said, "They didn't chase after us because they knew we would never get away. They knew because the whole town is in on it."

I asked, "In on what? I'm not following. Why would these rednecks care about you?"

He ignored me and said, "We got back to town. I told her we should leave right there, right then. She wasn't as scared as I was. She was scared at that moment, but the moment had passed. So, she shrugged off the whole thing like she was used to it. She insisted we stay and eat at the diner like we had planned—this diner. So, we came in here and didn't utter a word about the rednecks. We just wanted to eat. She insisted we continue our honeymoon. She said we could just stay on our side of the town and enjoy our time."

He fell silent again and peered around the diner like he was looking for the waitress or anyone who was familiar, and then he said, "We had a different waitress. This one is Latina. She's the only minority I've seen in this whole town. I hadn't noticed it before. Faye hadn't noticed it. Or maybe she had. I'm not sure."

I nodded. I had also noticed it. I remembered thinking that it was unusual, that having no minorities was strange. This is the South, but not one minority in any population is strange nowadays.

I understood what Matlind was telling me, but I still wondered what it had to do with the rednecks and his wife. I looked at him with an expression that said, "Continue."

He acknowledged it and said, "We sat over there."

He pointed to a booth on the other side of the diner, near the entrance.

He said, "Waitresses never came to us. Not one of them. They ignored us. I kept waving them over, and they never came. The patrons never acknowledged us, either. No smiles or cheery hellos. The strangest part was that they weren't rude. They didn't shout rude comments or give us rude stares. Not like the rednecks. They simply didn't look at us. We sat there for over twenty minutes, and then I grabbed the manager. He had walked by and didn't even acknowledge that we'd been sitting there with no menus or drinks. I was furious. I shook the guy. I asked him what the hell was going on! Why the hell was everyone ignoring us! Faye grabbed me by the arm and insisted that we leave. I was so angry. I shook the manager even harder because he said nothing. He was a young guy, and I guess he could take it, but he finally looked at me and asked me to leave. He asked me to leave."

Matlind took another drink from his coffee, a long one, and then said, "I was furious. I mean, what the hell? And now I remember he hadn't acknowledged Faye, either. He never looked at her. He said that he was going to call the sheriff if we didn't leave. So, we left."

I nodded.

"We went straight back to the motel and packed and went to the car. I started it, and then it broke down right as we were passing through town. I mean, it just died. I pushed it into a service lot—a little old shop. The mechanic must have had it in his family for generations. He came out to the lot and helped us. He never really looked at Faye, either. He just talked directly to me. He looked under the hood and told me it'd be a day or two before he could fix it."

I asked, "Is it done now?"

"No. Every time I go there, he says it'll be another week." He looked deep into my face with complete desperation and said, "Widow, the very next morning, I woke up in my motel room, and she was gone. Vanished. The door was wide open. I could hear the sounds of passing cars, but my wife was gone. I called to her and called to her, but she had vanished. Not a note. Not a message. Nothing. She was gone. I checked with the old guy in the office. He never actually saw her. And she'd left no message."

I asked, "What about your cell? Did you call her?"

"My cell phone was gone. I have no pictures of her. No contacts. All of my numbers were in there. I can't call anyone. I can't remember anyone's number, and the phones in the rooms don't work." He paused a beat and then said, "No one in town will let me use a phone. Don't you think I tried? I went everywhere and begged and pleaded. No one will help me! I'm a prisoner here! I can't leave! I can't call out!"

Matlind took a deep breath and paused again, and said, "That little manager remembered me. He called the sheriff, and the sheriff came. He brought one of his deputies right here to my door. I thought, 'Thank God! Finally, someone was going to help me find my wife!'"

I stayed quiet.

"But that's not what happened! Not at all! It was the most shocking thing! They threatened to arrest me! Said I was acting erratic and indecent! Said that the manager from the diner had filed a complaint!"

Matlind caught himself as his anger grew. I watched him sit back in his seat and take a deep breath and let it out. He took one more and let it out and then said, "So I told the sheriff about my wife. He took my statement right out front. I had to sit in the police car and give him the whole story. And he didn't believe me. He said maybe she left me. Right in the middle of the night. She just left me."

*The sheriff*, I thought. The man I was looking to meet—the connection to my mother. I was stunned by what he said. I asked, "He didn't ask questions? Do an investigation? Fill out reports? Put out an APB on her?"

Matlind shook his head. He said, "No way. Nothing. He did nothing. I mean, sure, he asked the staff here. He spoke to the manager, but the guy just claimed I was being unruly. He told him I grabbed his arm and harassed him and the other patrons. And he claimed no one had seen her. They only saw me. Like she was a ghost. He acted like I'd made her up! My own wife!"

"What about the rednecks? You told him about that?"

Matlind shrugged and said, "I did. He even made a big show of driving me out there with one of his deputies."

"And?"

"And the deputy was related to them somehow. He was their cousin or something. I know because of the way he talked to them, serving as the redneck liaison or something. It was weird. The oldest male, I guess their father, came outside and spoke to the sheriff for a long time. I had to remain in the back of the squad car as if I were a prisoner. I tried to jump out of the car to hear what they were saying, but the door was locked from the outside. The deputy had locked me in!"

I nodded. My jaw didn't drop, but I was a little shocked. The police work sounded shady, but the entire story was tough to swallow except because there had been three rednecks in his motel room. They had broken down his door, had broken his nose, and had tried to abduct the guy. If I hadn't seen that with my own eyes, I'd think he was crazy. But the rednecks had been real. He didn't fake them. He didn't conjure them. I had seen them with my own two eyes.

He looked down at his shiny, new wedding band for a moment. And that, too, was real. I had never been married, but I had known married people in my life. Some liked it. Some didn't. I had been to weddings, and I had seen happy couples. I had also been to many murder scenes and seen dead husbands and dead wives. Many, many times, one spouse was the one who had killed the other, and many, many times, the spouse never even tried to hide that fact.

Matlind twisted the wedding band around his finger like a nervous habit and then said, "I've been here ever since. I've tried looking for her everywhere. I don't know what else to do."

I asked, "Did you call the Feds?"

"No one in the town will let me use a phone. I told you that! I'm a prisoner here! I can't leave! I can't call out!"

"Calm down."

He listened and immediately obeyed. Then he said, "I dealt with the sheriff already. What's the FBI going to do?"

I nodded. He was right. The FBI would probably reprimand the local sheriff's department by calling the governor, who'd call the mayor, but that would be the extent of it. The FBI dealt with kidnappings, but there was no proof of a kidnapping. There was no ransom, and all the witnesses claimed his wife didn't exist. I could see his problem.

Even if the FBI or the state police got involved, the sheriff would say that Matlind was crazy, and so far, he might've been. I had no way to be sure, not yet. A gut feeling told me that this guy was telling the truth, but I had no hard evidence that his story was real. All I had were three rednecks, a distraught husband, no eyewitnesses, and a wedding band that could be fake. I'd gone forward on less. I'd seen prosecutors go on less, but in a military tribunal, less is needed.

Matlind drank the last of his coffee, stared at the tabletop, maybe at the cracks in the wood, and then said, "Those redneck assholes. They took her. I know it."

I said, "I don't understand. You said that they stared at you and Faye like it was with some kind of intense hatred, but I don't understand why. Why're you saying that they took her? And what about that part about the lynching?"

Then I finally understood, as I was saying it. Before Matlind looked up and said one more word to me, I had gotten it. I knew exactly why he was so scared. I knew exactly what he was suggesting.

He looked at me and said, "Faye is black."

## 15

I FINISHED MY COFFEE, and Matlind stared at his empty mug. Maria came around and offered us a refill. I shook my head, and Matlind stayed quiet. So, she figured he wanted no more coffee. Not that it mattered. He was so wound up that I doubted the extra caffeine would've made any difference.

Matlind wasn't going to bed anytime soon.

Still, I said, "We should go. You need some sleep."

Matlind asked, "Can you help us?"

I heard the desperation in his voice. It tugged at me like the pleas of a helpless child. I nodded, not even thinking about it. I just reacted, second nature.

He paused, took a deep breath, and closed his eyes for a moment. Then he said, "Thank you! Thank you so much!"

I said, "I'll stay longer. We'll sort this out, and then I'm on my way."

He nodded and thanked me again. A glimpse of hope shot across his face, like a meteor shooting across the night sky.

I said, "Don't thank me yet. Let's get her back first."

He nodded.

I said, "So the last thing that happened was that you woke up and she was gone? Along with both of your cell phones, but she left her luggage?"

He said, "That's right. Those rednecks took her!"

I shook my head. I said, "No. That makes little sense. Why did they take her while she slept, and yet they left you alone only to try to kidnap you last night? They could've just gotten you both at the same time. No, I wouldn't be so sure that they had anything to do with it."

"What about the way they stared at us? And why did they try to take me, anyway?"

I stayed quiet.

"Maybe they didn't want to do it in front of their kids during the daytime?" he asked.

"Maybe they weren't trying to take you at all. Maybe they wanted to get rid of you. I still think that we need to look closer at the whole situation."

"You mean like an investigation?" he said.

I said, "If the sheriff isn't going to help find her, then we'll have to do it ourselves."

Maria brought me the check. It only had a charge for the two coffees on it. I peeled out a ten-dollar bill and left it for her. And for the second time that day, I left her a good tip.

Matlind had walked out of the diner, but I had stayed inside to say goodbye to Maria. I waited, standing up near the long counter, and looked around the diner. The few other customers paid me no attention. They were all staring at the TV that hung above a cracked mirror.

The volume was low, but the closed captioning was on. There was a news report showing a town in Texas called Crosscut. Most of the town was burned to rubble. A story was running about a drug kingpin who had his men burn their properties to the ground. The kingpin was Oskar Tega, the name that kept popping up in the news lately.

Suddenly, Maria burst out of the kitchen and walked over to me. She asked, "Do you need any change?"

I said, "No. It's yours. I didn't want you to think that I wasn't going to call you. I have your number still."

She said, "You left it on the table earlier."

I said, "I memorized it."

"You memorized it?"

"Yes."

I stared back up past her and watched another scene of the burning rubble in the destroyed town of Crosscut.

Maria turned and looked back at the TV as well. Then she said, "Crosscut. That whole thing is a mess. I'm from a different part of the state, but my family tells me Crosscut is all anyone can talk about. It's just so hard to believe that a Mexican drug lord had a major operation in the middle of a small town like that."

A moment passed, and she smiled and then asked, "So you memorized my number? What are the last four digits?"

I said, "One eight six four."

She smiled again and asked, "How do you remember that?

I said, "Well, 1864 is the year before the end of the Civil War. In 1864, Lincoln implemented a strategy that would win him the war and crush the Confederacy."

"With what, more guns?"

"No, the victory wasn't about guns or bullets. It was about economics."

Maria had a puzzled look on her face. And honestly, I wasn't sure if it was out of genuine interest or because she couldn't care less about the American Civil War.

I said, "Old Abe and Grant used *total war* to win the Civil War. It means they won by crushing both the armed forces and the economy of the South."

She nodded and then changed the subject. Apparently, she wasn't interested in American history. She said, "So you do know my number. You gonna call me?"

I said, "Wait and see. I might."

I smiled at her, and she looked up at me, stared into my eyes. She said, "You have nice eyes."

I smiled bigger.

She leaned to her right and looked past me at Matlind, who stood outside. "That guy you're with. He's so sad. I heard his wife left him. She disappeared."

I asked, "What do you know about him?"

She said, "Well, he was in here the other day, claiming to be looking for his wife. He went off on the manager. He was delirious."

"Did you see her?"

"No. I was off. I only heard about it."

I asked, "Did any of the other waitresses?"

She said, "The ones on the day shift are old ladies. They've lived here forever and worked here forever, and they love to gossip, but they only talked about how crazy he was. Never mentioned a wife. And I didn't ask."

"Do you believe she's real?"

She said, "A man like that, he's bent out of shape about somebody. He's not faking that part."

"Would you ask around for me? Don't push the issue. Just casually?"

"I can try, but I don't really talk to the other girls. The only person here who ever talks to me is Andrew, the cook. And he's kinda slow. Something's wrong with him."

I nodded and said, "Can I ask you something else? Have you noticed that there aren't any minorities here?"

She said, "That was the first thing I noticed when I moved here a month ago. Came here by accident, trying to start a new life sort of thing. I'm from Texas and wanted to run away. So, I drove until I found this place. I liked the lake and thought I had never lived in a small town, so why not?

"I noticed right off the bat that because I'm Latina, people here treat me different. I mean, sure, the folks here have been nice to my face. And the fishermen who come through are friendly, but the store and bar owners didn't seem to want to hire me. They smiled and took my application, but no interviews, and no one even looked at my application. At this one place, the electronics store, I even handed the guy a blank application. Didn't even write on it just to see if he'd say anything. He never even looked down at it.

"Finally, I walked in here and demanded that the graveyard manager talk to me. He said that the people in this town were old and had old ways of thinking. He said it wasn't anything personal. He never used the word 'racist,' but he implied it. He said it like, 'They don't like outsiders.'

"No one here has said anything inappropriate to me or anything, but I'm telling you, Widow, that they are some of the most racist people. They keep it to themselves, but it's there under the surface.

"I mean, there are no black people here. There are no Asians—no other Hispanics. There are gay people. I mean, there must be. One person out of ten is gay. Odds say that there have to be some, but if there are, they stay closeted. No way are they going to risk coming out in this place. It's like the land that time forgot."

I nodded. I didn't know what to say or think. I had never in my wildest dreams imagined that a place like this still existed, even in the South.

"I'm the only minority in this whole town."

I nodded and thanked her and turned to walk away.

Over my shoulder, I heard her say, "Goodbye."

I stayed quiet and walked out of the diner. I stepped out onto the sidewalk and nodded at Matlind. We turned and walked along the streets in somber silence, headed back to the motel.

MATLIND HAD an expression of relief on his face. I guess having someone believe him had made him feel like there was hope.

For the last eight days, he had been on his own, scared and alone, and now he was no longer alone. Now there were two of us.

We made it back to the motel. He stopped outside in the parking lot and stared at his broken doorframe. I saw the fear on his face.

I said, "Take my room. I'll sleep in yours. We can start looking in the morning. We aren't going to be able to accomplish anything tonight, and you need rest. Right now, rest is the best thing you can do for yourself. Tomorrow, I'll look around."

"Can you find her?"

"I'll find her."

He paused, and then he asked, "Do you think she's alive?"

"She's alive."

"What makes you think we'll find her?"

I said, "They don't know about me. No one does. Not really. Except for the rednecks."

"What if they have her?"

I said, "They don't."

He asked, "What if they do?"

I said, "They don't. And if they do, at that point, they'll wish that they had never made such a grievous error."

He nodded, stayed quiet. He just looked down.

I said, "Matlind, go to sleep. Take my room." And he did.

I went into his room and pushed the splintered door as far closed as it would go. I went into the bathroom, past all the luggage and piles of dirty clothes in the corner. There were female items spread out all over the bathroom—makeup, mascara, a box of tampons, fragrances, one bottle of perfume, one razor, and two sets of toothbrushes. A pink razor, a nice foldable one, rested on the side of the tub. A bottle of girlie shaving cream sat on the ledge next to it. The lid was off, and a dab of white residue that must have once been cream hung out of the tip of the can. On the bathroom shelf, near the sink, were bottles of Midol, aspirin, Motrin, some prescription pills, and an asthmatic inhaler.

I looked up from the countertop and stared at myself in the mirror. I looked tired and less threatening because of it.

I rubbed my eyes.

I used the bathroom, washed my hands, and dried them off on a towel that hung near the shower curtain. Then I walked over to the bed, left my clothes on, and fell on top of the covers.

Lights out.

## 16

I woke up late in the morning. I rolled over and looked at my burner phone. It read 10:34, but the four switched just as I looked at it. Now it was 10:35—close guess.

I got up and headed out the door. I checked in on Matlind. He was in a deep sleep. There was a bottle of Ambien next to his wallet on the nightstand.

I backed out of his room and left him to sleep. No reason to wake him. He slept like the dead, and he probably needed it. Besides, I needed to investigate alone. I was better alone. And I had my own agenda to follow. Not likely that my mother's killer, the missing girl from my town, and now his wife were coincidences.

Matlind forgot to lock the door. So, I flipped the lock on the knob from the inside and closed it behind me.

For most fishermen, the day's catch had already come and gone because fishing was an early morning sport. Best started before the sun came up. The sun was high in the sky, and the trees creaked in the wind. The air was warm, and it smelled fresh and clean.

I set out to explore the town and to search for Faye Matlind.

I had no photograph of her because someone had taken Matlind's cell phone, where he had kept all of his pictures. I had no real clues except for the rednecks. They were my only lead. I walked on, took out my phone, and unlocked it. I skipped the missed messages, calls, emails, and voicemails, and pulled up the internet and looked up the name "Faye Matlind." I figured that she probably had a social media account of some sort. Something with her picture on it. So, I searched all the popular primary search engines and social networks. I found nothing. I found a Facebook page for Chris Matlind, but it must've been ancient. Maybe only used once. He had no profile pictures—no photo albums. He had only a dozen friends, and his last post was four years ago.

I gave up. I didn't need her picture, anyway. She was a black woman in a town full of white people. She would stick out with no trouble at all.

I continued into town.

I hadn't eaten since dinner the night before, but I skipped breakfast. I wasn't interested in lunch either. The only thing I wanted was to find Faye. Enough time had elapsed already, with no one looking for her.

I walked the roads and through the suburbs, past the school, the post office, the public safety complex, the people on the sidewalks, and the cars parked along the sides of the streets, and past a dismal public library with a parking lot that could've been a graveyard for old cars—the only cars in it were from the seventies or earlier. I continued walking past bait shops, a couple of gun stores, two hardware stores, and a four-wheeler store. Then I came up on the other side of the diner. I had walked the long way around it from the night before.

I continued walking past two gas stations, one with a liquor store attached, and one with a broken car wash that probably hadn't worked since 1980.

I walked past a small grocery store, an old chain store. I recognized the name, but I thought the whole chain had gone out of business over a decade ago.

I took one more glance at the Eckhart Medical Center and got a better look at the clinic attached to it. It was open for business, and it was busy because the parking lot was full. Across the street from the clinic was a small plaza with another grocery store, this one smaller than the others I'd seen, and it had a tiny drugstore attached at the corner. The drugstore had a drive-through window, but the window was closed and dark inside, and the lane to drive through it had been roped off.

Walking through the downtown area, I searched for store clerks, attendants, cleaners, anyone who held a blue-collar job. I wanted to find people who made less money than everyone else, people who might be more talkative. People who would be more apt to answering my questions. First, I planned to chitchat with them about pleasantries, and then ask them if they had seen a young black woman a week ago. I found a few townspeople who fit the bill. I inquired about Faye's whereabouts, but no one had seen her.

They hadn't lied to me. Most people had the common sense to give me the information I asked for and to do it quickly. Even if I acted polite, which I usually did, they told me fast. Most people didn't want to risk being discovered in a lie. Not by me. And not about something as serious as a missing woman.

By noon, I came across a lady walking a French poodle—an older lady, grandmotherly. She was as sweet as could be.

I asked, "Ma'am, do you know anything about a young black woman who came to town last week? She's missing."

The old lady replied, "Oh, dear. Missing? Oh, dear."

I said, "Ma'am, have you seen her?"

She shook her head in an early *Exorcist* movie fashion, like it was about to spin around and around, but it didn't. Instead, she said, "I heard about that poor fellow who's looking for her, but I haven't seen her. I hope it works out. Poor thing."

I nodded. The woman was telling the truth. She hadn't seen Faye or Chris. She knew nothing—just gossip. The old birds probably had some sort of phone tree. One would call another one and spread the latest rumors—that sort of thing.

I didn't want to be one of those rumors. And I didn't want to lose the element of surprise. I didn't push her any further. I shrugged, thanked her, and moved on.

I neared one church, the one with the short steeple. A bell sounded from inside. I looked at the shadows on the ground. It was late afternoon.

I had run out of places to search.

There were still the rest of the places around the lake, which looked to be just houses and neighborhoods. I figured I would spend the rest of the day retracing the Matlinds' hike around the lake and end at the rednecks' compound. That way, I could take my time, make sure there were no other places for answers. By the time I reached the fork at the southwest side and the redneck compound, it would be dark.

And that was where I shined—in the dark.

## 17

Before I set out to trek around the lake, I needed something to eat. It occurred to me to go back for Matlind, but after eight days without sleep, the guy deserved to sleep the day away, so I walked toward the diner. I was hungry, and I kept thinking about this guacamole steak burger I saw on the menu. I wanted to try it, but the diner was at the center of town and was surrounded by buildings. Before I went to eat, I wanted to get a look from the lake's shore and plan out my route. I walked the two blocks to the lake and then head to the diner.

It only took a few minutes for me to reach the lake. I stopped and stood near the edge. The lake was full of boats and fishermen. A couple of Jet Skiers were chasing each other in a wide circle. On the little stony beach, kids played, and parents fished and drank beer with the labels covered by bottle koozies.

I ignored all of that and scanned the shoreline. I followed it from left to right. Most of the eastern side seemed to be residential, lake houses, woods, and not much else.

It was a lot of area to cover, a lot of area for a new bride to go missing in, and a lot of area to hide a body. Then there was the lake itself. I wasn't familiar with its depths, but it looked deep enough to sink a body. If it was deep enough, it could be years before a body resurfaced. I shrugged. I didn't want to think about her as dead. The clock ticked away, but I had the right perspective. Right now, this was a rescue mission, not a recovery. To think of it as a recovery was to give up hope Faye was alive, and that would condemn her to death.

I turned and left the shoreline behind me.

I walked two blocks past a row of shops to the corner in front of the drugstore, and I stopped. My animal brain switched on, and my primal instincts surfaced. At that moment, at that exact second, I stood on the sidewalk, watching a normal and frequent daily occurrence take place, one that pissed me off.

A man was hitting on a woman. She rejected his advances, but he continued. She rejected him again and again, making it obvious from where I stood, she was clearly uncomfortable and wanted to leave.

I saw her just as she stepped out of the drugstore, a small bag in her hand and a purse on her arm—and then I saw the man. First, he was cruising in his car down the street with his head hanging out of the driver's side window. He rubbernecked at her and then pulled over into the parking lot, left his car running, and got out. He went over to her and stopped her by just standing dead in her way.

He kept hitting on her, and she kept on rejecting him. She tried to walk around him, but he followed her to her vehicle and continued to harass her.

She continued to reject him, and she even started raising her voice.

He ignored her rejections, and in a rural accent, like one of those fat rednecks, he taunted her.

This was a common everyday occurrence in America and around the world. A man hits on a woman. She rejects him. He harasses her. Typical everyday situation. Nothing new about that. Normally, I would've intervened when the guy had gone too far, which this guy had clearly done. Normally, I would've strongly encouraged the guy to apologize and to move along. But this situation was anything but normal because the woman who was being harassed was the beautiful woman, I had met yesterday morning, the one who was jogging around the lake. And the guy was armed—he had a Glock 22 in a plain brown holster on his belt. But far worse than that was the fact that this guy was a sheriff's deputy in full uniform.

## 18

THE DEPUTY LEANED against Sheldon's car door, hindering her from getting in and driving away.

Staying on the sidelines and ignoring an injustice wasn't in my nature. I crossed the street and walked straight up behind the cop.

A flash of recognition came across Sheldon's face.

I stood four feet from the guy before he heard me. Not the greatest situational awareness.

Uniform or no uniform, cop or no cop, I talked to him like he was just another guy. I said, "The lady said she isn't interested in talking to you. She made that clear."

The guy turned to face me. He was startled. Some kind of cop training or ancient predatory urge to defend an imaginary territory came over him because he immediately reached for his gun. He left it holstered but rested his hand on the butt. It probably made him feel safer. Whatever.

He wasn't going to draw on me. Not here. Not in front of witnesses on a relatively busy section of street in broad daylight. Just then, several customers left the drugstore behind him. A mother with three young kids walked to their car from a shoe store in the plaza. No way was he going to draw now, especially when he was the one in the wrong.

He opened his mouth to speak, but before he let out a word, I smelled his breath. He smelled like he had bathed in alcohol. I detected rum and whiskey and probably beer on his breath. Everyone must have attended that party.

The guy had probably been up all-night doing shots. He'd probably never gone to bed. But he wasn't wasted. Not completely. Badly buzzed, but mostly coherent.

He asked, "Who the hell are you?"

I said, "Me? I'm nobody. Just a passerby."

He looked puzzled. He obviously hadn't been at the top of his class.

I said, "But you... you're a cop. A sheriff's deputy, by the look of your uniform. You're supposed to uphold the law. You're supposed to make your department look good. And right now, I'd say that you're failing. Miserably."

The cop looked at me with fury in his eyes. He said, "I'm talking to this lady. She's not your concern. I'm gonna let you walk away now before you get hurt."

"Hurt?" I asked. "I agree. One of us will get hurt. But it won't be her, and it certainly won't be me. And that only leaves you. You could pull that gun on a couple of innocent people. And you could slip, and the gun could come out of your hand. It could go off and hit you in the leg or the arm. And then you'd have to go to the hospital ... and explain how it all happened."

He asked, "Are you threat'nin' me?"

He gripped the gun's handle. He didn't brandish it, just grabbed it like a gunslinger waiting for the count of three.

He said, "Threat'nin' an officer of the law is illegal here."

I said, "Harassing a citizen, especially sexually harassing a female one, is illegal everywhere. Now get your hand off your gun. As of right now, we're just a couple of guys talking. Having a verbal dispute. A disagreement."

My hands hung harmlessly by my sides. No sudden action. No threatening motions. I knew all the signals that cops were trained to look for, and at that moment, I displayed none of them. Even so, I stayed within grabbing distance of the deputy, in case I needed to take the Glock from him before he hurt someone with it.

I said, "Two guys having a verbal disagreement are just that—two guys. Not friends. Not enemies. Just two guys. If you pull that gun out, then we'll be enemies. And you don't want to be my enemy. Trust me."

The cop stood there frozen. He stayed quiet. He wanted to pull out his Glock and arrest me—I could see it in his eyes—but he didn't. With witnesses everywhere, he'd never be able to charge me with anything that would stick. Whatever bogus charge he came up with would get dismissed in court, and he'd be suspended for sure. Probably lose his job whenever Sheldon's testimony came up.

The guy moved his hand away from his gun as he looked around the parking lot and realized I was right.

I smiled and took a glance at his nameplate. Gemson. Strange name. Stranger than mine even.

I said, "Good call. Why don't we just keep this between us?"

He nodded.

I said, "And in the future, why don't you just steer clear of this woman? If I were you, I'd leave your squad car parked where it is, take the keys out of the ignition, and get on your cell phone or radio. Call the dispatcher and tell her you've suddenly come down with a stomach bug. Then walk or call a cab and go home. Get some sleep and sober up."

Gemson said, "I'll see you again."

He said nothing else, just looked around to see if anyone had paid any attention to what had happened. No one seemed to have picked up on it. Satisfied, he walked away. Not fast. Not slow. Just a normal speed until he was gone from sight.

I walked over to the cop car, opened the door, sat down, and pressed the brake. I shifted the gear to neutral, and then I gripped the roof and the side of the car and pushed it over to the curb. It was a fire lane, but, hey, this was a police vehicle. Then I popped the lever back to park and reached down and turned off the ignition. I tossed the keys onto the seat, not much caring if someone came along and stole the car. Not my business.

## 19

I HADN'T NOTICED BEFORE, but Sheldon had dropped her shopping bag while trying to get away from Gemson. Her purchases had spilled out all over the ground. She bent over and began recovering them.

I walked back up the drive to the parking lot, knelt down beside her, and began helping her pick up the spilled contents.

I put my hand on a box marked salbutamol, and there were various other pharmaceutical items. There was a box marked Elavil, an antidepressant, and another that said Ambien, a sleep aid. There were a couple of boxes of Norflex and Flexeril, both muscle relaxers, and there were various other medications I had never heard of, along with gauze and other medical supplies.

I said, "That's a lot of medications. And salbutamol, that's for asthmatics. You don't have asthma. No way. Not how you run and the shape you're in. Are you a drug dealer or something?"

She scooped up the boxes of pills quickly and then smiled. She said, "No. And what do you mean about the shape I'm in?"

I shrugged and said, "Don't take this the wrong way. But your body is immaculate. I'm guessing you don't have an ounce of fat on you. No way does someone with severe asthma workout and run as much as you do."

She smiled, nodded, and said, "I work at the clinic. This is a supply run."

I nodded and smiled back.

She stood up and straightened out the bottom of her romper. The bottom was short, well below her fingertips if she had reached them down by her sides. It looked new and had a tribal pattern. The back had a V shape cut down from her neckline. She wore her long, blonde hair down. The breeze scooped it up and blew it behind her.

She looked comfortable and magnificent all at the same time.

I said, "You don't dress like someone who works in a clinic."

"What's wrong with the way I dress?"

"Nothing. You look good. Really good. Is it your day off?"

She said, "No. I have clothes at the clinic. We have lockers. I keep my scrubs there."

I nodded.

She smiled at me. She said, "Nice seeing you again. Very nice." She looked me over.

I said, "I know that you have to bring all that stuff in, but would you like to have lunch with me?"

She paused a beat and looked down at a slim wristwatch that hung from her left arm. Then she frowned. She said, "I really can't. I'm sorry. I have to get to the clinic. Raincheck?"

I nodded and stayed quiet.

She said, "You can find me there."

I smiled and said, "Give me your phone number."

She gave me the digits. I didn't write them down. I memorized them without a problem. She pulled a pair of sunglasses out of her purse and slid them onto her face, pushing the top to the bridge of her nose. They were big and bulky, like actresses wear.

Then she got into a new model BMW, started the engine, and pulled away. I watched as she turned the corner and was gone. I thought nothing more of it. It was time to grab a bite to eat, so I headed off toward the diner.

## 20

STARBUCKS IS a company that has grown exponentially, from a single coffee bean to the largest coffee empire in the world. There is more than one reason for its success. First, coffee is addictive. Second, Starbucks provides a place for people to get together. Whatever the reason, Starbucks all over the world are hubs for people to gather, to talk, to read, and to work on whatever people do on their laptops.

Black Rock didn't have a Starbucks. This meant that, in this case, the place that served as a hub was the diner, and that was where I was.

I sat in the same booth as before. Hazel was my waitress. The place was busy. It was the middle of the day, and the lunch crowd was here—hell, the entire town was here. The place was filled with restaurant sounds—the clinking of plates, the tinkling of silverware, and the humming from the ovens in the kitchen.

I drank a coffee and devoured a grilled chicken sandwich.

The diner was full of fishermen in from a morning on the lake. They swapped stories of their catches and gloated over those who had caught nothing. In the corner, across from me, sat a group of firefighters. They wore blue T-shirts with the town of Black

Rock's crest on the front and "Fire Department" written in big, bold letters on the top.

One of them looked somewhat old to be a firefighter, but I doubted they saw much action here. I figured that the towns-people were safe for now.

At another table sat a pair of office types, and across from them, nearer to the bathrooms, there was a blind guy with a younger man and a well-behaved golden retriever, a service animal.

I took the people in the booth next to me to be city officials of some sort. They wore suits and talked about town ordinances and spoke ill of the public by making the occasional joke about some lady who had apparently filed the wrong forms.

I googled the Matlinds again and see what else I could find out.

I took my cell phone out of my pocket and checked the internet. I googled both Matlind and Dr. Matlind. No results. Then I typed in Faye's name. Nothing. I searched for combinations of their names and the word "married." Nothing.

I checked a website related to local arrests and crimes. There was nothing about Faye, and nothing about Chris. There was a good bit about the missing girls, but nothing new to me. The cops were baffled before, and they still were today. They suspected the girls were targeted because they had traveled alone on lonely highways and interstates.

The only thing that caught my attention was a website that had posted pictures of the missing girls, which was good because I could memorize their faces. Most were young. Some were white. Some black. Some Hispanic. The only thing that jumped out at me about them was that they were all beautiful. Not simply attractive but beautiful—like models in real life. They were drop-dead gorgeous.

The website also mentioned a missing teenage girl from my town —Ann Gables. There was a picture of her with an amber alert on the website. She was a minor, and she was black and stunningly beautiful. That was interesting. She was black, and Faye was also black.

Whoever was behind their disappearances had obviously picked them because they were so good-looking, but I was sure this was information the FBI and local sheriffs already had. If Deputy Gemson was any sign as to the quality of the local sheriff's office, I wasn't surprised they had found none of the girls yet.

I thought about Faye's connection to the missing girls. Perhaps it was related, or perhaps Chris was right about the rednecks. Or maybe she had left him. It happened.

I switched my phone to standby and slipped it back into my pocket. Then I sat back and tried to pick up on any clues I might have missed.

An old guy was seated across from me at the next booth. He wore a red trucker's hat and blue overalls. He tilted a white coffee mug all the way back until its contents were emptied. Then he stood up and thanked Hazel and left money on the table.

I watched him leave the diner and looked back at his table. He had left behind today's newspaper. I had seen guys leave their newspapers behind before. They left them for the next reader, like the change left in one of those take-a-penny cups at the gas station. They just paid it forward.

I scooted out of my booth, stood up, and reached across the aisle. I swiped up the paper—it was *USA Today*—and began skimming through it. It wouldn't have local stories, but that didn't matter. I was interested in the cover story. There was a giant photo of a Hispanic man. In large print above his picture, it read, "*WHERE IS HE?*"

The article was about Oskar Tega. The DEA was having a real problem finding him. They now believed he had escaped by private jet. They thought he was in Cuba but hadn't ruled out the possibility he was still in the US.

The article recapped how Tega had escaped capture and landed in a small town in Texas. One of his farms was located there. His men had stocked up on whatever drugs he manufactured and then had burned the entire town to the ground—some kind of scorched-earth policy.

That was when I noticed the four sheriff's deputies outside. One of them was Deputy Gemson. They had rolled up to the front of the diner, light bars flashing. The Dodge Intrepids with the police package, a good deal. Finally, they were getting their money's worth.

The other patrons stared out of the diner windows. They didn't react. I supposed no one knew what to do. Many of them had never seen the cops use their light bars before, not in this town.

The cops jumped out of their cars and lined up behind them outside of the diner. They drew their weapons and pointed them at the front doors. Two shotguns. Mossberg 590s. Both had pistol grips, and both were deadly—probably department-issued. Not good for their target. The other two deputies, including Gemson, held Glocks.

I saw one of them get on his radio. There was some inaudible chatter, and then the guys ran for the door. They had decent moves. Probably practiced their entries at least once a week. One shotgun and one deputy with a Glock covered the front door, and Gemson and the other deputy ran around the building and out of sight. I imagined they were covering the back door.

In seventeen seconds from start to finish, they were in the diner. It took sixteen and a half seconds before I realized they were there for me.

I had spent my summers training with my mom, and I knew the routine. I knew the score. There wasn't a doubt in my mind that these country boys were here for me. Gemson hadn't heeded my advice. Instead of going home and sleeping it off, he had gone and rounded up his cop buddies.

I finished my coffee and stood up. Hands raised.

Gemson entered through the back, with the deputy carrying a shotgun. The other two came in through the front at a nice speed, sweeping the room and scanning the other patrons, all of whom had dropped as low as they could. Hazel hid behind the counter. One guy in the kitchen stuck his head out and then pulled it right back in half the time it had taken him to stick it out.

The first deputy with the shotgun screamed at me to get down. He screamed it over and over. "Get down! Get down!"

I stayed standing. I wasn't going to get down. No way. I had just cleaned my clothes the night before, and I wasn't about to get them dirty on this floor. These guys could forget about that.

Gemson eyeballed me and moseyed on over. I noticed immediately that he had listened to me, partially because it was obvious he'd gone home. He'd showered and changed his clothes before grabbing the cavalry—he didn't stink of booze anymore. He probably hadn't wanted them to notice it. It would've been harder to explain to his cop buddies that he had been intoxicated on the job. It would've made my defense more plausible.

He moved closer. Too close. If I'd wanted to, I could have lunged for him. I could've grabbed his Glock and shot him in the chest before he knew it, before any of them knew it was happening.

These other cops would not fire. Not in here. Too crowded. There were women and children present. Even if they did fire, I could swipe the gun and duck and roll and get enough shots off to kill the one who had run in with Gemson. He'd be dead, and I would've shot my way out the back, but I did nothing. I stood still with my hands up. Then I lowered them and held them out in the universal gesture for "cuff me."

And Gemson did. He stepped up like a hero and slapped the cuffs on me—tight.

He said, "I got ya, city boy."

I smiled for three reasons. First, he had cuffed me in the front. Rookie mistake. Second, he had gotten close enough that I could still have taken his weapon from him. The third thing, I said out loud, "I'm not a city boy. I grew up in a town smaller than this, but you probably think that I'm from the city because I can read books and speak with big words."

He sneered and said, "Ya under arrest, boy. Silence is one of ya rights, and I suggest ya exercise it."

*Boy?* That's what he had called me. I smiled. I hadn't been called that in a long time. Silence was something I was good at. So, I stayed quiet.

## 21

GEMSON MADE sure that he drove me. I sat in the back of his car, handcuffed in the front. He talked the whole time, but I didn't listen. I thought about Matlind. He wouldn't be okay on his own. I had to get out of this somehow.

Always try to find the good in any situation—that was my motto, one of them, and that was what I did. The police detained me, but they had zero on me. Witnesses would've sworn to that.

We got to the station house. It was in the Public Safety Complex I had seen yesterday. Gemson turned off the light bar as we pulled into the parking lot. He parked the car and got out and waited for the other three cops to pull up before getting me out. The four of them took me into the building. Each had one hand on me. On my arms. My back. Restraining my movements. Wise choice.

It was a ghost town inside the station. Their dispatch center must have been in another part of the building because there were no employees there except for the cops who had brought me in.

One of the other deputies said, "Step this way."

I followed his instructions. When they saw I was complying, they took their hands off me.

Gemson and one of the other deputies went into another room, while the two remaining cops took me into a back room and fingerprinted and booked me. I ended up in a holding cell in less than fifteen minutes. Normally, I would've been impressed, except that these guys had nothing else to do. I was their top priority. I was their only priority.

I sat on the rear bench in my cell. No bed, just a hard bench made up to look like a cot. It thrusted out from the wall. I stared through the cell bars, imagining Chris and Faye Matlind, newlyweds who had taken a detour through Mississippi and ended up in a peculiar small town with hatred for people who were different.

I had witnessed no mistreatment, not like Matlind had described, but I couldn't justify the fact that there were no minorities here except for Maria. She almost didn't count because she worked late nights when the town was asleep, and she probably stayed indoors when they were all awake. Most people probably didn't even know she lived here. If the rednecks were guilty of abducting Matlind's wife, perhaps they didn't know about Maria either, or perhaps she was too visible and didn't make for an ideal target.

Suddenly, I heard a noise. Down the hallway from my cell, there was a thick metal door, painted white to match the walls. The door creaked open, and a man nearing sixty entered. He had deep blue eyes and slicked-back white hair. The guy limped slightly, not enough to require a cane but enough to slow him down in a foot chase. He walked slowly over to my cell and stopped out in front of it.

He said, "I'm the county sheriff. My name is Ty Grady. You can call me Ty. I don't mind."

*This is him, the sheriff,* I thought. *This is my chance.*

He said, "The law says you're innocent until a judge says otherwise. So, until he says otherwise, we can be on a first-name basis, right?"

I stayed quiet.

He said, "Exercising your right to remain silent? Well, that's okay. It is your right."

I nodded.

He said, "Stand up, so I can get a good look at you."

I remained seated for a moment. Then I decided that cooperating might get me out faster, maybe even today, if I was lucky. I stood up and walked closer to the bars.

Grady backed away after he saw me stand up.

My eyes were icy blue, like a wolf's. I had been told by girls a few times in my life that I had nice eyes. Maria had told me. She had used the word "nice," but my eyes could also be terrifying. I was good at it—years of practice in the Navy SEALs. And right then, that's what they were. I had mastered the ability to stare any man down.

Sheriff Grady felt that cold stare. It burned him like dry ice. He was a veteran sheriff and had probably seen it all, but now he was trembling. It was slight, but it was there.

He said, "So you aren't going to talk? That's fine. Like I said before, that's your right under the law, but just because you're going to be silent doesn't mean you can't listen." He paused. "Your name is Jack Widow? That's what your passport says."

I stayed quiet.

He asked, "What are you doing here in Black Rock?"

I stayed quiet.

"Jack, this will go a lot better on you if you cooperate at least some."

I paused for a second and thought about it. I decided I needed this to go faster, so I said, "Widow."

He said, "Pardon?"

"My name is Widow. No one calls me Jack."

"Widow? Last name? Like in the military?"

I nodded.

"You got relatives here? A wife?"

"I had a mother," I said. This was my opportunity to get some answers, to feel him out.

"Had?"

"She died. She was also a sheriff."

He looked at me with renewed interest.

He asked, "A sheriff? What was her name?"

I said, "Deveraux."

His jaw dropped. He said, "Deveraux? I know." Then he stopped. He waited, and then he said, "I knew your ma. She's passed on?"

I nodded. He seemed genuinely surprised by it. I was pretty good at spotting a liar, not that there hadn't been liars out there that were better than me at hiding their lies.

His jaw closed, and he said, "I'm sorry to hear that. I saw her about two years ago at a conference in Tupelo—excellent woman. I didn't know she had a son."

I nodded. I believed him. Still, I didn't want to tell him what I was doing there.

"Well, that might make the judge a little more lenient. I believe he met your ma once."

I stayed quiet.

"Do you know why you're here?"

Still quiet.

He said, "Assault."

I grinned, and then I said, "Your deputy started it."

Grady looked confused, and then he asked, "Deputy?"

I said, "Yeah, from earlier today. Your deputy picked the wrong man to mess with, and I wouldn't call it 'assault.' Maybe his feelings got hurt, but I hurt nothing else."

"I'm not sure what you're talking about."

I said nothing more.

He paused and shrugged, and then said, "I'm talking about the three guys from your motel room last night. You sent two of them to the clinic."

## 22

Ty Grady was well spoken for a country sheriff, more literate than his deputies seemed to be. I suspected he had been educated somewhere else and had then moved here. Grady wasn't a common Mississippi name.

He wore an official county sheriff department's jacket even though it was May, like a symbol of his profession. On his belt, he had an old web holster with a Glock 22 in it. All I could see was the butt of the gun. It glimmered black in the dim lights and looked well maintained and well oiled.

He said, "Those boys say that you attacked them."

"I attacked three armed men?"

"They were armed?"

I said, "One had a Louisville slugger."

"A baseball bat? You took on three heavyset guys, put two in the clinic, and one had a baseball bat?"

I said, "That's about the sum of it. Except I didn't attack them."

"You didn't?"

"No. They attacked my neighbor at the motel. The guy in room thirteen. You should check on him."

"Yeah? Why is that?"

"His wife is missing. She was abducted, and those guys had something to do with it."

He said, "Those boys didn't abduct anyone."

I said, "They were trying to abduct him."

"They mentioned nothing about a motel room. They said you attacked them in the parking lot."

"They must be confused. I attacked no one."

He nodded and then said, "Well, you're here for the day and night. The judge will hear your case in the morning. He's on the lake today. Will be the whole day, I'm afraid."

I said, "Grady."

He leaned in close to the bars.

"You need to check on Chris Matlind, the guy in room thirteen at the motel. He'll be in my room today—room fourteen. His wife is missing, and he's scared. He thinks the whole town is in on it. Claims no one will help him. Not even you."

"That guy you're talking about never came here with any wife. We investigated and questioned him and multiple eyewitnesses. No one saw any woman with him."

I said, "Sheriff, she's a young black woman. Could be the rednecks took her because of it, or could be that her disappearance has something to do with all of those missing girls. Might be that those rednecks you're protecting are into more than you think."

He said, "Those boys might be into making moonshine and stockpiling illegal guns—maybe even cooking meth—but that's the extent of it. They'd never hurt anyone."

He turned to walk away, but stopped. He didn't turn back but said, "I don't give a shit if anyone is black or purple. No one here has taken her, because she isn't real. Period." He continued walking. He made it halfway down the corridor.

I said, "Grady, my mom was a sheriff. I know the cop life. It's your duty to check on every crime that's reported to you, no matter how much you don't believe it. I'm telling you that Matlind is telling the truth. I saw it in his eyes. That guy lost someone, and she might still be here. She might still be alive."

He stopped but never turned around. He said over his shoulder, "I will go by and talk with him."

He turned and walked down the hall and was gone from sight.

One thing that I had learned from years in the military was during downtimes, go to sleep. You never know when the next chance will be. I hit the makeshift cot and closed my eyes.

## 23

THE FBI's Domestic Investigations and Operations Guide covers policies and procedures on how the FBI deals with domestic crimes such as kidnappings. Traditionally, officials are strictly bound to stay within the confines of the law in order to recover a kidnapped individual, but the Patriot Act changed that. It gave authorities considerably more room to maneuver—within the law —to secure abductees.

In abductions, there was an unwritten rule—the forty-eight-hour rule. If an abductee wasn't rescued within forty-eight hours, the kidnapping part was over, and the rescue turned into a homicide investigation. Chances were the victim was already dead. Not good for Faye Matlind. Even worse was that there had been no ransom demands—not one. If she had been taken by the same people who took Ann Gables or any of the other missing girls, Faye was as good as dead.

I knew that. I hoped Matlind didn't.

I woke up to a dark hallway and an even darker cell. The lights had shut off. I estimated that the time was somewhere around 10:30 at night. Not sure about that, but it seemed right. I had gotten no evening meal.

I got up from the bench and stretched my arms out as far as they would reach. The muscles in my body had cramped up from resting on the hard, tiny bench. I stood up and walked over to the bars. I craned my head and peered down the hallway. A single fluorescent light blinked in front of the door to the corridor. There was another light above my cell. It flickered once and then went out. I didn't imagine they came down here often to do maintenance.

I closed my eyes and listened hard. Surely someone was supposed to be guarding me. I heard nothing but the hum of an air conditioner somewhere outside my wall, probably a large outside unit.

I sat back down on the bench and thought for a bit, then went back to sleep.

## 24

I SLEPT for another hour and woke to a faint noise that sounded like keys rattling in someone's pocket. I got up and peered into the darkness. The single dim light still flickered by the door to the hallway. The door was wide open. As my eyes adjusted to the dark, I saw someone standing by my cell door. The door swung open in an abrupt, fluid motion, and the light above it flickered once. In that brief flash, I saw two things that unsettled me.

First, the man was a short stranger I had never seen before. No uniform, so not a cop. Not one redneck. My first thought had been that maybe they had gotten their cousin-deputy to let them in and had come for me in the quiet of the night—small towns were known for that kind of corruption. But the stranger I'd glimpsed was definitely not one of them. He was Hispanic.

The second thing I noticed that stirred me up inside was that at the end of a short arm, in a gloved hand—outstretched and pointed right at me—was what looked like a Heckler & Koch P30 with a suppressor attached to it. Possibly a P30L or LS, but I thought P30L. Not a common gun in this area except among collectors. A good weapon, but better when not pointed directly at your gut.

I remained still. I had the chance to dive to the right-hand side, roll, and come at the guy with a fast right hook. It was dark enough that I had a good chance to make a connection before a novice shooter fired his weapon, but I wasn't sure how much of a novice this guy was. And there was also the chance that he might fire blind. Even a novice could fire randomly into the dark and hit something, especially in such a confined space. I was fast, but I wasn't faster than bullets—the distance between where I stood, and the cell door was about eleven or twelve feet. I might make it. Maybe. But I didn't want to get shot.

Better to wait and learn his intent, then react—unless he fired. At which point, it didn't matter the odds or the questions that boiled in my head. If he fired a single shot, I'd react. Self-preservation demanded it.

He didn't fire. Instead, he clicked on a flashlight he held in his left hand, killing my chances of using the dark to my advantage. He shone the light right in my eyes, letting me know immediately he was not a novice. I had made the right decision in refraining from action.

In a thick Mexican accent, he said, "Stand up."

I stood up. I asked, "What the hell is this?"

He stayed quiet.

I repeated, "What the hell do you want?"

He tucked the flashlight between his cheek and shoulder like it was a telephone and then reached his left hand toward his center to remove something from around his body. It was something thick and bunched up, like he had been holding onto a snake.

He tossed it at my feet.

I looked down as he returned the flashlight to his left hand and pointed the beam at the coiled object on the ground. It was what looked to be about a seven-foot coil of extension cord, orange, and bright under the beam from the flashlight.

He said, "Tie it into a noose."

I didn't move.

He said, "If you don't do as I say, I'll find more people you care about and kill them."

That was when I knew I should've reacted sooner.

## 25

THE FIRST TIME I'd seen the Public Safety Complex in Black Rock, I had thought it was a new building. I'd been half right. Most of it was new—new brick, new doors, new roof. But the building was old. It had been remodeled and added onto, and then years later, it had been remodeled again. From the outside, I hadn't been able to tell. It had looked brand new—a fine job. But now that a short Mexican I had never seen before was pointing a solid Heckler & Koch P30L with a sound suppressor at my head, I realized it had been remodeled and wasn't new like I had originally thought.

I realized this because the Mexican guy seemed intent on forcing me to hang myself from the thick, brand-spanking-new sprinkler line above my cell. As I stared up at the metal pipes that ran along the ceiling, I saw that the tiles above me were newer and lower than the walls, as if the ceiling had been built only to split a larger floor in half. I saw paint distortion and pieces of chipped-away ceiling fragments that were obviously much older than the rest of the building.

The Mexican guy said, "Throw the cord over the pipe."

I tossed the cord over the pipe.

He said, "Loop it around the pipe and tie the other end around the bars. Make sure it's tight."

I did as he said. The cord was tight, and the pipe was strong enough to support my weight.

He said, "Jump up and grab the pipe and hang from it. Like monkey bars."

My mind raced as I evaluated the situation. I couldn't come up with a plan to escape that didn't involve bum-rushing him and getting shot in the process. I jumped up and hung from the pipe.

He said, "Now slip your head through the noose."

I followed his instructions.

I nodded, while a long, long moment passed. Sweat dripped from my brow.

He said, "Hang yourself."

I didn't move.

He fired the gun, and the muzzle flashed brightly in the blackness. The sound popped and echoed through the station house. A gun suppressor didn't silence bullets to a low ping sound like in the movies. The amount of sound that was silenced varied from gun to gun, but in a small room like a jail cell or a quiet station house with cement walls, the sound was much louder than someone breaking a window with a baseball bat.

The bullet zipped past my head and embedded deep into the ceiling above. Small chips rained down on me. I cringed.

He said, "Hang yourself, or I will shoot you, and you'll be dead, anyway. Then I'll find more people you love, and they will die too."

I didn't move.

He pointed the gun downward, aiming at an area where no man wants to get shot.

I took a deep breath and let go of the pipes. The drop wasn't far enough to break my neck, which was an immense relief, but my feet dangled above the ground. And that was enough to strangle me.

I was calm at first, but soon enough, I felt the lack of breath and the fear of death overpower me. I clawed and grabbed at the cord.

The stranger watched, but he didn't stay quiet. He said, "Good. You die now. No more of your family left."

I couldn't speak, but those words meant something. What did he mean by no more of my family left? Then it hit me. Earlier, he had said, I'll find more people you love. More.

He had killed my mother. I knew it. This was the man. He had found me.

My legs kicked violently and flailed around. The guy dodged to avoid them. He kept the flashlight beam in my eyes, and he kept the gun pointed at me. He watched as I struggled to breathe, to live, and in less than a minute, my body was limp.

The man who had shot my mother had watched me hang to death.

## 26

THE MEXICAN HAD FIGURED that I knew how to tie a hangman's noose. And I did. I knew how to tie all sorts of complicated knots. I had been in the Navy SEALs. Of course, I knew knots—all kinds of knots. Knots have many uses. Some of them are the uses that most people don't think about. Once I had dated a local girl from Japan. She liked knots a lot. She had told me, "The usefulness of a Navy man is his ability to tie a knot." She was a lot of fun. But this wasn't the time to be thinking about her.

In order to tie a fake hangman's knot, first tie a hangman's noose but lengthen the short-end and swap it as the long end. The sliding end has to be hidden inside the coil, so there's no risk of the noose tightening. The surrounding coil has to be loose enough to ensure it can be pulled free. To the casual observer, it will all look the same. I had tied the trick knot. But if the Mexican had turned on the overhead lights, he might've seen this. He might have lived longer.

He came in close to me to check to see if I was breathing. I wasn't. Then he waited for a long minute to make sure I was dead. It appeared I was dead. That was when he lowered his gun and turned his back on me—his mistake.

I squinted, barely opening my eyes, and peeked out. The guy's back was turned to me. So, I opened my eyes all the way and peered up. I reached up, grabbed the pipe overhead, lifted my body upward, and slid my neck out of the noose. It throbbed and ached from the fall when my neck had dropped and was caught by the cord, but my trick knot had worked. Any greater a drop and my neck might've broken, and I would be dead, but I wasn't. I was alive.

I dropped to the floor, landing on my bare feet, which kept me completely silent. Slowly, I tiptoed, staying in a low crouch. The floor was hard and cold. I snuck up behind the guy, closing the distance as fast as I could without alerting him. The guy fell for my charade. Still, he was no amateur. This guy was not just a hired gun, and it showed because he sensed that someone was sneaking up behind him. In a burst of fear and experience, the guy spun around fast, gun ready to fire, ready to kill whomever else was in the jail with us. He blind-fired once into the darkness, and the bullet whizzed past me. I heard it hit the opposite wall. The guy saw me in the muzzle flash, but it was too late. Terror beamed across his face. He had made a huge mistake.

I never played baseball in my life, but I always liked the sport. I respected the high-speed throws of major-league pitchers. And I was fascinated at how many miles per hour some fastballs clocked in at. A hundred miles an hour was fast, faster than most people ever drove their cars.

I couldn't hit a fastball like that, much less pitch one, but I was fast and strong—stronger than most guys, that was for damn sure. I swung a vicious right hook through the air so fast and so hard that it knocked the guy off his feet. It may not have been as fast as a major-league fastball, but I doubted a fastball would've knocked the guy's head clean off. I hadn't knocked it off either, but I had come damn close. The intruder smacked into the wall on the other side of the hallway about a second after my punch connected with his face. The sound echoed throughout the corridor. I felt the vibrations of breaking bones and snapping teeth through my knuckles. The guy hit the wall hard—hard enough that if the force of the punch hadn't killed him, the solid surface of the wall would have.

I yelled, "Are you the asshole who shot my mom?"

I picked up the flashlight.

He had dropped it, and it had rolled and stopped against my feet. In its beam, I could see that one of the guy's shoes was still laced up and, on the ground, where he had been standing. The gun had flown back a few feet and landed in the center of the hallway. I moved the beam up to the guy so I could get some answers, which I wouldn't get. Not from him. Because not only was his head still attached, but it had turned around a little farther than it was meant to, like it had been screwed on wrong. Either my punch had broken his neck, or it had broken when he bounced off the wall. I wasn't sure which. Regardless, the guy was dead.

I picked up the gun and pointed it at the open door at the end of the hall. In case he hadn't been alone. No one rushed in after him. No one came to see what the loud noise had been. He had no backup. No one checked on us.

I bent down and checked the guy's pockets. I found his wallet and IDs and sifted through them—all totally phony. A silenced Heckler & Koch P30L, gloves, nice clothes, clean-cut, able to make his way into the station house and steal the keys to the cell, and the fake IDs were good. This guy was a professional hitman. No question.

*Who the hell sent you? And why did you kill my mom? Who sent you?*

There was far more to Faye Matlind's disappearance than a clan of Mississippi rednecks.

27

I PICKED UP THE GUN. It was a Heckler & Koch P30L. I detached the suppressor and slipped it into my pocket. I wasn't concerned with stealth. Not anymore. I sat on the bench in the cell and slipped my shoes on one-handed. I had kicked them off before I went to sleep. The strings were still laced up and tied.

I walked past the holding cells and out of the hallway and then checked the bullpen. No one was around. I searched for my belongings and found them in a manila envelope marked "Widow," sitting in an evidence cabinet with a tiny steel drawer that squeaked when I opened it. My passport, ATM card, and cell phone were the only items in it. I tore it open, emptied the contents, and returned them to my pockets.

I stood up and explored the rest of the station, clearing each room as I went. Nothing. Then I wondered where the hell the night watch deputy was. Surely someone was assigned to watch the jail while I was there. But there was no sign of life anywhere.

No matter what happened next, I wasn't going back in the cell. No way. That was for damn sure. I tucked the gun into my waistband and exited the police station.

The night air was clammy and gusty. Thin, almost nonexistent clouds moved fast overhead like someone was speeding up time.

Through the breaks in the clouds, I could see the stars. One perk of living in a small town in the country was seeing bright stars.

I could see the lake off in the distance, a couple of blocks beyond the Eckhart Medical Center. It looked quiet.

The streets were quiet. I heard the faint whines of a steel guitar from the country bar down the street. To the north, I heard the sedate buzzing of one of those pesticide trucks that drove up and down the street at night, spraying for insects, almost like a pest itself as it buzzed through the silent town.

I began walking through the parking lot when I noticed something irregular. One more sound hit my eardrums. It was a beeping sound. No, it was a dinging sound—a familiar sound like a car's seat belt alert.

I crouched down low and looked around the parking lot. I positioned my hand near the butt of the P30L, ready to draw it quickly if I needed to. I looked left. Looked right. Checked all around me. The building was empty, but the parking lot still had cars. There were five police cars and two trucks, all with reflective, official markings on the doors, and all quiet.

One car had no light bar on the roof, and across from the cars were two civilian vehicles. All the cars were parked in two neat rows—all except for one. One police cruiser was stopped in the middle of the parking lot, facing the street.

I stood up tall to get a better look at it. The passenger door was wide open, but no one was in it. From this distance, it appeared unoccupied. The open door was tripping, the seat belt alert in the dash, and it beeped and beeped.

I crept over to the cruiser, staying close to the rear of the parked cars for cover. I hadn't drawn the Heckler & Koch, not yet. If there was a cop inside or nearby, he would've been within his rights to shoot me without warning if he had seen a gun in my hand. As far as he knew, I was an escaped armed fugitive. No judge in the world would convict him of a wrongful discharge of his weapon under those conditions.

I neared the car and gasped. Inside, sprawled across the front bench, was Gemson. Blood covered the dashboard toward the passenger side, like it had been sprayed across the front of the car. He had been shot in the head.

I drew the P30L out of my waistband and scanned the area. There was no one in sight. He must've been shot by the Mexican guy. That was how the guy had gotten the keys and access to my cell. Then I stopped, frozen in place. Just to be sure, I ejected the magazine and counted the rounds. Missing a round, plus the one fired back in the cell.

Great. Now I was holding the weapon that had shot a cop. And a cop I got into an altercation with in public. With witnesses.

Why had the guy tried to get me to hang myself if he had just shot Gemson? I had no idea. The best I could figure was that it was a message or some kind of sick turn-on the guy had. Like he got off on making his victims kill themselves. A lot of hired killers in history had their own signature styles. Maybe suicide was the Mexican's.

Since Gemson was an armed deputy, I guess the guy hadn't wanted to take a chance with him, so he put a bullet in his head. I lowered the gun and swung the car door open. I leaned in and checked Gemson's pulse. Suddenly, his left hand grabbed my wrist. He was still alive.

## 28

GEMSON BREATHED IRREGULARLY, but he was breathing. He had grabbed my wrist and then passed out. I examined his wound. He'd been shot in the head, but it turned out to be just a graze—deep but not fatal. He was lucky the Mexican guy hadn't double-tapped him.

Careless, but lucky for Gemson.

Blood loss was a different story. He had lost a lot of blood. I couldn't tell how much, but his skin color had faded. He wasn't quite blue like a corpse, but wasn't far from it.

Most police cruisers were equipped with a first aid kit in the trunk, so I popped the trunk and scrambled back to it. I looked inside and found the kit. It was a small green case with a white cross on the lid. I grabbed it and closed the trunk. Then I returned to Gemson and opened the case. I pulled out a long strand of gauze and medical tape. I wrapped his head several times—tight. Then I taped it off. I tilted his head to one side. Gravity should slow the bleeding.

I grabbed the radio, clicked the button, and put the receiver to my mouth. Pressing down on the call button, I asked, "Is anyone out there? Officer in need of urgent medical assistance!"

I released the button and waited. Listened hard. Static, and then I said, "Respond!"

Static again.

I said, "Respond! Officer down!"

No response. Gemson was on his own tonight.

I thought maybe if he needed backup; he was supposed to call for it on his cell phone. I dug through his pockets and found his phone, and searched through his contact list. I found Grady's information, hit the call button, and waited. Dial tone and then a ring. Two rings in, and the sheriff answered. He was groggy. Probably asleep.

He said, "It's late. This had better be an emergency."

"Gemson has been shot."

Silence on the other end.

Grady asked, "Who is this?"

I said, "You need to come! He's dying! He's been shot!"

Grady asked, "Widow? How'd you get out of your cell?"

I said, "There's no time! He's been shot in the head. He's lost a lot of blood. Get over here! Now!"

Then there was silence on the line. I imagine that Grady's brain was still half asleep and trying to process the information.

He said, "Take him to the clinic. It's only two blocks south of the station. I'll be there."

He hung up.

I looked around, then looked at the car keys hanging in the ignition of Gemson's cruiser.

I could've left him in the clinic parking lot and driven away. I could've been miles away in their police car before I'd have to dump it. Under the cover of darkness, I might've passed the state line. I could've driven straight north and crossed over into

Tennessee. The state had a lot of back roads—plenty of places to dump a car. I could've been back on the road and leaving this nightmare behind, but a voice in my head said, *You must do the right thing.*

It echoed over and over like some kind of predetermined destiny, some kind of instinctual voice set deep in my bones, something that had started with my ancestors and cursed my line for all time.

I looked down at Gemson's dying body in my arms and reached across him and slammed the passenger door closed and turned the key and fired up the car and hit the gas. I was there in seconds. Seven of them.

## 29

I WAITED on the street in front of the Eckhart Medical Center on the clinic side.

The building was two stories with thick windows tinted black. I imagined it was to protect the occupants from sunlight. The clinic was attached to the largest building, and the rest of the complex was surrounded by the barbed wire fence. The back of it faced the lake. At the end of the street, there was a boat launch and a shabby little pier with one boat tied to it. It rocked slowly on the water.

I waited outside of the squad car; my back planted against the rear on the driver's side. The P30L rested on the trunk lid next to me.

I had switched the light bar on so that the red and blue lights lit up the night sky. The colors reflected off the storefront windows and parked cars as the lights spun in a clockwise rotation. A long extension of the lights fell across the lake like a lighthouse beacon and rotated back across the street. A low fog rolled across the top of the water. The red and blue lights were magnified in the mist.

Minutes later, I heard distant police sirens blaring through the quiet town like a banshee on the moors. The wailing noise was deafening in the silence. Eight and a half minutes after that,

Sheriff Grady pulled up in an old department-issued Chevy Tahoe. The light bar on the roof waned and flashed in sync with a set of smaller lights buried deep in the front grille, and the tires squealed as he braked to a stop. They died off in a quick hiss as they screeched to a stop across the road in front of the Eckhart Medical Center.

Two seconds later, his deputies rolled up in their patrol cars. Both had one driver and no passengers. The two cops jumped out of their vehicles. The only one who wore a shred of his uniform was Sheriff Grady. His deputies wore department-issued jackets with sheriff badges patched on the right arms, but none of them wore the proper uniform. I guess they hadn't had time to change. They were probably in their pajamas when Grady had called them.

Sheriff Grady jumped out of the Tahoe with his Glock drawn. He pointed the gun at me from about thirty yards away. His deputies followed suit. The sirens had stopped the moment all three vehicles stopped.

Grady yelled, "Stand up with your hands up and walk toward us."

I said, "Sorry, Sheriff. I'm not doing that."

Grady said, "Widow, this isn't a game. Now follow my directions." He waited a moment and then repeated his orders.

I stayed behind the cover of the police car. I looked at him and shook my head. I said, "Not going to happen." Silence, and then I said, "Grady. Your man is dying. I didn't shoot him. Another guy attacked me in my cell. He had Gemson's keys. He tried to kill me, but he must've shot Gemson first. You're wasting time. He's losing blood."

Grady looked at Gemson. The guy wasn't moving, but he was pressed up against the closed passenger door.

I peeked in on him. His coloring wasn't good.

I said, "Ticktock, Sheriff. You can try to come and get me, a course of action that none of you will survive—that I can promise.

That I can pretty much damn guarantee. Or you can holster your weapons and help me get Gemson inside the clinic before he bleeds to death."

Grady remained where he was.

One of his deputies looked at him. The guy said, "Gemson looks bad."

I said, "I'm telling you the truth. Faye Matlind is missing. And now someone just tried to kill me. You need to believe me, or this is going to turn bad for you, Gemson, and a whole lot of other people."

At that exact moment, in the silence of a standoff, I heard the most recognizable sound in modern police combat. It was the ultimate conversation stopper—the last word.

A pump-action shotgun had cocked somewhere near us. We all froze as we heard *Crunch! Crunch!*

The four of us looked over toward the clinic's entrance.

Grady said, "Doctor, go back inside."

I saw a pair of small, feminine hands holding a Remington 870 pump-action shotgun with a pistol grip and a collapsible stock. One of the best shotguns ever made. Beyond the barrel of the shotgun, there was a beautiful woman with long blonde hair and a muscular frame, like a fitness model.

Sheldon.

She said, "Widow. Grady. You boys, stop all this nonsense and bring Gemson inside before he bleeds to death. And before I shoot all of you."

Grady said, "Dr. Eckhart. Now don't do anything stupid."

Was Sheldon a doctor? And an Eckhart? She had said that she worked at the clinic. What she should have said was that it was her clinic. Her last name was on the sign.

Sheldon said, "Ty, I'm not asking. I'm telling."

## 30

ONE DEPUTY HELPED me carry Gemson. He wasn't particularly heavy for either of us, but he had completely passed out. Deadweight was harder to move than a half-conscious person. We half carried, half dragged him into the clinic.

Sheldon pointed to a room opposite the waiting room at the same time she leaned the shotgun back somewhere out of sight behind a shelf filled with boxes of feminine hygiene products. We carried Gemson past a reception area, where two people sat behind a long countertop, past a public water fountain and some bathrooms, and into an examination room. We laid him on an examining table.

Sheldon unwrapped the gauze I had wrapped around his head and began inspecting his wound. She told the sheriff that he should call Oxford and ask for a medical chopper. Gemson needed hospital attention, not the care that Sheldon could provide in a small-town clinic. Grady left the room to make the call.

Sheldon wore a pair of blue scrubs and was all business. She reached up and pulled her hair back into a ponytail with a scrunchie from her wrist. When she finished looking at Gemson, she wrapped his head tight and tilted it in a way that reduced the bleeding. She injected him with something, and he was suddenly conscious.

He babbled nonsensically.

She looked at me and said, "He needs to stay conscious. You saved his life."

I nodded and stayed quiet. I figured he wouldn't have done the same for me, but that didn't matter. It only mattered what I had done.

## 31

WE WAITED for the helicopter for twenty-five minutes. It was coming from Oxford General Hospital. It was an MD 520N, a fairly decent chopper used for police and rescue operations all over the world. This one was painted white with a dark-blue stripe right across the middle. A red light blinked from the bottom of the canopy. We stood outside and watched as it flew over the trees. The rush of wind from the rotors blew the treetops in firm gusts like the oncoming winds from a tropical storm. The chopper pilot maneuvered the helicopter over power lines and streetlights. It yawed as it descended at a steady pace. The skids landed on the street with a low thud. The main rotor and tail blades kept turning. Debris from the road flew up into the air and drifted away behind the chopper, swept up into the night.

The deputies lifted Gemson and helped a pair of paramedics strap him to a gurney. They strapped him in tightly and loaded him onto the helicopter. We stood outside and watched as the chopper lifted off the ground and flew away.

Grady looked at me and scratched his nose. He said, "Widow, would you wait inside for a moment. Doctor, is that okay?"

Sheldon smiled at me and said, "Of course."

Grady pointed at one of his deputies and said, "Take him inside and watch him for a moment."

I put my hand up and said, "That won't be necessary. If I wanted to run, I would've."

Sheldon said, "Ty, I think Widow has proven himself."

Grady leaned forward and put his hand on her shoulder like he was trying to say something out of my earshot, but I heard him fine. He said, "I don't trust him."

Sheldon said, "If it weren't for him, Gemson would be dead."

Grady shrugged and made a kind of retreat. He backed away about a foot and stared at the ground for a moment, like he wanted to phrase his next statement right.

Sheldon never gave him the chance to speak. She said, "The bullet did more than graze his head. I think it fractured his skull. At the very least. And Widow could've walked away and left him to die."

Grady thought for a moment, conflict on his face. Finally, he faced me and said, "For now, you're no longer under arrest. I appreciate your helping my deputy. But don't you be leaving just yet. I need to know what the hell is going on."

I said, "All I know is that I was asleep in my cell, then I woke up, and some Mexican guy was waving a gun in my face."

A confused look fell across Grady's face. He asked, "Mexican guy?"

I nodded and said, "A dead Mexican guy now."

Grady cocked his head and looked at me. "So, there's a dead guy in my jail?"

I said, "Dead as he can get."

Then I paused a beat, reached into my pocket, and pulled out the P30L. I handed it to him—butt first. He stared at the gun, and his brow wrinkled and created several slopes across his forehead.

I said, "The Mexican was armed with this."

Grady inspected it and sighed, and nodded. He slipped the gun into the back of his waistband.

"Okay. For now, you stay here with Dr. Eckhart." He looked over at his deputy again and said, "Stay with them."

The deputy nodded. I shrugged and followed Sheldon and the deputy into the clinic.

Grady and the other deputy left their vehicles on the street with the light bars on and went on foot back to the Public Safety Complex. I guess they wanted to block the street from any traffic, or from me getting away in a vehicle. The road they were parked on was the only way out. Not that it mattered because I wasn't going anywhere.

## 32

SHELDON STOOD at the reception counter. Even in her scrubs, her muscular frame made its presence known. It called to me like a siren. I tried to look away, but she was like a vortex, and I was in danger of being sucked in.

She caught me staring. Leaning against the countertop, she heaved herself up and sat casually on its edge, her legs swinging back and forth like a teenage girl's.

"What're you staring at?" she asked.

"I was remembering my mother."

She tilted her head, and then she asked, "What? I remind you of your mother? That's weird."

I smiled and said, "No. Nothing like that. She died recently. And I was just thinking that when I was a kid, my mom was beautiful. I used to beat up the kids at school because they said things about her."

She looked perplexed. Strands of blonde hair from her ponytail fell across her left shoulder. "I don't understand what that has to do with you staring at me."

"I was thinking that I would hate it if you were mine."

Her smile diminished. She asked, "What?"

I said, "I'd hate for you to be mine. Like my girl."

"Why is that?"

"Because of all the fights, I'd get in over you."

She smiled wider.

It wasn't a line. I meant it. I had just met Sheldon, and already I was fighting over her. I said, "A beautiful woman can be a deadly thing. Look at Cleopatra or Helen of Troy. A beautiful woman can destroy the world."

"I'm like Cleopatra?"

I smiled. Then I said, "Cleopatra ain't got shit on you. That's for damn sure."

She paused and smiled and looked away, like some far-off realization slapped her across the face.

I asked, "What is it?"

She turned back and smiled again. "I like you. I think."

"You think?"

She said, "I mean, we just met, but you're different. A lot different from these small-town people."

"Aren't you from here?"

At first, she shook her head, and then she nodded.

I was confused.

She said, "I've only lived here for five years. I got a special grant to open this Medical Center, and it had to be here, so I came here."

"So, where are you from?"

She hesitated for a second and said, "Here."

"Really?"

She said, "I moved away for a while. I actually went to school abroad. I fell in with the wrong crowd and then got my medical degree and came back."

I looked around, starting with the walls, which were full of medical posters and plaques. Boxes of unused medical supplies were piled up like there wasn't enough room for them in a storage closet. There were boxes of feminine medical supplies and hygiene products—skin products, birth control pills, Plan B tablets, and female contraceptives.

I said, "Wow. Lots of female stuff here."

She cracked a smile and then said, "Country women have a lot of needs."

I looked down at the computer screens behind the counter. I guessed that this was the nurses' station. The screensavers danced on the monitors like flickering candlelight.

A low humming came from down the hall. I saw several open doorways. All were dark. Probably examination rooms.

I said, "Looks like you've done pretty well for yourself."

She stayed quiet and then said, "Wasn't always like that. Believe me, there was a dark time in my life. But sometimes you have to do things you don't want to do in order to do good things."

I asked, "Is that why you stay here in this small town? Something bad from your past?"

She said, "It's hard to escape a place like this."

I smiled and nodded. I knew something about feeling stuck in a small town in Mississippi. I had felt stuck in Killian Crossing once.

"When I was abroad, I met a nice guy. We got to know each other, and he offered to fund a clinic and a research facility for me. He paid for my schooling, and so I'm under obligation to maintain this facility. I only have another year, and then I'll be free and clear."

It seemed to me like she was too old to still be obligated, but I'd heard of people who started school late or graduated late. And I knew nothing of the track that it takes for a person to become a doctor.

I asked, "What will you do then?"

She said, "I'll move away. Maybe to one of the coasts. I like Florida. I don't know."

"You sound unhappy."

She smiled and shook her head. Her eyes closed and then opened. They were an unforgettable shade of gray. I'd never seen it before.

She said, "Don't get me wrong. I'm grateful. But I've got some moral objections."

I asked, "With what?"

"The research side."

"Animals?" I asked.

She looked off into the distance for a second. Her eyes stared at one of the medical posters on the wall—a poster about pregnancy.

She said, "Right. Animal testing. Gotta pay for this clinic somehow."

## 33

I SPENT the better part of an hour with Sheldon, and we talked like a pair of teenagers who had never kissed before.

I could've talked to Sheldon all night. She was an amazing woman. Truly sensational. Why she was single, I had no idea.

The one thing I wanted to do more than talk to her was to stare at her amazing beauty. The only thing that I wanted to do more than that was to kiss her. Everywhere. At that moment, she was the only thing I cared about.

She asked, "You're the reason I had so much business yesterday? I was setting broken bones all morning."

I smiled and said, "Sorry about that."

She smiled back and then said, "Don't worry about it. This town is full of backward people. They don't like outsiders. Gemson isn't any different. Women. Blacks. Hispanics. People here don't care."

I said, "I grew up in a place like this. Don't judge the South by the people here. Where I'm from, my community has its racial scars too. But there are good people."

She nodded and then changed the subject. "Was your mother really the sheriff?"

I nodded.

She said, "My parents are dead."

I stayed quiet.

She trailed off into her own thoughts, lost in some distant memory.

I asked, "What is it?"

"What is what?"

"You're thinking about something. What is it?"

"Nothing. Just glad I met you."

I smiled.

Three things happened next.

First, Sheldon Eckhart leaned forward and kissed me with a pair of lips that were sweeter than any fruit. Her kiss was incredible. It whooshed through me like a hurricane. My hair tingled, my skin perspired, and my heart beat faster.

I kissed her back and gently caressed the back of her head. I kissed her, and she matched me—move for move. Her lips were wet, and her skin was smooth and soft. She smelled good, like a wet rainforest. Her kiss was alive.

She mesmerized me. If Sheldon had stopped kissing me right then and said, "Stay with me," I would've considered forgetting about my mission and stayed the rest of my life. It would've meant spending the rest of my life in seclusion, yet surrounded by people I didn't belong with. But I would've been happy to do it. I might've done anything for her—like Cleopatra.

The second thing that happened at the exact time we were locked in a passionate kiss was that I remembered Matlind, and I realized that I had gotten sidetracked.

And the third thing that happened ended our kiss. Sheriff Grady walked in with a less than cheerful look on his face. He stood inside the doorway with an accusatory look in his eyes, like he had just caught me with his wife.

We were silent for a moment.

He interrupted the silence and asked, "So, who is the dead Mexican in my jail cell?"

I said, "I got no idea. All I know is that he tried to kill me, and he is definitely a professional hitman."

## 34

SHERIFF GRADY STARED at me with a kind of sullen look, like he had grown tired of me. I couldn't say that I cared. One of his deputies walked up behind him and stopped about three yards away. He rested his hand on the butt of his holstered Glock.

These country boys still didn't trust me. I couldn't say I blamed them.

I faced the sheriff. I needed to get back to Matlind. It had been most of a day, and he wasn't safe on his own. Not if this professional hitman was somehow related to his missing wife, which was the only thing that made sense to me. I had kicked a hornets' nest, and it had to be because of Faye Matlind's disappearance. She was the only thing that connected me to a Mexican hitman. Had to be. And in that case, Chris Matlind was at the center of something. I doubted if Grady was going to take him seriously. It was best that I got back there.

I said, "I need to go back to the motel."

Grady said, "You need to stay in my custody."

"Am I still a prisoner?"

"You're a witness. There are a lot of unanswered questions here."

I said, "You don't need me. And you can't take me back to the jail, not after what happened."

"So, what do you suggest? That I let you go?"

"Take me back to my motel. At least there I can get some sleep before morning."

Grady paused, like he was searching his brain for the right answer. He knew I was right. I couldn't go back to the jail. It was a crime scene now, and it wasn't safe there, but then again, it wasn't safe anywhere at that moment.

Grady looked at his deputy—not Mike, but the other guy. He said, "Lewis, take him back to the motel and stay outside in your car till I call you."

Lewis came all the way into the room. He looked at me and made a "come here" gesture with his hand. I ignored him and looked back at Sheldon.

I held her hand in mine. She slid off the countertop and stared up at me with those gray eyes like storm clouds brewing—beautiful and dangerous.

The lights above hit my back and cast a shadow from my body over her. It consumed her like she stood in the wake of a tall tree. She was tiny next to my frame.

I asked, "Will I see you later?"

She smiled and said, "I hope so."

## 35

DEPUTY LEWIS and I drove back to the motel in his police cruiser. I sat in the back. We didn't have to go far. Maybe ten minutes. He drove with the light bar off. There was no rush in getting me to the motel.

He hadn't spoken until we came to a traffic light. It was one of those times when the light turned red for us, and we were the only car on the road. After we stopped at the light, Lewis reached up and adjusted his mirror. I saw his eyes in the reflection. The light shone red across the top of his face.

He said, "Ya saved my friend's life, but ya're the reason that he got shot. I reckon I owe ya some justice for that, but I can't do nothing to ya—the sheriff said so. But that don't mean I can't tell ya that I don't like ya."

He spoke without an accent but still slurred his speech in a backwoods sort of way, just like Gemson. Maybe that was how he had gotten the job in the first place, like he came off as the smart one.

I asked, "Do a lot of backwoods justice here?"

He said, "When the situation requires it. We've been known to take a bad guy out into the woods and teach him a lesson before we book him."

"You abuse your prisoners?"

"We don't hurt anyone who ain't got it coming. And sometimes prisoners like to run. We gotta teach them a lesson."

"So why are you telling me this?"

He asked, "Maybe ya want me to pull over before we get to the motel? Maybe ya want to run?"

I said, "Sheriff told you to drive me to the motel. I'm not a prisoner. You're escorting me like I'm a VIP. Kind of like a chauffeur."

He scowled in the mirror and stared back at me, and then said, "Ya may think that ya aren't a prisoner, but ya'll end up back behind bars soon enough. I'd bet my badge on it."

I stayed quiet.

He asked, "So ya wanna get it over with now? I'll pull over, and we can get out and settle this."

I said, "You pull over, and only one of us is getting back in the car. The other is going to need that medical chopper to come back for him."

Lewis paused. He almost said something, but the light turned green, and he continued on to the motel.

We stayed quiet for the rest of the way.

The motel was dark and quiet. The parking lot was half full. Every car was silent and still. A family of raccoons rustled through a dumpster in the next parking lot over.

Lewis stopped the car in the parking lot to let me out.

He said, "Get out. I'll be sitting in the car. Sheriff's orders."

I paused.

He said, "What? Do ya need me to check your room for ya? Are you scared?"

I ignored him and reached into my pocket and pulled out Gemson's cell phone. I tossed it on the backbench. I didn't bother to explain. I just got out of the car and shut the door behind me. Not hard. I didn't want to slam it. I wanted him to know that his remarks hadn't affected me, which they hadn't.

I went to room fourteen, the room I left Matlind in the night before. I only hoped that he had stayed put and waited for me to return like I'd asked.

I knocked. No answer.

I knocked again—hard. No answer.

I reached down and grabbed the handle and twisted the knob, and pushed the door open. The room was dark. I flipped on the light. The room was empty. No sign that Matlind had ever slept there. The bed was remade as though it had never been slept in. The only thing left in the room that didn't belong was my phone charger. It was still plugged into the wall.

I left the room, left the door open, and checked next door. Maybe Matlind had returned to his own room to wait with his own stuff. Maybe he needed to shower and needed his own belongings.

The doorframe was still shattered, and it would probably stay that way for weeks. Judging by the state that the motel had been in, I doubted the owner got around to fixing things in a timely manner.

A dim light shone through the cracks between the curtains and the splinters of the door. I pushed the door open. It creaked, and more splintered wood fell from the top of the frame. The light that dimly lit the room was from the bathroom. And the reason Matlind had not answered me was because he was dead.

His body lay flat across the bed. His arms were twisted out and away from him. The fingers on his left hand reached out to me like he wanted me to take his hand and follow him. A Beretta Px4 Storm weighed down the tip of his index finger. It had a black, rubbery look to it and lay on the bed like a snake, coiled and waiting for action. The smell of gunpowder lingered in the air. At the top of the bed and partially on the wall were dried stains—part blood, part brain, and part skull fragments.

Matlind had blown his brains out.

He had woken up and found that I had abandoned him, too. He had set his hopes on me, and I had let him down. First, his wife vanished, and then I did.

He took his own life.

# 36

I STUDIED Matlind's corpse and scanned the motel room carefully. On the cold, hard tile at the foot of the bed was a shell casing. I knelt and inspected it without picking it up. I got down on my hands like I was preparing to do a pushup and went all the way down, eye level with the brass so I could see the head stamp.

The bullet was a nine-millimeter. I bet that if I ejected the magazine out of the Beretta Px4, it would have been loaded with nine-millimeter parabellums. That was the most popular bullet being used in the US. It was used in over sixty percent of police firearms.

I pushed up and got back on my feet. I looked over the corpse, inspecting Matlind's entry and exit wounds. He had put the gun barrel in his mouth, and the muzzle of the gun must've pushed in all the way till he involuntarily began swallowing it because the exit wound had taken out the top part of his brainstem and the bottom of his brain.

I looked at the fingers on his left hand. I saw gunshot residue on his left hand and clothes. It was all the way to his forearms. I couldn't recall whether Matlind had been left-handed. Maybe.

He hadn't killed himself. The suicide had been staged. I knew that for sure. It seemed like his fingers weren't broken—that was a typical sign of a faked suicide. But that didn't mean he wasn't forced to pull the trigger or hadn't been coerced in some other way.

I saw no visible evidence that he hadn't done it himself, but I knew that was the case because I had met a man who'd tried to get me to commit suicide. I was positive that he had murdered Matlind first. That was how he knew about me.

He came here after I left and questioned Matlind, probably convinced him he killed Faye, and then murdered him. The dead Mexican who had tried to kill me was connected to Faye's disappearance somehow. Had to be—no other logical explanation.

I stepped back to the door and opened it wide with my foot. Lewis saw me and turned on his headlights and then his light bar. I wasn't sure why he probably thought it would irk me. His engine had still been running. He was parked in the lot, facing my door. The cones from his light bar lit up the room every time they rotated by.

This time, I was the one using my hand to gesture for him to come. He got out of the car and approached.

Before he reached the door, he said, "What? You need me to tuck you in?"

I stepped out of the doorway to let him see the room and the dead body.

I said, "No. But you might need me to do your damn job for you."

His jaw dropped open, and he stared at the corpse. He said, "Oh, God!"

I said, "You'd better call the sheriff over here."

## 37

We waited outside for Grady to arrive. Deputy Lewis hadn't known what to do—that much was obvious. Under normal conditions, he should've locked down the crime scene as best he could. He should've locked me in the rear bench of his car, but he hadn't done those things. The only thing he had done was to move his car closer to room thirteen and adjust his light bar so that it spun faster. No siren, only the blue and red lights. I guess the faster spin was to signify more immediate danger.

They flashed and lit up the motel's exterior. The other guests started opening their doors and peering out of their windows. It was after midnight, and the bright lights from Lewis's police cruiser had awakened them.

Lewis had said nothing to me since he saw Matlind's body. Two dead bodies in one night must have been plenty for him.

I felt bad. I had seen plenty of corpses. That wasn't what bothered me. What bothered me was that I had been responsible for Matlind's death. I could've stayed with him or brought him with me. The only reason I had left was to let him sleep, and now the guy would never wake again. Stupid on my part. The guy's wife was missing, and some rednecks had tried to take him. I should've taken this more seriously.

I still wasn't quite seeing how a Mexican hitman and the rednecks were connected. A drug-related arrangement?

Sheriff Grady pulled up in his Chevy Tahoe. The light bar rolled and flashed out of unison with the lights from Lewis's squad car. The Tahoe's tires squawked as Grady pulled it into the parking lot. He got out and walked over to us. He gave me a look like "What are you doing out of cuffs?" But he said nothing about it.

He went past us and into the room and looked over the crime scene, the body, the brass, touching nothing. He came back out of the room a couple of minutes later and stepped out into the parking lot. Reaching into his jacket, he pulled out a half-empty pack of Newports. He opened the pack and slid a cigarette and a lighter out, and then lit the cigarette.

He took two drags and said, "Widow, you're bad luck."

I nodded.

He said, "I never even heard of you until yesterday, and now I have two dead bodies and a wounded deputy. One guy tried to kill you in jail, and another shot himself in the head. Both strangers."

I stared down at him; his eyes covered by the brim of his hat. Even with the police lights flashing, darkness covered his face. I got a glimpse of his facial features only when he took a drag, and they were illuminated by the dim glow from his cigarette. The brief light revealed the gray stubble of a man who had a long day.

He said, "Well. Looks like suicide. Did you touch anything?"

"No," Lewis said.

"I'm talking to Widow."

I stayed quiet. He waited until the silence was awkward, and then he asked, "Well? Did you touch anything?"

I said, "No. But I had a look."

"And?"

"Don't take this the wrong way, but you know dick-all about crime scene investigation."

"How do you mean?"

"I was never in law enforcement as an employee, but I've seen some things. And there is a clue that stands out. Don't you see it?"

Grady took a last puff of his cigarette and then tossed it onto the concrete. He asked, "What's that exactly?"

"You're going to kill yourself. How would you do it?" I asked.

"Gun, I guess."

I said, "That's the most common method of suicide among men Matlind's age."

"So?" he asked.

I said, "I'm asking."

"I don't know."

"Do you know how many people killed themselves last year?" I asked.

He said, "I don't know. Ten thousand?"

"Try twenty-two thousand one hundred and seventy-five."

He asked, "How do you know that?"

I ignored his question and asked, "Do you know how many people died from automobile deaths?"

"I don't know," he said.

I said, "Eighteen thousand. That's fewer people who died last year in automobile deaths than suicides. And do you know how many suicides were men?"

"The majority," he said.

I nodded. I said, "More than sixteen thousand. That's seventy-three percent."

He nodded. "So, seventy-three percent of Americans who took their own lives last year were men."

I asked, "Know how many were from guns?"

He said, "Most?"

"Fifty percent were from self-inflicted gunshot wounds. The rest were suffocation and poisoning."

He nodded.

"Do you know how many doctors killed themselves from gunshot wounds?"

He shook his head.

I said, "Not many. About four hundred doctors commit suicide every year, and guns are the method used least often. They overdose. Doctors self-medicate. It's the ideal way—write yourself a prescription for a painless and deadly drug. Overdose. Easy as anything."

He shrugged.

Then I asked, "What else?"

"What else what?"

"What else do you see?"

The sheriff looked back over the crime scene and said, "Look, the guy's wife left him on their honeymoon. She ran out. So, he got depressed, and he shot himself. End of story. I see nothing else here."

"Look at the gun," I said.

He looked and paused over it.

I said, "You don't have an investigation unit here, right?"

He shook his head and said, "No."

"Then it doesn't matter if you pick it up if no one else is coming to inspect it."

Grady said, "I do all the homicide investigations in this town. I know how to conduct a crime scene."

I nodded, like I was apologizing.

"We don't get a lot of murders here. At least we didn't before you got here."

Grady reached into his jacket pocket and pulled out an old bandanna. It was red with black tribal symbols dotted all over it. He wrapped it around his hand like a glove. He picked up the gun and smelled it.

"It smells like it's been fired recently. Safety is off. The ballistics would probably match the bullet in his head. There's gunpowder residue on the area around his left hand."

I stayed quiet.

"So, what am I missing?"

I paused and asked, "Why was I arrested?"

"Assault on those boys."

"Three guys."

"So?"

"Three tough rednecks."

"So?"

"So not a challenge for me. Obviously."

"What's your point? That you're tougher than three idiot rednecks?"

"Tougher than those three, apparently. Tougher than a short, wiry doctor from the Gulf Coast, definitely."

"What the hell are you getting at, Widow?" Grady asked.

"The gun. Does it work?"

The sheriff nodded, and then he asked, "So?"

"It works. You just said it's a working firearm. It looks pristine, well kept. And it works. It fired a bullet tonight that killed Chris Matlind."

"Yes. Yes. I can see that. So, he killed himself."

I said, "No. He didn't."

"Just say what you're getting at."

"Why was I arrested?"

"Assault!"

"Those rednecks were here to attack Chris. They wanted to drag him out of his room and abduct him against his will. They made that fairly obvious."

"So?"

"Chris was afraid for his life. He was terrified. I saw it."

Grady shrugged.

"First, a man who wants to die is not afraid of three men. Second, a man who has a perfectly good gun isn't afraid of three men. Certainly, he didn't need my help if he had a gun in his room."

Grady nodded. He seemed to understand.

"Chris Matlind didn't have a gun eight hours ago. I'm willing to bet that Chris Matlind had never fired a gun in his life. He certainly had never fired a Beretta Px4. Look closer at his hands. There's no initial powder on them, only some residue. He didn't fire that gun. Not point-blank. And putting the gun into the back of his throat was as point-blank as you can get.

"Plus, one thing that struck me about this motel when I saw the rooms was that they have tile, not carpet. I've never heard of a motel with tile instead of carpet. I'm just starting this traveling thing, but that seems unusual to me."

Grady asked, "What does that tell you?"

"The casing from a Beretta Px4 ejects from the top right-hand side of the gun. The Beretta Px4 Storm spits it out of the top fast. It's so fast that if you blink, you'll miss it."

"Okay?"

"This type of casing doesn't just fall to the floor directly after being ejected. It would've landed farther away and then rolled because of the tile. But the casing here is lying directly beneath his feet and to the right-hand side. The bullet was fired point-blank and from inside of his mouth. But he wasn't the one who fired it. Someone else stood over him and forced it down his throat. I think that whoever murdered him grabbed a handful of his hair and jerked his head back. The killer shoved the gun down his throat and fired. And that's why the brain and skull fragment patterns are spread across the wall and not the ceiling. If you put the gun in your mouth and fire upward, the remains will spray across the ceiling, not the wall. I'm also willing to bet that if a medical exam was conducted on him, it would find that one or several of his fingers are broken."

"And you don't think that we would've looked that far into it? We have Dr. Eckhart. I'm sure that she would've found such a thing."

"I'm sure she would have. She certainly is competent enough. I don't think that the man who murdered Chris cared about that. It would've been after the fact. I don't think he planned on staying in town. He just wanted this to pass for suicide for a couple of days at the most. It's buying himself time. He's passing through."

"You're the only stranger here," Grady said.

I said, "Not true. There's another stranger here."

"Who's that?"

"The dead guy in your jail."

38

We left the motel, but Deputy Lewis stayed behind to guard the crime scene. Grady had instructed him to set up crime scene tape around the rooms in question and told him to remain alert and stay in the parking lot all night.

Grady hadn't handcuffed me. No one had read me the Miranda rights. As far as I could tell, I wasn't under arrest. I was free, but Grady had made it clear that he didn't want me out of his sight.

We drove in the Tahoe. The wheels rocked and bounced as he took tight turns around corners. The same traffic light from earlier had turned red for us as well, but Grady ran it.

He said, "Since you aren't safe anywhere, and I don't trust you, you and I are partners in this thing."

I asked, "What do you propose?"

"I disagree with your assessment of Matlind. I say his wife left him and he then killed himself. End of story. She might even be shacked up here with a local or a tourist. The lake is full of young businessmen on vacation, far away from their wives. Just because you made a couple of interesting observations doesn't mean shit," he said.

"So how do you explain the Mexican?"

He shrugged and said, "He followed you here. You brought some kind of trouble to my town. Whatever."

I stayed quiet and thought about the idiots that can be found in small southern towns. I thought how they're the ones that give the rest of us a bad name. "So, why are we back here?" I asked.

We had pulled back into the Public Safety Complex's parking lot.

"We're going to have a better look at your Mexican friend. You say he tried to kill you and that he killed Matlind. I don't see any connection between the two. But let's see that mind of yours prove me wrong."

He parked the Tahoe, killed the motor, and stepped out. The driver's seat squeaked as he got out like it had probably done a million times. He opened the back door and let me out.

We walked into the building, past the reception area, past the bullpen, and down some steps to the door to the hallway with the holding cells. Grady flipped a couple of switches, and the holding cells lit up brightly. Lying against the wall, neck still broken, was a tangled mess of limbs—the corpse of the man who had tried to kill me. Grady went over to the body, reached into his back pocket, and pulled out his wallet.

I said, "I already checked his IDs. They're good but fake. That's the biggest clue that he's a professional. IDs like that must've cost good money."

Grady asked, "So, who is he?"

"Some kind of Mexican hitman. Like I told you."

"How do you know he's Mexican?"

"Was Mexican. And I don't. Not for sure. Just a hunch."

"Share your theory?"

I shook my head, and said, "Not yet. I need more first." Which I did, plus I didn't want to reveal my cards.

Grady nodded and searched through the dead guy's other pockets. He found a backup pair of surgical gloves besides the ones the dead guy wore.

"I bet that if you send the gun from Matlind's motel room and those gloves off to a crime lab, you'll find strands from the glove on the gun," I said.

"Gloves aren't uncommon. It proves nothing."

"This guy killed Matlind, and you know it. Case closed. You just don't want outsiders poking around. If I'm right, you'll have to call the state police. Probably the FBI too. I know that you small-town types don't like the Feds, but this is out of control now. It's time to call them in before this gets any worse."

Grady stayed quiet. He frowned and stared at the gloves.

I said, "Faye could still be out there and alive. This is big, too big for you to handle on your own. You need to call the Feds. And call them now."

"Who is Faye?"

"Haven't you been listening? Faye Matlind is the missing wife. She's still missing. Whoever this guy was, he's connected to Faye somehow. He wanted to shut us up. It's the only thing that makes any sense. He probably killed Matlind, and he tried to kill me."

Grady stayed quiet. At first, he nodded like he agreed. But then he shook his head and said, "No. I never saw Matlind with any woman. No one else in town saw her either. I've been sheriff here for fifteen years. These people are good, quiet folk. They aren't concealing some big conspiracy about a missing woman.

"I know these people. I know those rednecks. They bring barbecue in for the tourists to buy every Sunday. They're good, quiet people. The whole town is full of people like that. We don't need some outsiders here poking around in our business.

"Matlind came into town and started trouble at the local diner one day. That has been my only exchange with him. There is no wife."

I shrugged and gave up. It was like trying to convince a brick wall.

He went on, repeating what he'd just said. He said, "Mr. Matlind's death was tragic, but there's no wife. No one remembers her being here. This is a small town. Don't you think someone would've remembered her? A black woman? In case you haven't noticed, Black Rock is full of rural white people. Someone surely would've seen a black woman walking around. Hell, she would've been the talk of the town. But no one saw her!"

I breathed in and breathed out. He was heated. I could see that.

Then he said, "I think we've had enough of you."

He tossed the gloves back onto the corpse. They landed on his stomach. I glimpsed the dead man's face. Even in death, he seemed to grin at me.

Grady wiped his hands together as if done with the investigation. He said, "As unfortunate as this day was for Mr. Matlind, you've caught a break."

I asked, "What do you mean?"

He said, "Our jail is a crime scene like you said. We've got two deaths. I don't see any reason to hold you on an assault charge, being that we have nowhere to hold you. So, you're free to go."

I shook my head and said, "I'm going nowhere."

"It's not open to debate. Lewis'll take you back to the motel to pick up your belongings. Then he'll drive you out to the highway."

I paused a beat. I didn't want to leave. That guy in the jail might've been the one who shot my mom, but there had to be more out there. Someone paid him for it. And how did he lure her out to that road?

Grady looked at me, waiting for an answer. I couldn't think of a way to get out of leaving, not without fists and broken bones. I said, "I don't have any belongings."

"No baggage?"

"Nothing."

Grady got on his radio, and hailed Lewis. He gave him instructions to return to base. There was a crackle from the radio, and Lewis gave an affirmative response.

Grady looked up at me, and said, "Then the highway is your next destination." He paused a beat and said, "Never come back."

## 39

DEPUTY LEWIS ESCORTED me out of town in his police cruiser. We drove in silence. The wind rushed around the cruiser as we picked up speed, sending a hot marshy odor from the lake through the vehicle's interior.

I needed to stay, but what choice did I have?

The sky had been calm most of the night, but now it was waking. Mammoth storm clouds crawled slowly toward Black Rock from the north. They looked like wispy, dark creatures swarming across the sky, lethargically but steadily creeping in over the town. Lightning cracked in the far distance.

Lewis drove across the land bridge. I gazed out over the lake for what I thought would be the last time. Dark shapes appeared across the surface as my eyes adjusted to the blackness—night fishermen, most likely. Most of them began cranking their motors, planning to head back to their boat launches to escape the encroaching storm clouds.

We drove past the land bridge and onto the dusty two-lane road that headed out of town. I glimpsed the end of the jogging track where I had met Sheldon. A wave of disappointment rolled over me as I realized I would never see her again. I turned in my seat and stared out the back window until the track was gone from sight, then turned around and faced front again.

The police cruiser slowed as we came to the fork in the road. We stopped on the northwest side of the fork. I looked over to the left and saw the enormous Confederate flag through the tall pine trees. It flapped violently on the flagpole.

I said, "Your friends had better take down their flag, or it'll get rained on. Probably ruined."

Lewis looked at me in his rearview mirror and first grinned, then gave me a scowl. He opened his mouth like he was going to say something, but a kind of low snarl came from his mouth before he turned his sights back to the road and headed south.

I looked to the east and thought about Hank and his dog and wondered if they were still at the cabin. I hoped he had gotten his fill of fishing. The old guy had dealt with two storms in three nights, but I remembered him saying he used to be a pilot in the Navy. He had probably flown missions in Vietnam. I was sure he could handle a little rain. I realized he might be crazy enough to go out there and fish during the storm.

I turned and looked out of my window. The land moved past me. Sparse trees turned into groves of trees and then thinned out again. After fifteen minutes, we hit Highway 35. Lewis skidded the car onto it and headed west. He picked up speed.

The highway was barren. We saw a passing car here and there, but not much else in the way of nighttime travelers. Lewis gunned the motor, and the car got up to ninety miles per hour. After about twenty minutes, we were nearing Interstate 55. Lewis turned the light bars on, and the red and blue lights flashed. We came up on a couple of trucks that took up both lanes, moving side by side, but they saw Lewis's police lights and pulled over to opposite shoulders. Lewis floored it past them, turned onto the loop for Interstate 55, and headed south.

I could hear the wind howling even though my window was rolled all the way up. It whistled and hissed like it wasn't sealed properly.

We drove for a few minutes more before Lewis slowed the cruiser and pulled over to the shoulder. Another interstate cloverleaf lay in front of us. He left the light bar on, the engine running, and got out of the car, walked around the hood, and came over to my door. He opened it and stepped back, staying well out of my reach. I got out of the car and stretched my legs and my arms.

He rested his hand on the hilt of his holstered Glock. A move I had gotten used to by this point. Then he said, "From here, ya can head in any direction ya want. Ya can get on 278 and hitch a ride east er west. Ya can stay on 55 and head north er south. It's up to you. But don't come back to Black Rock."

Lewis got back into his car and sped away onto the off-ramp on the cloverleaf and crossed under the overpass. I lost sight of him for a moment, and then he was back on the other side of 55, headed north. Back to Black Rock. I watched as his light bar switched off and his red taillights faded into the mist. Then I turned and looked at the cloverleaf and scanned in all directions. Five minutes later, I headed west on 278. I could head back to Killian Crossing, meet with LeBleu. I'm sure I had enough to get the FBI involved.

I had gotten the guy who killed my mom. I guess I didn't need to be involved anymore. And I had enough of Black Rock.

I walked on for a ways. I didn't want to stay at the cloverleaf. A hitchhiker standing there might look confused about the direction he wanted to go.

I was trying to convince myself to go back to Killian Crossing, but my gut wanted to return to Black Rock.

I told myself, *You're on a mission. What difference does it make what happened in a small backwater town? Forget about it. Matlind is dead. You found the guy who pulled the trigger.*

I reached into my pocket and pulled out my cell phone. I had a signal. I went into the internet browser and searched for bus stations. The search took a while. My face was lit up in the darkness by the phone's screen as I stood on the border of the blacktop and the shoulder. A car sped past me. I missed it because at that moment; I wanted only to find a bus station and forget about Matlind and his wife—real or not.

My phone showed that the nearest bus station was in Clarksdale, about thirty-five miles west.

The good news was that my phone light had garnered the attention of a van driver. The guy pulled over on the shoulder about thirty yards in front of me, the brake lights shimmering in the darkness. I put my phone back into my pocket, didn't check the battery. I walked to the van. As I neared the rear, I saw the vanity plate. It read, "ISWHTIS." Which I guess meant "It is what it is." I hated that saying because everything in life is what it is. A monkey is what it is. And so on. But I wouldn't pretend that it didn't fit my current predicament perfectly. And then I realized— it wasn't my predicament. It had been Chris Matlind's. It had been—and maybe still was—Faye Matlind's. And it was Sheriff Grady's. And it was Sheldon Eckhart's predicament. It had nothing at all to do with me. The town of Black Rock and all of its problems were just that. Their problems.

I got to the passenger door of the van and opened it. The driver was a young, scruffy guy with a soul patch and no other facial hair to speak of. He held one finger to the front of his lips, the universal symbol for shush.

The driver said in a low voice, "Quiet." He motioned to a sleeping girl in the van's rear. He whispered, "My wife. Where are you headed?"

I said, "West Mississippi."

He nodded and smiled. Then he said, "That's close to where we're headed. Hop in."

I smiled because I was terrifying in the darkness, more than in the daylight—like a crazed killer or the guy who only came out after dark—and I was glad that someone had stopped for me in the middle of the night. I'd been afraid that no one would pick me up and figured I'd probably be out walking the entire night.

Besides my looks, I was also concerned about my smell. I realized I hadn't showered in days. I had cleaned my clothes two nights ago. They didn't smell clean anymore, but at least they weren't filthy. But I had spent several hours yesterday sleeping in a jail cell, and jail cells aren't known for cleanliness. My fears of stinking up this guy's van disappeared when I realized this couple was a pair of hippies or rockabillies. They smelled of marijuana. That smell killed every other odor inside the van.

I closed the door, and the guy sped off. He wasn't the most cautious driver, but I didn't complain. The guy's wife must've been used to it because she slept deeply on a bundle of bedspreads and laundry. His swerving from the slow lane to the fast one hadn't even shaken her awake. And she was definitely not wearing a seat belt. He wasn't either. I reached for mine, found it, and slipped it on. Better safe than sorry.

The guy talked and told me about himself and his wife. I listened, thinking it might distract me from thoughts of Black Rock. Occasionally, I acknowledged him with a polite nod.

We drove for more than an hour. The guy pushed the van hard—it wasn't a vehicle known for speed. It topped out at around seventy miles per hour.

He had his window rolled down. Hot air blew in.

Close to 4:00 a.m., we neared Clarksdale.

I said, "You can drop me off at the next exit."

The guy said, "Nonsense. We can take you into town. Where are you going?"

I said, "The Greyhound station."

He nodded. We drove past the next mile marker and then turned off at the Clarksdale exit. His wife snored loudly for a minute and then rolled over and was silent again.

We stopped at a traffic light and turned west. Then the driver pointed at a blue street sign with the Greyhound symbol on it. The arrow pointed south along a service road that was lit by numerous bright streetlights. He turned onto it and drove another two hundred yards, past a gas station, an all-night McDonald's, and a small two-story motel with three burned-out letters on its neon sign. The Greyhound station was across the street from a doughnut shop.

The guy made a U-turn and pulled up to the front of the station. He looked at me and smiled. He extended his hand and said, "I never told you my name. It's Hank."

I smiled and thought about Hank from Black Rock again. Small world.

I extended my hand and took his in mine, which swallowed his up like a whale swallowing a dolphin whole. I said, "Widow." And then I turned, opened the door, and stepped out into the hot night. I shut the passenger door and waved Hank goodbye. He drove off.

I went into the bus station and walked up to the counter. The woman behind it had a paper cup full of steaming hot coffee in front of her. Her head was propped up on her hand like she was falling asleep. I cleared my throat loud enough to wake her.

She looked up at me and asked, "Can I help you?" There was a tone in her voice, like she didn't want to be bothered.

I looked up at a huge monitor above her. It displayed available destinations and times that the buses ran. The next departure was for Little Rock. It was in thirty-four minutes.

I said, "One ticket. Little Rock." I didn't say please.

She gave me the ticket and stayed quiet. No "Thank you." No "Sit over there, sir." Nothing.

I walked over to a row of chairs that were connected on the bottom by a black metal bar. Several other people already waited there. Most of them were asleep. One girl was probably a teenager. She slept with her head down and a hoodie pulled over most of her face. I could only see her profile. She had no luggage, only a pink knapsack with a teddy bear sewn onto it.

I took a seat and waited for the bus. As I waited, I thought about my mom and about the stranger who was my dad—anything to keep my mind off Matlind and Black Rock. I held my bus ticket and breathed in and breathed out. Then I looked back at the sleeping girl again. Hood down. Face now buried in her arms. She looked uncomfortable. Tired. Frustrated.

Maybe she was running from something. Maybe I was running from something.

I looked around the room. An enormous clock on the wall said it was now 4:15 a.m. The bus for Little Rock would arrive soon. No time to nap now. I'd nap on the bus. I wasn't tired, anyway. Not in the slightest. I was too wound up. Too tense.

I looked at the other people waiting. Young. Old. All had some kind of luggage. Brown bags with handles. Black bags with handles and wheels. Some old. Some new. Then there was that girl. I looked at her again. She had no bags. Nothing but the pink knapsack.

And I had no luggage. No luggage.

Normally, women carried things. Female travelers always carried more items than men—new clothes, toiletries. And they needed space for additional items purchased and souvenirs.

Faye Matlind had been on her honeymoon. She had packed. I had switched rooms with Matlind and had seen plenty of luggage in his room. There had been female items—lots of things.

I sat up straight in my chair. I dug into my pocket and pulled out my phone. I unlocked the screen and examined it—low battery. I clicked the phone icon and dialed Grady's number from memory.

It rang, and he answered. I could hear the confusion in his voice, the kind when someone answers a call from an unfamiliar caller.

I said, "I swapped rooms with Matlind. Night before last. I stayed in his room, and he stayed in mine."

"Widow?"

"In his room, there was extra luggage. Girlie luggage. There were perfumes, an extra toothbrush, razors, some female medications, makeup, and a box of tampons."

Grady said, "Widow, it's over. Matlind killed himself. He was crazy."

I said, "You still think Matlind invented his wife? That he imagined a woman, and he brought luggage along for her? No one does that! Faye Matlind is real."

There was dead air for a long moment, and then Grady said, "Widow, this isn't your fight. It isn't your business. I'm the sheriff in this town. Wherever you're headed, keep on going! It's not your concern!"

Grady hung up.

I stared at the phone. The screen flashed a warning: "Battery critical." I pocketed it, leaned back in my seat, and stared at the gigantic clock on the wall. It was now 1:20 a.m.

*Why should I get involved? It's Grady's problem.*

"You will do the right thing," my mom had told me. Her voice and her frail, dying body haunted me in my memories for a long moment.

Then a man's voice in the distance said, "Now boarding for Little Rock."

## 40

THE BUS WAS COLD, and I was too big for the seats even though they were like captain's chairs. Two to a row. And they reclined a hundred fifteen degrees.

I had my own row, which was good because I had legroom, but I was still too tall for the seat. There was no way to recline because an older couple sat behind me. I didn't want to be right in their faces. So, I just stayed upright.

I pulled out my phone and checked the battery. It would die soon.

I started thinking about Ann Gables. I wondered if it was my responsibility to solve a cold case. Then I thought, *What was the connection between her and Faye Matlind?*

So, I pulled up the internet and did a local search on Ann Gables in the news. Images came up of her high school yearbook pictures and her Facebook, and I found stories about her and the other missing girls. The FBI had thought she was one of the victims. If she was, then so was Faye. No doubt about it.

I searched for a few minutes and then stopped. I realized these stories wouldn't tell me anything. So, I looked through other news, just the headlines. Then something caught my eye. It was about the manhunt for the criminal, Oskar Tega. I shrugged. I might as well try to read about something else since I was on a bus out of Mississippi and had no plans of returning to Black Rock.

I clicked on the article and skimmed it. Tega had eluded authorities, escaped by sea, and was thought to have come to Texas and burned one of his farms to the ground. Nothing I didn't already know. The end of the article said that it was thought he hadn't escaped by boat but by seaplane.

My brow furrowed and I stared at the screen. Seaplane?

Hank, the old guy, the airplane mechanic from two days ago, had talked about a seaplane. He had explained the difference between a seaplane and a flying boat. The flying boat was also called a water bomber, those planes that fly over a forest fire and drop tons of water over the flames. I thought back to what he had said. He had driven from Jackson to Jarvis Lake to refuel some rich guy's seaplane. But actually, it had been a flying boat. He had said the guy was flying his rich friends in for some fishing.

I thought back to my conversation with Maria. What had she said about Texas? Oskar Tega had visited Texas, taken back his product, and then murdered his employees. And the thing that stuck out was that he had used a scorched-earth policy. His men had set fire to the farm and most of the town. They had destroyed the evidence, but the police knew it was them.

So why cover your tracks and hide that you were even there when it was so obvious that it had been Tega? I couldn't understand why anyone would go through all that trouble to destroy evidence when it hadn't changed the fact that everyone knew it was him.

I read some more, but there was nothing new in this article. I moved on.

What was the name of the town in Texas?

I was sure Maria had told me, but I couldn't recall, and that was rare for me. I usually remembered everything. I returned to the home screen on my phone and dialed Maria's number from memory. The phone rang and rang, and I got her voicemail. I hung up and left no message. A few seconds later, I received a text.

"Who is this?"

I replied, "Widow. Can you talk?"

She texted, "At work. 'Sup?"

I texted, "Battery dying. What's the name of the town in Texas with Tega's farm?"

She replied, "?"

"Granjas?" I texted.

Time passed, and I figured she had gone back to work.

Then she replied, "Crosscut."

I texted back, "Thanks."

I went back into my internet browser. The low battery warning popped up again. I ignored it and searched for Crosscut. The phone searched and offered several results. I scanned them until I found what I was looking for. Crosscut was a small town in West Texas, far from any major urban areas. It was nothing but desert and tumbleweeds, the perfect secluded place to hide drug manufacturing in the US.

In the case in question, there had been no evidence of the product left behind. There had been no evidence of any drug manufacturing. Therefore, I reasoned that it was logical to question how the DEA knew that he trafficked drugs. I researched and sifted through articles and old clippings about Tega as fast as my eyes and mind could process them—and that was pretty fast. But I found nothing. No evidence to conclude that Oskar Tega was a drug dealer. The only connections that the cops had made between his operations and drugs were from his known associates —drug cartels—but there was no evidence that he himself manufactured anything.

Then I had another idea. I searched for missing girls in and around Crosscut. Sure enough, the county had numerous reports of missing girls—travelers, mostly. Same as around Black Rock.

An alarm went off in my head. That was the connection—Tega.

I dialed Grady again. The phone rang and rang. I heard a beeping noise, and then Grady answered.

"What?" Grady had known that it was me calling.

"The guy in the news, the drug lord."

Grady asked, "What guy?"

"Oskar Tega."

"Tega? What about him?"

I said, "He's not selling drugs."

"What?"

"Tega isn't in the drug business. He's not dealing drugs."

"What the hell are you talking about?"

I said, "Oskar Tega isn't dealing drugs. The Feds have him all wrong."

"What the hell does he have to do with anything?"

"I rode into Black Rock with this old airplane mechanic. He said that he was meeting a rich guy on the lake. The rich guy had a seaplane."

"What the hell does that mean?"

I said, "Oskar Tega escaped from the DEA from his beach house in Mexico. He escaped by seaplane."

Silence on the other end. I took the phone away from my ear and checked the screen. A red battery symbol flashed, but the connection was still there.

"Grady?"

"Are you saying that he's coming here? But why?" Grady asked.

"Look up 'Crosscut, Texas.'"

He said, "I know about Crosscut. It's been on the news." Another pause. Then Grady asked, "You think that he's making drugs here? In my town?"

"I don't think that he's in the drug business at all. Think about the missing girls, Grady. Girls from all around your county. And the neighboring counties."

"Yeah."

"Enough missing girls to raise suspicion but spread out over four counties so that no one can pinpoint an exact location that might be connected to them."

He wasn't making the connection.

I said, "Think, Grady. They're spread out to hide the fact that they're all going to the same place."

Silence.

Then I said, "Think about why Tega torched his own compounds in Crosscut after he left. What was the point? The DEA figured they belonged to him, anyway. So why torch them for no reason? And what difference would it have made if the cops connected the farm to him? He had already cleared it out and was long gone."

Grady stayed quiet.

I said, "And the Mexican hitman. Why send him? Why try to kill me? Why kill Matlind? What was the point?"

*Why'd he kill my mom?* I thought. It was because she got too close.

Silence, but I could hear Grady breathing. I could picture his expression as he was trying to figure out what I already knew.

He said, "I don't know."

"To shut me up. He sent the hitman to silence both of us."

"So, he didn't want either of you talking? But why? What did you know?"

"It wasn't what I knew. It was what one of us or the cops would figure out later."

"What's that?"

"Tega isn't a drug dealer. He isn't destroying evidence and killing witnesses to hide who he is. He's destroying evidence and killing witnesses to hide what he is. He's coming to Black Rock, and he's going to kill everyone involved and burn your town to the ground just to keep his secret."

"What secret? What is...?"

Then silence—not dead air, not static, but cold silence—fell over the phone. No sound.

I waited a long moment, and then I shouted, "Grady! Grady!"

I looked at the phone. It was dead.

Shit!

Oskar Tega was going to Black Rock—or he was already there—and he was going to leave the town in ashes.

## 41

DARKNESS LOOMED IN THE DISTANT. The night sky was all around me, it was thick and grim and stood out like a lone dark cloud on a sunny day. I was east of Jarvis Lake, the small town of Black Rock, and a brewing storm.

I was on a bus about forty miles from Clarksdale on Interstate 61. The ride was smooth, and most of the passengers slept. They were seasoned bus riders.

I couldn't sleep. All I could think about was Black Rock and Faye Matlind, and I felt an overwhelming sense of guilt, as if I had left the scene of a car crash and ignored a dying survivor.

It had been fifteen minutes since I'd spoken to Grady on the phone. This was his problem. It was his jurisdiction, and I wasn't even in law enforcement. It was none of my business. Or at least that was what I kept telling myself. So why did I feel the burning urge to return?

I supposed it was my Widow blood.

In the last four days, I had felt two types of urges that I couldn't quell by doing nothing. The first was traveling, and the second was correcting the uncorrected. I couldn't walk away. If I continued on this path of looking the other way, I would never feel right. So, I leaned over the seat, reached up, and pulled the emergency stop. I jumped out of my seat and began trekking up the aisle toward the front of the bus.

The passengers were all abruptly woken up. Most of them had skipped the usual disoriented phase and kicked into full alert as if they had awakened seconds before a fatal crash.

By the time the driver turned to interrogate me about why I had pulled the cord, I was already standing at the door to exit.

I said, "Open it! Now!"

I used the cop voice that my mom had taught me. I'd heard her use it many times before. Lots of sound and fury. It wasn't about yelling. It was about meaning and power.

As always, it worked. The guy jumped into action and flipped a black handle on the center console. The doors opened, and I leaped off the bus to start the long trek back to Black Rock.

## 42

I WALKED NORTH on the 61. Jarvis Lake was about thirty-five miles northeast of me, but I had already combed through the roadmap in my head. There was no straight shot back. I had to take 61 and then cut west on 278. This route would take me about twenty-five miles out of my way, but it was the quickest way back.

I walked the long stretch of road with my thumb out. I walked at a fast pace but didn't run because I didn't want to scare away any potential rides. I hadn't had a lot of experience with hitchhiking, but I doubted anyone would stop for a male of monstrous stature running down the road. It would be difficult enough to wave down a ride in the middle of the night, and I figured walking at a brisk pace gave me better odds.

I walked for more than an hour before taking a break. I had seen cars, big trucks, one delivery truck for a soda company, a pair of twin pickups with the same logo on the side, and another Greyhound, but none stopped for me.

So, I walked on. The highway was dark for a while, and then a set of red lights sparkled in the distance behind me. As they got closer, I heard the whine of a siren. It neared, and I saw it. It was an emergency vehicle, an ambulance. It sped past me. The woods to the east echoed its screeching until it finally faded off into the distance, a small white ghost sailing along the blacktop. I hoped it wasn't headed to an accident up ahead because that would delay any vehicles driving north, the direction in which I wanted to go.

I walked on for another twenty minutes and saw no one. I rounded a bend past a grove of trees and walked under an overpass. Then I saw the line of taillights—all stopped on the interstate. There was an accident. It was fresh. A lone cop was setting up road flares. He sparked one up and tossed it on the road to what looked like a two-car crash. A black pickup had t-boned a sedan. I couldn't tell the make or color of the sedan. It was crushed like crumpled paper. The paramedics were pulling the driver of the truck out of the passenger side. From the looks of the sedan, they would need the fire department to get the occupants out, but it looked like it was already too late for them.

Brake lights filled my side of the highway. Seconds after I neared the end of the line of taillights, a second cop arrived on the scene. And then another one. All state troopers. Sirens howled and lights flashed in unison.

Maybe I could get a ride from one of the stopped cars. They might take pity on me. Sometimes seeing the pain and suffering of others ignites certain helpfulness in people. So, I walked on the white line of the shoulder, glancing in each car as I passed.

The new cops started guiding the closest cars around the accident. The cars adjusted their course slightly and drove on the shoulder to get around the accident.

The cars in front of me pulled forward. The car I had just passed was alongside me again. I peered into the window. The driver was a middle-aged woman. Brown hair cut short and spiked. She had a tough military look to her. But she couldn't have been more than a hundred pounds. She sat in her seat, close to the steering wheel. The car she was in was a little thing. Maybe a Kia? I wasn't sure about the symbol on the front. Her car was blue.

She looked back at me. There was no interest on her face, but she rolled her window down. She leaned out and said, "Hey, you."

I turned to her and smiled, not too wide, just a good normal smile.

She asked, "Where ya headed?"

I said, "Black Rock."

"I don't know where that is."

"Jarvis Lake?"

She nodded and looked forward. The cars in front of her were moving again. Their brake lights had lit up the inside of her cabin, but now the interior of her car was turning black. The details of her face—lips, eyes, nose, and cheeks—vanished in the darkness.

She said, "Quick. Get in."

The car in the neighboring lane took advantage of her stalling and jumped in line to follow the other cars around the accident.

I opened the passenger door and dumped myself into the seat. I had to cram my legs into the footwell, and my knees were pressed against the dash. Her car wasn't made for someone my size. But I wanted to get the door closed and the car moving before I concerned myself with comfort, so I shut the door. The moment I did, the car behind us honked.

The woman next to me looked in her rearview mirror and shook a fist in the air. She said, "Hold on!" Then she paused for a second and said, "Seat belt! We are safe in my car."

I obeyed her instruction and pulled the belt around me. There wasn't much slack after I had latched it into the buckle.

She pressed the gas, and the little four-cylinder car jumped to life. We passed the cop directing traffic, and then she got in the fast lane and hit the gas. Just twenty-seven minutes later, I was back near Clarksdale. My driver was headed in a different direction than me but was nice enough to drop me off at a gas station before going on her way. I didn't protest.

The only problem was that the gas station was closed. Only the pumps were dimly lit. Automatic credit card machines were the source of the light.

Luckily, Highway 278 wasn't far. I set out toward it. I cut through a short field that had been freshly mowed. The smell of cut grass lingered in the air. I made it to the interstate and began walking along the shoulder. I stuck my thumb out every time a car passed, but all they did was pass. No one stopped.

The storm clouds were some distance from me, which was good because I didn't want to walk in the rain. But it was bad because that meant that I was far from Black Rock. I ran the math in my head. I figured I was somewhere around seventy miles away from where I needed to be. So, I walked on for another thirty minutes and only saw eleven cars.

I needed to get a ride—and fast. I walked on, hoping someone would feel my desperation and take pity on me. Before long, I heard tires speeding along the pavement behind me, the hollow sound of a car going over the speed limit. I turned and glanced over my right shoulder. The car switched on its high beams. Maybe the driver was sizing me up, or maybe he was trying to avoid hitting me. I wasn't sure. Within twenty-five seconds, the car had flown by me without slowing. It had Alabama plates.

I walked another fourteen minutes, and the sound of distant tires came up again behind me. This car had the high-pitched shriek of a squealing drive belt and the labored sound of a struggling engine. I stopped and turned. This time, I stood completely still and stuck my thumb way out.

*Stop! I need you to stop!* I thought.

The driver must've seen me from far away because he slowed. I heard the whining of the bad drive belt slow with the vehicle. The car was an ancient Corvette driven by an old guy. It slowed and came to a stop right behind me. The guy had decided to pick me up even before he'd sized me up. That was a first.

I walked up to the hood. It had more than a few dings in the grille. The paint had rusted and chipped sections. I imagined that at one time; it had been a beautiful cherry red.

The guy stuck his head out and glared at me. "Ya gonna stand thar s-s-s-s-starin' or ya g-g-g-g-g-gonna get in?" he stuttered in a thick, redneck accent.

I jumped to it and scrambled to the passenger door and climbed into the seat. Immediately, I noticed the guy's old flip-style cell phone resting in the cup holder nearest me. I stared at it like it was the object of a long quest. I thought about asking him to borrow it, but I dismissed the thought and just looked away. I looked around the car like I was admiring it.

The guy hit the gas, and we took off. He asked, "Where ya headed?"

I said, "I need to get to Black Rock. It's urgent."

The guy said, "G-g-g-g-good. I'm headed t-t-t-t-to Memphis. I c-c-c-c-can d-d-drop ya off after... I g-g-g-g-get on 55 n-n-n-n-north."

He hadn't asked why it was urgent or for any other details. He pushed the accelerator harder, and the Corvette sped up. The belt whined so loud and steady that it almost became an ambient noise, like the sound of a well-oiled jet engine.

Before I knew it, we were nearing a hundred miles per hour, and I wondered if the drive belt would last under the pressure. The driver didn't seem to care, though, and it was his car, so I figured he'd know better than me.

The guy checked a bulky, black device suction-cupped to the windshield. It was a radar detector.

I looked out the windshield and gazed into the storm ahead. I knew that Oskar Tega would be there. He didn't know I was coming. I hoped Faye was alive, and I hoped I would make it in time.

## 43

THE GUY in the corvette had been a nice driver, like all the others I'd met so far. Too bad my mind had been on my destination.

He had turned north on 55 to let me out on the side of the road. There was an off-ramp up ahead that veered off to the east, and he told me to take that ramp. It led to 35, and that went straight into Jarvis Lake from the west. I had already reconfigured the route from the west in my head, but I let him tell it to me, anyway. He stuttered. But that was no big deal. He had been a lifesaver.

He let me out, but not before he had asked me twice if I was sure. He had seen the storm clouds on the horizon. They were low and ominous, even in the dark. The center and darkest part of them was in the direction I was headed.

I reassured him I'd be fine, thanked him, and went on my way. The clouds were bad, but so far, there hadn't been a drop of rain. No thunder and no lightning either. Only clouds.

I walked down 35. I calculated Black Rock was still over five miles away, and I was tired as hell. But I was full of grit, and I was determined to get there. I figured it would take me less than an hour and a half, maybe sooner, if the weather held out.

I walked along the empty and lonely stretch of highway. The road was old and badly kept. It was bumpy, with lots of potholes. I walked in the middle of the road because I didn't figure there was much danger of getting run over out here. If any headlights came hurtling down the road, I would see them from more than a mile away because the highway was as straight as a bullet's path. Plus, I would hear any car driving up because there was no noise except the rhythmic sounds of crickets, the flutter of night birds flying from tree to tree, and the smooth rustling of leaves blowing in the night's wind.

There was no sign of human life. Not a car. Not even the distant outside lights of a country house. I passed a couple of dilapidated buildings that had once been stores. Now they were nothing more than a bunch of boarded-up windows and food for termites.

I walked on. There was an airport sign with a turnoff. I looked over the distant trees and could see the lights of a small airport, but there didn't seem to be anything going on. That reminded me of Hank Cochran and Link, the border collie. I guess Tega had used Hank because of his knowledge of Tega's particular seaplane.

I kept moving, looking back only once more before I was one mile from Jarvis Lake. As if on cue, a thick fog rolled in from the direction of the lake, like dark smoke rising from an active volcano. I put one foot into the blanket of fog, and a chill rushed through me. I walked another five minutes into the fog and could barely see twenty feet in front of me. Then I saw a flash of lightning off in the distance, and a second later, I heard the rumble of thunder. Another lightning bolt cracked through the sky, lighting up the land with a giant white flash. The fog seemed to multiply in intensity, and all I saw was white.

I heard another thunderclap. It was high and far away at first; then it rolled across the sky like a sonic boom. A moment later, two more lightning bolts charged across the sky. Then another low, thunderous rumble. This one was slower than the others. It continued to grow louder and louder and sounded like it was coming from over my shoulder to the southwest. I gazed back and looked up at the sky as I walked.

Then I stopped suddenly and squinted through the fog. The new sound wasn't a thunderclap. It was the sound of twin plane engines roaring. It was coming in low over my head. I saw the underbelly of a plane, painted black as the night, like it had been designed for stealth missions. It had no blinking lights on the bottom. It was too dark, and the fog was too thick to tell if there was a tail number. I saw no visible landing gear, but it flew low like it was coming in for a landing.

*The flying boat*, I thought.

It was Oskar Tega and the rest of his men. It had to be. He was arriving to get the rest of the girls and kill any remaining employees. That meant that Faye was probably still alive, and she was probably still on the grounds in Black Rock. The plane flew in, passed overhead, and vanished into the fog ahead.

Another lightning bolt flashed in the distance, and I got one last glimpse of the tail of the plane as it descended over the lake. The lightning vanished, and the darkness returned. I lost sight of the plane.

There were two things I regretted.

The first was swiping the Corvette driver's phone. I reached into my pocket, pulled it out, and palmed it before I'd gotten out of the car. And I felt bad about it, but I needed it. I had wanted to ask if I could borrow it, but what would I have said? Can I borrow your phone for a day or so? I'll mail it to you when I'm finished. It was a cheap phone, and hopefully he wouldn't be too bent out of shape about it.

I flipped open the phone and dialed Grady's cell number. The phone rang and rang and then went to voicemail.

I said, "Grady, it's Widow. Meet me at the rednecks' compound. I'm going to save Faye Matlind. Call me back at this number."

I hung up, searched my memory banks for Sheldon's number, and dialed it. The phone rang once. She picked up like she had been waiting for the call. She sounded wide awake and alert. Maybe she was an early riser. Very early.

"Hello? Who's this?" she asked.

"It's Widow."

"Where are you calling from?"

"The road."

"The road?"

I said, "Yes, I'm on my way back. I think I know what's going on. There's a really bad guy in town. I saw his plane. It just flew overhead."

There was a pause. Then she asked, "Plane? What the hell are you talking about?"

I said, "Sheldon, I didn't tell you the truth about me. I told you my mom died. But I didn't tell you how. She was murdered."

Silence fell over the line.

I said, "She was a sheriff in another town. My hometown."

Sheldon was silent, but I could hear her breathing heavily.

I said, "I'll explain later. Where's Grady?"

"I'm not sure. Did you try calling him?"

"Voicemail."

"He must be on the other side of the lake. Out of reach."

"Come get me, okay? We'll have to make a stand without him."

"Make a stand? What are you talking about?"

"I'll explain when you get here. Just come and get me. And Sheldon..."

She paused a beat, then asked, "Yes?"

I thought about that nice pump-action shotgun she had aimed at Grady and me and said, "Bring your gun."

And at that exact moment, the second thing that I regretted happened.

It started raining.

44

Ten or fifteen minutes had passed. The skies opened up, and it came on like a biblical flood. The sky dumped buckets of water over Jarvis Lake and its surrounding counties.

I had no time to prepare. Maybe the lack of sleep and the expenditure of energy were slowing me down, but I failed to get the flip phone into my pocket before it got soaked. The screen shut down first, and then the phone made a buzzing noise. It was ruined.

I had heard that you could cover a wet phone with rice and let it sit overnight to fix it. I wasn't sure how it worked, but it didn't matter. It wasn't my phone, and I could never return it, anyway. So, I tossed it off to the side of the road.

The rain came down so hard and thick that I couldn't even make out individual drops. I pulled my shirt up over my head like a hood. It didn't help, but at least it was something to slow the water getting into my eyes. The rain was cold this time, colder than the weather had been. I was in danger of hypothermia. I held a hand over my eyes like a visor, trying to shield my eyes so that I could see, not that there was anything to see. The rain came down even harder. It was a torrential downpour.

I started shivering. My skin got goosebumps, and my jaw started chattering. My shivers turned to an intense shake. I wanted to run to the trees and find cover, but I had to press on. Then I saw a pair of headlights coming toward me. An SUV with bright high beams drove up slowly. I waved my arms in the air to flag it down. The vehicle drew nearer and came to a stop in the middle of the road. The high beams switched to low beams, and I saw Sheldon behind the wheel.

I scrambled around to the passenger door, opened it, and dumped myself into the seat. I slammed the door, tugged my shirt down, and gave her a wide smile. Regardless of what was happening in her town, I'd never been happier to see someone. And my smile told her exactly that.

She said, "You're soaked."

I shook my head and hair like a wet dog. Water droplets sprayed across her dash and on the inside of the passenger window.

"Towel?" She had a towel in her hand, outstretched to me.

"Thanks."

I grabbed it and dried off in a flutter of hand movements. The towel was soaked by the time I'd finished. And I was still wet.

She asked, "Where to?"

"Redneck compound. And go as fast as possible."

She made a U-turn and headed back in the opposite direction. Water splashed up and away from the tires.

I asked, "Did you bring your gun?"

"Glovebox."

*Not the shotgun*, I thought.

I reached forward and popped it open.

The gun inside was a CZ 52, not a great firearm. It was Czech made, had terrible aim, and the firing pin was easy to remove. It was barely better than no gun at all. I would've traded anything for the shotgun.

"This is your gun?"

"Yes, I bought it for protection. Why?"

"It's a piece of crap. Terrible. Where's the Remington?"

"I had no shells for it. I was bluffing."

I scowled as I looked down again at the piece-of-shit gun she had brought me. I tilted it in my hand and studied it in the dim light from the dashboard lights.

*Guess I can throw it at the bad guys*, I thought. I asked, "Where the hell did you buy it? The Soviet Union thirty years ago?"

"I bought it in an auction."

I sighed, and then I asked, "Historical?"

"Partly. Why? A gun is a gun."

"Unless you can pull it on your attacker at point-blank range, it won't do much good."

"The guy told me it was a great deal."

"It was if you paid for it with pocket change."

She said, "Well, that and the shotgun with no bullets are all I've got. I'm not used to needing a gun."

I said, "The shotgun with no shells would've been better. At least we could have bluffed like you did."

She stayed quiet.

Then I asked, "Does it fire?"

"I've fired it before. Like I said, I wanted protection... just in case."

I shrugged. I couldn't be mad at her for it. But I sure hoped I wouldn't need to fire it. It'd probably blow up in my hands.

I checked it out. The safety was switched to the on position. I turned it over and examined the butt. On old European-style guns, the magazine ejector was on the bottom. I ejected the magazine and inspected it. It was loaded. I replaced it and pulled back the slide. A bullet chambered. Ready to fire, if it would fire. It was heavy in my hand. The frame was all steel, and there was a bulky back end between my thumb and index knuckle. Despite being an old relic, it'd been well maintained. Clean. Oiled. It looked like Sheldon had kept up with it. I guess I'd have to trust her.

I asked, "So what about Grady?"

"Something's going on across the lake. And now they've got to deal with the weather."

I nodded and said, "We're on our own."

She asked, "What exactly is going on?"

"You know the rednecks?"

"Of course."

"And you know about Chris Matlind?"

She nodded without taking her eyes off the road. She was glued to it like our lives depended on it, which they did. The rain wasn't letting up.

I said, "They're the ones who abducted his wife. They've been taking women all over North Mississippi."

"Taking women? What? Why?"

I paused and said, "This is a small town. There are no secrets in a small town."

"What are you saying?"

"I think you know something. You all know something. No way have they been doing this in complete secrecy."

She said, "They're a bunch of idiots who drink beer and shoot squirrels. No one knows anything about women being taken."

"Come on, Sheldon. Tell me the truth. What've you heard?"

"Only that they grow weed. Maybe cook meth. But no one says anything else. They keep to themselves. It wasn't until you blew into town that they started making a ruckus."

I said, "They do more than cook meth."

"Like what?"

"Second night I was here, they tried to take Matlind. It's deeper than meth. And it's more than random abductions. They're part of something bigger."

Sheldon looked doubtful. She asked, "Like organized crime?"

I nodded. "More like an international crime syndicate. Has to be."

"Are you serious? Most of them barely passed high school. A couple of them can't even read."

"Yeah. They aren't rocket scientists. They're walking redneck clichés, but they aren't the brains behind the operation."

"Who is?"

"Have you heard of Oskar Tega?"

Her eyes flashed at me. She said, "Yeah. The guy from the news. He escaped capture in Mexico, right?"

"That's what the media was saying, but tonight I was on a bus and checked the news. Now they're saying that he's thought to have escaped on a seaplane. And a compound in Texas was half burned to the ground. His complex. The guards, equipment, and even the immigrant workers there were all burned. The drugs and any cash were the only things missing," I told her.

"So, what does that mean?"

"Do you remember the old man who's staying on the lake? The day I first saw you, I was with him."

She nodded.

I said, "He's an airplane mechanic. He was paid to drive here from Jackson. He said that he was coming here to refuel a special type of seaplane."

"A seaplane?" she asked. The car veered to the middle of the road. She turned the wheel and let off the gas to fight a quick skid. She regained control and continued on. Then she asked, "So the seaplane is Oskar Tega's, and the rednecks are selling drugs for him?"

"The rednecks are well financed. I saw their compound when I first got here. They drive brand-new F-150s. They have a new brick house and a brand-new barn. I noticed the barn has motion sensors hanging above it. Those sensors are attached to expensive-looking floodlights. And that giant Confederate flag? The flag itself might've cost a few thousand dollars, but that steel flagpole had to cost a fortune. It's huge. I've seen nothing like it. Where else are they getting the money? Not from selling weed to tourists. No way. And I doubt it's from cooking meth. Now, I believe they are cooking meth, but that's not how they're making their money."

She said, "So you think that they're cooking meth, but they're making their money from kidnapping women? Like for a ransom? But no one has been asked for a ransom for any of the missing girls."

I shook my head and said, "They aren't selling drugs. Not to Tega. And they aren't kidnapping the women for ransom money. They're taking the women for Tega because that's his real business. They aren't drug dealers. They're human traffickers. Tega isn't a drug dealer. He's a human trafficker. And he's been paying the rednecks a percentage like a finder's fee. And that's where they're making their money."

She looked over at me, an incredulous look crossing her face.

I said, "We have to get there before they do."

She asked, "They?"

"The old guy said that his client was flying in with a group of guys. Plural. Tega's coming, and he's not coming alone. The old guy said the plane seats eight on the rear bench. So Tega probably has at least five guys with him, depending on how much cargo he has."

"Cargo? You mean the women?"

I nodded.

She paused and then said, "This sounds crazy. Are you sure about this?"

"Sheldon, Oskar Tega escaped in a flying boat. It's a huge seaplane."

She nodded.

"And just before I called you, I saw a flying boat. It flew just over my head, and it was headed to the lake. It was landing. Oskar Tega is already here. My bet is that he's headed to the rednecks by now and plans to take what's his and kill everyone else."

She turned her head, took her foot off the gas, and stared at me with shock in her eyes.

I nodded.

"What are you going to do?" she asked.

I said, "Whatever is necessary."

She stayed quiet. She pressed her foot harder on the gas and accelerated the SUV. Ten minutes later, we were at the fork in the road.

45

WE PARKED on the side of the road down from the compound. A patch of trees hid Sheldon's SUV. She killed the headlights and left the engine running. The windshield wipers swept the light rain off the glass. The sound echoed through the cabin like a slow, loud clock. Rain fell slower now. I took advantage and scanned the compound as best I could from our position.

Sheldon broke the silence. She squeezed the steering wheel. I could hear the nervousness in her voice. She said, "Oh, take this." She reached into her center console and pulled out a hands-free set. "It has Bluetooth. It's already paired with this phone." She handed me a smartphone.

I stared at it.

She said, "I have two for work."

I placed the set in my right ear, and she pulled out a second phone and called me.

I clicked the tiny button on the back of the Bluetooth. I said, "Hey."

She said, "Okay. I can hear you."

I looked back out over the compound. The rain had slowed some more, but the fog was still thick. I could see the rednecks' pickups. A couple of other vehicles were parked near them. I couldn't make them out. More trucks, probably.

Sheldon asked, "What's the plan?"

"I got no idea."

"What're you going to do?"

I looked at her and smiled. Then I held the gun and got out. The door opened smoothly, but a rush of cold air blew in some rainwater. It misted across the seat behind me. I reached to shut the door, but the wind pushed it out of my grip. A wind tunnel sucked it closed. The door slammed. The wind outside howled, and the trees waved. A colossal bolt of lightning crashed across the sky and over the direction of the lake. The storm was loud enough to camouflage any door slamming.

The fog lit up with a giant flash-bang of lightning across the sky. Even though it was bright and white, its thickness camouflaged my movements like a blizzard would in snow country.

Sheldon's voice came over my earpiece and said, "I'll stay here and try to contact Grady again. I'll keep you on conference calling."

"Good idea. If you get him, tell him to bring everything he's got. I'm sure these rednecks are armed to the teeth. If I don't come back out or this goes sideways, drive to the other side of the lake and find him."

"What are you going to do?" she asked again.

"I'm going to sneak in, grab the women, and sneak out."

"What about Tega? What if he's there?"

"He's not. His plane just landed. In this weather, they'll still be trying to find their car. Besides, the cops can deal with Tega. All I want to do is keep my promise to Matlind." I said, "Sheldon, if a firefight starts, you drive away."

"Okay."

She said nothing else.

"Forget about the conference calling—radio silence for now. I need to concentrate. I'll call you if I need to."

I clicked off the Bluetooth.

## 46

THE RAIN HAMMERED down in one torrential rush like an invading force. Then it slowed suddenly. A minute later, it stopped. I was left in the cold, damp night with only the fog as cover. It would have to be enough.

I snuck through the trees and made my way to the edge of the compound's erratic circle of buildings. I ran up to the closest one and pressed my back against it. It was wood. It smelled of wet boards and had the odor of animals inside. There was no sound.

I shimmied along the wall and up to a window. I crouched underneath it and didn't risk peeking in. This window was near the back door. Nine times out of ten, that's the one where someone is waiting inside with a shotgun. I tiptoed to the second window and peeked in. The room was quiet and empty. It seemed to be some kind of bedroom. I saw no personal effects—no pictures, no jewelry on the vanity, no sheets on the bed. No sign that anyone lived there. The closet door was wide open—no shoes on the floor. No clothes were hanging on the bar. Empty. It wasn't clean, but it wasn't dirty. It appeared to be just an extra building. The only distinct thing about this building was an animal smell, but I saw no dogs and no cats. No animals at all.

I went around to the back door and tried the knob and got lucky. It was unlocked. I twisted the knob and opened the door in a quiet rush. I threw myself against the outer wall in case someone inside had a gun pointed in my direction. Nothing. I entered the building with the CZ 52 drawn.

I'd been raised to believe that if you pointed a gun, you'd better be ready to fire it. I wasn't really ready because that piece-of-shit gun wasn't worth firing. But in the dark, a gun barrel looked like a gun barrel, and I could at least scare someone with it. So, it was better than nothing.

Luckily, there was no one in the building. It took only a few seconds to confirm that. The structure had only four rooms in total. And they were all small. The only thing of use I found was a Maglite flashlight. It was a foot long, hefty, and could be dangerous as a club. So, I grabbed it. It would be more useful than the Cold War relic that Sheldon had given me, especially in close-quarter combat.

I left the little house and headed to the main one, the next closest one. The fog began thinning, and I saw the outlines of vehicles and the other buildings. The main house was the only one with lights on. In order to get there, I'd have to travel through the center of the front yard. It was about a hundred feet. I couldn't be sure—it was too dark, too foggy.

I slipped the CZ 52 into the waistband of my jeans. No reason to run with it. No reason to even have it out. The Maglite would work just fine.

I kept the light off, crouched, staying low, and scrambled across the yard. Halfway to the main house, I could make out its red brick. From a distance, it had looked brand new, but now that I was closer to it, I saw it wasn't. It was an old, two-story house. The newest addition was a grayish wooden deck that had been slung around the front. A porch swing rocked and swayed in the breeze. The porch lights were on, but they were dimmed by the fog. There was one light on in the house. That was all. It was late at night, so the darkness inside wasn't unexpected. I figured that the house's occupants weren't expecting visitors, least of all Tega. And I was sure that Tega meant for his visit to be a surprise.

I had run through two-thirds of the yard when I heard a strange sound. It sounded like the bell from a buoy off in the distance. A slow ding. Ding. Ding. The sound was ominous in the silence. I stopped and turned around to see what the source of the sound was. Then I realized it had come from above me, from the flagpole. I gazed up into the darkness. My eyes followed the giant steel flagpole. It towered over me. At this range, it was even more massive. It was like standing underneath the Washington Monument and looking straight up. The top of it was hazy in the weather, but I could make out the flag. It was drenched, and it flapped like a wet bag in the breeze.

They left it up?

That didn't sit well with me. Rednecks were not only known for being fanatical, but also for being patriotic. Usually, they were more fanatical about their patriotic beliefs than anything else, at least enough to have the flag and to raise it every day and take it down every night. But they left it up in this nasty weather? That seemed unusual.

I pressed on. I scrambled for the porch and the front door. No lights came on—no signs of life. I peeked through a man-sized window—still nothing. Then I reached for the doorknob and turned it. It was unlocked. The door creaked open with a high-pitched, whiny squeal.

No one came rushing out. No guys with guns. None of Tega's men. No one.

I clicked the Maglite on and swept it across the downstairs. The house had an open layout. The staircase was wide and impressive, curving up from the first floor of the house to the second. I spot-lighted every inch in my line of sight with the Maglite. Nothing.

I walked upstairs. I wasn't silent. I wasn't loud—just a normal but careful pace. At the top of the stairs, I saw that there were three doors. All bedrooms. All wide open and empty. There was no one in the house unless they had hidden in the attic or the cupboards. I couldn't understand it. Where was everyone?

I returned downstairs. The beam of the flashlight fell across the bottom steps as I descended, and then swept across the floor. I moved it around the living room to get a better look. There was broken glass against the back wall. Furniture was splintered and knocked over. I'd been in too much of a hurry before to notice. I should've seen it. There were signs of a struggle all over the living room. A long Persian rug near the front door was stained with wet shoe prints—multiple prints.

*Dumb, Widow,* I thought.

I clicked the Bluetooth on. A computerized female voice asked, "Call whom?"

I said, "Sheldon Eckhart."

The voice replied, "I don't recognize that name."

Sheldon probably hadn't programmed her own name into her own phone. So, I thought for a second, and then I said, "Call back."

The voice said, "Calling."

Sheldon had been the last person to call this phone so that it would dial her number back. The phone rang, and she answered.

I said, "We're too late. The main house is a wreck. There are signs of a struggle. Broken furniture and glass."

"That doesn't sound good."

"Stay back. I'm headed to check the barn."

I looked around the house quickly. There were no guns. I thought that unusual for a family of rednecks. I imagined that most had rifles perched across the top of the fireplace like trophies, but these people had none.

I shrugged and clicked off the Maglite and held it in my left hand. Then I pulled the CZ 52 out of my waistband and held it in my right and clicked the safety to fire and kept the muzzle facing downward. I had to be careful tramping through the house with a loaded, untested gun. Matlind had said that there were kids here.

I left the house and turned around the back corner. I saw the barn in the distance, over a hill, and around some trees. A gravel path led up to it. When I had driven in with Hank, it had looked closer to the house, but now I saw it was farther away. I moved along the path, making very little noise. Halfway down the path, I saw other houses that looked more like family-style dwellings. They had backyards with swing sets and animal pens.

I saw no signs of life.

I scrambled the rest of the way up the path and made it to the barn doors. They were shut. The barn was a two-story wooden building painted white, matching the brick on the house. Parked off to the side, near the trees, was another SUV. The lights were off, and the vehicle was empty.

I said, "Sheldon, get ready. We may have to move quickly."

Her voice was crisp in the Bluetooth set. She asked, "Why? What's wrong?"

I neared the barn doors. They were about twenty feet in front of me. I said, "The motion sensor lights. They aren't coming on."

I waved my left hand in the air to get their attention. The sensors clicked and rattled, but never came on—no bright lights. No sound. Just darkness. I switched on the Maglite and stared up at them.

"The bulbs have been shot out," I said.

I saw bullet holes in the light casings. The motors whirred and sputtered and tried to switch the lights on, but nothing happened.

"There's something else."

She asked, "What?"

I shone the light across from me at the rear of the parked SUV.

"I'm staring at Grady's truck."

His Tahoe was parked right there in front of me. The light bar was as lifeless as the rest of the cold machine.

Sheldon said, "Oh, my God! Is he involved?"

"I don't know. I don't think so."

She asked, "What's in the barn?"

I stayed quiet. I moved in closer to the doors. I left the Maglite's beam on and scanned the door with it. Then I reached out and rapped on the door: not a loud knock, just a couple of moderate taps. No one answered. I put the Maglite underneath my arm, gripped it tightly in my armpit, and held the CZ 52 with the hand of the same arm. With my free hand, I reached out and grabbed the barn's door handle and jerked it open. The door swung out. Next, I reached over and jerked the other one outward. It swung out easily. The two massive doors were light on their hinges.

I squinted my eyes, trying to adjust to the lack of light inside. Past the darkness, I saw several figures swaying high above me. I stood fast, burying my feet into the wet, muddy soil, and I jammed the gun outward, two-handed, ready to fire. The Maglite dropped out of my armpit and sunk into the mud.

I shouted, "Freeze! Freeze! Freeze!" I used a powerful cop voice, like before, only this time, loudness counted.

None of the men in front of me responded. I couldn't make out any details from this distance, but it looked as though they kept on swaying.

I shouted, "Stay put! Stay put!" I dropped quickly to one knee and scooped up the muddy Maglite and lifted it and scanned the men inside. I counted more than a dozen. But I couldn't tell who they were. I couldn't see enough through the fog and darkness to tell if they were even armed. But I figured they were obeying my directives because no one shot at me.

I got up from my knees and moved in fast. I stepped inside the wide entrance, took a few strides into the barn, and then froze. Grady was there. So were the rednecks—the ones I had met in Matlind's room. It looked like all the able-bodied men in town were there. The sheriff's deputies. Lewis.

The air was filled with an awful stench. It was strong. I shone the light around the room and saw flasks, giant pots, and an expensive air filtration system. The rednecks had definitely been cooking meth here. Evidence of that was everywhere. It looked like I had caught them all red-handed. That was what it looked like, but that wasn't what had actually happened. Not at all. Not by a long shot.

I slipped the gun back into my waistband and reached up to my ear and cupped it to block out any outside noises. I said, "Sheldon?"

"Yup. Did you find the women?"

"Nope. I found the rednecks and Grady. And his deputies."

Silence fell over the connection. Then she asked, "You found them? So, Grady is involved?"

I said, "No, he's dead. They're all dead. They're in the barn. Someone bound their hands and feet and hung them from the rafters."

She paused and gasped. "They're all dead? All of them?"

"Yes. Dead as anything. It was done recently."

"I thought you said that Oskar Tega had just arrived. How could he have gotten here so fast?"

"He must've had help. Guys already here. He sent a guy into my jail cell to kill me. I thought he was a lone man—a hitman—but maybe Tega had a group here already. Maybe he had a kill team. They knew they were going to be coming here a week ago. I bet he had already sent guys here ahead, the day before the DEA raided his house in Mexico. The sheriff and the rednecks are casualties."

She asked, "So the sheriff wasn't in on it?"

"No. Neither were the rednecks. From the looks of this barn, they were busy with their own operation. Grady probably had stock in their meth business. I was wrong. Someone else was taking those girls. We're looking at two separate operations. The rednecks dealt in meth, and Oskar Tega dealt in humans. That's why Grady was reluctant to call in outsiders. He was protecting the rednecks. Everything must have gone sour between them."

She was silent.

I looked at the dead faces. I said, "Tega is here, and now it's time to clean up. That's what he's doing. His men killed these guys either to cover his true operation or to get rid of loose ends. I don't know. Probably he wants the cops thinking he's a drug dealer. That's what has worked for him so far. He'll be taking the girls international. We have to find them before that happens, or no one will ever see them again."

Sheldon stayed quiet.

I walked out of the barn. I returned the CZ 52 into my waistband and lowered the Maglite. I stared off into the distance. "Where else could they be?" I asked.

From the main house, I hadn't been able to see the lake, but now the fog was rolling out like a living creature, as if somewhere out there, a giant was inhaling it. It was now low to the ground. Some storm clouds still hovered in the air, but the thunder had quieted.

I stared across the lake, and my jaw dropped. I saw bright orange and red lights rising toward the sky. It was a fire. Across the lake, it roared and burned high above the buildings. Orange hues tornadoed up into the sky. Black smoke merged with the storm clouds. And then there was an explosion. The fire had reached a gas tank or a propane tank. The sound ripped across the horizon, and the blast burst upward in a horrifying ball of smoke and flame.

I looked on in horror as the fire consumed the Eckhart Medical Center. One thing came to mind. One condition burst into my head—asthma.

Faye Matlind had severe asthma.

## 47

THE RAIN STARTED AGAIN. It was slight—just a sprinkle. No thunder. No lightning. Just the raindrops. I stood there collecting my thoughts and lost track of time. It could have been a minute. It could have been fifteen.

I stared at the roaring fire across the lake. It grew and spread. It devoured the buildings in the Eckhart Medical Center and moved to the perimeter fence. Steel wires from the barbed wire fencing snapped, and the sharp sounds jetted across the water. The freed wires whipped up into the air and down again like the giant tentacles of some alien metal creature. The fire grew and roared and consumed everything in its path. A transformer exploded from the heat. Sparks of electricity fired into the night sky like a fireworks show with only one color—the sharp white flash of electricity.

I spoke into my earpiece. "Sheldon?"

She didn't respond. Instead, a voice within earshot and with a thick Latin American accent said, "Mr. Widow."

I turned to my left. My right hand went straight for the CZ 52. It came out fast, and I aimed it in the direction of three short men.

I'd been so distracted by the explosions across the lake and the thoughts of Faye Matlind's asthmatic condition I hadn't noticed them approaching. They got the drop on me—not an easy thing to do.

*Careless*, I thought to myself.

They saw the CZ 52 in my hand, but none of them reacted.

I didn't fire.

The guys were dressed in black. Black jeans. Black rain slickers with hoods slung back. Their heads and faces were exposed, and the light rain misted down on them.

The guy in the middle, the one who had already spoken, said, "Toss the gun."

An idiotic move for any man to make, even when he's outgunned. If I obeyed, I was as good as dead. No way was I ridding myself of my only leverage. But there was one enormous factor to be considered—aside from the fact that two of the men were armed with FN P90s, excellent submachine guns. Accurate. Reliable. Deadly. The piece of leverage that they had over me was that the guy in the middle had a Five-Seven pistol in his hand, and it was pointed at Sheldon Eckhart's head.

## 48

THE THREE GUYS in front of me were Mexican. Short, wiry, and deadly. They had me dead to rights, and they knew it.

The sprinkle turned into a drizzle. Water trickled harmlessly from the sky in a kind of misty vapor. The wind blew, and the treetops swayed and sagged under the pressure, but the thunder and lightning had stopped.

The middle guy said, "I am Oskar Tega. You're Mr. Widow."

I wasn't sure if he was asking me or merely stating a fact. So, I nodded.

Tega pushed the Five-Seven pistol closer to Sheldon's head. The muzzle pressed into her skin.

"This is your woman?" he asked. He jerked her by the tuft of her hair, pulling her close to him. She let out a whimper. His lips moved inches from her ear.

I stayed quiet. I looked at the guy on the left-hand side, then the guy on the right-hand side, and then back to Tega. Oskar Tega wasn't anything special. He was older than I had pictured. Maybe early fifties. His hair was black and gray and slicked back. Stubble had besieged his face. Earlier, I had thought he wore black, but I was wrong. He was dressed in a dark-green slicker. It looked black in the dark. From what I could tell, he was a thin guy. So were his friends.

I stared at Sheldon. I never lowered the CZ 52, even though I was pretty sure it was useless.

Sheldon said, "I'm sorry. They were going to kill me."

Tega nodded and whipped her around and pointed the Five-Seven at her head.

"Toss the gun, Mr. Widow, or I kill her."

Sheldon stared at me with tears in her eyes. She begged, "Please. They'll kill me."

I thought about salbutamol again. I thought about asthma, and I thought about Faye Matlind and her dead husband. And then I thought about Sheldon's body. Immaculate. I pictured her in my mind, jogging around the lake. With a body like that, she must've run and exercised six, maybe seven days a week.

I kept my eyes open. Gun trained on Tega.

Asthma. Salbutamol. Faye Matlind.

Then, in a quick movement, I pointed the gun straight at Sheldon, center mass, and said, "Not if I kill her first."

I squeezed the trigger.

Sheldon's face turned white, but she didn't close her eyes. She didn't flinch.

The gun hammer fell back, and the empty air was filled with a snapping metallic sound like a mousetrap. It echoed into the trees and was lost in the distant sound of the roaring fire from across the lake. Nothing else happened. No gunshot. No bullet. Nothing. The gun hadn't fired. I tossed it to the ground and dropped the Maglite. I didn't raise my hands like a prisoner, but lowered them to my sides. Let them relax.

"You removed the firing pin," I said. I shook my head and looked at the CZ 52 as it sank down in the grass and mud. I looked back up and said, "I knew the gun was a piece of shit. One thing about the CZ 52 is the easily removable firing pin. No way does a woman like you live here in this town, own a Remington shotgun, and not know anything about guns. You set me up. Probably led the sheriff here, too. But you probably could've just left the firing pin in that stupid gun. You could've left it alone. That shitty relic probably would've blown up in my hand."

Sheldon's eyes turned cold, and Tega released her from his grip. She stepped forward. She asked, "How did you know?"

I stared at her, emotionless, and said, "You met a man abroad? A benefactor?" Then I turned to Tega and said, "Tega, I wondered when you'd show your face. I thought for sure it would've been after we made it to the Medical Center."

Tega asked, "Where?"

"The Eckhart Medical Center."

He nodded, pointed the Five-Seven at my chest.

I said, "Sheldon works for you. She always has. That's how you got so many girls. She's the one who looked after them. They'd need a medical doctor to keep them healthy. To keep them sedated. To keep them calm. To keep them prime for your customers. And she was probably the one abducting them. I mean, who's more trustworthy than a doctor? And a woman doctor? No one would suspect her."

Sheldon said, "How did you know? When?"

I said, "The day I met you. In retrospect. But I was slow. Too slow. I liked you. I ignored my suspicions. You ran around the lake like an Olympic runner. In immaculate shape. Great body. You could compete nationally. But it was the salbutamol that gave you away. I saw you buying it."

Tega cocked his head and looked at me questioningly. He tried to pronounce the word but couldn't.

Sheldon said, "Salbutamol. It's a medication for severe asthma."

I asked, "Who would you be buying that for? Yourself? You don't have asthma. No one with serious asthma could have a body like yours. No way! You fed me that bullshit that you were buying it for the clinic, but you only had one box. No, that medication was for someone in particular—a patient, but not one from this town. If it were a regular patient, then you would have bought a lot more. Might as well stock up on it instead of having to return to the store constantly and buy more.

"And you had all kinds of female products stacked up in your clinic. Boxes and boxes. Enough for an all-girl community. Who's that for? The women who live here? No offense, but I've been around this town, and it's a pretty boring place. No one here is having that much sex. You didn't need it for anyone living here—you needed it for Tega's girls.

"You needed salbutamol to treat Faye Matlind. She is real. I saw her medications in Chris Matlind's motel room. She's asthmatic. You had to take care of her. You were in-charge of taking care of all of them. Tega can't use his stock if it's dead or pregnant, can he?

"Plus, why does the Eckhart Medical Center need a barbed wire fence? Not because of animals. That place was surrounded like a prison because it is a prison."

A devastating silence fell between us, like Sheldon and I were locked in time. Finally, I said, "You were my mom's contact. She must've reached out to you. Being the local doctor and an outsider and a woman. She didn't trust Grady. But she trusted you. How did she figure that? Did you know her?"

Sheldon shook her head. To be fair to her, there were signs of tears in her eyes—a symbol of remorse, but that didn't affect me—not one bit.

She said, "Deveraux figured I might've seen something. She figured maybe I had knowledge of some man buying up supplies of medication. Like maybe a stranger was holding Ann Gables somewhere and needed feminine medications to keep her healthy."

I nodded. It made sense. My mom had reached the same suspicion that I had. But what were the odds that she'd reach out to the one person who was a part of it?

Tega interrupted. "So, you figured it all out. You know why I'm here?"

I said, "You're here to pick up your human stock. You aren't into drugs. That's all smoke and mirrors to keep the cops guessing. You deal in sex slaves. You're scum. The lowest of the low. I'll admit that at first, I thought the rednecks were keeping the girls, but you're too smart to trust a bunch of rednecks. They aren't the best at keeping secrets. If one of them got caught, they'd roll on you the first chance they got. But you bought drugs from them. They cooked your meth—meth that Sheldon used to keep the girls tweaking.

"I'm guessing they're already loaded on your seaplane. And they're tweaked out of their minds. Probably have no idea what day it is, let alone where they are or what's happening to them. "You used Sheldon to take care of the girls for you. You trusted her. And who can you trust more than a doctor?"

Silence fell across us. No one spoke for a long moment, and then Tega said, "Good for you. You got it. For a gringo, you're quite smart."

Sheldon looked away for a moment, and then she looked back at me. It was a cold, uncaring stare.

Tega moved his finger into the Five-Seven's trigger housing.

I said, "Before you kill me, tell me, how did you recruit her? Was it money?"

Sheldon said, "How do you think a small-town girl gets through medical school? Especially in this backwoods state? He paid for my education. He paid for the Medical Center." She paused. "I belong to him."

I nodded and said, "He paid for your schooling, and in return, you had to host his criminal enterprise here in a small town."

She nodded. It was as simple as that. I didn't condone it, not by a long shot, but I understood it. I had grown up in Mississippi. Parts of it were still bordering on the third world. I understood wanting to escape, but not like this. Then I said, "All of those lives—Matlind, Grady. And none of those women will ever make it out alive. You know that. I hope it was worth it."

Tega said, "Sheldon was my first girl." He reached out his right hand, lowered the Five-Seven with his left, and caressed her face. There was some obvious sentimentality there.

I nodded again. I got it. They had met when she went out of the country. Became lovers. She probably had dreams of being by his side in Mexico, living out their days on a Mexican beach. She'd work some kind of local clinic, and he'd run his operations from Mexico. They would travel together under the guise of her Medical Center's name, doing medical charity work. But the reality was far darker than she had predicted. And now she was just as guilty as he was.

Tega said, "I'm afraid it's time for us to go. But I'm so impressed with you I will give you the gift of a painless death—a quick bullet to the head."

Tega raised his gun again, aimed at my head, and prepared to fire.

49

LAST REQUESTS WERE ALMOST ALWAYS a means of stalling. But ninety-nine times out of a hundred, they were frivolous. The same end always came. A man headed for death always ended up at the same place.

I was about to die. I had fallen for this woman's tricks and gotten myself caught in an ambush. What the hell?

So, I asked, "Last request?"

"What?"

"Don't I get a last request?"

Tega thought for a long moment. Then he lowered his weapon. "Make it quick," he said.

I stepped closer to Sheldon.

Tega quickly raised the Five-Seven again and followed me with it. The two guys at his sides followed suit, but I moved slowly so they'd know that I wasn't planning an attack. And I wasn't. Not yet.

I said, "Give me some of your goods. One last time."

"What?" Sheldon asked.

"Come on. I'm about to die. Let me touch you one last time. Let me kiss you again. Like last night. You liked it. I know you did." I looked at Tega and said, "The sounds that she made. You should've heard her."

Anger flashed across Tega's face. It came from deep within. It came from a place of extreme mistrust. No matter how composed he was, that primal instinct to protect what was his ran deep. He couldn't hide it. Not from me. Before, he had been a man of stoic composure, always in control. But Sheldon belonged to him. He knew it, and she knew it.

"You slept with him?"

Sheldon said, "No!"

I said, "She wanted to. We didn't have time."

Tega stared at me and asked, "What are you trying to do?" He wasn't stupid.

Sheldon said, "I kissed him, but it was for you. For us. I played a part. Baby, I'd never betray you." She looked at him and put her hands on his face. She said, "Kill him and let's go."

Tega looked at her, taking his eyes off me for a second, but there was nothing I could do. His guys had me in their sights.

The drizzle had stopped, and the air dampened to a sticky dew.

Tega wanted to do more than shoot me. I saw it in his eyes. He wanted me to suffer. Then he looked over my shoulder. He stared at the barn and smiled. He said, "You just lost the luxury of a painless death. Get in the barn."

I turned, and Tega and his men followed me back to the barn. We walked through the gloom to the barn doors. They were still open. Grady and the other dead bodies still hung by their necks. They swayed slowly, like a room full of eerie marionettes. Tega stepped into the barn, past me. His men looked straight at me, never losing their focus. One of them stepped up close to me and motioned for me to follow Tega deeper into the barn. We walked to the middle, close to the hanging corpses. Whatever he had planned for me, they'd seen it before. They knew the routine. I hoped he didn't plan to hang me like he had the rest of them.

Tega searched the barn. He looked at all the walls, and then he said, "This is the only way in or out. There is a steel padlock on the outside of the doors. Do you know why?"

I shook my head.

He said, "To keep people out. Do you know what else a lock like that is good for?"

I shook my head again.

He said, "Keeping people in."

Then he said, "The rednecks cooked meth in here. Do you know what can happen when there's a lot of meth?" He didn't wait for me to respond. He said, "It explodes. It's flammable. But the padlock is not. The logic of these rednecks fails me."

I stayed quiet.

Then he asked, "This word 'flammable'—you know this word?"

I stayed quiet.

"I love this word. Americans make so many things that are flammable, like products used to cook meth. As you figured out, I do not sell or make drugs. I'm not in the drug business. I am in the sex business." He nodded to Sheldon. He said, "I would not know which of these chemicals was flammable if it were not for the label."

He walked over to a row of plastic barrels and looked at the labels and smiled, coldly. He kicked hard at one barrel. It fell over, and the lid came off. The liquid contents spilled out across the floor of the barn. Tega moved on to the next barrel and kicked it over, and then the next, and the next. The air filled with the sharp smell of chemicals.

A terrible suspicion of what they were, crossed my mind. I suspected one was probably ethanol.

He said, "Do you know what I am going to do to you?"

I said, "I have no clue."

He said, "You are lucky. Really. If I had more time, I'd stay and do a slow job on you. But I don't have that kind of time. I am going to lock you in here and let you burn alive."

Tega backed out of the barn. He lowered his gun. Then he looked at his men and said, *"Hazlo."*

Everyone stepped out of the barn except for me.

Tega said, "Goodbye, Mr. Widow."

I waited in the barn as Tega's men locked the padlock. Two minutes later, the barn was a roaring inferno.

# 50

Tega had spilled flammable chemicals all over the floor of the barn. Tega had smiled at me as his guys closed the doors. I heard the rustling of a chain and then the click of the padlock.

A few minutes later, the walls on the north and south sides started smoking. Flames ate through the wood. It wouldn't be long before they connected with the chemicals. I'd be burned alive.

I heard more noises outside, voices, but I couldn't tell what they were saying. I looked around the room and searched the corners and the tables and checked the corpses for weapons, but found nothing. Then I found the keys in Grady's pocket. If I got out, I could take his Tahoe.

The flames sparked onto the floor. The blaze ate up the walls. Wood splintered, and the fire scratched at the outer walls like a pride of lions trying to get in. I had to get out.

I kept calm and focused. There was no reason to waste time wondering how I had let Sheldon get the best of me. There'd be plenty of time for second-guessing later once I escaped.

I looked around the barn again. I looked up at the roof. There was a closed hatch on the upper south side, but it might as well not have been there. It was twenty feet above me, well out of reach. Then I turned away from the corpses in the direction they had been looking before they died. And that was when I noticed a difference. The sheriff and the deputies hung facing the direction of the doors, as if Tega's men were the last thing they saw before they died. But the rednecks were looking in a different direction. They stared down to the left-hand side of the barn. Their gazes were fixed on a huge wooden table.

I rushed over, tossed the table over on its side, and jerked up the rug from underneath it. I had hoped I would find something, and I had. There was a loose wooden plank under the rug. I pulled it up, and I saw my salvation. On the floor was a thick concrete trap-door cover. I grabbed the short, worn rope attached to the top and pulled. The concrete was heavy, but I got the door up. I peered in and found a small bunker with a crawl space. It was too dark to tell how far back it went, but I figured I could follow the walls by touch. It was dark and damp, which was good—the damper, the better. I might be safe in there. I hopped in and pulled the cord behind me. The concrete block slid back into place.

I listened as the fire ripped through the walls of the barn. It didn't take long for the flames to reach the batch of spilled chemicals. I pulled down on the cord with all of my strength and weight. I wanted to keep the concrete cover closed tight.

I heard an explosion. Heat and smoke sprayed through the tiny cracks around the concrete. I hung by the cord a couple of inches off the floor. My knees were tucked under my body. The fire had stayed out of the bunker, but the heat was intensifying. It was like being in an oven set too low—it was hot but not hot enough to cook me. Not yet.

I hoped the explosion would take most of the flames outward, and it did. I'd wait a few minutes and then surface. Tega would most likely be gone by then. But just then, the cord snapped beneath my weight, and I fell. It was only a few inches. Not a big deal. I rolled over and got up on my knees. My head nearly bumped on the ceiling. Dust from the concrete ceiling sprayed down into the chamber as a second explosion blasted from above. It sounded louder than before. I hoped that was the last of it.

A tiny row of lights along the bottom back wall of my underground crawl space flickered to life. Maybe they were automatic. Or maybe the tremor from the blast had shaken them on. They barely lit the crawl space. But in the dim light, I saw two things. First, the bunker wasn't a bunker at all. It was small, and there was no food stored in it. Plus, there was no bathroom. No kitchen facilities. No visible power source. There was barely room for one person to stretch out and sleep. The second thing I saw made me smile ear to ear. It wasn't a bunker—it was a weapons cache.

## 51

ANOTHER EXPLOSION ROCKED the concrete walls, and the dim lights went out. I waited in the thick darkness. The fire above me devoured huge chunks of the barn. I heard a section collapse. I had to get out before the rest of it came down. The roof might've been blown off by the explosions, or it might've been hanging by a board. I couldn't wait for the whole thing to collapse on top of me. I could be trapped in this prison.

I closed my eyes and pictured the gun collection in my mind. I scanned through it. It was impressive, that was for damn sure—assault rifles, long guns, handguns, and even some classics lined the walls. There were magazines stacked on the ground by each gun. Some of them had been fired regularly, either for fun or target practice, or just to make sure that they were kept in good working order.

I grabbed a modern assault rifle—the M4 Carbine. It was the A1 version, an improved version from the previous design. It was the basic design. No scope. No flashlight. Also, I grabbed the nearest magazine, loaded it, and readied it for use. I clicked it to fire a three-round burst. For a moment, I palmed an extra magazine and then I slipped it into my back pocket. I lowered the gun and carried it by the handle. Then I prepared to open the concrete lid.

I planted my feet firmly on the ground and pushed up on the block with my shoulders. I used the muscles in my legs, knees, and calves and pushed. The block wasn't weighed down by any obstructions, which was good, and it moved up easily and slid back. I crouched back down, aiming the gun at the opening in case someone was waiting. No one was.

The smoke was thick, and the heat rushed across my face. Until this point, I had felt both unlucky and foolish. I had been ambushed, betrayed, chased away and forced to hike all the way back. I had abandoned Matlind's quest. I should've never done that.

*Always do the right thing,* my mom had said to me. She was right.

But just then, something good happened, something to help me. It started to rain again. It was subtle at first, but within seconds, it was a strong downpour. The rain before had been cold. But now it was warm. The rain came down and put out a part of the blaze.

I smiled. I quickly lifted my head out of the hole. No one was there, just remnants of what used to be the barn and some lone dancing flames. I scrambled out of the bunker and rolled. I came up on one knee. Fire danced in my cone of sight, but there was no other movement. No bad guys.

The fiery barn walls surrounded me, but a single clear path lay open from my position to the double barn doors. The doors them-selves had exploded off the hinges and shot outward somewhere. I didn't know where. So, I stayed crouched for a moment and then rushed through the opening while I had the chance. I rolled again and came up with the M4A1, ready to fire at anything that moved.

Nothing moved but the dancing fire.

The fog was thick, but the fire lit a good thirty-foot radius. To my left-hand side was the rear of Grady's parked Tahoe. I crouched and scurried over to the bumper. I put my back to it and flicked the M4A1 through the area again, staying low and scanning once more. Suddenly, I heard a noise a little way down the path—a rustling sound. I moved up to the front of the Tahoe and peered through the glass. One of Tega's guys was coming up the path. He had a flashlight attachment on his FN P90 and was using it to search the area opposite me. I had no idea why he was here. Maybe he had run from the explosion and was returning to check things out.

I stayed put. I'd let him check that side and then come to me. I didn't want to fire, but I had no problem with shooting the guy in the back. No problem at all. My main problem was that I wasn't sure the guy was alone. The M4A1 was a loud gun. Even with the background noise of the barn fire, the gunshots would be heard by anyone nearby.

So, I waited.

The guy searched the area, and then he approached Grady's Tahoe. He walked at normal speed, not really expecting to find anything. When he was almost there, his cell phone rang. He paused and reached into his pocket, letting the FN P90 drop to one side in his left hand. The light's beam made a tight circle at the guy's feet. He pulled out his phone and answered.

The guy started speaking Spanish, which I didn't understand, and then he switched to English. He said, "He's dead, boss." He paused and listened, and then he said, "I'm looking for his body now." He paused again, listened, and said, "I call you when I find him."

I grinned because the guy had just told me he was all alone.

He hung up the phone.

I wasn't a fan of firing a gun for the first time when my life depended on it. That wasn't an ideal situation. But if I had test-fired it, the guy would've made me. I took a deep breath and readied the M4A1 to fire a quick burst. In one fluid motion, I stood up, knees straight, shoulders loose, ready to fire. I aimed down the sight, and squeezed the trigger. Three rounds fired at him, but all I'd needed was one. All three bullets hit him in an uneven pattern, right in his heart. An explosion of red burst through his back and sprayed out the front of his chest. The guy flew back like he'd been jerked by a bungee cord being pulled by a high-speed train. His FN P90 hung in the air for a moment and then dropped to the ground. I didn't have to touch it to know it was cold. He hadn't had the chance to fire it.

I walked over to the guy. Checked him to make sure he was dead. Not that I needed to. I ignored his pockets because I wasn't interested in their contents. The same went for his FN P90. I ignored it because I was satisfied with the M4A1. I lowered the M4A1 and gripped it by the top-mounted handle. Then I turned and looked at the fiery barn one last time, and then sprinted back to Grady's Tahoe.

I dug in my pocket for the keys and felt a lot of splintered pieces of plastic. Curious, I pulled out the phone Sheldon had given me. It had been shattered. I dropped the pieces to the ground.

I checked my mom's phone—it was fine—and then dug around for the keys again. I found them and took them out. I pressed the unlock button on the key remote. The Tahoe unlocked.

I hopped in, tossed the M4A1 on the passenger seat, shut the door, and fired up the engine. I popped it into reverse, backed up, and hit the gas. The tires turned, shooting up mud, and then the truck took off.

## 52

I SPUN the Tahoe's steering wheel as I turned the vehicle to catch up to Oskar Tega. The path curved and pitched. Tall, menacing pine trees flapped along the sides as if warning me to turn back. The rear tires skidded through the mud, splashing wet orange muck across the back window. Hard rain beat down on the roof. The pounding echoed through the interior. I had the wipers working overtime to keep the rain and the mud off the windshield. I kept the light bar off and the high beams bright.

Oskar Tega had left before I escaped the barn, but I wasn't sure how long it had been or at what speed he'd traveled. I had no way of calculating how long it'd take to catch him. I knew they hadn't started the seaplane. Not in this rain. But it would happen soon. They would be gone forever at the first opportunity they had for clearer conditions.

I pushed the Tahoe as fast as I could, without losing control. I had experience driving in the mud. This was Mississippi, after all. I was fifteen years old when my mom had taught me how to drive. I'd driven a police cruiser on a dirt road obstacle course. I knew how to handle these conditions. My hair whipped across my face as I bounced and shifted in the seat.

I turned a sharp corner and sprung up onto a paved road. Loose items in the front console jittered. Coins fell across the footwell. Up ahead, I saw the tail end of a convoy of F-150 pickups. It was Tega and his men. They drove cautiously through the weather. They had given me the advantage.

I sped up. The Tahoe's engine roared and charged like a chariot of horses. I pulled up to the convoy, several car lengths behind them. Their taillights flickered in the rain. The red beams were visible every time that the rear truck braked, which was often. Then they faded into the fog.

I stepped on the gas. The engine roared, and the gas pedal shook. Thunder roared overhead and then softened into a low rumble. I reached over my left shoulder and grabbed the seat belt. I pulled it down and snapped it into the locking mechanism. Then I tugged to make sure it was fastened. The Tahoe had come with the police interceptor package, which meant that Grady's vehicle was armored and reinforced and built to withstand damage. Another prominent feature was the battering ram on the front grille.

I caught up with the convoy. At first, they must've thought I was one of them—the guy Tega had left behind, probably—because they continued to drive slowly. But as soon as I got close enough to see their license plates, the two F-150s hit the gas. The passenger in the rear truck leaned out of his window and started firing at me. Bullets sprayed and darted across my hood. Two pierced the window and zipped past my head. If I had a passenger in the front seat, he'd be dead. I swerved to the left-hand side of the road and out of the bullets' path.

The passenger fired again and again in rapid succession. The rain and the fog hindered my vision, which meant that his sight was also hindered. He continued to fire off course. Bullets whizzed past me and into the weather behind. He followed my high beams, adjusted his trajectory, and fired. The front right head-light exploded in a burst of broken plastic and glass. The bulb went dark. I reacted and shut off the other light. I ducked down behind the wheel and darted the Tahoe back to the right-hand lane.

The guy firing thought I had stayed in the same place. I heard bullets spray across the hood again as I traversed into the right-hand lane. One bullet just missed my head as I swerved to the right. It flew through the interior and shattered the rear window. Cracks from the bullet holes in my front window spider-webbed across the glass until I could no longer see. I drove closer to the rear of the back truck and slammed into the back bumper. I disengaged my foot from the gas and let the truck in front swerve and skid. I braked. In this weather and at this speed, the truck would've flipped if I had rammed it and driven full force ahead. I didn't want it to do that.

If the truck flipped, it would've rolled over my hood and probably crushed my head. That definitely wasn't the plan. So, I let the driver regain control. Then I leaned over the console and grabbed the M4A1. I lifted it, switched it to full auto, squeezed the trigger, and fired through the windshield. The glass shredded, and the left half flew forward and broke off. It was tossed off to the right-hand side, and the wind sent it flapping behind me. The rain beat down and blew through the opening. The wipers were mangled and whipped up and down on the hood like broken insect antennas.

The passenger reacted to the sound of my gunfire. He had regained control of his aim and started firing his FN P90. The first sequence of shots rang out into the night. I fired the M4A1 into the rain and the fog and the darkness. Everything seemed to happen in slow motion.

Moving at a speed that was dangerous in these conditions, but I maintained control of both the Tahoe and the M4A1, even with the recoil. Driving and shooting at the same time was difficult, but I managed well for being out of NCIS training for years. And I wasn't just firing blindly like the guy in front of me had been. I had one major advantage. My headlights were dark, so my vehicle was camouflaged by both the night and the weather. But I couldn't disengage the brake lights. The guy firing from the passenger seat didn't know my exact position—he only knew that I was behind him. But I knew exactly where he was.

I fired the M4A1 in a tight horizontal arc, right to left— point A to B. Seven rounds rocketed out of the M4A1. Once I reached point B, I rested my trigger finger for a second and then repeated the process from point B back to point A. Six rounds spent. I knew instantly that I had hit the driver in the back because I didn't make it back to point A. The truck jerked to the left, and the truck's right-side tires came off the ground. A half second later, the truck flipped. It bounced and rolled on the pavement. Glass shattered. The roof crushed inward, and the vehicle skidded along the wet road. Sparks flew from beneath the roof as it slowed to a stop.

I slammed on the brakes. The Tahoe skidded and fishtailed violently. The rear swung around to the front, and I stopped perpendicular to the road. Quickly, I released the steering wheel, raised the M4A1, two-handed, and pointed it at the wreckage through the passenger window. No movement. I pressed the button on the seat belt's locking mechanism, and the belt shot up and raked across my chest.

I popped open the door and stepped out. Using the Tahoe for cover, I stood on the step bar and pointed the M4A1 across the roof. I looked through the sight. Nothing moved from the flipped truck. I watched the taillights of the front F-150 as they faded in the distance. They hadn't even stopped to check on their friends. Tega must've been in the forward truck. No way would his men have left him behind. He was their paycheck.

I kept the crashed F-150 in my line of sight and walked through the rain toward it. It was dark except for the brake lights. They were still bright, like the driver's foot was pressing down on the brake pedal. I scrambled to the back of the downed truck. I checked the passenger side first since I knew he'd been armed, and I had gotten the driver with at least one round.

The F-150's bed was mangled and crushed. Glass shards crackled beneath my feet.

I peered into the passenger side through the sights of the M4A1. A short Mexican guy hung dead from his seat belt. His head was twisted too far over his left shoulder. He was wide-eyed. His neck had been broken in one swift snap. Must've happened when the truck bounced. His FN P90 had been broken into two uneven pieces. Hard to do.

I smiled—at least one down. I walked around the hood. The underbody was caved in. Engine fluids leaked, cascading like a waterfall. They pooled on the ground and mixed with the mud and the rain. The battery sparked.

Better make this quick.

*Don't want it to explode*, I thought. I scrambled over to the driver's side.

The driver was crawling out of the front of the truck. He used his hands to drag himself out across the concrete. Rain fell and beat against his small back. Blood trailed behind him in a curved, smeared pattern. He had no visible weapon. His left arm was broken. His legs were broken and mangled, dragging behind him like dead weight. Two bullet holes gaped near the small of his back. He had lost so much blood that I doubted he'd live much longer.

As I got closer, I realized my horrible mistake.

He was a she. It was Sheldon.

## 53

Sheldon's hair was wet and matted from blood and rain. She had hit her head hard when the truck flipped.

I lowered the M4A1 and held it down and low and knelt beside her and gently rolled her over. I held her head up and cradled it in my palm.

I frowned and set down the M4A1 on the concrete and stared at her. I said, "Sheldon."

She looked up at me. One of her eyes was swollen shut like she had been punched hard.

Her front teeth were missing, and blood spilled out of her mouth.

"Why? Why did you do this?" I asked.

Sheldon gasped. She said nothing.

I said, "Tell me what to do. Tell me how to save you."

She said, "No."

"Please. Tell me something. Anything."

"No. There's nothing. I'm dying."

I couldn't respond.

She said, "Widow, I'm... I'm sorry."

"Don't say that. Where's your phone? I'll call for help."

She reached out with her one functioning hand and touched my chest. I thought she was trying to reach my face like my mom had four days ago. Only she had no strength left, and then she said, "Don't let them on the plane. If Oskar gets them on the plane... you lose."

She froze suddenly, like a block of ice. Her eyes remained wide open, but her lips stopped moving. Her chest stopped breathing and her life faded away.

I heard the battery from the flipped truck spark again. I had to move.

I knelt down farther and picked up her body. I left the M4A1 on the street and tucked her in close to me. Her head rolled back and hung over my arm. I ran as fast as I could with her in my arms. I wanted to get her body away from the vehicle. I knew it was only a matter of time before it caught fire and exploded. With all of that spilling gas and the sparking battery, it was bound to happen. And it did as I ran with her.

A bright flash of electricity sparked, and the truck exploded behind me. A ball of fire erupted and propelled into the sky like a surface-to-air missile launch. It was followed by a giant force of air, which erupted out in all directions from the explosion. It hit me square in the back and launched me forward and off my feet. I dropped Sheldon's body and rolled just at the tree line, hitting my head hard on a loose rock when I hit the ground. I rolled some more. And then everything went black.

## 54

I woke up in the dirt and fog. My head pounded like someone had hit me with a baseball. I had no idea how long I'd been out. It'd been long enough for the rain to slow to a light drizzle again.

Sheldon was near me. I touched her hand as I sat up. I looked over at her corpse. Her good eye stared up at me—lifeless.

There was no time to be sad. I had to save Faye. And then there was Oskar Tega. I was going to kill him. That was for sure.

I jumped to my feet. Suddenly, dizziness struck me like a blow to the head. I touched the top of my head—pain shot through me. I shuddered and then studied my hand. No blood. That was good. But I had hit my head hard. I didn't have a concussion—at least I was fairly confident I didn't. But I was definitely going to be sore for a few days—no doubt about it. I stood still for a moment to let the pain subside. Then I shook it off.

I looked down at Sheldon for a long moment and trekked back to the truck. I wanted to recover the M4A1 or at least find a working firearm. The truck was burning, and the fire rose and lit the area like a floodlight. I hunted around but saw no sign of the M4A1.

The trees around the truck were on fire. The flames had climbed while I was unconscious, and now the tops had burst into flames.

I wouldn't make it back to the Tahoe. Not through the smoke and flames. I turned around and stared east. The rain had slowed, and the fog started rolling off toward the lake, but the road was visible.

Tega's truck was gone. He'd be a couple of miles up the road at the lake house.

I knew Faye would be unharmed and alive. He needed her that way. She was a valuable commodity. But I worried about Hank. I hoped I'd make it in time. I doubted Tega would leave him behind. That wouldn't be in accordance with his scorched earth policy.

I gave up worrying about my head and started running.

## 55

My head hadn't reset. My phone was dead. I didn't know the time, but it was obviously early morning. The sky was still grim, but the thunder had stalled, and I hadn't seen a lightning bolt in a long while.

I neared the driveway to the lake house. The stolen F-150 was parked behind Hank's fuel truck. I scrambled behind the loading bed and crouched down. I scanned the front yard. The trees blocked most of the house from view, but I could see the garage doors. The house had a three-car garage. One door was wide open.

Tega had posted no visible sentries. I had only my bare hands to use as weapons. That was all that I needed.

I reckoned if there were no guards posted in the front yard, the open garage door was a trap. A wide entrance, inviting and unguarded. Had to be an ambush.

I crept out to the cover of the trees and away from the driveway and stopped at a suitable spot along the middle of the yard, in line with the front door. I stayed where I was and stared through the open garage. The garage was dimly lit by a utility lantern. It hung near the garage door and left a gigantic shadow of darkness near the rear. That was where the guard would be. He would sit there and stare out toward the yard. That's where he would wait for me. He'd use the shadows as cover, knowing that I wouldn't spot him until it was too late. He was probably sitting there wearing night-vision goggles, ready to put bullet holes through my chest before I even knew he was there.

I studied my other options. That was when I noticed the fuel truck. Its long hose was uncoiled and extended from the truck's rear. I heard a motor kick on, and the hose thickened as it filled with fuel. The hose stretched out from the truck, traced along the driveway, and vanished into the open garage. They were refueling the seaplane. A very long hose had been used, and it led through the garage. It may even have been run through the kitchen and the backdoor of the house or an open window. I wondered if they had even posted a guy in the cone of shadow in the garage. Maybe they'd just left the door open so that the hose could feed through.

The front door and the gate on the side would be locked or guarded. I thought about how I could draw a sentry out of the shadows if he was there. If there was someone hiding there, he was bound to be good. But in the dark, I was better.

I got down. Really low. I crawled on my elbows and knees through the mud and wet grass until I reached the walkway between the garage and the front door. I crouched and hid near the bushes. No one came out either the front door or the garage. I skulked over to the edge of the garage, staying out of the line of sight. In the darkness, I stood up straight, and put my back in line with the wall, but I didn't touch it. Slowly, I shimmied past the first garage door, then the second until I made it to the edge of the open one. I stayed out of the light. I studied the ground for moving shadows. There was nothing. So, I crouched and moved out toward the fuel truck. Then, I got down on the ground and lay flat on my stomach and moved along the concrete until I was under the front of the truck and behind the tire. I hid in shadow, and I peeked out from behind the tire. I waited and stared into the garage.

Inside, there was a van parked half in the shadows. The side of the van had the Eckhart Medical Center logo stretched across it.

More proof of Sheldon's guilt. The back doors of the van had been left open. One swung back and forth slowly, like someone had burst through it only seconds ago. They must've used the van to transport Faye and the others after they set the Eckhart Center on fire. I wondered how many girls were here. They wouldn't have used a van for only one. There must've been more.

I smiled because I realized that more than one girl was going home tonight. It was then that I saw the guy in the shadows near the driver's side of the van. He was crouched down and leaning against the back wall. I saw his silhouette and that of his rifle. I couldn't tell exactly what it was but assumed it was an assault rifle or another FN P90. It was too big to be a smaller submachine gun. I could see his head—no night-vision gear, which was to my advantage.

I squirmed forward, taking my time so I could remain undetected. One wrong move and he'd shoot me dead. Finally, I made it to the rear of the truck and shuffled over to the side, closer to him. I was about to be in the guy's line of sight, but only for a moment. I would quickly pull back after I did what needed doing. Cautiously, I rolled over onto my back, reached up, and grabbed the bottom side of the truck. Then I leaned out, reached up quickly, and grabbed the nozzle from the hose and pulled as hard as I could. The hose ripped off the fuel truck, spraying fuel across the back tire and onto the concrete. I removed my hand quickly and rolled back into the darkness under the belly of the truck. And I kept rolling until I was on the other side of the truck, out and away from his view. Quickly, I scrambled to my feet but remained crouched behind the rear passenger-side tire.

I waited until I heard his footsteps. He'd taken the bait. I swiveled and peeked up past the edge of the tank. The guy had his gun pointed outward, ready to fire. He walked out of the shadows and scanned the area.

I stayed hidden.

He came to the driveway and let out a loud gasp at the sight of the tank leaking fuel. He scanned the area again. The guy wasn't dumb, not completely. He lowered his weapon, pressing the suppressor's end into the concrete. Then he knelt down and grabbed the hose, lifting it like he was going to reattach it to the open end of the tank. He never made it that far.

I grabbed his head with my hand. I slammed it into the side of the fuel truck as hard as I could. Once. Twice. Three times. I pulled his head back, prepared to do it again, and saw a bloody mess of protruding nasal bones, mangled teeth, and smashed eyes where his face had been.

I thought of Matlind, and I thought of Grady, and I thought of Sheldon. It made me mad. Rage boiled under the surface of my skin. I pulled his head far back like a bowler, cocking back to bowl a strike, and I slammed it once more into the side of the truck. I heard his skull crack like a clay flowerpot. The force of my slam was so powerful that his head bounced off the truck, and I lost my grip. He fell backward. His legs twitched one time, and only once, and then the guy was dead.

Two down.

Three, if I counted Sheldon as one of them. But I didn't.

I picked up the guy's gun. I left the fuel line on the ground with the tank spewing out fuel.

I entered the garage.

## 56

I HEARD noises coming from the backyard, but the interior of the house appeared empty. Tega had at least two guys left, I knew that. I had killed two. There had to be more than that, but not too many more. I felt good about my chances of survival.

I checked the downstairs living room, the kitchen, the pantry, the bathroom, and the closets. It wasn't until I got to the back bedroom that I smelled the stench of a dead body. I hoped it wasn't Hank. I liked that old guy. But he would've been expendable to Tega.

I pushed open the door and gasped. There was a dead body lying on the floor at the foot of the bed, but it wasn't Hank. They had shot Link, the border collie. I bit down hard. My teeth ground together, and the bones in my temple tightened. I liked dogs. It was senseless. They would pay for it, like everything else they had done.

I spun around and headed back down the hall to the kitchen. As I rounded the corner, the back door swung open, and a small Mexican guy stepped in. He had a handgun stuffed into the front waistband of his jeans. The guy wore a gray T-shirt and baggy blue jeans with white sneakers. And he was young and inexperienced, but he had a gangster-like quality about him, like he was newly minted. Maybe he was an American member of Tega's outfit, freshly recruited from the streets. I had no idea. And I didn't care. I gave him those few seconds of thought and nothing more.

I stepped into the kitchen—fast. I walked up to him plain as day and big as a horror movie slasher. Then I reached out with one hand, grabbed his shirt, bunched up his collar, and jerked him off his feet into the kitchen. He made a low yelp, but it wasn't loud enough for anyone to hear. Before he could make another sound, I raised the FN P90 one-handed over my head like a club and smashed him square in the face with the hilt.

It was a solid and vicious blow. His nose cracked. He went limp, and I let go of his shirt. He grabbed his nose and whimpered. Before he made another sound or went for his gun, I fired two rounds into his neck and shoulder. The bullet went straight through his throat and onto the floor—a messy through-and-through shot.

He grappled at the entry hole with both hands. He tried to scream, but he was inaudible. As he writhed around on his back like a headless snake, I turned back to the door and pointed the gun at it, readying myself for another guy to enter and check on his buddy.

I waited for an entire minute.

The sounds of the guy behind me wriggling around were all I heard in that minute, and then he fell silent. I twisted back to check on him. He was dead. There was a pool of blood around him so big that I could've filled a bucket with it.

I whispered, "You shouldn't have killed the dog."

Then I walked over to the door. I left it open and clicked the gun to full auto. I switched off the kitchen lights and peered outside. No one noticed me. I know that because no one shot at me.

The first thing I saw was the flying boat. It floated in the water at the edge of the dock, rocking up and down over the waves caused by the storm. It was majestic, painted all black with a red-tipped nose. The black color camouflaged it perfectly with the dark lake beyond. The number on its side was painted white and stood out from the darkness.

I stopped, and scanned the people in the backyard.

At that exact moment, the twin engines cranked to life. They started dull at first and then revved up to a gentle roar. A light clicked on in the cargo area of the plane. The side door was wide open.

I took the opportunity and scrambled away from the kitchen door, taking cover behind a bricked-in grill. I put my back to the brick side and breathed in and breathed out. No one had noticed me. I leaned over to get a better look at the surroundings.

Tega was near the door to the plane. He shoved a girl inside. Two other girls stood waiting, the second one I recognized. She was Ann Gables, alive. I couldn't believe she was still here. She moved slowly, like a zombie. All three of them did. They had obviously been doped up.

Ann went into the plane and swiveled left. Then Tega grabbed the final girl by her arm and pulled her toward the plane. She turned back to the house as if she wanted to run, but was too weak. It was Faye Matlind. Had to be. She was black, about Chris's age, and she was stunning. Even with no makeup and hair in complete disarray, all three girls were naturally beautiful. That's why they had been picked, I supposed. Tega must've been one of the finest dealers of sex slaves in the world.

Faye got on board the plane, and Tega waved at the only other guy he had left.

Tega said, *"Ve por el piloto."*

*Get the pilot.* That was the best I could translate.

I glanced over my shoulder, back at the kitchen door. Either the young guy or the guy in the driveway had been their pilot. I wasn't sure. What I was sure of was that in about ten seconds, this guy was going to make it to the kitchen and see the dead gang-banger, and I would be made.

I peeked back over the grill and saw the one guy well enough. I could hit him from here. No problem, but Tega was in the seaplane's doorway. Too far away. And with the fog and rain, I couldn't be sure about the accuracy.

But it didn't matter. Not anymore. It was now or never. So, I jumped up and aimed and took the shot. The first guy saw me and reacted fast. He went for a sidearm he had tucked in a holster clipped to his belt. I saw the hilt of what looked in the darkness to be another Beretta Px4. It was just like the one that had killed Matlind.

It was the fraction of a second, I took to process that thought that caused everything to go wrong.

I got the first guy with three twenty-eight-millimeter rounds fired through the suppressor. These were the same rounds a Five-Seven pistol used, but the muzzle velocity of a twenty-eight-millimeter bullet fired from the FN P90 was something around twenty-five hundred feet per second. That would be hindered slightly by the suppressor, but I wasn't worried about that.

I knew the last Mexican guard could not outrun bullets. I squeezed the trigger, and the gun fired fast. The recoil was pretty manageable, one perk of the bullpup design. Five bullets burst into the guy's center mass. Not one shot missed.

One of the purposeful designs of the FN P90 was to fire high-velocity rounds with hollow points. This should stop over-penetration of the bullet. Therefore, the gun promoted minimal collateral damage. It was rare that one of these rounds fired all the way through a target or ricocheted. It was the perfect urban submachine gun.

Everything was going perfectly until I moved to kill Tega. Hank Cochran, the old mechanic, stepped out of the back of the plane.

He'd been in the cockpit starting the plane, probably checking the systems before they took off.

Tega hadn't heard my gunshots, but he'd seen the explosions of red mist that burst out of his guy's chest. He reacted fast. Faster than any of his guys had. He pulled out an FN Five-Seven pistol, and in two quick seconds, he moved sideways, grabbed Hank, and ducked behind him, using him as a human shield.

I lost my aim. I had no clear shot. If I fired, I'd hit Hank and kill him. I released my finger from the trigger but kept it in the trigger housing.

Tega fired the Five-Seven in my direction.

I ducked behind the grill again as bullets sprayed across the opposite side. I heard the metal-on-metal sound of the bullets hitting, reminding me of when they'd been firing at the hood of Grady's Tahoe earlier. A few bullets sprayed over my head and shattered two large windows in the house.

Tega stopped firing. If he'd been reloading, that would've been my chance to return fire. But that wasn't what he was doing—he was doing something else. And I figured it out only a microsecond before he did.

He was aiming at the propane tank beneath the grill.

I jumped up and dove to the right-hand side. He fired the Five-Seven, and two bullets ruptured the tank. The smell of gas filled the air. He fired again, and the tank exploded. A small fireball erupted into the air. That was the third or fourth explosion that night. I had lost count.

I rolled away from the fireball and back to my feet, full stance, and took aim. Tega's head was in my sight, but his body was behind Hank. He stood tight behind him. And they were over thirty feet away. I had no clean shot.

I screamed at Tega. "Wait!"

Tega pointed the Five-Seven at me.

Tega shouted, "Gringo? Is that still you?"

He didn't fire, not yet. He knew if he missed, he'd have to reload, and then I'd have him. I was too far away for him to get a good aim. At least I hoped I was. He had done well with the propane tank.

I knew his gun had to be getting low on ammo. The Five-Seven held a good number of rounds—I couldn't recall the capacity of a standard magazine—but I was pretty sure he had fewer bullets than I had. The FN P90 in my hand held fifty rounds. I had the advantage in that department, but that advantage was of little use right now.

He shouted, "Mr. Widow, you're a hard man to kill."

I didn't respond.

He shouted, "You know, who was also hard to kill?"

I stayed quiet.

"Your *madre*, amigo. I hear she died slow. She fought for her life in the hospital."

I ignored his taunts. I understood their purpose. I shouted, "No one else has to die. Let him go."

The twin engines of the plane hummed and vibrated in their casings, ready to go. Suddenly, I realized Tega couldn't shoot Hank. He needed him. His pilot was dead. He'd need Hank to fly the plane. I wasn't sure if he had realized that yet, so I shouted, "Your men are dead! Your pilot is dead! You aren't going anywhere! Not without that man to fly your plane!"

Tega shouted, "I'll kill him! I don't care! I'll find another way out!"

Tega wasn't bluffing. He was rich and connected. He'd find another way. I had only one play left. I had to gamble.

I said, "You can still leave, Tega! Let them go!"

Tega shouted, "Drop your weapon, and I'll let them live! Hell, I'm so impressed with you, gringo, that I'll let you live as well!"

I waited. I stayed quiet.

He tilted his head. Then a crazed look came across his face, and he shot Hank just to prove he wasn't bluffing.

## 57

THE WEATHER over the lake was about as good for flying conditions as it was going to get.

Hints of morning sunlight pierced through the cloudy sky. The bottoms of the storm clouds turned a dark gray as the sun's rays shone through them.

On a normal morning on Jarvis Lake, the early bird fishermen would've been waking up and readying their boats and trailers for the drive to the boat launch. But it hadn't been a normal night. The only emergency employees left in the town of Black Rock had to be the fire department. I was certain they had their hands full with the fires. Across the lake, the Eckhart Medical Center was still blazing. The fire had spread to the nearby buildings. No way was the fire department available to help anyone else right now.

Oskar Tega had shot Hank through the leg. The old guy had screamed a blood-curdling scream that tore through my ears and echoed across the lake. If it had been a normal morning, I was sure that everyone on the lake would've heard him. Probably the gunshot, too. But there was no one on the lake—not today.

Tega shouted, "Throw it away! Or the next one kills him!"

I shouted, "Okay! Okay!"

I tossed the gun aside and raised my hands. I wasn't sure what the next few minutes would bring. But I hoped Tega wouldn't shoot me. Not yet.

Tega moved Hank aside and stepped out onto the dock. He approached me, keeping me in his sights the whole time. He got about ten feet away. I was at his mercy and was sure I was about to die, but Hank saved my life.

Tega looked down the barrel of the Five-Seven and took aim. Then he glanced over his head, back at Hank. It was a quick glance—not long enough for me to rush him, but long enough for him to see that Hank limped over to the gun of the guy I had shot a moment ago. Tega fired in the air over my head. Hank froze.

Tega kept the gun on me and shouted, "Old man! I will make a deal with you. You fly my plane and give me no more trouble, and I will let him come with us. I'll let you both live."

Hank stopped limping. He turned back to Tega. I could tell he was thinking it over. He took a long minute.

"Make up your damn mind, old man!"

Then Hank said, "Give me yer word?"

Tega rolled his eyes. Then he shouted, "What? You don't trust me, old-timer?" He paused a beat and said, "I give you my word."

Hank said, "Den you got yerself a deal."

Tega lowered the Five-Seven and said, "You're a lucky man, gringo. Come on. Let's go! I'm on a tight schedule."

Tega motioned for me to move toward the plane. He stepped back, maintaining a ten-foot distance from me, well out of my reach. He was a smart guy. I guess that was how he had lasted so long in his world.

I stayed quiet and followed his instructions. Kept my hands raised high and walked toward the open door of the seaplane. I stopped by Hank and helped him hobble back to the plane. He was hurt, but he'd survive. We boarded and Tega followed.

The engines were much louder from inside the plane. This plane was bare bones. It had a cockpit and two rear benches. Metal. No seat belts. No modern luxuries. It was like a military plane.

Tega shouted over the roar of the engines. "You sit in the seat over there at the front of the plane. I want you far from me and always in my line of sight."

I followed his instructions and sat down on the bench.

Tega remained standing near the back of the plane. He slammed the door shut and locked it. The metal sound echoed in the interior chamber even over the engine noise.

He kept the gun on me. Then he shouted, "Try anything! *Querido Dios!* I'll shoot you dead!"

I nodded.

He shouted up to Hank, who had made it to the pilot's seat and buckled himself in. "Old-timer, take us up!"

Hank nodded back and started pushing buttons and moving levers. Then he tugged on a handle from above. The plane's engines roared louder, as if changing gears. It shifted and moved forward. Hank took it out on the water and then turned the plane to face the longest stretch of the lake. He accelerated forward.

He shouted back at Tega, "Ya'd better sit down!"

"Don't worry about me, old-timer. You just fly the plane."

Hank smiled and pushed another lever, and the plane jetted forward in a powerful push. The plane shot across the water—fast. I felt the vibrations of the engines through the metal bench. My ears rattled.

I looked out the plane's window and saw the trees on the shoreline as we flew by. Water splashed up. We bounced once. Twice. And then we were in the air, climbing up into the low storm clouds. Off in the distance, a lightning bolt flashed and crackled. The underbelly of the storm clouds lit up.

We climbed farther and faster.

## 58

Tega hadn't let his gun hand rest. But how long could he hold it up? Not forever. Probably not even too much longer. I was already impressed by how long he managed to hold the Five-Seven. The weight must've been really straining his wrist by this time.

I looked over at Hank. His leg was bleeding badly.

I shouted back to Tega, "His leg is bad. If I don't clean him up, we won't make it very far."

Tega breathed heavily. Then he acknowledged I was right. But he shouted, "Not you. Faye, you do it."

Faye was the least doped up of all the girls.

"You're a nurse, right?" he asked.

She nodded and stood up. She was woozy. Anyone could see that.

Tega patted her on her butt. He looked at me, smiled, and said, "You can assist, but stay away from the controls."

I nodded and moved to the jump seat behind the cockpit.

Faye moved up and stopped close to me.

In a regular voice, which sounded like a whisper in the noisy chamber, I said, "Faye, Chris sent me."

She looked at me. Her eyes faded in and out, but she was coherent, mostly. She asked, "Chris?" Her voice held plenty of recognition.

"Yes."

She walked to Hank and smiled at him. She said, "I'm going to look at your leg."

She plopped down into the copilot's seat. Then she leaned over and started checking his wound.

I leaned in and acted like I was only watching, but I spoke in a low voice to both of them. I said, "I'm going to get that gun from him. As soon as I make a move, open the rear cargo door."

Hank glanced over at me from the corner of his eye. He said, "Are ya sure? Ya could get sucked out."

"Don't worry about me. If we fly out of the country, we're all dead, anyway."

I turned back. I was going to bum rush Tega. Of course, I'd probably get shot, but I had no better option.

And then Faye reached back and grabbed my arm tight. Her nails dug into my right forearm. She said, "Wait. Let me distract him."

Before I could object, she made her move. She stood up and wobbled over to him.

Tega shifted his weight and pointed the Five-Seven at her.

She stopped and said, "Relax. I need the, um..." She scratched her head. "I need the first aid kit. It's under the bench."

Tega glanced down. A bright-orange case was stuck beneath the bench, just as she had said. He nodded and motioned with the gun for her to grab it.

I clenched my fists and flexed the muscles in my legs. I was ready to pounce.

Tega returned his aim to me.

Faye knelt down, still acting dopey. Or maybe she really was. I couldn't tell. She grabbed the case, unhooked it from the bench, and then she swung it around in a fast and vicious backhand. The case nailed Tega square in the face. The bottom swung open, and the contents flew out. No first aid stuff, only a flare gun and a bunch of flares. The flare gun bounced onto the floor near the other girls.

Hank hit the button to open the rear door, and I leaped up toward Tega. A bright warning light came on and flashed red across the interior of the plane. A loud warning sound buzzed. It continued to buzz as the back of the plane cracked open.

The winds outside were hard enough to increase the air pressure. Immediately, a blast of air sucked through the cabin like a vacuum. It was light at first, but became heavy and gained more power as the door continued to open slowly.

I reached Faye first. I grabbed her and flung her hard to the front of the cabin. I had no choice. She had a tiny frame. She was probably a size zero. The wind would have sucked her right out.

Then I swung blindly at Tega with a powerful left hook. I hit him square in the shoulder. He had the gun pointed in my direction. He fired it. But my punch flung him off balance, and several bullets whizzed by me. The Five-Seven takes the same rounds as the FN P90, with the same non-ricochet bullet technology. They slammed into the metal walls of the plane. No penetration.

The plane bounced, and the suction in the cabin grew more intense. I came back at him with a right jab, but it was hard to aim my blows. This one got him dead on the solar plexus. But it wasn't the most powerful blow ever—not my best work. Even if I hadn't had to fight in sketchy conditions, I was still exhausted from being awake for over twenty-four hours.

Tega dropped his gun and let out a loud shriek. He flew back against the starboard bench, and I felt the body armor he was wearing under the rain slicker when I punched him. He jumped up and came at me. I grabbed him and tried to throw him out of the plane, but he seized my collar and used the momentum of the throw against me. He returned with a fast-right jab and then a left hook. His fist was small, but he had some muscle. He knew how to fight, and he was fast—most little guys were. That was the biggest advantage small opponents always had over me. They were weaker, but they were quick.

He aimed for my face, but he missed and caught me in the chest. He would've been better off if he had gotten me in the face. Still, I was exhausted, and it hurt, but I didn't squeal, not like he had. I shook it off and reared my right fist back. But he fought dirty. He kicked me in the groin.

Any man anywhere has at least one major weak spot—the groin. I was no different. I pulled my punch and grabbed at my groin. It hurt like no kind of pain I had felt in years. But I didn't have time to worry about it. I tried to go at him again, but the pain hit me like a truck. I clammed up again.

Tega went for the Five-Seven. He got to it. He stood about six feet from me. We were both at the back of the plane. The rear door was now completely open. He pointed the gun at me. Once again, I thought I was a dead man. Game over.

Tega squeezed the trigger, but just then, from out of left field, a flare from the flare gun launched out of the barrel. It hissed past me and torpedoed in Tega's direction. It lit up the cabin in a bright orange flash. The flare flew right between us and shot out into the night. It exploded behind the plane.

A split second before it exploded, Tega had turned quickly and returned fire in the direction of the flare's origin. He had intended to hit Faye Matlind—she was the one who had picked up the flare gun, loaded it, and fired it at him. But the explosion caught him by surprise. It threw him off balance and caused him to misfire. Instead of the one bullet intended for Faye, Tega fired two rounds. And each bullet hit two different targets.

One round shot into the plane's gauges. It caused all kinds of noises and alarms to beep and ding.

The second bullet caused more damage. It did something very rare for one of those rounds—it penetrated the pilot's seat and went through Hank's chest. The old guy fell forward against the controls, clenching his sternum. The plane dipped into a quick nosedive.

The girls tumbled forward into the cockpit. They were all wide awake now. The adrenaline from all the danger had jump-started their bodies.

Tega stumbled a couple of paces forward, and I stood my ground.

Hank's head rose up. He pulled the controls back and got us out of the nosedive almost as fast as we had gone into it. Hank was a tough old guy. He had fought in the Navy. I remembered.

Tega jumped back to his feet and pointed the gun at me before I could attack him. He aimed at my chest and screamed, *"Te vas a morir!"*

Then Hank pulled back hard on the controls. Tega lost his balance and stumbled back a few feet toward the rear, near the edge.

I swiped at his gun hand with a fast backhand. The Five-Seven went flying into the air, and the slipstream sucked it out of the plane. Then I reared back on my heels, bent my knees, and leaped forward. Using every muscle from my legs to my neck, I delivered the most powerful headbutt of my life, far more powerful than the one I had given years ago on the football field, or since. My brow was rigid and powerful and landed flat against Tega's face, concaving it, crushing his nose and bashing his face to a pulp in one powerful and fatal blow. He was dead instantly. I knew it, but I'd never find out for sure because he went flying backward, and the night air sucked him out of the rear door. I almost got pulled out after him, but I reached up with both arms and locked my palms against the ceiling, bracing myself. I watched Oskar Tega's departure with great satisfaction. His body whipped around just outside the plane like a leaf in a storm, and seconds later, he was gone from sight.

I said, "Adios."

That was the last anyone saw of Oskar Tega.

## 59

THE SEAPLANE DIPPED AND BOUNCED. Hank tried his best to keep it steady, but the controls were damaged beyond the point of repair. He had bled all over the place. I knew he was going to die soon—no doubt about it.

I held my hands over his wounds—one over the hole in his back and one over the hole in his chest.

"Ya gotta get da girls outta da plane," Hank said to me, breathless.

I said, "Can't you land us? Or tell me how?"

"I've lived a long life. My kids are grown. My wife died two years ago. Dat bastard killed da last friend dat I had in dis world. I'm dyin'. Let me go."

I moved my hand and took a peek at his chest. He was right. Blood splattered and pooled out of the wound. There was no going back for him. Not under these conditions. Even a doctor onboard wouldn't be able to help him. He had a slim chance at a hospital. He wasn't going to make it.

He grabbed my hand with his and squeezed. He said, "Let go."

I nodded, pictured my mom, and then I let him go. He gripped his chest and tried to stop the bleeding as best he could.

He said, "I'm gonna fly low above da lake. You take da girls and jump out. And don't wait. I won't last." Then he took the plane down into a slow dive.

I grabbed his shoulder and said, "I'm glad I met you." I turned to the girls and said, "Ladies, listen up. The plane isn't going to land. We've got to jump."

Faye was almost fully alert. The drugs had worn off for her. So at least I had her help.

Then one of the other girls seemed to be more cognizant of what was going on. I confirmed that she really was Ann Gables. This was the first time I had really looked at her. She was still alive. Skinny but alive.

She asked, "Jump?"

"Ann, there's no time to explain, but you're going to have to jump and swim," I said.

Faye grabbed her and said, "Remember me? It's Faye. We're free now, but we have to jump from this plane. Can you swim?"

Ann's face came alive and alert at Faye's words. She said, "We're free? Yes, I can swim."

I said, "Good." Then I said to Hank, "We're ready."

Hank took us down above the lake. Thunder rumbled above us. He shouted back to us, "All right. Head all da way ta da back. Jump in ten seconds. No time ta waste."

He flew low over the lake like he was going to land. I pushed the ladies toward the rear. I grabbed the third girl, who was still woozy, and Faye helped Ann. At the rear of the plane, we felt the starboard engine explode in a sudden wave of fire and wind. The plane lurched through the air, and Faye and Ann both flew out the back before they were ready. I grabbed the other girl and leaped out after them.

We dropped through the air for not even three seconds and then crashed through the surface of the lake like boulders. We sank several feet down, and I started swimming with one arm. I pulled the girl with the other. I swam and paddled upward through the water with all my strength. I kicked and kicked. After a long moment, I burst through the surface. I filled my lungs with the warm, damp air. I sucked down the oxygen like it was my first time breathing.

The girl floated next to me, unconscious. Then suddenly, she was awake and completely confused. Second-nature kicked in, and she treaded water on her own. She coughed and gasped and stayed quiet. Then she started swimming away from me toward the shore. She might've thought I had abducted her or was trying to drown her. Neither would've surprised me. But she was alive. That was all that mattered.

I turned and swam in the opposite direction toward the other shore. Not sure why? I just followed my instinct, which was to paddle to the other side. I kicked and paddled and swam as hard as I could.

I heard my mother's voice. She said, "Do the right thing."

I heard her repeatedly in my head as I swam. "Do the right thing."

Eventually, I reached the shore and pulled myself up onto the rocks with my arms. I didn't stand up. Not yet. I just rolled over and lay on my back and stared up at the sky.

The sun had broken through the storm clouds. Thunder still roared every other minute, but the sunlight was there. Then there was one loud, thunderous sound that was a little different from the rumbling thunder. It was much closer. I looked up in the noise's direction and saw that it was the seaplane. It had exploded above the town of Black Rock. Pieces of the plane fell to the earth in a rainstorm of shrapnel and broken metal fragments. I thought about Hank, and then I thought nothing else.

I sat up and looked around the lake for signs of Faye Matlind. I didn't have to search for long. Directly across from me on the opposite shore were all three of the women—the drugged one I had jumped from the plane with Ann Gables and Faye Matlind.

They were holding each other and hugging like long-lost sisters who had survived a horrible plane crash and more, which they had.

I smiled.

Do the right thing.

I lay back down on the hard stones and closed my eyes. I had felt nothing more comfortable in my life than that bed of rocks.

## 60

It was well into the early morning hours. Cars had lined up to leave the town of Black Rock like it had an outbreak of the plague. The traffic to exit the town was heavy and thick.

Emergency vehicles from the neighboring towns, the state government and state cops, the FBI, the DEA, and the ATF were all lined up within twenty-four hours to get into the town of Black Rock. They had set up their own traffic stops and perimeters and security stations. The local motel, which had survived the fires, was fully booked.

The national media had canceled all of their regularly scheduled programs to report on both a small town in Mississippi that was on fire and a missing international criminal named Oskar Tega. He was now thought to have crashed his plane over Black Rock. It was also reported that he hadn't been a drug kingpin after all, but a human trafficker. He and his gang had allegedly been responsible for dozens of abductions of young women in the last five years along the highways and interstates in multiple counties.

Much, much earlier than all of this, I had left Black Rock. While all the government agencies were fighting to get into the town, I was already miles away. I stood on the side of Highway 82, just outside a small town called El Dorado. The sun was out, and it was hot. I had my thumb out when a bright-red Scion pulled over to the shoulder. I lowered my arm and started walking toward the car.

I was exhausted. I had slept for only about an hour on a bed of rocks, and my back was sore. My shoulders hurt, and I felt my bones with every step I took, but I had to keep moving.

I stepped up to the passenger door. I was so tired that, without even leaning down to meet the driver, I opened the door and dumped myself into the seat. Casually, I gazed over with sleepy eyes and then laughed. I laughed louder and heartier than I had ever laughed before because the driver was Maria from the diner.

She smiled at me. She looked good in the morning, but she also looked a little tired, but better than me, for sure.

She said, "Hi."

"Well, hello."

"I never thought I'd see you again."

I nodded.

Then she said, "I called you."

I shut my eyes tight, and a deep frown fell across my face.

She asked, "What?"

"My phone."

I pulled it out of my pocket. I was amazed because it was still in one piece, and it was dry, like my clothes, but surely the phone had been ruined.

"I was in the lake earlier. I forgot to take it out of my pocket."

She said, "Put it in rice. It'll work again."

I shrugged.

"Don't you have it all backed up, anyway?"

I said, "It's not my phone. Why are you here? Where are you going?"

Then I noticed that the back seat was loaded up with her belongings.

She smiled and said, "There's nothing for me in Black Rock, even when it wasn't on fire. I'm headed home. Back to Austin. What about you? Where are you headed?"

I looked around the car, and then I looked back at her. Our eyes connected. I could've headed back to Killian Crossing. I could've called Cameron, explained that I wasn't coming back to the NCIS. But then again, I didn't have to say anything.

I said, "Austin sounds great."

She nodded and smiled.

"Mind if I sleep a while?"

She said, "Not at all."

Then she took her foot off the brake, merged with the traffic, and drove off.

Before I dozed off, she asked, "Hey, you wanna meet my parents?"

I laughed again. This time, I laughed so hard that it hurt.

She laughed too. Then she asked, "Why are you going to Austin?"

I said, "I gotta be somewhere."

We said nothing more. I lay back against the seat, closed my eyes, and fell into a deep, deep sleep.

# A WORD FROM SCOTT

Thank you for reading GONE FOREVER. You got this far—I'm guessing that you enjoyed Widow.

The story continues in a fast-paced series that takes Widow (and you) all around the world, solving crimes, righting wrongs.

The next book, WINTER TERRITORY, takes us to an isolated Indian Reservation in the Wyoming mountains, where Widow goes undercover to stop an unimaginable terrorist threat, only things may not be as they seem.

The third installment, A REASON TO KILL, has Widow drifting along a sweltering Texas landscape. Everything is good until he gets charged with locating a missing child. His investigation leads to a deadly, political conspiracy. Widow races against the clock to save the child from dangerous murderers who will kill to keep the truth in the dark.

The fourth book (one of my personal favorites) is WITHOUT MEASURE. Hitchhiking all night. No sleep. Widow stops in a diner in a California mountain town. A chance meeting with a Marine officer. A short conversation. And an hour later, the Marine walked onto a military base, shot and killed five random people, and committed suicide. Now, the MPs want to know why. All suspicion is on the outsider, Widow.

In this exciting mystery, Widow digs deep under the surface to uncover the truth. As he turns over rocks, he finds dark secrets crawling underneath.

You can grab each book from Amazon.com. What are you waiting for? The fun is just starting. Once you start reading Widow, you won't be able to stop.

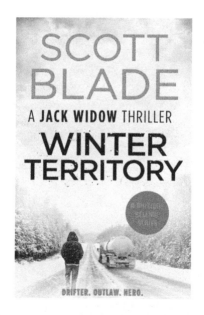

Out Now!

# WINTER TERRITORY: A BLURB

**A terrifying bioweapon...**

**A hidden terrorist...**

**Only Jack Widow can stop them.**

Out for good, former NCIS agent, Jack Widow goes undercover to stop an unimaginable terrorist threat in the second "electrifying" book in the Jack Widow series.

Deep in Wyoming, the dead of winter, CIA Agent Alex Shepard is desperate. A few days ago, he sent an undercover agent to the Red Rain Indian Reservation to investigate an unthinkable terrorist plot. However, when his man was supposed to check-in, Shepard heard nothing.

With a snowstorm fast-approaching, Shepard's secret mission is in peril. There is no time left, and lives are on the line.

Enter drifter Jack Widow--Shepard's one hope to recover his agent and stop the deadliest domestic terrorist plot in American history.

*Readers are saying....*

★★★★★ *A first-rate page-turner! -Amazon Reviewer.*

# WINTER TERRITORY: AN EXCERPT
## CHAPTER 2

JACK WIDOW WAS DOING what he loved best—wandering without a care in the world. This was what he thought was true freedom. A lifetime of doing as he was told had turned him into a man who no longer listened to anyone. He did as he wanted and went where he pleased.

Widow had spent the last several months doing more and seeing more of his home country than he had ever done or seen in his entire life. He had traveled from Mississippi, a place that seemed so far away and long ago in his memory, through seven states, across hundreds of highways, around thousands of cloverleaves, and over the southern part of the Rocky Mountains. He'd traveled all the way west until he couldn't go any farther unless he started swimming or chartered a boat or stole a submarine or bought a plane ticket. And even then, he was out of states except for Hawaii and Alaska, depending on whether you considered them to be west.

Over the last year, he had discovered three addictions. The first was the open road. There was nothing like the freedom of the American frontier. The second was coffee. Coffee was a drug he couldn't explain. Perhaps it was from being a Navy cop. Perhaps not. Or maybe it was just a drug that did what drugs do and did it well—it created an addiction. Whatever the case was, he didn't care. And the third was that he was constantly picking up old paperback books and reading them along his travels.

He had slept only about five hours the night before because he had met a girl named Farrah in Salt Lake City. The only person he had known with that name was the actress Farrah Fawcett, but when he'd asked the girl about it, she had denied being named after her. She told him she had been asked that question for her entire life but claimed never to have even seen a Farrah Fawcett film. As the girl was only twenty-four years old, that was probably true. Farrah had been dead for years and hadn't really done any acting in decades. The only thing Widow knew her from was *Charlie's Angels*, a horrible show in his opinion, from before he was born.

Farrah—the twenty-four-year-old and not the actress—had been a lot of fun for Widow. She was a part-time waitress and student, not at the University of Utah but at a community college. She was taking night classes to be a nurse, a trade that Widow admired. He admired anyone who was in the profession of helping others. The military, criminal justice, firefighting, the medical field, and even the clergy were all trades he respected.

Farrah was the complete opposite of Farrah Fawcett, but that didn't mean she wasn't gorgeous. She was absolutely gorgeous, far more so than the 1970s actress. At least that was Widow's conclusion. Farrah was six feet tall. She was dark-skinned with long, straight black hair and even longer legs. She was toned, but not in the way of someone who was into fitness. It was more of a youthful way, the way you are when you have good genes.

Widow had met Farrah while she was working at a local bar. She had thought it was odd that he was reading a book in a bar, and they struck up a conversation. He had asked her to have a drink after her shift ended, which they did. His time on the road had been lonely. Not that the isolation didn't appeal to him as well. He liked to be alone. And there was something romantic and resolute about wandering. He found peace. Widow accepted the aloneness, but finding the occasional friend was something he looked forward to.

After they had a beer together—some local craft brew—Farrah had invited Widow back to her place for another beer, which turned the one beer into an all-night thing, which was okay by him.

In the morning, Widow put his clothes on and said goodbye to Farrah as she slept. He wasn't sure if she had heard him or not, and it hadn't mattered. He was ready to be on his way.

He left her asleep in her bed in her ground-level apartment and locked the door behind him. He left without a phone number or without leaving her one in return. No email. No forwarding address. There was no point. He had no phone. No email. No address.

Jack Widow had been born in Mississippi to a single mom. She was an ex-Marine, which meant she was still a Marine. She was also the sheriff of the town in which Widow had grown up in until six months ago when she had been murdered while investigating a series of disappearances of beautiful women.

Widow had left his assignment as an undercover Navy cop to investigate her death, returning to the small town he'd grown up in. No one remembered him because he had left home when he was eighteen and joined the Navy. He'd spent sixteen years away from home and never called or wrote or spoke to his mother. His last two memories of her were the day she died and sixteen years before, when they had fought one of those life-changing fights. She'd admitted to lying to him his entire life about his father.

Widow had grown up thinking that his father had been a military war hero, a soldier who had died defending his country. But when he turned eighteen, she told him the truth. His father had been a drifter, just some guy. Widow had wanted to escape small-town life for his entire childhood, and that fight with his mother led him to run away with the Navy. Originally, he had planned to call her, but one month turned into two and then into six. Six months turned into a year, which turned into many years.

American families.

By the time sixteen years had passed, it took a tragedy for him to return home. When he returned to his old town, the people there had thought of him as a drifter. So he continued on to the town in which his mother had died and kept his drifter persona intact.

Widow knew about undercover work—that's what he did for NCIS. He stayed undercover to find out who shot his mother, and that led him down a dark path. At the end of which, he came face-to-face with a conspiracy he'd much rather forget.

After his mother died, the NCIS told him he had to come back. That was his only choice, but Jack Widow decided it was time to make his own choices. He put one foot in front of the other and never looked back.

What started as a quest to find the person responsible for shooting his sheriff mother had turned into a full-blown obsession, which turned into a way of life.

Along the way, Widow realized that the first part of his life had been to follow in his mother's footsteps. She was a Marine and a cop, and he had become a Navy SEAL and a cop. Now in the second half of his life, he was a drifter, like the father he had never known. Now he was literally following in his father's footsteps.

No possessions had been Widow's thing. It was because, in the Navy, Widow had carried gear everywhere he went. He had been trained to carry tremendous weight. After he joined the NCIS and went undercover with a secret unit, he had carried more than physical things with him. Living a double life had taken a toll on him. Now he carried nothing.

Widow didn't want possessions. Possessions meant commitment and things to carry and store. In Widow's mind, things to carry meant baggage, and baggage could hold you down and hold you back.

The things Widow carried now were his passport, his debit card, and a wad of cash, which was four hundred fifty-eight dollars at that moment. He tried to carry cash-money on him. He never knew when he would need quick access to it. In addition, using cash provided a lot more anonymity than using his debit card. And he liked anonymity.

The only other item he carried was a foldable toothbrush, which looked like a blue barber-style shaving blade. Instead of a blade that snicked out of the handle, there was a toothbrush. The bristles and plastic head folded down into the handle and flipped out like a switchblade. He carried the toothbrush but replaced it fairly often. Toothbrushes could be bought at any drugstore.

On the morning after Widow left Farrah for Salt Lake City, he ventured out to visit the unique attractions around the city, including the Temple Square gardens, thirty-five acres of land downtown that headquartered the Mormon Church. The gardens were world famous and had two hundred and fifty flower beds and seven hundred different plants from all across the planet. The gardens were replanted and redesigned every year, and it took hundreds of volunteers to finish them. But Widow couldn't get in to see them because the garden was only open in the summer, and tours were by appointment only.

So he spent the afternoon on a ritual he completed either daily or weekly, depending on where he was and how dirty he had gotten. He went to a cheap-looking old barbershop and said hello to an old guy with a jarhead haircut and photographs of himself with other guys, doing guy things, that were pinned all over a bulletin board near the entrance. The old guy said hello back and asked if Widow needed a cut. Widow nodded and told him he would like a buzz cut.

On the road, Widow had discovered the benefits of keeping his hair short, and he had quickly shed the long-haired look. Of course, in the winter months, it would make sense to let it grow long, but Widow was still getting used to the drifter lifestyle. For the last six months, he had been getting his head buzzed short and hadn't yet thought about the winter. He had figured he'd spend it in California, but he had gotten there earlier than he'd thought he would. Part of this new nomadic life was going with the flow, and the flow had turned him around at the Pacific Ocean.

After the jarhead barber had cut his hair short, Widow got out of the chair, paid the man, and thanked him. Then he left the barbershop and walked down the street along a cracked cement sidewalk to a side of town that was less than pristine. Potholes riddled the street, and old cars were parked along the street. Leaning telephone poles besieged the area like reminders of a forgotten time.

Widow walked on until he found what he was looking for, an old consignment store called America's Clothing Store. Not a catchy name for a consignment store, but Widow wasn't looking for trendy. He was looking for cheap.

Another thing he'd discovered was buying cheap clothes was better than owning one pair and rewashing them all the time. Laundromats aren't cheap. Detergent isn't cheap. Buying new clothes, wearing them, and tossing them in a Salvation Army bin after was like being a part of a subscription service. In his mind, it was like Netflix for clothes. He'd buy new ones, wear them, recycle them, and someone else would use them.

He walked into the store and nodded at a cute girl behind the counter. She was folding clothes and nodded and smiled back at him. He guessed she was barely an adult. She looked like a mixture of Asian and white. The girl wore a multicolored striped top with mostly gray in it and black chinos. She was petite, probably five foot one. Her hair was shorter than shoulder length, dyed pink, and shaved on one side. To Widow, she looked like a modern punk rocker, a style that seemed to return.

Traveling from state to state, city to city, Widow had come across young people of all types. In the urban areas, he'd noticed similar hairstyles, especially among girls. Although he was from a southern state, a conservative state, Widow couldn't complain about the new look. In fact, on her, it looked damn good.

He began wandering around the store. They didn't have a big and tall section—he had found that most places didn't. The big and tall sections of America hadn't vanished—there were plenty of them out there—but most of the stores that catered to bigger

SCOTT BLADE

people had become specialty stores. Expensive specialty stores. So Widow had often settled for XXL or XXXL if he could find it in tops. Fitting his waist hadn't been a problem because he had a thin waist for a guy his size—thirty-four inches, but he was six four with long legs and needed pants that were long enough. Usually, he'd buy a size thirty-six and let them ride on his hips.

Widow headed to the pants section and searched around. He looked at jeans first and found a pair of Levi carpenter jeans, size thirty-five. The legs were long. He grabbed them and walked over to look at the tops. He sifted through the selections and pulled out a long-sleeved white shirt. Then he turned and started toward a wall of shoes on display, but before he got there, he saw a nice gray fleece vest from the corner of his eye. He stopped and looked it over. He was thinking about heading northeast and realized he had no winter gear, and it was now the beginning of November.

He grabbed the fleece and looked at the tag. It was only an XXL, but it was a sleeveless vest, so he didn't need to worry about it having long sleeves that reached only to his forearms. Widow had abnormally long arms—long arms and long legs. His mother was tiny, so he assumed he had inherited them from his unknown father.

Widow grabbed his clothes and went over to the fitting room, which was in the back of the store. He dipped into a little hallway and came face-to-face with a young black girl who was barely out of high school. Like the girl from the front, she also had a punk rocker look about her. No pink hair, but she had three nose piercings and those huge pieces in her earlobes that looked like rims for a truck. They were black and rubbery looking. They opened her ears up to a size big enough to slide his pinkie through, which was more like the size of a gun barrel.

She asked, "How are you, sir? Want to try those on?"

Widow said, "Yes."

"How many items do you have?"

"I have three, but I want to grab a pair of shoes and socks, too. Can I leave these with you?"

She said, "Here, I'll take them and set you up in a fitting room."

She reached out with tiny coffee-colored hands and took his three items. She had to use both arms to carry them, and even then, she was swallowed up like a newborn wrapped in king-sized sheets.

Widow turned and walked over to the shoes. He paced back and forth, looking at them, studying them. With shoes, he had only one goal on his mind, and that was to locate a size fourteen, which was his shoe size. Locating a comfortable shoe was one of the hardest things about being a little taller than average.

He had walked one way up the aisle and then back again when he realized that the bigger sizes were all the way at the top of the wall.

Widow looked at the small selection of shoes in size fourteen. His choices were pretty slim. There wasn't much there, not much at all. Not in the way of comfortable shoes. But he had found it was better to look at the work shoes and boots. There was usually a larger selection of them. He picked up a pair of plain black boots that were comparable to Timberlands but without the name brand. The boots were worn, but still in good shape. He took them and returned to the fitting room where the young clerk had hung his clothes. She handed him a white-and-yellow tag that said "4" in a big block font, showing how many items he had with him in the dressing room.

He went into the booth and closed the door, tried on the clothes. Everything fit pretty well, including the long-sleeved white shirt. Widow rolled the sleeves down over his forearms and looked in the mirror. He looked okay. He ripped the tags off all the items and pulled the size stickers off, and walked out wearing them.

The girl looked him up, and down, smiled. She said, "Nice. Everything looks good."

"Thanks. I'll take them. I'm just going to wear them out."

The girl said, "That's fine. Where're your old clothes?"

"Right," he said. Then he turned and went back into the room and picked up his old clothes and shoes and the tag she had given him, and he came back out.

He handed her the tag, and she said, "If you take them to the front, Shelly will ring you up. Have a nice day."

Widow smiled and stayed quiet. He went to the register and paid for his new clothes, and walked out of the store. He stopped just outside the front door and turned to a Goodwill bin that looked like a giant blue city garbage can with a slot to throw old clothes in.

Widow bunched up his old clothes and tossed them in—no reason to waste them.

Then he turned and looked at the shadows on the ground. The time matched what he guessed it to be, which was about 2:45 in the afternoon. One skill SEAL training had taught him was how to tell time by the sun's shadows. He had found that this skill wasn't completely necessary since he liked watches, especially tactical ones, but he wasn't wearing one at the moment.

He had lost his watch. Probably left it in a motel room some-where, or maybe he left it at Farrah's. He thought about looking for a new one, but not from a consignment store.

He shrugged and figured he didn't need a watch. What was the point in knowing the time when you were always free?

# A SPECIAL OFFER

Get your copy of Night Swim: a Jack Widow Novella. Available only at ScottBlade.com

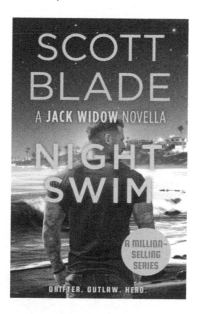

# NIGHT SWIM: A BLURB

*Under the cover of night, Widow swims through dangerous waters to rescue an FBI agent from a death sentence.*

**A blown cover for an FBI agent means a death sentence, unless Widow can stop it.**

Under cover of darkness along the Malibu coast, Widow takes a night swim. It's meant to be soothing and stress-relieving.

Instead, Widow's night swim turns deadly with the echo of gunshots over open water. A covert FBI operation is blown apart, leaving only blood in the water and a lone undercover agent exposed to a den of lethal international criminals. From the quiet night swim to a high-stakes criminal party at a mega millionaire's beach house, Widow faces grave danger to warn her.

Widow, the drifter who stands for justice, emerges from the waves. With literally nothing but his resolve, he faces unbelievable odds. Time is running out, the enemy is within reach, and for Widow, stealth and cunning are his only weapons.

*In this pulse-pounding Widow novella, the line between the hunter and the hunted blurs in a deadly game of espionage and survival.*

# THE SCOTT BLADE BOOK CLUB

Fostering a connection with my readers is the highlight of my writing journey. Rest assured, I'm not one to crowd your inbox. You'll only hear from me when there's exciting news to share—like a fresh release hitting the shelves or a can't-miss promotion.

If you're just stepping into the world of Jack Widow, consider this your official invite to the Scott Blade Book Club. As a welcome gift, you'll receive the Night Swim: A Widow Novella in the starter kit.

By joining, you'll gain access to a trove of exclusive content, including free stories, special deals, bonus material, and the latest updates on upcoming Widow thrillers.

Ready to dive in? Visit ScottBlade.com to sign up and begin your immersion into the Widow universe.

# THE NOMADVELIST
## NOMAD + NOVELIST = NOMADVELIST

Scott Blade is a Nomadvelist, a drifter and author of the breakout Jack Widow series. Scott travels the world, hitchhiking, drinking coffee, and writing.

Jack Widow has sold over a million copies.

Visit @: ScottBlade.com

Contact @: scott@scottblade.com

Follow @:

Facebook.com/ScottBladeAuthor

Bookbub.com/profile/scott-blade

Amazon.com/Scott-Blade/e/B00AU7ZRS8

# ALSO BY SCOTT BLADE

Made in the USA
Monee, IL
11 February 2024

53349090R00215